HIGHEST PRAISE FOR
DIAMOND HOMESPUN ROMANCES:

We at Diamond Books are thrilled by the enthusiastic critical acclaim that the Homespun romances are receiving. We would like to thank you, the readers and fans of this wonderful series, for making it the success that it is. It is our pleasure to bring you the highest quality of romance writing in these breathtaking tales of love and family in the Heartland of America.

And now, sit back and enjoy this delightful new Homespun Romance . . .

OUR HOUSE
by Debra S. Cowan

Don't miss Debra S. Cowan's previous Diamond Homespun romance, Almost Home, a touching story of the heart's triumphant journey to an unexpected love.

"Debra S. Cowan shows the beautiful p... of a rising star. Almost ... great piece of America... the couple's tragedie... oeur

Diamond Books by Debra S. Cowan

ALMOST HOME
OUR HOUSE

OUR HOUSE

Debra S. Cowan

DIAMOND BOOKS, NEW YORK

This book is an Diamond original edition,
and has never been previously published.

OUR HOUSE

A Diamond Book / published by arrangement with
the author

PRINTING HISTORY
Diamond edition / November 1994

All rights reserved.
Copyright © 1994 by Debra S. Cowan.
Cover appliqué illustration by Kathy Lengyel.
This book may not be reproduced in whole or in part,
by mimeograph or any other means, without permission.
For information address: The Berkley Publishing Group,
200 Madison Avenue, New York, NY 10016.

ISBN: 0-7865-0057-3

Diamond Books are published by The Berkley Publishing Group,
200 Madison Avenue, New York, NY 10016.
DIAMOND and the "D" design are trademarks
belonging to Charter Communications, Inc.

PRINTED IN THE UNITED STATES OF AMERICA

10   9   8   7   6   5   4   3   2   1

To my sisters,
Vicki Banta and Susan Crawford,
whose dreams inspired the heroine in this book.
Here's to your role
in the future of women in medicine.

Acknowledgments

Very special thanks to Mary Linn Bills of the Burton Memorial Library of Clarendon, Texas. Without her kind and generous help, this book would have been one big guess. If mistakes were made, they were mine.

Thanks to Melinda Metz, my editor, for the chance.

Thanks also to Jodi Thomas for her help with the obscure research.

ONE

West Texas, 1883

Blood soaked the ground, slashes of scarlet turned black in the night. Jefferson Grant clutched at the searing pain in his side, felt a wet stickiness slide over his fingers and knew it was his blood.

Get up, man. Get up. You've got to move.

He lay facedown, his mouth scratchy and full of Texas dirt. Clouds crowded the hazy summer moon as it cast a shimmering glow over the desolate land. The rancidly sweet odor of blood burned his nostrils. Sweat caked the red dirt on his neck and sun-weathered cheeks. A buzzing in his ears muffled the sounds he now recognized as Phipps's screams and the retreating hoofbeats of the outlaw's horse. Jeff had hit Phipps somewhere in the face just as the outlaw had fired on him.

Pain crashed through his body, numbing his arms and legs and mind. He struggled against the blackness reaching for him, desperately forcing his mind to work.

Awareness floated back. August 1883. Martin Phipps had ambushed him on the way to Clarendon, in retaliation for Jeff killing Martin's brother, Billy. Jeff repeated the information to himself, trying to keep a grip on consciousness.

Clarendon.

The letter.

1

Urgency burned through him. He had to move, had to get there. Jilly was counting on him. He clenched his teeth and managed to push himself to his knees.

Pain arched through him, as brutal and unrelenting as some of the men he'd killed. And killed for. He hung his head between his shoulders, panting for more of the suddenly thin air, wishing for a soft bed and a bottle of tequila.

His chestnut gelding snorted and blew a hot breath across Jeff's neck. He latched onto the horse's leg for support. He wasn't going to lie in this godforsaken stretch of land a couple of days from Clarendon and end up as buzzard bait.

He groped for his vest pocket and closed his eyes in relief. The letter was still there, as was the locket, his only connections to the past.

Supporting his shoulder against the horse's leg, Jeff staggered to his feet. Warm blood trickled from the wound and beneath the waistband of his denims.

Nausea and dizziness swept over him in a cold wave. The chill rippled down his back and he bit off a cry of agony. Clenching his teeth, he managed to turn the horse sideways toward him, then he sagged against the saddle. He buried his face in worn leather and gathered his strength to mount.

The night closed around him, thick and silky and warm. He wanted to sink into it as he would a woman, but he couldn't.

They were up there in Clarendon. Waiting for him.

"I want the barber," the old man rasped. A spasm of breath rattled his chest. Pain creased his lean, weather-worn features, and he clutched his stomach.

Dr. Abigail Welch reached out toward him again, and he pulled away. He had appeared at the clinic a few minutes ago, but upon learning the doctor was a woman he had demanded Jackson Swimmer.

Registering the fever-dulled eyes, flushed skin and colorless lips, Abby had followed him to the barber's. "Please, Mr. Sweeney, let me help you. I assure you I am a trained medical doctor."

"No . . . woman . . . doctor." Despite his obvious pain, the old man wouldn't yield. He lowered himself gingerly into Jackson's chair and leaned back, his eyes drifting shut.

Jackson stepped up, his round beef-red face shiny with sweat. "Abby, you heard the man. Now, go on and quit pesterin' 'im."

Abby stood, torn between anger at their ignorance and compassion for Mr. Sweeney. Jackson knew a little about healing, but even he had scoffed when she tried to convince him of the dangers of bleeding. Despite the danger, she couldn't very well sit on Mr. Sweeney and force him to accept treatment.

"Go on, now," Jackson said gently.

The other gentlemen in the shop, Joe Lomas and Tom Ardington, stared balefully at her, but said nothing.

The usual frustration scraped at her. After another moment, she left and went back to her office. She had thought Texans might be more receptive to progressive ideas, and most in Clarendon were. But several, mainly men, shared Mr. Sweeney's belief that women shouldn't be doctors.

Her thoughts crashed back to the day two years ago when she had bleakly realized that her fiancé, Neil, had his own prejudices concerning women in medicine. She knew now he had been attracted to her only because she was a novelty.

Once he learned she intended truly to practice medicine and not simply serve as a doctor's wife, he had broken their engagement. She had come west, from Philadelphia, hoping for a chance to be accepted for what she was, what she had always wanted to be.

Rachel waited for Abby on the porch of the clinic. The little girl's soft voice jarred Abby's thoughts. "Is that man going to be all right?"

"I don't know, honey." Pushing the past aside as she would a pesky spiderweb, Abby followed Rachel into the spotless front room of the clinic and watched as Rachel joined her sister. At the sight of the two little girls, joy and love ached in Abby's heart.

Rachel, the oldest, stood in front of Hannah, who sat on

a bench, chubby legs dangling. Late afternoon sun glinted through the freshly washed windows, scalloping the edge of Rachel's plain blue dress and picking out strands of gold in Hannah's dark hair.

Rachel held Abby's stethoscope against Hannah's stomach.

"Higher," Abby instructed, grinning. "Unless you want to hear Hannah's stomach rumbling instead of her heartbeat."

Rachel moved the listening tube above her sister's breast.

Hannah's blue eyes rounded. "Can you hear it, Rachel?"

Rachel's brow puckered in a frown then cleared instantly. "Yes! I can hear, Abby! I can hear Hannah's heart swooshing."

Abby laughed and tugged at the little girl's braid. "You'll make a fine doctor, Rachel."

"Me, too?" Hannah demanded, swinging her legs.

"You too, sweetie." Abby dropped a kiss on both dark heads and walked to the examining table in the center of the room. She moved her microscope to a small table and reached for the solution of Lister's carbolic acid and hot water she had mixed earlier. Taking a sterile sponge, she began to wipe down the table.

Thoughts of Mr. Sweeney nagged at her. Without examining him, she couldn't determine the problem, of course, but he had a deep cough. That and the violent flush of fever on his face made her wonder if he had pneumonia.

She hadn't heard of any other cases, but Mr. Sweeney worked for Strat Kennedy on the Rocking K. Knowing Kennedy's attitude toward women doctors, she would be the last to hear.

"You are very sick." Rachel spoke in a serious tone to Hannah. "I'll have to give you an infection."

Abby grinned. "It's *injection*, Rachel."

"What's an injection?" Hannah pronounced the word carefully, her face set in solemn lines.

Rachel answered in a hushed tone, "It's the needle."

Hannah squealed and jumped off the bench, running over to hide behind Abby.

Abby grinned and rumpled Hannah's hair. She held out

her hand for the stethoscope. "Go wash up for supper. I might need your help taking medicine to Ruth Ann tonight."

Immediately both girls darted to the back where Abby had installed a pump. She watched them go, her heart swelling. *Thank you, Jilly, for trusting me with them. You, of all people, knew how I regretted giving up a family. I miss you, dear friend.*

Thoughts of the girls' mother brought an unwelcome reminder of the letter Abby had written. For a moment, a spike of uncertainty penetrated her soft musings, then she reassured herself.

Jefferson Grant wouldn't come.

He hadn't come in the preceding years when Jilly had needed him. He certainly wouldn't come now when she was dead.

A shadow sliced through the light in the clinic, interrupting her thoughts. She pasted on a smile and turned.

A tall, bearded man, with shoulders as wide as the door frame, slumped against the door. "Need doctor."

"Yes." Abby rushed toward him. "I'm a doc—"

He toppled to the ground, freezing the words in her throat. His body slammed into the planks with enough force to vibrate the floor. Abby winced as she knelt beside him.

A few minutes later, she had managed to get him on the examining table with the help of Sheriff Gentry, who had seen the man ride into town.

Once she began stripping off the man's clothes, the sheriff had politely backed out and closed the door. Abby was too busy with the patient to miss the help.

The man's blood was smeared all over her, from her forearms, where she'd rolled up the sleeves of her gray daydress, to the apron she wore over her skirt. He was lucky.

The gunshot wound was clean, entering in the front at the base of his ribs and exiting through the lower left thorax and lumbar region. Though the wound was dirty and the edges of the star-shaped hole were shredded, there was no infection and no remaining bullet or fragments.

After cleansing the injury with carbolic acid, she deftly closed the wound with tiny, even stitches. Her mind absently took stock of the man as she worked.

A light sheen of sweat covered him. He was a magnificent specimen, big and brawny with no spare flesh. His back was bronze, but from the waist down, his skin was lighter, the color of half-baked bread. Broad shoulders angled to a lean waist. All over he was hard and smooth with muscle.

She prayed he would stay unconscious until she finished. With only a few stitches to go, he moved suddenly. Muscles flexed in an oak-hard arm as he groped for her hand.

Abby froze. His large, calloused hand closed over her much smaller one and squeezed hard—as though seeking life, willing her to help him live.

She stared at their hands clasped together, hers nearly obscured, his blanched white with the power of the grip. Her breath lodged in her throat and unexpected tears stung her eyes.

His arm shook, and he sucked in a labored breath through his teeth. After several seconds, his grip relaxed and his hand fell limply away.

A quick fear shot through her. "Please, please don't die," Abby whispered.

She'd felt such strength, such urgency in his grip. Shaking from the impact of his touch, she resumed her stitching.

Please, please don't die. The memory of a woman's voice, gentle and pleading, floated through his consciousness.

Then the deeper strains of his father's voice.

The shock was enough to startle Jeff out of his pain-induced sleep. He opened his eyes slowly, slitting them against the glare of the sun. Through the fog of sleep and pain, his eyes and mind slowly focused.

He lay on a cot in the corner of a large room. A curtain prevented him from seeing his surroundings, but he could hear movement from the other side. The white bed sheets smelled of starch. Plank walls glistened with cleanliness or newness, he couldn't tell which.

Across the room, four beds hugged one wall. He could see a glass-front cabinet neatly lined with bottles of pills and powders and a handful of shiny brass and silver instruments. The glass doors of the cabinet shone like a mirror.

He'd been headed to Clarendon when Phipps had ambushed him. There were no memories after that.

He ran a hand over his bare chest and looked down. White strips circled his waist and glowed against the darkness of his belly. Someone had bandaged his wound and taken off his clothes.

Being without clothes didn't bother him. Being without his gun did.

His shirt, pants and vest were on a chair next to the bed. Easing himself over, he reached for them, fingers groping for his pistol. Pain arrowed through him and he tempered his stretch.

The pistol was buried beneath his denims and shirt, which were freshly laundered. He laid the gun beside him and reached for his pants. He managed to get his legs in and pull them over his hips, sweating with the effort. The pain sharpened, shooting through his side and down his leg, in a wash of weakness. He buttoned three buttons and left the top two undone.

Where was he? Had he reached Clarendon? Memories of Jilly and the letter surged back. The girls. He had to find Rachel and Hannah.

He pulled his shirt over his head, easing it gingerly down over his arms. He searched his mind for some image that might help him remember how he'd come to be in this bed.

"You look considerably better today," a feminine voice said lightly from the open end of the curtain.

Jeff's gaze shot to the end of the bed. A dark-haired woman stood there. Suddenly the voice clicked in his memory. *Please, please don't die.*

Had the soothing plea come from this woman? She stepped closer to the bed, a tiny frown puckering her brow.

"I don't want you trying too much. That wound was quite deep and had to be stitched."

She was young and fresh looking, wearing a light gray dress and white apron. The apron was smeared with dark stains, and she wiped her hands on a still-white corner.

His gaze locked on her hands and another memory surfaced. Cool hands on his body, easing the pain, sending strength into him. Her hands? He hoped so. "G'day, ma'am."

She smiled and he felt suddenly stronger. The ache in his side eased. There was a freshness to her oval face, a striking intelligence in her eyes.

"Any dizziness?" she asked.

His gaze skipped over her, taking in the full breasts, trim waist, the gentle flare of her hips. "No, ma'am."

"Nausea?" She crossed in front of him and leaned down to pull up his shirt and peer at the dressing, her fingers floating gently over his back.

Her eyes were violet, a deep blue-purple color like a mountain sunset, and even more noticeable because of her mink-brown hair. He grinned, never having seen violet eyes before.

Her gaze searched his face. She clasped her hands in front of her, her skirts brushing his knee in the enclosed space. "You'll want to rest for a couple of days. You've lost a lot of blood."

"Did I make it to Clarendon?" Jeff buttoned his shirt and reached for his holster.

She nodded, watching him quietly.

"Good. How long have I been here?"

"Two days."

"Two days?" He had to get to the girls. Moving slowly against the stiffness and pain in his back, he brought his holster around his waist and buckled it.

She looked him over, her gaze lingering on his gun. When she looked at him, the friendliness in her eyes wavered.

He pushed himself off the bed, wincing as pain jabbed his side. A quick flash of dizziness assailed him then disappeared. "Maybe you can help me."

"I really think you should rest longer." She held out her hands as though to catch him, then dropped them to her sides when he stood on his own.

"I can't. I'm looking for someone." He picked up his vest and dipped his hand in the pocket to withdraw the letter. "Maybe you could tell me how to find—" He glanced at the name signed neatly at the bottom of the letter. "Dr. Welch. Dr. A. Welch?"

A sudden stillness stole over her features, and the hair on the back of Jeff's neck prickled.

"I'm Abigail Welch."

His gaze skated over her then paused on her cheeks. They flared with color at his blatant perusal. "I've never seen a woman doctor before."

"You wouldn't believe how many times I've heard *that*."

Her words were dry and sharp. Jeff felt a stab of warning and said warily, "I'm Jeff—"

"Jefferson Grant." She bit off the words acidly, as if pronouncing a disease. Her eyes darkened, first with shock, then with definite disapproval. "I didn't think you'd come."

A muscle in his jaw tightened. There was a price to be paid for having a reputation that stretched across Texas, and he was used to the sudden distance from people when they learned his name, especially women. Usually, he shrugged it off. For some reason, he couldn't dismiss the censure in this woman's steady violet eyes. Annoyed and now impatient, he stepped to the foot of the bed. "Well then, if you'll just get the girls . . ."

"I will not."

"Pardon?" His voice was quiet and deadly low, yet he wasn't surprised she had refused. The ache in his side returned, and for an instant the ground tilted beneath his feet.

She studied him for a minute, seeming to search for words. "It's not . . . quite that simple."

He thrust the letter under her nose. "It says here that Jilly left her two girls to me."

"Rachel and Hannah are their names."

"I know their names," he barked. "I've come for them, in response to your letter."

"Yes, I know, but—"

"What's the problem, Miss, er, Dr. Welch? Have you done something with the girls?"

"Of course I haven't," she snapped. "I just didn't think you'd come."

"Yes, so you said—"

"Everything okay here, Dr. Welch?" The front door opened and a deep nasal voice boomed in the room.

Jeff turned to see a whip-thin man with a shaggy dark mustache watching him through narrowed eyes. The man's holster was slung low on his hips, and one hand was poised above the handle of a revolver. But Jeff's gaze was riveted by the tin star on the man's vest.

"Yes, Sheriff Gentry. I think so." Dr. Welch looked surprised, but quickly recovered and gestured at Jeff. "This is . . . Mr. Grant."

"Jefferson Grant?" The sheriff's even voice revealed none of the sudden turbulence Jeff saw in his eyes.

Jeff answered flatly, "The same."

"I've heard of you." The sheriff straightened, his wiry muscles taut and ready.

Jeff's hand itched to cover the butt of his gun, and the sheriff glanced there as if he expected Jeff to draw. "Flattered."

"Don't want any trouble here. Clarendon is a peaceful town and we work hard to keep it that way. You might want to check your hardware over at Rosenfield's."

"I don't think so, but thanks just the same," Jeff said tightly, silently vowing not to be without his gun while in this town. "There won't be any trouble. I only came—"

"For Jilly," the sheriff finished.

Jeff slanted a glance at Dr. A. Welch. "I suppose the whole damn town knows."

"She *was* a part of this community, Mr. Grant." Dr. Welch drew herself up, somehow managing to look taller than she really was. Despite her size—the top of her head barely reached his chin—he figured she could probably intimidate a lesser man.

"I'll be watching you." Sheriff Gentry stared hard at Jeff then turned to Dr. Welch. "Holler if you need me."

"Thank you."

The man backed out the door and closed it softly. Jeff noted a small group of people gathered outside the door and heard the low murmur of voices.

He raised an eyebrow at that.

Dr. Welch smiled tightly. "They're concerned. They didn't think you'd come either."

"Well, I did come, so you can fetch the girls."

"You can't take them." Dr. Welch looked desperate, almost afraid, but also seriously determined.

Jeff angled his head, tamping down a spurt of anger. "What's that?"

"Your sister gave me the girls, too."

"She what?" Blood roared in his ears as the implication hit him. The ache in his side moved to his temple. "How can she do that?"

"They're her children. She can do whatever she wants."

Jeff pulled a wad of money from his vest pocket. "I'm willing to pay you for any trouble—"

"You just put that money away, Mr. Grant." She tilted her chin at him. "Those girls are like my own."

"Well, they're not yours." Jeff narrowed his gaze at her and locked his knees against a surge of fatigue. Was this woman crazy? Did she really think Rachel and Hannah belonged to her? Why would she want someone else's children?

"They're not yours either," she shot back, her eyes flashing fire, a startling combination of purple and blue.

"They're my blood. They belong to me." Jeff felt as if the ground were sliding out from under him. Hell, he didn't know what to do with two little girls. And he didn't know what to do with any woman doctor. Jilly had wanted him to come and he had.

"So, you came after all?"

The voice behind Jeff froze him. Though he hadn't heard

it in years, the deep, rich timbre shot regret and longing and pain through him all in one shattering moment. *Dad?*

Jeff thought he might have passed out again, but he saw a brief flicker of compassion on Dr. Welch's face and knew he was very much awake.

Marcus Grant had disowned him fifteen years ago. Fifteen years in which Jeff had never considered going back home. Fifteen years in which Jilly, ever hopeful, had never stopped urging him to do just that.

He turned, swallowing as anger arced painfully across his chest. Where once Marcus Grant's hair had been black, it was now streaked with iron gray. Deep lines were etched around his shrewd silver eyes, but the face was still smooth, still handsome. Jeff *had* heard his father's voice while unconscious.

Jeff's voice was hoarse, the muscles in his throat clenching on each word. "Where the hell did you come from?"

"I notified him." Dr. Welch stepped around Jeff and between the two men. She turned to Marcus Grant. "You know he's been wounded. Please don't upset—"

"Wounded on one of your 'jobs'?" his father snarled.

Jeff barely kept himself from swinging at the old man. He hissed at the doctor, "Why the hell did you send for him?"

"Stop cursing," she snapped, anger coloring her cheeks. "Rachel and Hannah don't need to hear that kind of talk."

For the first time, he noticed the two little girls on either side of Marcus Grant. Both were dark-haired, with rose-and-cream skin, both beautiful.

The taller one had to be Rachel. She had Jilly's black hair and silvery eyes and a stubborn tilt to her chin. Her body was tight as she clung to her grandfather's hand, and her eyes blazed with fire. Jeff's gaze drifted to the other one.

Hannah was obviously the younger, and as he stared at her, he had the oddest sensation of looking at himself. She had a pert nose, but wavy black-brown hair, just like his, crystal blue eyes just like his and a little scar on her upper lip. His was on the left and hers was on the right, but for an instant Jeff felt as if he were staring in a mirror. Her chubby legs peeked out from beneath a neat red calico dress and pinafore.

Emotion slammed him in the gut. He'd planned to keep them, but now he realized he couldn't walk away no matter what. How he was going to deal with Dr. A. Welch, he didn't know, but he wasn't leaving these girls. They were his blood. They were staying with him.

He shook his head, trying to clear the pictures of him and Jilly swinging on a rope into the river, him and Jilly and Justin racing new ponies on Justin's birthday, Jilly stomping her foot in anger when he and Justin refused to let her come along to their secret hiding place. He saw that anger in Rachel's face, a sweet uncertainty in Hannah's and fear in both. Abruptly, his head cleared.

"Hello," he said gruffly. "I'm your uncle."

Hannah scooted farther behind his father's leg, but Rachel looked questioningly at Dr. Welch. After a slight hesitation, the doctor nodded. Rachel looked back to Jeff, staring at him with big eyes. Waiting.

Jeff felt as unprepared as if he'd been asked to lay down his gun and take up needlepoint. "I think we'd better get this straightened out." He looked at Dr. Welch, jerking his head toward his father. "Why is he here?"

"I told you, I didn't expect you to come."

"Why wouldn't I come? Jilly was my only sister."

"Why, indeed," Dr. Welch muttered.

Jeff's father interrupted, "No one's ever sure what you're going to do, Jefferson. And, quite frankly, you're not fit to have these darlin's."

"Wait just a minute—" Jeff began, his voice rising as he stepped forward.

Dr. Welch pushed between them, turning her back on Jeff. "Marcus, if you'd be so kind as to take the girls back to supper?"

"He won't agree," Marcus Grant said in the patronizing tone Jeff had never been able to forget.

Jeff felt disoriented at seeing his father, as though he'd come to a familiar place only to find nothing familiar. He watched as the older man led the little girls back down the hall. "Won't agree to what?"

Dr. Welch turned back to Jeff and her gaze halted on his gun, hanging low on his hip. She stared for a full minute, repulsion streaking through her eyes.

He couldn't resist taunting her. "It's a gun. A Colt."

"I know what it is, Mr. Grant. And what it's used for." She turned away. "I think perhaps your father has a point."

"About?"

"You're really not . . . equipped to care for children, especially little girls."

"What equipment do I need, Dr. Welch? And what makes you so sure you have it?" He made his voice deliberately pointed and felt a rush of satisfaction when her neck colored.

"Your job is hardly conducive to raising children."

He narrowed his eyes at her, anger throbbing with the pain in his side. "Jilly didn't object to my job, Dr. Welch. And it doesn't matter a good damn to me whether you do or not. I came for those girls and I'm leaving with them."

"No, you're not." His father reappeared in the doorway.

Dr. Welch looked as if she were on the verge of tears, and she glanced over Jeff's shoulder to Marcus Grant. "Jilly wanted him to have the girls, too, Marcus."

"What about your claim? You don't have to give them up."

Jeff muttered a curse and pivoted to face his father. "Dr. Welch can see them anytime she wants. I'm not trying to keep her from it. I'm just trying to do what Jilly wanted."

"What your sister wanted," Marcus ground out, "was that you both raise them."

"Both!" Jeff barked, suddenly unsteady. "Not together?"

"That's what she said and that's what she meant." His father leveled a sharp glare at him.

"I didn't think I was fit," Jeff reminded him caustically.

"You aren't." The words came from Dr. Welch. They were quietly spoken, but she tipped her chin at him and held his gaze.

"I'm as fit as you are. And if Jilly wanted me to have the girls then you can damn well—"

"Mr. Grant—" Dr. Welch tried to interrupt.

"—bet I'm going to take them."

Marcus stepped into the room from the hallway. "What can you offer them? You have no experience with children. You can't lug them around the country with you."

"I'm planning to stay here. Jilly left the house for the girls, and they won't have to go anywhere."

"I'm more prepared to care for them. They've been living with me since Jilly . . . passed on." Dr. Welch's voice caught then strengthened. "You can see them anytime you're in town."

"They're going with *me*." Jeff's voice echoed off the planked walls.

"We don't want to! You're mean!" The outburst came from just outside the hallway door, and all the adults spun to see Rachel standing there, her big eyes sheened with tears and her chin sticking out defiantly. Hannah stood beside her, clutching her sister's hand.

The lady doctor threw Jeff a look guaranteed to poison water and hurried to the little girls. She dropped to her knees in front of them. "He's not mean, honey, just loud. He won't hurt you."

"We don't want to go with him, Abby."

The doctor gathered both Rachel and Hannah close. "Oh, sweetheart."

"Oh, damn," Jeff muttered. He closed his eyes, feeling like an ill-tempered bear. The pain in his side gouged at him.

"Enough of this." Marcus joined the others in the hallway. He wore a hard-edged look, one Jeff had seen many times in court. Dread slithered up his spine. "If you both want the girls, you're going to have to agree to take them. Together."

"What?" Jeff and Abby burst out in unison.

"It *was* Jilly's last request," Marcus pronounced in a grave voice.

Abby rose to her feet, her hands closing over the girls'

shoulders. "But . . . but—" Her gaze flew to Jeff, pleading.

"Using guilt?" Jeff said silkily, twisting the words like a knife. "How unlike you."

Marcus Grant locked his hands behind his back and began pacing, a definite courtroom habit. Jeff groaned inwardly. His father was on the offensive now and nothing would do but blood. Marcus strode the length of the room as though in front of a jury box. "Rachel and Hannah have had both natural parents taken from them. They need stability, which you can't give them, Jeff—"

"Jilly thought I could."

"And they need a male influence, which you can't give them, Abby."

"That's ridiculous. What about my father? They already think of him as their other grandfather."

Marcus ceased pacing and faced them both. Jeff stifled the urge to squirm, long leftover from his childhood. Stern silver eyes bored into Jeff and Abby. "You'll marry or neither of you will get them."

"Each other?" the doctor whispered, her face going as white as her apron.

"The hell we will," Jeff grated out, feeling the walls press in.

"That's . . . absurd!" Dr. Welch cried.

Jeff started toward his father, his fist clenched over the butt of his gun. "I'm their blood. They belong with me."

"I'm their blood, too, Jefferson. No one would trust those girls to a hired gun. That visit from the sheriff proves that. Not to mention that new wound you're sporting. I'd win and you know it."

"You'd take this to court? Typical."

"It's my way or no way."

"Just like always, right, Father?" Jeff spat. Sweat tunneled down his back, itched his neck. Even after all these years, his father had to control Jeff's life.

"Please, don't do this to the girls." The doctor's voice was hoarse, edged with pain. "I'll give them to your son. Please."

"No!" Rachel and Hannah cried in unison, clinging to the doctor. "No, Abby! Don't make us go with him!"

Jeff's heart seized up at the anguish and fear in their voices.

Marcus Grant drove on relentlessly, speaking to both Abby and Jeff. The little girls sobbed, their faces pressed into the doctor's skirt. "It's in your power to change it. You can give them the home they need. All you have to do is provide one."

Jeff turned to Dr. Welch. She'd seemed brave, courageous. Wouldn't she have to be to become a doctor? Desperation forced out his next words. "You can live at the house with us. You can have claim to them. We don't have to marry to do that."

She looked mortified, actually wobbling as she held tighter to the girls. "Your reputation may be in tatters, Mr. Grant, but mine is not. I've worked hard for the respect I have, and I'll be darned if you'll come along and take it away. No one would set foot in this clinic again."

"Is that more important to you than the girls?"

She drew in a sharp breath as though he'd punched her. "No."

"That option is not acceptable to me either, Jeff," Marcus Grant put in. "As much as you don't want to, you will consider my feelings. And your sister's. You're going to give those girls a home, a real home. I said marriage and I meant it. As much for Rachel and Hannah as for Dr. Welch's reputation."

Jeff studied his father, fighting the urge to surrender his claim and walk away. Jilly's faith in him kept him rooted to the floor. He'd known his father too long and too well to believe he was bluffing. Marcus Grant never bluffed. Jeff's gaze slid from the tearstained faces of the little girls to the pasty white one of Dr. Welch.

The doctor had been there for the girls when their mother passed away. Jeff hadn't. He wanted to be there for them now. He had no intention of letting Jilly down, in spite of his father. His father, Jeff knew, was expecting him to refuse, to walk away, proving again that he wasn't fit to carry the Grant name.

He bucked at the imposed restriction of marriage, the sense that his father had backed him into a corner, that this Welch woman would be sticking her nose into family business. But the little girls came first. Chafing even as he knew what he must do, he gave a curt nod of agreement.

Abby looked from him to the girls. Pleas ravaged their small faces. She drew in a deep breath. "All right."

Jeff had no doubt that Dr. Abigail Welch considered this as much a sacrifice as he did. For some reason, that annoyed the hell out of him.

Jilly, Jilly, what have you done?

He'd come for the girls, to honor a pledge. In return, he'd lost his freedom, saddled with a woman who didn't appear to like the sight of him. And all because of the man who'd driven him from home.

TWO
❧

Jeff watched his father slam out the door, and anger slashed through him. A fiery orange sun hovered on the horizon, painting the street in glimmering rose and gold. Marcus's shadow weaved in and out of the color as he walked across the street and behind Rosenfield's Mercantile.

Damn! Even after all these years and all the distance, his father still hadn't forgiven him for leaving.

Jeff moved to the window, one hand closing over the butt end of his revolver, the other gripping the wall for support.

Dr. Abigail Welch stepped up next to him, Rachel and Hannah wrapped like vines around her legs.

He slanted a glance at the doctor and grated out, "Why didn't you tell him you had someone else?"

"Because he knows I don't," she said sharply, her gaze steady on Marcus Grant's back as he disappeared into the tiny frame building used as both church and school. "He has a law practice here now."

"He lives here?"

"Yes."

The information slammed into Jeff and increased the throbbing in his head. He stared blindly at her.

She kept her gaze focused out the window. "Why didn't you tell him you had someone?"

"He wouldn't give a da— care if I did."

She turned her head slightly and met his gaze. Her own was steady and burning with the same helpless anger he felt. Jeff's gaze returned to the street, narrowing on the spanking white clapboard building where his father had gone to speak to Reverend Carhart. Damn his father!

"Will he really go through with it?" Dr. Welch turned to him, her features pinched and white. Those amethyst eyes stood out in startling jeweled color against the pale face.

Jeff willed himself to soften. She was cornered, just as he was, by her feelings for Jilly and the girls. "You mean take them legally?"

She hugged Rachel and Hannah close to her. "Yes."

He gave a curt nod, his gaze dropping to his nieces. Hannah pressed closer to Abby, her blue eyes huge and frightened. Rachel's face was powder white, but there was defiant anger behind the fear and uncertainty.

Dr. Welch hustled the girls toward the hallway. "Rachel, would you and Hannah please start cleaning up the supper dishes?"

Hannah locked onto Rachel's hand, and the girls shuffled to the hallway door.

Rachel turned back to find Abby.

"I'll be right there," Abby reassured.

"Promise?"

"Promise." She waited until Rachel and Hannah had disappeared, then she spun. Her spine was stiff and straight, her eyes blazing. "There's got to be another way."

"I wish there was. Believe me." He studied her, grudgingly recognizing the determination in her voice, admiring the way she addressed the problem. "Don't make the mistake of thinking my father won't follow through."

"You've known him longer than I have, but . . . surely he can see how this would hurt the girls."

"It's done. We'll just have to live with it." His gaze paused on the rigid set of her jaw, the angry flush on her face and neck. The rapid flutter of pulse in her throat gave away her uncertainty. "Unless you're willing to give them up?"

"Or you are." She stared him down, her violet eyes unflinching.

No coy cajoling, no fluttering, no hysterics. He bit back a smile of admiration. "We've already danced this dance, Doc."

"So we have." Her jaw tightened then she sighed, turning to look out the window once more.

The curve of her neck was elegant and slender, her jaw sturdy but in a challenging way, not unappealing. Jeff frowned, annoyed for noticing. It hit him then, what he'd just agreed to do.

Marriage! Suddenly the walls closed in. Suffocating Texas dirt clogged his throat, blocking all air. He had to get out of here. His voice was rough and impatient. "I'd like to see Jilly."

The doctor studied him, mistrust sharp in her eyes. Her gaze lit on his gun, and again her face closed in disappointment. "She's next to Dave, in the town cemetery. It's just to the east, across Carroll Creek and at the foot of the bluff."

"Thanks." One stride carried him to the door. "I'll be back tomorrow. Do the girls need anything?"

"No. Aren't you going to wait for your father? You know, to see what time—"

"He'll find me." The words burned Jeff's tongue, as bitter and coarse as ashes. How he used to wish his father would look for him and find him, but he never had. "We'll move your things tomorrow. We'll be living at Jilly's."

"No." Anger edged her voice.

Jeff looked over his shoulder, his side aching dully, his head pounding from the astonishment of seeing his father. Fresh anger ripped through him, merging with the frustration and helplessness he felt at his father's threats.

She held his gaze. He saw a core of steel behind those violet eyes. "It's not practical for me."

Jeff considered arguing then dismissed it. "Yes, ma'am." Her eyes widened at that, but she still regarded him warily. "I need to be close to my patients, and the girls are already settled here."

If he had to pack her himself and carry them all out, he would. No bossy woman doctor was going to dictate to him. He deliberately let his gaze stroke her, pausing on her breasts. "Yes, ma'am."

At his blatant perusal, she folded her arms across her chest, but didn't back down. "So you won't make us leave?"

He wasn't going to fight with her. Not today. Not when he felt as weak as a kitten and muddled after seeing his father. His gaze skipped over her, noting the slat-stiff set of her shoulders. "See you tomorrow."

He shut the door without a sound and mounted up, heading east of town.

"Dad's here. I guess you know that." Jeff grimaced at his sister's grave. "If I didn't know better, I'd think you had planned this."

He fell silent, his throat burning. Somehow he had withstood the shock of seeing Marcus Grant, and now he had come to say good-bye to his sister.

He stood inside a wrought-iron fence with the waters of Carroll Creek at his back. An easy breeze blew across the rolling hills. He removed his hat and stared down at the stone marker that bore his sister's name. *Jilly Claire Parker.*

Jilly. Guilt and pain rampaged through his tired body. His only sister, his best friend after Justin had died. Jeff knew he should've tried to visit her more. In the last ten years, he'd seen her once, just after her marriage to Dave Parker, when they were on their way to Texas.

Even when Dave had been trampled to death by a wild steer, Jeff hadn't come to Clarendon. Jilly had told him to stay away because the old man was there. Jeff had allowed himself to be convinced, and it was an indulgence he now regretted.

He'd never forget his sister's stubborn chin, those silver eyes the color of their father's. She alone had understood that Jeff wanted nothing to do with the family tradition of becoming an attorney.

Justin, his older brother, had loved law just like Marcus Grant, and had a brilliant mind. But after the War Between the States, Justin was gone, killed at Shiloh.

Marcus Grant had turned to Jeff to carry on the family tradition. For a year and a half, Jeff tried. But it wasn't in his blood. He could appreciate the mental battles and victories, the shrewdness of a quick mind, but those things were not for him. When he'd finally told his father he couldn't do it, that he wanted to leave Kentucky and make his way in the West, Marcus Grant had reacted much more violently than either his son or daughter could have imagined.

It had been that way since the death of their mother six months before. Jeff knew his father felt as if he were losing him forever. He tried to explain that he would be back, but his father had accused him of deserting the family and forbidden him ever to return.

Jeff left in anger that night. He'd been seventeen then, greener than a new shoot and just about as tender.

He palmed the sweat from his brow, his thoughts returning to Hannah and Rachel. Now, when he could use a little tenderness, he had no idea where to find it.

He angled his body and regarded the town from his perch on the hill.

Clarendon. Or Saints' Roost, as the cowboys were wont to call it.

The irony of his situation was not lost on Jeff. A hired gun settling in the mainly Christian colony in Donley County? A bitter smile twisted his lips.

The newly named county seat, built at the mouth of Carroll Creek, nestled in a sandy valley surrounded by hills and cedar-studded canyons. The road to Tascosa, one of two other settlements in the Panhandle, served as the main road of Clarendon. The road to Mobeetie and Fort Elliot ran alongside the cemetery where Jeff stood and over a high bluff just above the creek.

From here, he could see the doctor's office situated between the stage stand and the sheriff's office. The setting sun painted streamers of red and gold over the doctor's pale blue two-story building. His gaze scanned the brick-hard red dirt street and the line of buildings that were mostly that same dirty red.

Established four years ago by a Methodist minister named Carhart, Clarendon had businesses, several law offices, a church, restaurants, two hotels, a blacksmith, a newspaper office, and a doctor's office. There wasn't one saloon, gambling house or dance hall in the whole town.

The town fathers of Clarendon wouldn't sell lots to anyone unless they agreed not to sell liquor. A damn nuisance, Jeff decided, though he supposed it might be a good atmosphere for kids.

Two little girls.

How the hell was he going to raise two little girls? Apprehension, the first he'd felt in years over anything besides a gun barrel pointed in his direction, curled in Jeff's belly. The prospect of being responsible for children was more daunting than leaving home had been so many years ago.

Ignoring the pain in his side, he settled his hat back on his head and turned to his sister's marker. His throat tight with desperate determination, he said, "I don't know how, Jilly, but I won't let you down this time. I swear."

Abby stood on the porch of the clinic, able to see the gray felt hat and wide shelf of shoulders on the man at the cemetery.

Anger, though futile, still throbbed inside her. Marry Jefferson Grant? Absolutely not. Especially after the insulting way he had looked at her, as though she pleased him, as though she were a . . . woman.

No man had looked at her like that since before her decision to attend medical college. Once she had declared her intention of becoming a doctor, men always regarded her as if she were crazy or loose. She was neither. Or they regarded her as Neil had, like a novelty, something to be admired and studied because of its differences, then discarded when the newness had worn off. It was just as well she had not married him.

But she didn't want to marry Jefferson Grant either.

There had to be a way out, a way without hurting the girls.

Well over six feet tall, sturdy as an oak beam, Jefferson Grant was as dangerous as any epidemic she'd ever seen. It wasn't his dirty clothes or shaggy dark hair and beard that disturbed her. Danger pulsed from the man, evident in the frigid ice-blue eyes, the barely leashed rage when he'd confronted his father.

And she'd heard the rumors about him, the whispers of his lethal ability with a gun, his coldness in the face of death.

Now that she'd seen him, she believed. Even injured and weak from loss of blood, his shadow had swallowed the room, netting her with an invisible threat. His eyes had been hollow, empty until he'd looked at the girls.

By simply answering her letter, he had managed to turn her world upside down. His presence resurrected old memories of Jilly. And the guilt.

Abby knew she hadn't learned of Jilly's tumor in time to help, but she still berated herself for not seeing the symptoms. Of course Jilly, in her stubborn way of protecting those she loved, had hidden her illness from everyone.

Stubborn. In that way, Jefferson Grant was definitely Jilly's brother. Both had the same ruthless determination as well. And though his eyes were the clear, undiluted blue of the sky on a cloudless day and Jilly's had been a soft silver-gray, both could still turn as slicingly cold as a Panhandle winter when enraged.

Anger jabbed at Abby yet again. Frustration and resentment crowded in. Jefferson Grant was dark, forbidding, his name infamous in this state. What would that do to *her* reputation?

"That's him, huh?" Lionel Welch stepped up on the porch, his gaze following the direction of his daughter's.

The lingering scent of dust and man and horse hung in the air, and the clinic seemed suddenly and strangely empty. A fresh jolt of irritation surged through her. "You already heard?"

"Yep. Gentry came by the hotel."

"He actually checked on me. Maybe I'm starting to be accepted by some of the men." She kept her gaze locked on Jefferson Grant's broad back as though she could will him to disappear. "Help me think of something, Papa."

"Think of what—"

"Papa Lionel! Papa Lionel!" Rachel and Hannah tore out the door of the clinic and onto the porch, hurtling toward him.

He knelt, arms outstretched, and caught them up, hugging them fiercely. "How're my little fillies today?"

Abby barely heard him. Normally, his newly acquired vocabulary annoyed her, but not today.

Hannah giggled. "We're not fillies, we're girls."

Rachel stared somberly at Lionel. "Our uncle came today. He's going to take us away."

Lionel and Abby exchanged a look over Rachel's head then he turned his attention back to the girls. Hannah was patting her chubby hands over his shirt front and leather vest. "Now, Hannah, what are you doing?"

"Looking." She grinned up at him. "Did you bring us something? Did you?"

"I bet it's in his vest," Rachel suggested, having forgotten her uncle for the moment. She stuck her hand inside his pocket and withdrew a clump of wood. "I found it!"

She held the awkwardly shaped piece of mesquite triumphantly for a moment. Both girls stared and their brows furrowed.

Hannah frowned up at Lionel. "What is it?"

"What is it!" he exclaimed, shifting the girls on his hips. "What is it!"

"A . . . bear?" Rachel offered, studying the one recognizable feature, a long snout.

"A bear! Who ever saw a bear that looked like that?" Lionel declared indignantly.

"It's a puppy," Hannah guessed eagerly.

Abby grinned. So far, the girls hadn't been able to figure out one of her father's carvings. Neither had she, for that matter. Whittling was just another skill he'd wanted to learn after he'd retired from practicing medicine and moved with her to this vast land two years ago. He'd also grown a beard, begun dipping snuff and was learning to rope a steer. All in the name of fitting in and broadening his horizons.

"A puppy?" he snorted. He gave the girls a little shake, making them giggle. "It's a wolf is what it is. What's the matter with the schoolteacher in this town? Don't she teach you girls about animules?"

"It's *animals,* Papa Lionel," Rachel corrected with a grin. She squinted at the awkwardly shaved and gouged piece of wood in her hand. "I guess it's a wolf, if you say so."

"Well, I do." He squeezed both girls and slid them to the floor. Reaching into his vest pocket, he pulled out a peppermint stick for each of them. He winked and said in a loud whisper, "Don't let Abby catch me giving you these."

True to the ritual, Rachel tucked hers carefully in the pocket of her pinafore for later. Hannah popped hers straight into her mouth, giving a two-eyed wink back to him.

Lionel swatted them on the rear and turned them toward the door. "Now, you girls run along inside and let me talk to Abby."

When they stepped inside, Rachel turned. "Are you going to talk about us, Papa Lionel?"

"I reckon so, sweetness." He chuckled as they disappeared.

Abby's heart clenched at the sight of them, Rachel too serious for her years, Hannah too sweet and shy to fend for herself. She loved them as though they were from her own body and would do anything for them, but did that include marrying a man she didn't know or like?

Her father turned, the white of his newly grown beard startling against the weathered bronze of his face. His blue eyes, usually smiling, clouded with concern. "What's happened? Did Rachel mean what she said about Jefferson Grant coming to take them away?"

"Yes. I told him I had claim to them, too." She squinted into the sun, remembering his reaction. "I think he was shocked by that, though it was hard to tell."

"He's not planning to stay, is he? Won't you be able to keep them?"

"No. At least not by myself." She explained what had happened when Jefferson showed up and the resulting scene between him and his father. Her voice rose and she gripped one of the porch posts. "And now Marcus has gone over to speak to Reverend Carhart about performing the ceremony."

Lionel Welch frowned. "Will he really do it?"

"Jefferson thinks so."

"Well, I'll be jumped up."

"Papa," she groaned. "Don't give me any of that silly cowboy talk. Not now."

"Is this such a bad thing?"

"How can you even ask that? I don't even know Jefferson Grant, and what I do know of him I don't like. He's a hired gun." Her voice rose another decibel. She wrapped her arms around her waist, warding off the feeling that she'd been sliced open and her nerves exposed. "The whole state of Texas and beyond probably knows about him."

"You could always let him have the girls. He is their uncle."

"I will not! Rachel is scared to death of him and so is Hannah."

"That's only because they don't know him. Hannah is scared of everyone at first."

Irritation flickered in her at his observation. "You know what he is, Papa. What he does."

"I've heard of him." His frown deepened, and he leaned against the wall of the clinic, studying her. "I've never known you to judge a person based on that. Or on things you've heard yourself."

"I know about all those letters Jilly wrote to him. He didn't come to her, not once when she needed him." Shame pricked at her for judging anyone so harshly, but she was still angry and stunned and feeling threatened. "Why would he be any more reliable with the girls?"

"He came for them, didn't he?"

She pressed her lips tight and remained silent.

"Didn't he?"

She glared at him and walked inside the clinic. A square

of linen lay next to the examining table, and she picked it up, ripping a piece with her teeth to make a bandage.

"This could be a good thing." Lionel followed her inside, his tone as optimistic as if he were deciding on a horse to buy. "You've wanted a family for a long time. You just might get one."

"The girls and I are a family. We don't need him."

"Then don't do it." Her father's tone turned brusque, as it did with patients who refused to cooperate.

"If I don't, Marcus will take them. I couldn't stand that. Rachel and Hannah have been through too much already. There's got to be a way out, but I'm not sure what it is."

"Abby, don't overlook what's right under your nose. You have it in your power to make a home for those girls, give them love and stability. Maybe yourself, too. Why can't you see that?"

"With him?" The idea of a hired gun settling down and providing a home was almost laughable. And yet . . . She stared at her father. "That's almost exactly what Marcus said."

"You can make the best of any situation. I've seen you do it all your life. It's the one thing that made you a doctor."

She tore another strip from the cloth, biting back a scream. "Papa, that's different."

"I haven't seen you this het up over anything since you were trying to get into medical college. You didn't let a little setback get in your way then."

"I wouldn't call marriage to a hired gun a setback." She tore the cloth with her teeth and ripped another strip. "Besides, he's a total stranger."

"My point is, you want a family and it's within your grasp to have one."

She dropped the linen onto the table. Disappointment and frustration edged into her mind. "We're only doing it for the girls. I tried to tell Marcus that, but he wouldn't listen."

"It's a noble reason."

"That doesn't make it right. I don't love Jefferson Grant, Papa. He doesn't love me. Don't the girls need that as much as anything else?"

"You can't have everything at once."

She stifled a groan and gripped the linen in her hand until it burned her palm. "He's no more interested in this marriage than I am."

"You might be surprised."

"I don't think so. He was pretty plain when he left here." Once again she saw the cold blue eyes, the latent rage simmering there. But, too, she remembered the flicker of love and uncertainty in his eyes when he'd looked at the girls.

"Once you get to know him, you might like him."

"I don't want 'like,' Papa. I want what you and Mama had."

"Your mama, God rest her, would've been the first to tell you that some marriages have started with less."

"I don't see how," she muttered, rolling a bandage neatly into quarters.

"Some have had only the physical side of love and it's turned into something everlasting."

"The physical—" She sputtered, dropping the bandages and jerking her head toward him. "There will be none of that!"

"Don't close all the doors, Abby. You're doing what's best for the girls and so is he. He can't be all bad."

She picked up the bandage, threw it down again and planted her hands on her hips. "Are you defending him?"

"No, I'm just saying give the man a chance."

"Doesn't it matter to you that I've been blackmailed into marrying a—a hired gun? How can you be so calm?"

"I don't like it, but Marcus has a point. Hannah and Rachel do need both of you. And you can't deny you've longed for a family."

"Not like this," she said firmly.

Lionel gently took her shoulders and turned her to face him. "If Marcus really thought his son was so terrible, do you think he would force the issue?"

"I . . . I—that doesn't make me feel any better." Her throat ached with a frustrated anger that shredded her control. "There has to be another way."

"You've just told me the girls must come first. If there is another way, I'll help you."

The front door opened and Marcus Grant stepped inside. Abby froze, gripping the edge of the table. Silence draped the spacious room, and she thought she could hear each torturous thud of her heart.

Marcus nodded almost imperceptibly at Lionel, his gaze fixed on Abby. "The ceremony will be at ten o'clock tomorrow morning."

She bit her lip, apprehension clawing through her. She met her father's gaze, and anger exploded within her. Her chest ached. In her mind, she ran out of the clinic and over to the creek. Away, far away. Visions of Hannah and Rachel danced through the mist of rage, drawing her back.

Abby stared out the window, oblivious to the blazing late-day sun, the lengthening shadows that teased with the promise of coolness.

There had to be a way out.

She repeated the words the next morning as she stood side by side with Jefferson Grant in front of Reverend Carhart.

The wedding was small and short. Only one pew was occupied, making the small room hollow. That hollowness gnawed at Abby's insides. Tension hammered the room with each word from the pastor's lips.

Honor. Cherish. Obey.

Mistake. Mistake. Mistake.

In her mind's eye, Abby saw Jilly as she lay suffering on the exam table, asking Abby to take the girls. Panic blinded her and she partially turned. Enough to see Rachel and Hannah sitting between her father and Marcus Grant. Harriet Beasley, the schoolteacher and a dear friend of the Welches, sat next to Marcus. The only other guest was Sheriff Gentry. He stood at the back of the church, his gun in plain sight as though he anticipated trouble.

She could still leave, just turn away and walk out. Her muscles tensed, and for a split second she considered doing it.

Then she heard the rustle of cotton on the pew and Hannah's low whisper, "Will they be married like Mama and Daddy were?"

Abby couldn't bring herself to do it, couldn't abandon Rachel and Hannah to a man she didn't know or trust. Beside her, Jefferson Grant stood stiff and unyielding. She found it difficult to picture him as the same man who'd collapsed at her feet three days ago.

His color was better today, and he smelled of strong lye soap and summer sun. Though he looked almost handsome, there was still an edge to him, a harshness that splintered all her good intentions.

She didn't want him to touch her or look at her. She tried to concentrate on the beeswax freshness of the wood in the one-room schoolhouse that doubled as a church, but all she could smell was the tantalizing muskiness of *him*. The uncomfortable awareness knotted her stomach and rendered her as jittery as when she'd performed her first surgery.

His dark hair, a shade shy of black, was thick and gleaming and waved over his collar. He'd trimmed his beard close, but instead of giving him a refined appearance, it only tightened the high-slashed cheekbones and darkened his copper skin. His crystal-blue eyes gleamed like polished stones.

Abby didn't realize until Reverend Carhart bowed his head for a prayer that she'd spoken the vows that would forever tie her to Jefferson Grant. The preacher pronounced them man and wife.

She glanced sideways at Jefferson and met his gaze. Anger still burned behind the vivid eyes, but there was also speculation. His gaze fell to her lips then rose again to meet her eyes. A blush heated her neck, but she didn't look away. He wouldn't kiss her, would he?

He tipped his head down and her breath jammed in her chest. He was going to!

"I'll be out front with the wagon in ten minutes."

She blinked, startled at his words. She managed a small nod and watched as he turned and strode from the church without a glance at anyone.

Relief washed over her followed by a small sting of indignation. Why hadn't he kissed her? Was he, like nearly every other man she'd met, intimidated by her? The thought disappeared as quick as rain in July, and relief washed over her.

She didn't want him to kiss her. His mouth looked hard and forbidding. There didn't seem to be much kindness in his broad, calloused hands or in that expansive, sturdy chest, either. Besides, Reverend Carhart had studiously omitted that instruction.

A small, awkward pause filled the room as all eyes followed Jefferson out the door. Abby, determined not to upset the girls, smiled and moved forward as the five guests rose. Marcus Grant stared stony-jawed after his son while the girls hurried up to Abby. She guided them outside, grateful to find her father and Harriet waiting.

Harriet, reed-thin and supple in a jaunty moss-green chintz that set off her auburn hair, took Abby's hands. "My dear, I'm afraid I don't know quite what to say."

Trust Harriet to speak plainly. Abby refused to look around for her husband. "I don't think anyone does."

"That won't be a problem once you leave today," Harriet said dryly, tipping her head toward town.

Following Harriet's gesture, Abby looked out at the street. The entire town had turned out for the wedding, though not in the conventional way. People were huddled in groups on the sidewalks, faces pressed to the windows, and bodies strained over balconies. She caught several looks full of compassion, and others cold with anger.

She gripped the girls' hands and marched across the street.

Harriet bustled along beside her, shielding her eyes from the mid-morning sun. Jefferson pulled the wagon to a halt in front of the clinic and climbed down, a gray felt cowboy hat now covering his dark hair.

"He doesn't seem a harsh man," Harriet said quietly to Abby.

She shot a sharp look at her friend, surprised. Though Harriet was usually a good judge of character, Abby thought

Jefferson seemed harsh. Rough and dangerous as well. The women halted in front of the clinic and Jefferson tipped his hat to Harriet.

Abby performed introductions stiffly, amazed when Jefferson smiled at Harriet and actually bowed over her hand. The effect was . . . disorienting.

Teeth flashed white against the dark mustache, drawing Abby's attention to lips that were now curved in a charming smile. The cold eyes warmed, hinting at fire and humor beneath the glacial depths. His face appeared younger, almost pleasant. Abby remembered the look of pain that had flitted through his eyes at mention of his sister, and supposed maybe he wasn't all harshness.

He stared at her, eyebrows arched, holding open the door of the clinic. "Ready to go?"

She gaped at him. "But you said—"

"I told you to be ready this morning."

"When you left, you sounded as if you agreed with me!"

Harriet interrupted. "Perhaps you'd like me to take the girls inside?"

Without waiting for an answer, she led Hannah and Rachel into the clinic.

Abby stepped closer, glaring at Jefferson. "Yesterday, you acted as though it were settled."

"No, you acted as though it were," he reminded quietly, irritation sparking his eyes. "I told you what I intended to do."

"Do you go around spouting out orders and expect them to be followed?" she demanded hotly. The sun baked her back, but her blood was boiling. Was that amusement in his eyes?

He pushed his hat farther back on his head and regarded her as though she were some sideshow in a circus. "Yes, I do."

"Well, that's ridiculous. I'm not one of your victims or jobs or whatever your father called it!" Fury flashed in his eyes and Abby felt danger lick at her. She balled her hands into fists, keeping them pressed to her sides. "When I gave you my reasons for staying here, I assumed you had agreed."

"Yes, ma'am," he drawled, sparking a shiver across her neck. "And I assumed they were just excuses so you wouldn't have to live with a hired gun."

She couldn't stop the heat crawling up her neck, embarrassed that he had read her so easily. "They were valid reasons."

"Yes, ma'am."

"Stop saying that," she gritted out, struggling to keep her voice down.

"I acknowledged your point," he said tiredly. "Do you want to get your things or should I?"

"You had no intention of letting us stay here."

"I told you that yesterday."

Abby stared at him, fighting anger and tears and the absurd notion to call her father into this. Fighting Jefferson, she could see, would only bring misery to the day and make it worse on the girls.

With a deep breath, she squared her shoulders and marched past him. "Make yourself useful and bring me those boxes from the kitchen."

THREE

Two miles west of Clarendon, the tiny log cabin sat in a waving sea of thigh-high grass. As Abby climbed down from her buggy, she stared blankly at the small house she would soon be sharing with Jefferson Grant.

Chipped and weathered, the logs were crudely made, but tightly fitted together. A small chimney allowed smoke to pass out, and two windows in the front let in sunlight.

Abby knew what she would find before she stepped inside. A large front room and two bedrooms, one for the girls and one for . . . someone else.

Dread knotted her stomach. With a glance back at Jefferson as he helped Rachel and Hannah from her buggy, she pushed open the door of the log cabin.

Ever since her father had referred to the possibility of "physical love," Abby had fretted. She hadn't wanted to marry Jefferson Grant in the first place. She was most definitely not sharing that other bed with him, no matter where she had to sleep.

A dry, burning wind swirled through the little room as Abby opened the door. Sunshine flowed in, glittering off cobwebs and turning dust motes into floating pieces of gold.

The front room, used as kitchen and parlor, was dominated by a carved pecan table, Jilly's pride and joy. An inch-thick film of dust silvered the table and six matching chairs in the afternoon sunlight. Dust and cobwebs draped the cookstove that stood on the left wall. The stove was flanked by a washbasin and a sink fitted with a pump handle. A tall, slender cupboard backed against the opposite wall. In the month since Jilly had died, the place had dulled with dirt and neglect.

Abby set a basket of clean linens on the table and reached behind the door for the broom.

From outside she heard the murmur of voices, the girls' high and sweet, Jefferson Grant's low and masculine. A shrill scream pierced the still afternoon.

Hannah! Abby's heart lurched and she dropped the broom, rushing outside.

A scene from hell greeted her. Hannah sat on the ground in a froth of skirts, wailing the ear-splitting cries of a hurt child. Rachel charged at her uncle, her small fists flailing against his powerful thighs.

"You hurt Hannah! You pushed her!" Rachel screamed, pummeling him with her fists. Tears streaked her face, red with heat and anger.

Jefferson gripped her arms and hauled her up until her face was level with his. "Rachel, I didn't—"

"No!" Abby cried when he shifted Rachel as though he would spank her. She rushed toward him and jerked Rachel out of his arms. "Stop it!"

"A-A-Abby, A-Abby, h-h-heee psssshed . . . me!" Hannah sobbed, her words barely distinguishable. She huddled in a heap of yellow gingham.

Rachel buried her face in Abby's neck and sobbed. "He hurt her, Abby. He's mean. I told you."

"Just a damn minute!"

Abby glared at him, rage swelling through her until her chest ached. She rushed over to Hannah and held out her hand. "Come on, sweetheart." She hitched Hannah up on her other hip and stalked to the door of the cabin.

Jeff stepped in front of her. "Hold on, Doc—"

Rachel and Hannah burst into fresh tears and gripped Abby until their nails dug into her skin like fiery talons.

Their little bodies trembled against her. Through their thin cotton dresses, she could feel the bones of their fragile shoulders.

Abby's anger exploded. "Get out of my way."

Blue eyes, cold with fury, burned into hers, and she nearly faltered.

Jefferson clenched one huge hand at his side, clearly struggling for control. White lines of rage bracketed his mouth.

She pressed forward, and amazingly he moved away.

Still seething with fury, she settled the girls down. She checked Hannah and found no bruises or welts, then instructed the girls to stay inside until she returned. Steeped in anger, barely aware of her movements, she stalked back outside and shut the front door so the girls couldn't overhear.

His big body taut with tension, Jefferson hauled crates and boxes from the wagon, dropping them methodically onto the ground.

Abby marched over to him. "What is the matter with you? What did you do to her?"

He straightened and forced that cold blue gaze on her. "Don't ever question my authority again." His tone was low, but bone-chilling. Lethal.

A warning sounded in her head, but rage pushed her on. "I realize you've never been around children, but even you can't be that cruel. What did you do to Hannah? And Rachel was simply frightened. She didn't deserve a spanking."

"If I think Rachel needs a spanking, I'll give it to her." He reached into the back of the wagon, jerking a crate full of Abby's medical books toward him. His eyes were bleak and empty. "If you ever interfere again, I'll do the same to you."

"Don't threaten me, Jefferson Grant." Rage hazed her vision, and her skin heated. "I'm not some little girl you can bully around."

A muscle flexed under his close-cut beard, but he yanked up the crate, hefted it in his thick arms and started for the door.

"I don't see how you can be Jilly's brother. You don't

have an ounce of compassion in you. Is violence the only way you know to solve anything?"

He shouldered open the door, dumped the box on the table with a loud clap and spun, heading for her. His blue gaze speared her. Wicked, unleashed fury crested on his face as he moved toward her, his quick, smooth motion like that of a snake shadowing its prey.

Abby suddenly realized she'd crossed some invisible line. She stepped back, but thrust her chin at him. "Don't think you can handle me the way you handled them. I won't stand for it."

"Shut up." His hand whipped out and grabbed her arm.

She fought him, trying to pry his iron-bar grip off her as he dragged her across the yard. He halted abruptly, bringing her to a teeth-snapping stop. "Look."

She struggled against him, damning his size and hers, wishing for a syringe to stab him with.

"I said *look*." Long, unmerciful fingers captured her jaw, and he forced her head toward the spot where she'd found Hannah.

She jerked her chin from his fingers and stared down at the ground, looking, searching. Anger clouded her vision, and for an instant sickly brown grass blurred into reddish dirt. Then she saw it. About four inches long with a dull gold shell, a scorpion lay on the ground. Its narrow, venomous tail curved toward its head, crushed in the attack pose. The creature lay motionless, but Abby took a reflexive step back.

Frowning, she looked up at Jefferson. "I don't understand. Was she—"

"Hannah was about to step on that thing. I pushed her away and that's all. I guess Rachel didn't see the scorpion either." A muscle flexed in his jaw and anger flushed his neck. He dropped her arm then turned and strode for the wagon. "For the record, I wasn't about to spank her."

Abby swallowed, staring at the vicious bug, relief and comprehension flitting through her. Her anger evaporated, replaced by embarrassment and shame. She wanted to go in the house and pretend this had never happened.

Instead, she walked over to him, as uncertain as if she'd landed in the middle of a cattle roundup. "I'm . . . sorry. I didn't know." The words were pitiful and weak. She felt foolish even saying them, but knew nothing else to offer. "I thought—I heard them crying and I—"

"Thought I was hurting them. Of course you did. Silly of you, though, for such a smart woman," he chided, his voice harsh, lashing at her. "Don't you think I would use my gun if I wanted to hurt them?"

His tone mocked her, but she saw the quick flicker of pain in his eyes, just as she'd seen it yesterday when he'd come for the girls. She swallowed and clenched her fists to still her own shaking. "I misunderstood. I don't know what else to say."

"You don't really need to say anything, do you?" he drawled, his blue eyes shuttered against her. He dragged the last crate across the wagon bed toward him and hefted it, stepping around her. "You've made it pretty clear how you feel about me without saying a word. As hard as you've tried to keep your reputation lily white, you got yourself conned into marriage with a gunslinger. Must be pretty bitter medicine, huh, Doc?"

She clenched her teeth and knotted her hands into fists, knowing she deserved his anger. "This isn't easy on any of us. It's going to take a little time for us to get used to each other. I— What's happened to you?"

His head swiveled toward her, rage still firing the blue eyes.

She rushed toward him. "You're bleeding! There's blood on your shirt."

He lifted his left arm to peer down at his waist. Blood soaked through the light material of his shirt, sticking the cloth to a spot on his back just below his ribs. He swore.

She reached for him. "You must've torn the stitches loose."

"Probably moving your damn books." He turned away, dismissing her, and shifted his way through the front door, angling the bulky crate to fit inside. "Don't get excited. I'm not going to die."

"You're bleeding, Mr. Grant. Let me look at it." She followed him inside. Wedged in the tiny cabin between the door and his body, she was able to block his way.

"I'm fine."

"Sit down." She pushed at his massive shoulders, urging him toward one of the chairs at the table. "I need you to—sit down," she said again when challenge flared in his eyes.

Irritation washed through her at the stubborn flex of his jaw, but she carefully kept her face blank. She reached for his shirt. "Take this off. I want to look at that wound."

He sat down silently, but rage vibrated from him, coiled in his body. He made no move to remove his shirt, but slitted his eyes against the pain as he plucked the blood-soaked cloth from his skin.

Abby swallowed, trying to ignore the tension and rage pulsing from the man in front of her. The cabin shrank even more. The air, thick and hot, was stifling. She opened her bag with one hand and reached for his shirt with the other.

"I can do it," he growled, batting her hand away.

Blood spread across the shirt in a thick streak, close to his waist on his left side. He quickly jerked the shirt over his head and tossed it on the table.

Even though she'd originally stitched the wound, Abby hadn't really noticed his chest. She'd seen farmers, cowboys, even a highly conditioned boxer once, but she'd never seen a chest like Jefferson's. It was deep and broad, smoothly muscled with a dusting of dark hair. His pectoral muscles were distinctly defined, rounded and hard with muscle and wiry sinew, tapering to a rigid abdomen. A thin line of dark hair trailed from his navel to disappear into the waistband of his denims.

A sudden warmth moved through her, unnerving her, obliterating any professional distance she might have had. Her glance flickered upward and met his. Blue eyes, cold chips of ice, bored into her. His jaw tightened. She jerked her gaze away and knelt beside the chair. "Lean a little so I can see it."

He did so and moved his arm to rest on his thigh, out of

her way. The tear was at the base of the wound, in the fleshy part of his waist. Or what flesh there was. Though broad in the shoulders and chest, with powerful thighs, he was hanging-rope lean, no spare flesh on such a large frame. The tightly closed wound had split and gaped wide at the base.

She couldn't stop the sudden rush of distaste as she was again reminded of his violent way of life, but she pushed away her feelings, concentrating on the wound. Close examination revealed that he'd torn out more than half of the stitches.

"It's pretty deep," she commented, keeping her voice neutral. She had never thought to ask why he'd gotten the gunshot. Was it a quirk of fate that her letter about the girls had reached him at all? She dragged her bag closer and reached inside for a brown bottle.

"What's that?" he asked tightly, his gaze glued to some spot across the room.

"Carbolic acid. I need to sterilize the wound." She removed one of her clean bandages and doused it with the liquid antiseptic. With a gentle but brisk touch, she cleaned away the blood until she could clearly see the wound.

His stomach muscles cinched at her touch, but otherwise he didn't move. She removed another sterile bandage from her bag and held it out to him. "Press this against the wound while I get my sutures."

Mildly surprised that he didn't question her, she relinquished the job to him. He held the pad as she had instructed, but his blue eyes, hard and full of contempt, swept over her once then moved dismissively away.

She was suddenly reminded that she had accused him of hurting the girls. Regret coursed through her. Sweat dotted her palms and her stomach gave a strange lurch, but Abby ignored it. She washed the needle with carbolic acid then removed the catgut from another sterile bandage. Though there was still a raging debate in the medical community, Abby was a firm believer in sterilizing everything.

The strong scent of the antiseptic stung her nostrils. She glanced up and saw that Jefferson had paled under his copper skin and dark beard. Speaking quickly, she kept her voice even as she explained, "I'll have to re-suture. You still have a high risk of infection, especially now that the wound has broken open again."

His eyes narrowed, but he said nothing.

She quickly splashed carbolic acid over her hands and dried them with a clean towel. He sat as still as the wild apple tree by the river, his body taut with anger. She knelt and withdrew the bandage, now covered with blood.

She gave him what she hoped was a reassuring smile. "I'm fast, I promise."

"Get on with it."

He stayed completely still, flinching only the first time she drove the needle into his flesh. His arm, close enough to brush her head, was steel hard with tension. Warmth pulsed from his body. His skin was smooth and supple under her fingers, but she noticed these things only peripherally. With quick, even stitches she closed the wound.

As she worked, she spoke soothingly to him, as she did to all her patients. Her fingers flew, sure and brisk, and her confidence, which she realized had been in question before, returned. "You'll need to keep this clean."

She tied off the sutures then blotted the wound again with carbolic acid. Refusing to allow her fingers to dawdle over the smooth warmth of his skin, she briskly bandaged him and stood. "There. I hadn't planned to, but we can share the bed—"

"Well, thanks, Doc." His voice was as sharp as her surgery knife, but his eyes were cloudy with pain. He vaulted out of the chair, snatched his shirt from the table and stalked out. "But I wouldn't sleep with you if you were naked and begging."

For one brief instant, she was stunned speechless. She had probably just saved his life and that was the thanks she got!

Fury boiled through her, scraping against her pride and her common sense. She'd been offering him the bed, not herself. He had misunderstood, but she was too angry to care. "I guess we'll never have to worry about that, will we?"

With stiff, jerky movements, she gathered her instruments and the bloody bandages. A tiny voice inside her, her doctor voice, reminded her of the pain clouding his blue eyes, the deep, ragged hole in his back.

But his acid declaration taunted her and she refused to follow him. If Jefferson Grant wanted no part of her, fine!

Abby had the bed to herself, but the knowledge gnawed rather than reassured. Her anger hadn't diminished even when the sun set. There was no question in her mind that Jefferson would sleep in the bed, but she wouldn't offer again. He had disappeared shortly after supper, and now, three hours later, he was still gone.

The girls had long since fallen asleep, snuggled happily in their own bed. Abby rearranged her teacups, put away the rest of the dishes and unpacked a few of her medical books.

She changed into her nightdress and crawled into bed. Perhaps he had left. She couldn't imagine him leaving the girls, but after everything that had happened today, perhaps he had.

Where could he be? There were no saloons or gambling houses in Clarendon, but the Rocking K ranch backed up to Jilly's land. Strat Kennedy was renowned for his wild and woolly cowhands and hired gunslingers, most of them having come from Tascosa. If Jefferson was looking for a friendly place, he'd most likely find it with other men just like him, men who lived by the gun, by a coldhearted code she didn't understand.

It was none of her business, of course. And she had what she wanted—this bed to herself. He was a grown man and could take care of himself. She rolled to her side and closed her eyes.

But Abby's conscience flicked at her, rubbing over the sore point of her pride until it festered inside her. He was injured, regardless of how it had happened, and it was her sworn duty to take care of him.

A sudden noise startled her and she bolted upright. The door closed and she heard the unmistakable bump and thump of someone moving around. The first rush of blood at the sound calmed. Instinctively, she knew it was Jefferson.

She tensed, expecting him to open the door and claim the bed. His scathing words about her being "naked and begging" echoed in her head, igniting her anger again. But it was tempered by concern.

She waited for long minutes, her body tense, sweat clinging to her skin under the light nightdress. The shuffle of boots and the whispered sounds of him moving around died away. Silence wound through the cabin once again. Outside, she could hear the flutter of the wind through the tall grass, the clatter of a loose fence board.

She stifled the instant rush of pleasure that she was still alone, and forced herself to lie back down. But her conscience wouldn't rest. No matter what Jefferson had said to her, he should be sleeping in a clean bed.

She eased out of bed, plucking the nightdress away from her sticky skin. Her hair, rebraided for the night, had come loose in all her tossing, and now strands of it hung loose, streaming across her cheeks. She walked to the bedroom door, opened it quietly and stood for a moment, adjusting to the flow of moonlight through the windows.

Silver light washed over the table and part of the stove. Her gaze moved to the other wall, over the cupboard. The room appeared empty, and she took a step inside, her annoyance mingled with uncertainty. Where was he? Had he left again?

A click sounded in the stillness, as deafening as a crack of thunder. She froze, her mind going blank before she registered the sound of a gun being cocked.

Turning her head, she saw him. He lay sprawled on the floor in front of the fireplace, one arm crooked behind his neck for support, his chest bare and crisscrossed with streaks of moonlight. Her gaze moved down over his naked chest, the pristine bandages at his waist and the light quilt that bunched at his hips, before she locked on the gun pointed directly at her chest.

His whisper was harsh and spare in the quietness as he lowered the gun. "Shouldn't sneak up on a man like that."

She expelled a shaky breath, anger and fear merging. "You scared me to death!" she hissed. "Put that thing away and come to bed."

He eased up on one elbow and regarded her steadily. His eyes glittered in the darkness, and though she couldn't see, she knew they were focused on her body. Heat crawled over her. "Are you begging?"

"No, and I'm not naked either." She didn't allow herself to dwell on the words she threw back at him. With great effort, she evened her voice. "You should *not* be on that floor. It's dirty and you're increasing your risk of infection."

"Don't worry. I won't hold you responsible if I get sick and die." He laughed mirthlessly and lay back down, his pale gaze still fixed on her.

"I'd feel better if you'd come on." What could she say to get him to that bed? Her throat dried up, but she plowed on. "You misunderstood what I said before. I meant to offer you the use of the bed, not . . . me," she ended lamely. She fisted one hand and covered it with the other, resenting the damp palms and her second apology of the day.

He sat up then, leaning into a shaft of moonlight. His face was sharp and carved in the white light, the beard accenting his high cheekbones. Purpose glinted in his crystal eyes, mingled with the danger that curled around him.

Her heart skipped and she eyed him warily, poised to flee if necessary. She still bore the scars from that last encounter.

"When I come to your bed, it won't be to heal or to sleep. Understand, Doc?"

Her breath jammed in her chest and her mind blanked. A traitorous warmth fingered through her before she found her voice. "Thank you for the warning."

She pivoted and sailed into the bedroom, catching the door just in time to avoid slamming it. A low, deep chuckle floated through the wall, and she gritted her teeth.

Let the idiot sleep on the floor, she told herself. It's no more than he deserves.

FOUR

Damn woman doctor! Jeff yanked at a busted fence board then winced as pain stabbed his side. He eased off, cursing the wound that had forced him to stick to light jobs all day. He'd slept poor little last night, plagued by uncertainty and anger and just plain lust.

Lusting after a woman who hated everything he stood for! It had been too long since the blond in San Antonio.

He wasn't sure what had surprised him most yesterday— that the doc had believed he would purposely hurt the girls or what he'd seen of her last night.

In the pale midnight moon, he'd learned something about Dr. Abigail Welch. She was all woman under those clothes. When she'd stood in the door of the bedroom, the moonlight had filtered through her thin nightdress, outlining every curve, shading every swell and secret place. Thinking about it, his throat dried up like gunpowder.

Mid-afternoon sun seared his fresh stitches. Sweat trick-led down his back and released the scent of medicine. His wound burned, shooting pain into his side. He felt old and tired. It angered him that Doc thought he would purposely hurt the girls, but a string of doubts circled in his mind.

Jeff wasn't sure what he had expected when the four of them had arrived at the cabin, but it hadn't been to be considered an outsider, an enemy. Despite his best intentions, he had frightened the girls.

Maybe his father was right. Maybe he wasn't fit to have them.

He balked at believing it, but he had handled the incident with Hannah poorly, the one with Rachel even worse. Truth was, he didn't know a damn thing about raising kids. Should he have given them up to Abby? Every stubborn instinct screamed no, but doubts hammered at him.

Today the doctor had gone out of her way to avoid him. She was polite, but distant. When they had taken lunch, the heavy quietness had been broken only by the sounds of utensils scraping the plates and Hannah's noisy slurps of milk. A sense of longing, for something he couldn't identify, tugged at him. He pulled his attention back to his sister's homestead.

The grass around the cabin was shorter, evidence that someone had once lived there. With Jilly's absence, straggling weeds had begun to grow back.

The cabin itself was in amazingly good shape. The barn and corrals were another story. Fence posts were broken or missing, the corral and pens were grown up with grass and weeds, the barn doors sagged on rusty hinges. All in all, the place didn't look nearly as profitable as Jilly had led him to believe it was.

Out behind the cabin, situated about one hundred yards away, stood the frame of a bigger house. The porch and porch steps were finished. The golden pine of the structure, hauled from Dodge City, had aged and turned a dirty color from sand-mixed red dirt. Part of the floor of the house was in good shape, although there was a hole as big around as Jeff's thigh close to what would be the front door.

Dr. Welch told him Dave had been building a new house for the family when he'd been killed by the wild steer. Weathered wood and stacks of lumber testified to a work in progress. The skeleton structure was naked, bare poles and supports and a floor, but it bore an expectant look, as if waiting to be given protection from the elements, an identity. As Jeff stared, it came to him that Rachel and

Hannah were like that, raw material to be shaped and strengthened by parents.

Jeff determined right then to finish building the house. And he wasn't giving up on the girls. Not yet anyway.

By damn, he just needed a plan. He could make friends with Hannah and Rachel. The doc was another story. All morning long, he'd been thinking about what he'd like to do to those soft rose lips, her creamy skin. Damned if he could figure it, because she treated him as countless other "ladies" had.

Distaste they didn't try to hide burned in their eyes. If he was on their side of the street, they crossed to the other, as if he might somehow infect them with an invisible pox. The one difference between Doc and other "ladies" was that she had told him to his face what she didn't like about him.

Before last night, he'd found her strong and intriguing. Now he wanted to forget her, especially how she had looked with her hair streaming in moonlit strands around her shoulders. But the gnawing in his belly and the vague, teasing pictures of naked limbs and silky flesh tortured him.

He wanted to slide his hands up those slender thighs and part them, delve into the magic darkness between her legs, use her, discard her—

"Whatcha doin'?" An angelic voice shattered his thoughts.

He started, jerking around violently. Pain ripped through his side. "Damn it!"

Hannah's eyes grew wide, and as if he'd laid a whip to her, she jumped, whirling to run in a swirl of calico.

"No, Hannah! Wait." Jeff turned slowly, his breath leveling as the pain subsided. The little girl slowed, still a safe distance away, watching him with wide, frightened eyes. "You startled me, that's all."

She swallowed and her voice wobbled out. "You cursed, but I won't tell."

"Thanks. I appreciate that," he said dryly. He eyed her warily, wanting to make an effort. What was he supposed to say to her?

She popped her thumb in her mouth and stared, but didn't

retreat. Jeff shifted, taking in her tightly braided hair, her scrubbed round face. They stood, separated by the rickety broken-down fence, silence forcing their senses to attention. Tension circled them. Each considered the other, sniffing out the territory.

Hannah broke the silence first, removing her thumb from her mouth with a loud *smack*. "Abby says you saved me from a nasty sting."

Her words were so obviously parroted that Jeff couldn't help a smile. "She did, huh?"

She stuck both chubby arms behind her back and nodded solemnly. "I would've been sick."

"Yes, very." Jeff eased closer, his movements fluid and slow, as they were when he approached a new colt. He wanted to win her trust, but wasn't sure how to start.

"Can I watch you?" Big blue eyes blinked up at him. "I'm not supposed to be in the way."

"You're not in my way. In fact, you can probably help me."

"Me?" A blinding smile spread across her face, and Jeff felt his heart tilt.

He pushed his hat back on his head and motioned her inside the corral. "We'll have to go easy, since you're new and all."

"Okay." She took a hesitant step, then another and finally met him at the fence.

He opened the gate for her and walked into the barn, expecting her to follow. Her short legs pumped to keep up. Inside the barn, dim light flowed around them, breaking the relentless blaze of sun. Fecund smells of manure and hay damp with age permeated the air.

He reached for the pitchfork. "I need somebody to tell me when the wagon is full. Think you can do that?"

"Yes!" She nodded eagerly and turned to the wagon. With her chubby arms straining and her short legs pushing against the ground, she tried to pull herself onto the floorboard of the wagon.

Jeff grinned and hooked his arm around her waist and deposited her on the seat. "There. We're going to clean out the old hay and put down fresh, so you tell me when it's time to haul off the wagon, okay?"

"Okay." She perched like a tiny statue on the seat, half-turned to see the bed, her eyes trained dutifully there.

Jeff grabbed the pitchfork and began tossing soggy, soiled hay into the wagon bed.

"I can count to twenty," she announced in the shadows without taking her eyes from the wagon bed.

Jeff glanced up, trying to look skeptical. "Aw, I don't believe you."

"I can! One, two, three . . ." She counted to twenty-three while Jeff worked.

He found himself grinning at the sweet, childish voice as she patiently and clearly recited the numbers. Her gaze never left the wagon bed, and she frowned in concentration a couple of times. She mixed up twenty and nineteen, but he didn't have the heart to correct her.

"It's about half-full," she announced.

"Think it's time for a rest?"

Her blue eyes wide, she turned to him and fanned herself with a delicate wave of her hand. "I am a little parched."

He heard Jilly's soft drawl in the child's words, and nostalgia stabbed him. He grinned. "Well, then I think we should take a break."

"Hannah, it's time to come in." Rachel appeared in the doorway of the barn and marched over to the wagon. She kept her gaze averted from Jeff and held up her arms expectantly for her little sister.

Hannah frowned at her sister then glanced at Jeff. "I'm helping."

Jeff thought she looked disappointed, and surprise joined the pleasure he felt. "We were just about to take a break, Rachel. Would you like to join us?"

"No, thank you," she said stiffly, not looking at him. She motioned to Hannah and swung the little girl to the ground. "We have work to do inside."

She clamped onto Hannah's hand and herded her out the door like an angry hen. Jeff leaned on the pitchfork and watched them go. At the door, Hannah looked over her shoulder to give him a sweet smile. He smiled back, his heart catching as an unfamiliar warmth spread through his chest.

He'd made some progress with Hannah. It wouldn't be too much longer before he befriended Rachel, too. He was going to prove his father wrong, after all.

The thought kept him whistling through the afternoon.

When the sun flattened into a red disk over the bluff, Hannah fetched him from the barn. His stomach growled as he stood inside the door of the cabin. The dark, rich scent of venison and toasty smell of bread filled the cabin. Hannah and Rachel were already seated at the big pecan table. Abby was pulling a pan of cornbread from the oven.

He stepped inside and removed his hat, running a hand over his face and beard, now damp from his quick wash. Abby turned and their eyes locked. She jerked away quickly, but tension sprang up in her as taut as a razor strap. Was she still annoyed over last night?

The girls were seated on either side of the table. Abby placed the cornbread in the middle and pulled out the chair at the far end.

Jeff took the chair at the opposite end and looked up, his gaze catching hers. Again she looked away, her mouth tightening. Annoyed, Jeff let his eyes sweep over the sweat-dampened curls sticking to her neck, the sheen of perspiration on her face.

She had rolled her dress sleeves up to her elbows, revealing smooth, slender forearms and delicate wrists. Fire stabbed his gut. He dragged his gaze up over her waist and full breasts, then fixed his eyes on hers. Abby's gaze dropped to the table in front of him then skittered away.

Jeff, too, glanced down and realized he had no plate or utensils. He saw Abby shoot a quick look at Rachel before she turned to the cupboard in the corner. She set the plate, fork and knife in front of him then walked to the other end of the table. "There, now I think we're ready."

Abby kept her gaze intently on the cornbread as she sliced it, and Jeff slowly felt the sting of understanding. Rachel hadn't set a place for him.

Abby had tried to cover it, but he'd seen the way she looked at Rachel. Jeff's gaze shifted to the little girl. Had she purposely omitted him? Probably, judging from the flush in her cheeks and the stubborn way she kept her eyes averted.

Uncertainty pulled at him again. Getting to be friends with the girls could be a lot harder than he'd thought.

In the next week, Jeff began to wonder just what he was up against. He found his boots hidden behind the stove, a work shirt stuffed behind a moldy bale of hay in the barn. Though there was a place set for him at the table, once he was missing a cup, another time a fork. Jeff had no proof that Rachel was responsible, but he suspected.

He was at a loss as to how to deal with it unless he actually saw her do something. There seemed no point in mentioning the incidents to Abby. The woman worked like the devil at a revival.

Since that first day, he'd barely seen her. But he hadn't forgotten the sight of her in that nightdress or the feel of those slender, competent fingers moving over his skin. Since then, he'd changed his own bandages.

During the day, the girls attended school. Either Abby was in town at the clinic or driving hell-bent in her rig, checking on patients anywhere within a hundred miles of Clarendon. It was after dark each night when he saw or heard any of them.

He made his own supper, washed his own clothes and in general lived just as he had since he'd left home fifteen years ago. Hannah was the only one to include him in anything, asking every night what he had done that day.

Jeff determined to make Sunday the exception. Having overheard Abby and the girls the night before, he was in the barn harnessing the wagon with every intention of joining them for church. He couldn't remember the last time he'd been to church and didn't particularly want to go now, but he wouldn't be ignored today.

"Oh. Hello." Abby's voice, stilted and confused, floated through the barn.

Jeff glanced up, taking in the three females with their fresh-scrubbed faces and fine starched clothes. His gaze moved to Abby's trim waist and full breasts, her long, creamy neck, admiring in spite of himself. Her violet eyes froze, and tension snagged the air between them.

She looked quickly from the wagon to the harness Jeff was placing over the gray's head, then back to him. Abby gathered the girls closer to her. "We're going to church."

"Sabbath school," Hannah announced, pushing forward to peer up at Jeff in the early light. "Wanna come?"

"I think I will, tadpole." He grinned with an effort, his blood sizzling at Abby's protective stance. She reminded him of a lioness guarding her cubs. He wasn't a threat to any of them, but so far he hadn't had a chance to prove it.

A small frown puckered Abby's brow, and uncertainty clouded her eyes. "You're going to church?"

"Any objection?" He arched an eyebrow at her, challenging her to tell him straight out that she didn't want him along.

She hesitated, pressing her lips together. "Of course not."

Rachel looked down, circling her shoe in the dirt, but Jeff didn't miss the disappointment on her face. Nor did he miss the flower-sprigged dress Abby wore. The dress was high-necked, but tightly fitted, gloving her breasts and waist like a lover's hand.

He raised his eyes to hers, reminded again of the shadowy curves revealed through her thin nightdress. Awareness flickered in her eyes, and a jolt of live lightning jumped between them.

She jerked her head away and moved toward the wagon. "We'd better hurry or we'll be late."

"Put me up first, Jeff," Hannah demanded, holding out her arms to be lifted.

He grinned and hoisted the little girl into the wagon. The spirited gray mare neighed softly as Abby approached and the doctor reached out to stroke the horse's nose.

Jeff watched, his throat dry, as her hands slid over the mare's nose, gently stroking. Long, slender fingers; competent, sure movements. Doctor's hands. He had a flash of those hands on him, stroking, pleasing, tempting.

He cleared his throat and turned to Rachel. "Want some help?"

An angry flush stained her cheeks, and she shook her head stiffly, stepping around him to pull herself into the wagon unaided.

Jeff pushed down his frustration, turning to the doctor. "Ready?"

Doc studied him warily, but allowed him to grip her elbow and help her up, though she held herself stiffly erect and away from him. Frustration simmered in him as he grabbed the seat and vaulted up. "Hannah, I might need some help this afternoon. Are you up to it?"

"Oh, yes." The little girl leaned over the seat and smiled up at him. "I was a good helper last time, wasn't I?"

"The best one I've ever had," he replied truthfully, picking up the reins.

"Somebody's coming." Hannah pointed out the barn door. "Look."

Jeff glanced up as a lone rider atop a nugget-gold palomino halted at the corral fence. When the rotund man dismounted, Jeff frowned, his hand going automatically to his gun.

"It's Strat Kennedy," Abby murmured, hopping down from the wagon and hurrying outside. "Mr. Kennedy, is everything okay at the ranch? Did you come about Mr. Sweeney? How is he?"

"Mr. Sweeney? Oh, Sweeney. He's fine, just fine. I didn't come about him, Miss Welch." Kennedy barely looked at Abby. His small whiskey-colored eyes, set deep in a ruddy face, locked on Jeff. "I came to see Mr. Grant."

Silence ringed the small area for a moment. Jeff climbed down and walked to the barn door, apprehension skittering up his spine.

"You came to see Mr. Grant," Abby repeated, the words clipped. Her shoulders stiffened and she shot Jeff a look of reproach. Anger fired her violet eyes, turning them a pure gem color.

Jeff looked from her to the burly-chested man with weed-thin red hair and jowls that sagged as though stuffed with marbles. Why was Abby upset?

Certain the man posed some kind of threat, Jeff let his hand close slowly over the butt of his gun. "If you didn't come to see the doc, what do you need?"

Strat Kennedy stepped up to Jeff, extending his hand. "This is the first opportunity I've had to welcome you to Clarendon. Thought I might come by for a visit. Your name's mighty known around these parts."

Abby spun on her heel and swept past Jeff to the wagon, where the girls sat quietly. "Mr. Kennedy owns the Rocking K, which backs up to Jilly's land."

Jeff pulled his attention to the man, apprehension playing at his neck, stringing his nerves taut. He could guess now what the man wanted.

Kennedy's next words confirmed it. "I'd like to talk to you about a job. Got a minute?"

Jeff glanced at Abby. She climbed into the wagon, eyes averted, but her jaw and neck were taut with anger. He knew she didn't want him discussing the job with Kennedy. Hell, what did the woman want? She didn't like his job, didn't want him to go to church with them, didn't approve of anything he did.

He hadn't cared about approval for a long time, but he didn't stop to consider that. A perverse need to show her he would do *what* he wanted *when* he wanted overtook him. He turned back to Kennedy. "Sure, let's talk."

She slapped the reins on the gray's rump. Leather snapped and the wagon lurched forward. Jeff barely pulled his feet out of the way in time, flattening himself against the door.

He watched as the rig bumped through the gate and down the road toward town. Tension hung in the air as thick as the dust churned up by the buggy wheels. At his missed opportunity with the girls, disappointment flared in him for an instant then stubborn pride kicked in.

Whether Doc liked his job or not, he needed one. He

wasn't changing for anybody or anything, certainly not a pair of violet eyes.

The sun had turned a glimmering buff yellow, washing the bluff and Carroll Creek in late afternoon light when Jeff rode into town, rage building to white heat inside him. Church couldn't last all day, even in Saints' Roost.

Before Kennedy left, Jeff had worked out a honey of a deal with him. There were some advantages to having a reputation that spread across the West, one being that Jeff could name his price and his terms.

He had agreed to take a twelve-hour day shift beginning at six o'clock in the morning, but refused to take the night one or live on the ranch. Because of Abby's erratic hours, he would need to be home with the girls. Despite the fact that they avoided him as much as possible, he felt responsible for them.

It was an odd feeling, arranging his schedule for someone else. He hadn't done it for fifteen years.

He would be riding fence, mainly on the lookout for rustlers and strikes by the cowboys. The more prosperous cattlemen in the Panhandle had organized and established their own set of rules. Back in March, in retaliation, the cowboys had formed their own organization of sorts and initiated a strike. It had lasted only thirty days, but since then, unrest had spread across the state.

Cowboys who before had been allowed to brand maverick cattle no longer were allowed to do so. Their low wages rendered them unable to start their own herds, and many had reverted to stealing.

Resentment had flamed furiously in the south and spread northward. Now many Panhandle ranches were feeling the effects, especially the XIT up by Tascosa, the two largest ranches in Donley County—the RO and JA—and the Rocking K.

After Strat Kennedy left, Jeff had ridden over the rest of Jilly's land, checked the fences, eaten lunch and worked on the unfinished house, determining what he would need to patch the floor and begin the roof. Since mid-afternoon, concern had gnawed at him. Where were Abby and the girls?

Was Abby still angry about his visit from Strat Kennedy? He rode to the clinic first, but it sat closed and silent. There was no sign of his father or Abby's father or any patients.

He pulled up in front of Rosenfield's store, listening for sounds from the church behind. There were no voices raised in song, no deep rumblings of a sermon inciting people to goodness.

Had Abby perhaps been needed in an emergency? Had there been trouble?

Although she had told him they had never had problems with the Indians, Jeff knew other settlements across the state had been raided and destroyed. Though the Indians had been confined to reservations since the winter of '74, it didn't comfort Jeff to know that Reverend Carhart had planned for Indian attacks by building a dugout large enough to protect the entire town if necessary.

Jeff stepped into Rosenfield's for the first time since he'd arrived. Due to the continuous flow of westward travelers, the store stayed open seven days a week.

Scents of lavender, rose, and sandalwood soaps, steaming from the late-day heat in a barrel just inside the door, teased his nostrils. There were also barrels of candles, apples, nails and candy. Leather goods lined one wall; shoes and boots marched along the floor underneath towering shelves.

A crowd of people, talking and laughing, faltered when they spotted Jeff. They grew as silent as the bluff beyond the creek, huddled into a corner as though he had herded them there. So they knew who he was. News traveled fast.

A handsome dark-haired man about Jeff's own age stood behind the counter, watching with slitted eyes. He lowered the copy of the *Clarendon News* he had been reading.

"May I help you?" The man didn't have the drawl that Jeff had noticed in the sheriff, or even the slight one of Abby's father, and his words were razor sharp.

"You Rosenfield?"

The man nodded curtly, moving stiff-legged toward the counter.

Jeff slanted a glance at the people huddled across the room, then stared at the man. "I'm looking for Dr. Welch and the girls. You seen them?"

Whispers erupted on the other side of the store then abruptly ceased. Mr. Rosenfield shook his head, his dark eyes cold. "No."

"You didn't see them when they came in for church?"

"I said I haven't."

Jeff clenched his jaw, measured the man then turned to the crowd. "Any of you seen them?"

Impassive faces with anger burning in their eyes stared back at him. No one moved or spoke.

A grin twisted Jeff's lips as he raised a hand to his hat. "Thanks for the help."

He turned and strode out the door, shifting his gun around his hip in a deliberate taunt. As soon as he stepped off the porch, the voices resumed, relief evident in the burst of sound.

The street was sparsely populated, and the sun was now a red crescent over the bluff. Jeff walked around the store and strode for the church.

Lewis Carhart was locking the door when he walked up.

"Good afternoon, Reverend."

"Mr. Grant, how are you today? Missed you in church." Reverend Carhart's eyes glinted warmly as he extended his hand.

After the welcome Jeff had received at Rosenfield's, he eyed the preacher suspiciously, but took the hand, giving it a quick shake. Evidently everyone knew his name. "I'm wondering if you could tell me where Dr. Welch is. I thought they would've been home by now."

"Well, it's such a nice day, they're probably picnicking."

"Picnicking?" Jeff frowned. How long could a picnic take?

Reverend Carhart smiled. "Often after church, Abby and her father take the girls for a picnic. They fish and swim. I've joined them on a couple of occasions."

"Where would this picnic be?" Jeff fought to keep his

voice even. He'd been worried about Indians or an emergency and they'd been on a picnic?

"It's past Jilly's house. The salt fork runs past there."

"Thanks, Reverend. I appreciate the help." Jeff turned for the clinic, where he'd left his horse. Abby had probably been deliberately avoiding him.

The preacher called behind him. "We'd sure like to see you in church next Sunday, Mr. Grant."

Jeff raised a hand in acknowledgment, but didn't respond. When he got his hands on Abby Welch, he was going to need a church!

FIVE

When I come to your bed, it won't be to heal or to sleep. Understand, Doc?

No matter how hard Abby tried, she could not dismiss Jefferson's words. In the last week, she had hardly seen him, but that hadn't stopped her mind from conjuring pictures of him. Pictures of his hand reaching for hers while she stitched him. Pictures of him sprawled on the floor, dangerous and luring at the same time.

She alternately cursed and blessed the night he had drawn his dratted gun on her. It had served to remind her brutally of what he was.

A hired gun. A man who was paid to take care of problems for other people, whether the problems were human or not.

She just plain didn't like the man.

But today, after Reverend Carhart's sermon about godliness and fairness, shame nipped at her. So she had sent Rachel to invite Jefferson to the picnic. Rachel said he had refused, thank goodness, but Abby had tried. Or so she told herself.

She knelt in the shade of an old cottonwood on the banks of the Red River. Tall prairie grass rippled in a gentle breeze. The scent of earth and fish twined in the wind. The rusty waters of the river chugged by. Down the rise behind her, the girls laughed and talked with her father, Marcus Grant, and Harriet. The six of them had eaten lunch and spent the afternoon fishing.

Proclaiming her skill with a surgical knife, the other five had nominated Abby to clean the fish. The truth was Marcus and Lionel were too busy with Harriet to be bothered. Hannah and Rachel were too young.

Abby placed another fish on top of the flat cutting board. A picture of Jefferson's broad chest flashed in her mind, fluid muscle, molded sinew. Annoyed, she slid the knife down the fish's middle, slicing it open. Gripping the knife tighter, she stared hard at the fish, wishing she could destroy the taunting pictures of Jefferson in her mind.

Harriet walked past, carrying the basket of leftover food and a bundle of quilts to the wagon. "Nearly finished?"

"Almost." She smiled, trying to dismiss the image of Jefferson Grant, wishing away the heat clinging to her skin.

Lionel walked up, his face flushed red-brown from the sun, his blue eyes sparkling. He held a crudely carved wooden heart out to Harriet.

"Thank you, Lionel." Harriet took the piece, holding it carefully. Her face pinkened. "This is lovely."

Abby grinned. "I can actually tell what it is, Papa."

"Hush up, you." With a flourish, he offered his arm to Harriet. "Care for a walk?"

"She promised to walk with me," Marcus put in gruffly, coming up beside them.

Harriet took Marcus's arm as well. "We'll all go." The trio started down the rise of the bank, and Harriet threw a saucy wink over her shoulder at Abby.

Abby grinned and shook her head. With a delicate slice of the knife, she separated the fish skin from the meat, leaving the vertebrae attached to the skeleton and the meat free of bones. She tried to concentrate on her task, but images of Jefferson pushed through. Blue eyes, hard and cold as the winter sky one minute, warm as sun-kissed water the next.

The gentleness she'd seen him exhibit with Hannah didn't reconcile with the things she'd heard about him. According to Sheriff Gentry and Mr. Rosenfield, Jefferson had once shot a man clean between the eyes when awakened out of a dead sleep. Another time he'd left a man accused of rape to die, cooking in the sun as he hung from a tree. He had driven families from their homes, frightened innocent women and children.

"How's it coming there, Abby?" her father called from the bank of the river.

She turned, waving the knife in the air. "I'm nearly finished. There should be enough for all of us to take some home."

"Not Harriet," Marcus Grant teased. "All she did was sit on the bank and tell everyone what to do."

"Well, somebody needed to. You and Lionel were so busy tossing your lines over each other, it's a wonder you caught anything at all."

Lionel and Marcus both protested, though the two of them and Harriet were laughing. Hannah and Rachel ran up, both holding shoes and stockings.

Abby turned back to the cutting board, curling her bare toes into the soft grass. The wet hem of her dress rested coolly against her ankles. Overhead, dry cottonwood leaves clicked together. She tossed the last of the fish bones in a pile under the tree and shoved the meat into a canvas bag. After tying it closed, she placed the bag in the water to stay cool until they were ready to leave.

Jefferson was hard and aloof, just as she expected a man like that to be. Since she had tried unsuccessfully to give him the bed, she hadn't mentioned it again. Neither had he. She had offered to help change his bandages, and he'd looked at her so coldly she'd practically thrown them at him. After that night, she had simply given him the bandages and he'd changed his own dressings.

She expected him to be callous and selfish and unfeeling. Things like that reinforced the stories she'd heard about him.

But his easy rapport with Hannah belied all of it. He had sincerely tried to befriend the little girl and was succeeding. Hannah, the shy one, the one slowest to warm up to anyone.

It had taken Abby herself a month to get Hannah to sit in her lap. Besides the similarities in their looks, Jefferson seemed to share something special with the child.

Rachel was another story, and Abby somehow knew Jefferson wouldn't give up on her. Was that why he'd wanted to attend church with them this morning? Her heart softened at his efforts, and she quickly reminded herself that despite his genuine interest in the girls, he was still a hired gun.

He had emphasized that fact this morning by choosing to talk with Strat Kennedy rather than attend church.

She didn't like Jefferson Grant. She didn't like the way he talked to her or the way he looked at her. When she was with him, all her senses tingled as though she'd been numbed with ether for the last several years and the medicine had only just worn off.

She wondered what his hands would feel like on her, his lips. If his beard would scratch or tickle.

He looked at her as no other man had since before medical college. Though she wasn't unattractive, Abby knew her chosen profession and take-charge attitude didn't sit well with most men. But it didn't seem to bother Jefferson Grant.

She didn't know what to do except avoid him. And avoid him she would.

She leaned over, washing her hands in the river then drying them on her wrinkled and grass-stained skirt. Pounding hooves shattered the quiet laziness of the afternoon. She turned, eyes widening, heart skipping as Jefferson came tearing over the hill.

From the corner of her eye, she was aware that her father, Marcus and Harriet also turned.

Hannah spotted him and skipped through the tall green grass, halting beneath an elm as he drew his horse to a stop.

Rachel took one look and sprinted off behind the tree.

Abby walked up, suddenly very aware of her bare feet and disheveled appearance. She'd worn her hair loose, and a light breeze blew the dark strands across her face.

He sat astride the chestnut gelding, his shadow stabbing

through the flow of sunlight. His broad shoulders strained at the seams of a well-worn work shirt, and the blue fabric mirrored his eyes. Large hands, long fingers she'd imagined on her skin since he'd taunted her, gripped the reins tight.

In a smooth, quick motion, he vaulted off the horse and started toward her. Dark trousers hugged his muscular thighs and cupped him blatantly between the legs. Again that unfamiliar heat coursed through her and tingled in her breasts.

Her breath caught in her chest, and Abby realized with disgust and shock why she'd been avoiding him. She was attracted to him!

Furious with the realization, she forced herself to remember what he was. "Working already? You certainly didn't waste any time."

He halted in front of her and gripped her arm, eyes blazing blue fire at her. "I want to talk to you."

"You're hurting me." She was more startled than hurt, but his touch burned clear to her toes. She pulled away from him, taking a step back. Tension curled through her body.

Behind her, Hannah said tentatively, "Hi, Jeff."

"Hi, tadpole." His gaze shifted to the little girl, and a quick smile tugged at his lips.

Relief gentled his hard eyes, and Abby felt the quiver in her stomach again. How could he be so cold one minute, so tender the next?

His gaze drifted over Hannah's head and his face changed to a harsh mask. Hurt flared in his eyes before he shuttered them against Abby.

Abby turned, spotting Marcus, Harriet and her father staring curiously.

Marcus spoke to Jefferson, his words tight. "You've frightened Rachel."

"Forgive me for intruding," he bit out.

Marcus started forward, and Harriet put a hand on his arm, speaking in a quiet voice. He stopped. The two men stared, anger lashing the air between them.

Jeff turned to Hannah, asking quietly, "Mind if I talk to Abby for a minute?"

"Okay," the little girl returned uncertainly, looking from him to Abby as she backed down the rise.

His gaze sliced to Abby, eyes fired to blue steel. "Somewhere private. I don't think you'll want an audience for this."

She frowned, her legs trembling despite her bravado. "Are you threatening me again? I don't like the tone of your voice."

"We're going to talk about what *I* don't like, Doc." He gripped her arm again, though not as tight this time, and tugged her toward the cottonwood tree and down into a tiny valley. "I've been waiting all afternoon, wondering where y'all were."

"You knew we went to church."

"It doesn't last all day. You could've let me know your plans."

"You knew where we were going to be." Rachel had said he'd refused the invitation, and Abby couldn't imagine why he had come now.

Hidden from view, they stopped behind the tree close to the bank where she'd left her shoes and stockings.

"I had to talk to Kennedy and you know it. I didn't think you'd be gone all day. I was starting to wonder if there'd been some trouble."

There had been no mistaking the gentleness in his eyes when he'd seen Hannah, or the relief. Seeing worry beneath his anger, Abby relented. "You could've joined us at any time. The invitation was sincere."

"I just found out where you were." He frowned. "Reverend Carhart told me."

"Reverend Carhart?"

"What invitation?" His gaze skipped over her, paused on her bare feet and lingered.

Her feet now felt conspicuously bare. And even her legs, though they were hidden beneath her skirts. She curled her toes into the sun-toasted grass. "I told Rachel to tell you—"

"Rachel?"

He really hadn't known. Suddenly Abby realized what had happened. Sighing deeply, she looked to the tree Rachel had ducked behind when Jefferson arrived. The little girl was gone and now Abby knew why.

"You sent her to tell me, didn't you?" His voice was quiet.

Abby met his gaze, wondering if she had imagined the loneliness in his blue eyes. Shadows shifted across his face. "I guess she didn't."

He shook his head.

Irritation and concern mingled. "I'm sorry. Really. I'll talk to her. I don't understand. She's never lied before." She bent to pick up her shoe.

Sturdy fingers clamped on her arm, and he drew her up to face him, his voice hard. "Don't blame it all on her."

"What do you mean? She lied."

"*She's* probably scared," he drawled, the lazy words underscored with steel. "What's your excuse?"

"Excuse?" Her own voice sharpened as she tried to tug away from him. Had he realized why she had been avoiding him? "I don't need an excuse."

"Look, Doc, I know you don't like this marriage any better than I do, but you have no right to keep the girls from me."

"Keep the girls—" Stunned, she felt her arm go limp in his grasp. "But I don't. I haven't."

"The hell you haven't," he growled, moving in so close she could feel his heat, see the sheen of sweat on his neck and chest. A patch of sunlight angled across his hat. "You've sheltered them all week and I'm tired of it. You may not like the way things are, but those girls are mine, too. I want a chance to know them, a chance for them to make up their own minds about me, not have you dictate to them."

"I haven't been dictating to them. I simply—" *Don't want to be around you.* She stopped, appalled at what she had nearly said. By avoiding him herself, she'd made the girls feel insecure around him, at least Rachel. He *was* their uncle, and continuing to avoid him would only do more harm.

His blue eyes were steady on hers, hot with anger. They lingered on her lips then drifted to her breasts before rising to meet her gaze again. Mockery fired his eyes, as though he knew exactly why she had kept her distance.

She'd been avoiding him with no thought as to what that might mean to the girls. Her motives had been purely self-preserving, but she wasn't about to admit it to him. "You're right."

His brows snapped together, surprise evident on his carved features. "What?"

"You're right." Abby pulled her arm away and stepped back, needing to rid herself of his touch. "I hadn't realized I was doing that and I'm sorry. I don't mean to take the girls away from you. What can I do about it?"

He looked as dazed as if he'd just been thrown from a wild steer. "Well . . . I don't know."

For a full minute, they stared at each other. The air, though cooler from the river, crackled with tension and uncertainty. She could hear the rush of the water as it flowed over fallen limbs, the rustling of leaves and the roar of her heart. Abby saw another side of the man, a vulnerability she had never expected.

After another minute, he said, "Give me a chance to know them; to do things with them, make mistakes with them." He added quickly, "I'm not saying I don't need your help. I do. I don't know a damn thing about kids, but I'd like a chance to learn."

"I think that's fair. I'm truly sorry for . . . the last week. I just didn't think." Which was true, Abby conceded. She'd been so confused about the feelings he stirred in her, she hadn't given one thought to the effect her behavior would have on the girls. "You really didn't know where we were?"

"Hell, no. I was checking the dugout in town for Indians."

"The children use that as a fort now." All too aware that this unforeseen agreement would force her to be with him, her stomach fluttered nervously.

"Yeah, I know." He looked into her eyes, and tension sliced the air between them.

Suddenly she realized their seclusion. Pushing her hair out of her face, she picked up her other shoe, gathered her skirts and started up the rise. "What are you going to do about Rachel?"

"Don't look so frightened," he said dryly as he fell into step beside her. "I'm not going to hurt her."

"It's not that." His shoulder brushed hers, and she laughed nervously, uneasy at the touch. "She lied to me. I think I should handle it."

Jefferson tensed beside her and fell abruptly silent. Abby risked a glance at him.

His attention was focused thoughtfully on the ground. "She looked pretty scared behind that tree."

"Yes, she did." Abby wondered what he would do. Would he spank Rachel? Abby wouldn't be able to bear it if he did. Rachel deserved some discipline, but Abby knew the little girl was just afraid and uncertain about Jefferson.

"I think you should let her tell you what she did."

Surprised, she swiveled her head toward him. "Let her tell me?"

"Yeah. I know when I used to do something wrong, my parents— my mother would just wait for the guilt to eat me up. Usually worked."

"You mean, she'll feel guilty and confess?"

"Something like that." He shrugged, uncertainty clouding his eyes. "What do you think?"

Abby answered slowly, "I think it's a good idea."

"You don't have to sound so surprised."

"I am surprised," she admitted with a slow grin.

He laughed, rich and full-throated.

A shiver jumped down Abby's spine. She stopped in the thigh-high grass, smiling in confused response at the sound of his laughter.

He walked to his horse and picked up the reins. "Looks like you might need a ride home."

"What?" Abby looked around, startled to discover that the clearing was empty. A quick glance at the river showed someone had taken the bag of fish.

"How about it?" There was laughter in his voice as she jerked toward him. "I'm going your way."

His gaze trailed over her again, a quick but definite

caress. Blue eyes met hers, satisfied and warm as though he knew how he affected her, as though he were daring her to accept the ride.

She hesitated, torn between the compromise she'd just made and the sudden urge to get far, far away from him. "I smell like fish."

"I won't hold it against you, though I can't speak for the horse."

She ignored the quivery feeling in her legs. She didn't want to get on that horse with him, didn't want to touch him. And she had the strangest feeling he knew that.

Refusing to let him see her worry, she smiled brighter. "All right."

She wanted him and Jeff knew it.

Since the ride home from the river last night, he hadn't stopped thinking about backing her into a corner and kissing her senseless.

He stabled his horse and strode to the cabin. Dirt and sweat stuck to him. He'd ridden miles of fence today, getting the lay of Kennedy's land. Once he had washed and they'd fed the girls and put them to bed, he intended to find out if Abby was as drawn to him as he suspected.

Oh, he knew she didn't like him. Not that it mattered. There was something stronger, something hot bubbling just behind those violet eyes, and Jeff meant to unleash it. He had been drawn to her since he'd arrived, but he had never realized until yesterday that she might feel the same.

It all fit. When he'd accused her of avoiding him to keep him from the girls, she'd agreed too quickly. Almost as though she'd been about to admit something else.

Their ride home on his horse had been a pleasant torture for Jeff. Each bump of the hilly terrain brought her backside into the intimate cradle of his thighs and bounced her full breasts against the arm anchored around her ribs. He knew she hadn't been unaware.

When they'd arrived home, her face had been as red as sunburn. After the girls went to bed, she hadn't avoided him by going into her bedroom, but by keeping her nose buried in some doctor book titled *Delafield and Prudden's Pathology*.

One kiss. That's all it would take, and he planned to get that in less than an hour.

He stepped up on the porch, grinning at thoughts of her violet eyes clouded with passion, her shoulders bare as he peeled away her clothes.

The voices stopped him.

"It doesn't matter what your reason, Rachel," Abby said softly. "You still lied."

"He was busy anyway," came the child's petulant tone.

"What he was doing doesn't matter. You told me you had obeyed me when you hadn't."

"Why do we have to be nice to him? He won't stay." Rachel's voice dropped to a quiver.

Abby murmured something Jeff couldn't hear, then, "You'll do Hannah's chores for a week and no story tonight."

"But, Abby—"

"Rachel, lying is wrong. You told me you would accept the punishment."

"I know." The little girl's voice wobbled then broke. "I'm sorry, Abby. But he scares me and I . . . I miss my mama."

"Oh, sweetheart," Abby crooned.

At Rachel's plaintive admission, Jeff's heart ached. He pushed open the door and found them sitting in a chair at the table. Rachel's face was buried in Abby's shoulder, and the little girl was shaking.

Abby swiveled to look at him, her eyes surprised and bright with unshed tears. He suddenly felt very uncertain, but driven by his own pain at the death of his sister, he took a step forward. "I miss her, too, Rachel," he said hoarsely.

She froze, the tears catching on a hiccup, then she raised her head slowly. For a long moment, she simply stared, her eyes a wet crystal gray, her face splotched.

Jeff's heart turned over. He wanted to touch her, but didn't think that would be welcome. He took another step forward, then another, going down on one knee beside Abby's chair.

Rachel stared at him, her chin still quivering, her eyes wary.

At least she hadn't turned away from him. He was searching for something to say, feeling inadequate and lost, when he suddenly remembered the locket. He withdrew it from his vest pocket and held it out to her. "I have something to remember her by. It helps a lot."

Rachel's gaze dropped to the oval locket lying open in his palm. Her eyes widened at the pictures of her mother and another dark-haired woman. "Who's that?" She pointed, her voice quiet.

Jeff glanced up to find Abby's gaze riveted on him. Uncertainty blazed through him again, and he pulled his attention back to Rachel. "That's Lottie, your grandmother."

The little girl stared at the picture of her mother then at the picture of Lottie Grant. "She's beautiful. She looks like Mama."

"You look just like them."

"Hannah looks like you," Rachel observed, her gaze tracing his features.

"Except for the beard," Abby put in gently.

A small smile wavered on Rachel's face. Jeff grinned.

Rachel sat back on Abby's lap, wiping at the tears on her cheeks. "Do I still have to go to bed without a story?"

"I'm afraid so. Now, scoot."

Rachel slid to the floor, her eyes averted once again. She cast a longing look at Jeff then turned for the room she shared with Hannah.

"Rachel?" He stood and stepped toward her, his hand clenching over the oval locket.

She stopped, glancing apprehensively over her shoulder.

He held out the locket. "If you'd like, you can sleep with this."

"Really?" Her eyes widened in awe, and Jeff realized it was the first time she'd looked at him without fear or anger.

He nodded, his throat too tight to speak. She took the

locket from him, cradling it gently as she went into her room.

He stared after her, lost in memories of Jilly and the sight of pain on Rachel's face moments before.

"That was a wonderful thing you did."

Jeff turned, surprised to see the softness in Abby's violet eyes. She had risen from the chair and stood only a foot away from him. The memory of the moment they had shared wrapped around them.

His gaze lowered to her lips, and Jeff remembered what he had vowed to win from her. She froze, as if reading his mind.

Testing, he moved closer, his heart thudding against his ribs. One hand closed over her upper arm and gently pulled her to him. Wariness skittered through her eyes, but she didn't resist. Her eyes now were trained on his, full of uncertainty but also desire. Triumph burned in his chest. He'd been right.

He lowered his head, and her breath feathered his. Lust tugged deep in his belly.

"Dr. Welch! Dr. Welch! Come quick!"

The yells and accompanying hoofbeats brought Jeff's head snapping up. Hell!

Abby slipped from his grasp and was out the door before he could stop her.

"What is it, Mr. Ardington?" She grabbed the reins of the cowboy's skidding mount as he struggled to halt the horse. "Is something wrong at the ranch?"

"Yes, ma'am," the man panted. "You-gotta-come-quick."

She and Jeff reacted at once.

"I'll get my bag." She turned and headed for the door.

Jeff started for the barn. "I'll hitch your rig."

"Hurry, Doc. It's Sweeney."

"Mr. Sweeney?" She stopped in the door, a stricken look on her face. "What's wrong?"

"He's out cold. None of us can figure it. He said he'd been feelin' poorly all day, but he just kept working. While ago, he collapsed on the floor, just fell over like a dead—"

"All right, Mr. Ardington," Abby cut him off. "Let's not panic."

Jeff led the rig out of the barn. Without thinking, he grabbed Abby's bag and set it on the floor, then reached for her. She allowed him to help her up.

Gripping the reins, she gave him an apologetic look. "You're on your own with the girls."

"True to your word." He attempted a smile, not wanting her to worry while she was at the Rocking K, but he had visions of all hell breaking loose once the girls learned Abby was gone.

Distant now, her mind on Mr. Sweeney, she snapped the reins against the gray's rump. Ardington spurred his horse, and Abby followed at breakneck speed right behind.

She was some woman. Jeff felt a surge of pride as he watched her go, but he also felt disappointment. Just another second and she would've surrendered.

"Jeff?" Hannah slipped her hand into his, her voice drowsy with sleep. "I need to go to the privy."

He glanced at the dust churned by the buggy and Abby disappearing into the dusky night. "Now?"

She danced impatiently. "Yes. Hurry."

Wishing Abby were back, he picked up Hannah and headed to the outhouse.

"You brung that goldanged woman?"

"Ardington brought *her*!"

"Travis should be here soon with Jackson."

Abby ignored the stinging words and followed Ardington through the crowd of men in the bunkhouse. Their whispered words were nothing new. She had more important things to concentrate on.

Sweeney was lying on a cot in the middle of the room, his teeth chattering. Someone had tried to make him comfortable by removing all his clothes except his long underwear. The red material was soaked with sweat. His skin burned and still he shivered.

Frowning, Abby forced away the grumbles and complaints behind her. Sweeney's pulse was thready, and she had to feel several times to be sure it was there. His eyes were dilated and fever-red. Sporadic breaths labored out of him.

She took out her stethoscope and listened. His breathing was shallow, the sound in his lungs muffled. Pneumonia, or something else? She quickly unbuttoned his long underwear, ignoring the sounds of indignation from the men behind her.

His chest was red with fever, but there were no spots or lesions. Abby swiftly took a bottle of rubbing alcohol from her bag and wet a cloth, stroking it over the old man's bony chest.

Ardington stepped up beside her. "Can I help, Doc?"

"Do what I'm doing." She handed him the bottle and another cloth.

He followed her lead. After several seconds, Sweeney bucked on the cot. Coughing seized him, severe enough to rattle the bones in his chest.

Dread froze in Abby's heart. "No."

She hadn't realized she'd spoken out loud until Kennedy's voice boomed beside her.

"What's that you're rubbing all over him? The man's sick. He don't need a bath."

A couple of men snickered behind their boss; others grumbled. She ignored them all, motioning to Ardington to continue rubbing down the patient. Sweeney's pulse was weaker and fading quickly.

She grabbed her stethoscope and placed it against his chest. His heartbeat and breathing were wheezy and growing faint. He bucked again on the table and went into a series of convulsions. Then he stilled.

Abby stared down at him, dazed by how quickly he'd died. The old man lay limp. She put her ear on his chest and was met with silence as she had known she would be.

"He ain't dead, is he?"

"Here's Jackson," someone announced from the crowd.

Abby stared down at Sweeney, feeling the same bite of regret and failure she did every time she lost a patient. The ranch hands behind her hovered like a chill, dark cloud.

Jackson Swimmer stepped up. "I came as quick as I could . . ." His words trailed off as he spotted Sweeney. "Is he—"

"Yes, he is," Kennedy snapped, turning to Abby. "I thought you were a trained medical doctor."

"I am." She passed a hand over her forehead, wondering why nothing she had done seemed to work.

"Then why couldn't you save him?"

"You didn't call me soon enough," she said evenly. "If he'd let me look at him the other day, perhaps I could've helped."

"What's wrong with him?" Ardington asked quietly, placing the bottle of alcohol back in her bag.

"I don't know." Abby studied Sweeney's blotched red face and cracked lips. "Mr. Kennedy, I need to do an autopsy."

"You mean, cut him open?" Kennedy exclaimed, shock creasing his ruddy features.

"It's the only way to find out what was wrong."

"You cain't go cuttin' up a dead man's body." A man protested from the back of the crowd.

Abby turned to Kennedy. "If he died of something contagious, some of your other men might have it."

"I thought you said you didn't know why he died."

"I don't. That's why I need to do this," she explained as patiently as she could, reaching into her bag for a syringe.

Kennedy considered Sweeney for a moment then agreed with a sharp nod. "Fine." To Ardington, he said, "You shouldn't have brought her."

"She was closer than Jackson," Ardington defended.

An old, shriveled cowhand named Tandy spoke up. "Sweeney might still be alive if you'd waited for the barber."

"Yeah, someone with experience," someone else added.

A man.

The words were silent, but Abby heard them anyway.

This was not the time to argue or defend herself. She felt like a failure, as she always did when she lost a patient. She drew a sample of blood and transferred it to a vial, then placed it next to another vial in the wooden holder in her bag. Picking up her bag, she glanced at Ardington. "Could you bring him to my office tomorrow?"

The cowboy nodded, and she made her way through the crush of men. Their gazes followed her, heavy with blame. Their silence flayed her nerves. Once outside, her eyes stung, but she didn't cry. She tortured herself with thoughts of why Sweeney had died so suddenly. She didn't know if she'd been able to ease any of his pain, and that hurt, too.

She guided the buggy home, letting the gray set the pace. The night wrapped around her as it drifted coolly across the plains and ravines.

She had taken an oath to preserve life, to ease suffering. She hadn't had a chance to do either for Mr. Sweeney. Or Jilly, the reminder whispered in her mind.

She didn't remember reaching the cabin, but long after she had unharnessed the horse, she stood outside the barn. Resting her chin on her hands, she leaned against the rough railing of the corral. She didn't want to see anyone, especially Jefferson.

The men at the ranch had been right, at least this time. She hadn't helped Sweeney. All her training, all her knowledge had been for naught.

"Abby?"

She had forgotten that near kiss with Jefferson. At the sound of his deep baritone, the memory flooded back. She stiffened, brushing away the lone tear that had slipped down her cheek. "I'll be in soon."

"Is everything okay?"

She stared out at the moonlit landscape, her throat burning. "I'd rather be alone."

"All right." His voice sounded strained and uncertain.

She heard him turn back toward the house. Feelings of inadequacy bubbled to the surface within her, and the words forced their way out. "Mr. Sweeney . . . died."

Jefferson stopped. "I'm sorry."

She clenched her fists, closing her eyes. "They didn't come for me soon enough. If they had, maybe I could've helped. But they don't trust me and I've done nothing to change that."

"What happened?"

"I wish I knew." She covered her face with her hands. "When I arrived, he was almost gone. He was burning up with fever and I couldn't do anything. I stood there, just like they did, and watched him die."

"Abby, it was too late. That wasn't your fault."

"I'm supposed to be able to help people, to ease their pain. I didn't. Not for him and not for Jilly," she choked out, burying her head in the crook of her arm. "I took an oath."

She needed to feel the warmth of another person, the assurance of a body next to hers, needed to hear that she wasn't a complete failure. But she didn't need it from Jefferson. Her father had taken the same oath she had. He would understand.

Jefferson touched her shoulder, sending a streak of heat through her, crumbling the little self-control she did have. She wanted to draw away from him, but found she couldn't. His touch was strangely calming. "Don't."

"Abby, you tried. That counts for something."

"I should've tried harder. He was in town last week. I should've checked on him." She pulled away, stunned at the sudden chill that swept her with the loss of Jefferson's body.

"You can't control everything. You're not God, Abby."

She swallowed back the lump of tears. "It was the same with Jilly. By the time I saw her and realized what was wrong, there was nothing I could do. I trained for this. I'm supposed to know." Tears slipped down her cheeks and pain sliced through her.

"Shhh. Hush now."

His voice was soothing, but it didn't comfort her. She realized then that he was shirtless, his bronze skin gleaming in the moonlight.

And she was in his arms, exactly where she didn't want to be.

SIX

Jeff held Abby snugly against his chest, his arms tight around her. She didn't want to be here like this with him. So why did it feel so right?

Torn between needing comfort and knowing she should push him away, she hesitated. The dark velvet night webbed around them. Far to the west, a coyote howled and an owl cooed a sleepy night sound. Grasshoppers hummed in the grass beyond the barn.

The wind caressed her, soothing and cool, easing the ache of her heart, the tension of her shoulders, moving gently, so gently upon her hair—

Her eyes widened. *His* hands were in her hair, stroking the satiny mass that flowed loose around her shoulders. Jeff's steady gaze met hers, comforting and completely unthreatening.

She felt the strength of the man, and another higher, more venerable strength. She couldn't make herself move, not yet. Unable to keep her gaze on his, trying to calm her knocking heart, she looked out over the landscape. When she arrived from Philadelphia, she had felt small and insignificant in this harsh, relentless land.

Now when she looked at the craggy faces of wind-carved

bluffs and ravines, the red dirt mixed with sand, the purple flowers and yellow grass, she felt strength.

Jeff stood quietly, not pushing, not talking, but silently understanding. She soaked in the strength of the night. Slowly her awareness shifted to the man in front of her. His bare chest nudged hers; his heat caressed her breasts, searing through the thin fabric of her dress. His hands soothed, stroking over her hair again and again, settling her nerves, easing her soul.

The fatigue disappeared. Thoughts of Sweeney and Kennedy slipped away. She was wrapped in the blanket of night and the comforting touch of a man she never would've sought.

"Are you going to sleep?"

There was a smile in his voice, and she answered with a slow one of her own.

She met his gaze. His hands streamed through her hair and kneaded her shoulders. When had he started touching her shoulders? She tensed, abruptly reminded of the moment between them before Ardington had arrived.

"No," Jeff said quietly. "Don't pull away."

She should run. Now. All her instincts urged that she politely thank him and go inside, away from his tempting warmth. His gaze fell to her lips, and hunger flared in his eyes.

He was going to kiss her.

She couldn't kiss him. She didn't even like him.

Even as the thought formed in her head, his lips touched hers. It was no tentative caress, but the heated one of a man tasting a woman, seeking a response. He took her bottom lip first, grazing it with his teeth. Then his lips covered hers. Liquid heat curled through her and she gasped.

Desperation stabbed the pit of her stomach. There was no thought of desire, only need. The need to feel him against her, around her, moving inside her. She'd never felt such unrestrained desire. And though she didn't understand how she knew, she was certain she felt the same need in him.

She wound her arms around his neck, pressing closer against his warm chest, aching with the virgin fire that shot through her body and stroked her nerves. In his lips, she recognized the hunger she'd denied, the craving he'd evoked. He clasped her to him, crushing her breasts against the sleek muscles of his chest. His arousal, heavy and demanding, burned against her abdomen and started a wanton wetness between her legs.

Abby thrust her hands into his hair, met his tongue with her own. There was no thought, no reason, only the need to feel and respond. With him, she was wild and unfettered, a feeling that had nothing to do with competence or acceptance but simply being, burning alive.

He claimed her, branding her with his tongue deep in her mouth. Her own tongue played with his, and her shocked mind was barely aware. She welcomed the shattering sensations she'd never felt with any other man.

Fever built inside her. Groaning, Jeff tore his lips from hers and moved to her neck. She gasped for air, digging her nails into the bare skin of his back, shocked at the power that moved through her.

His lips were on her neck, hot, seductive, and she arched to give him better access. Her heart pounded in her chest and swelled painfully. Tiny breaths tore from her. He laved wet heat against her neck, small kisses that weakened her knees and flicked her nerves with fire. His hands moved around her waist and up to cup the sides of her breasts.

Desire tingled sharp in her nipples, and she shifted, wanting to get closer to him, needing to feel the hardness of his body pressed against her, the satin-covered steel of his muscles. Drugged by the touch of skin on skin, she curved her hands over his shoulders. He felt as beautiful as he looked.

He nipped at her ear then trailed more kisses along her jaw. His beard scraped her neck.

Her hands slid over supple skin, feeling the flex of muscle beneath as he drew her nearer. She moved her hands around his waist and froze.

Powerless to stop herself, hating it even as she did it, she ran her fingers over the spot again. The stitches.

He didn't flinch, but went as still as she had. She opened

her eyes. His gaze, glittering silver in the night, impaled her.

She felt stripped, her soul bared to the implacable light in his eyes. Finally reason soaked in. She shook her head and tried to step away.

He tightened his arms around her and lowered his head again. "No. Stay with me."

"Don't." Her voice was sharper than she'd intended. On the edge of panic, she pressed her hands against his chest, willing herself not to caress him. "Please. That shouldn't have happened."

"Why not?" His voice, still hoarse with passion, lashed her. "Because you don't like what I am?"

"Jefferson, please. Just admit we made a mistake and let it pass."

"The hell I will. What's the matter, Doc? Can't you believe you came alive that way for me?"

"Stop it." She turned to go into the house, not wanting to hear the words she herself had thought. "I was . . . not myself. You knew that."

"You wanted me." He grabbed her arm. "Admit it."

"No." She tried to pull away from him, swamped with feelings of uncertainty, fear, the vestiges of desire.

"Are you trying to tell me you melt like that for every man who kisses you?"

She gasped and pried at his hard fingers. "Let me go."

"Would your response bother you so much if I were a rancher or a lawyer or a doctor?"

"Stop it!" She whirled, her chest nudging his, her voice raspy with nerves and hysteria. "I *don't* like what you do or what you are. Nothing will change that."

"You didn't seem to mind what I was *doing* a minute ago," he pointed out bitterly, pain flashing through his eyes.

"I'm sorry." Her voice caught. "That was wrong."

"Maybe, but I bet you don't forget it. I know I won't."

With that, he strode past her and to the cabin. Abby closed her eyes, flooded anew with feelings of inadequacy and loss. He had offered her comfort, and she had thrown it back in his face.

That in itself shamed her, but it was for the best. She

couldn't allow herself to get close to a man she didn't
respect. Or to think about that kiss. Especially that kiss.

For the hundredth time, Jeff willed himself to forget the
honeyed sweetness of her lips, the moist heat of her tongue
on his. Even after swapping the night shift with Murdoch,
Kennedy's other hired gun. Jeff's mind still burned with
images of Abby molded against him. His body should have
been numb and tired by now, but it wasn't. Every nerve,
every aching muscle throbbed with pulsing awareness.

How could she deny what was between them? As much
as he hated the thought, he wasn't able to. Somehow he
would get her to admit to the same potent, raging need he
felt.

Damn the woman anyway! He hadn't been able to stay in
the cabin last night, knowing she was on the other side of
the wall. After working all night at the Rocking K, he'd
arrived back at the cabin just after sunup and decided to
work on the house.

Now bathed in the first pink-yellow light of day, he
finished repairing the hole in the floor, then went to the side
of the house for planking to start on the walls. The rumble
of hoofbeats drew his attention. He turned, making out the
form of a man on horseback in a cloud of dust.

Jeff lowered the wood and walked slowly toward the
cabin, tucking his work gloves in his waistband and sliding
his hand over his holster for reassurance.

Sheriff Gentry drew his strawberry roan to a halt and
climbed down, his movements unhurried but taut.

"Sheriff." Jeff's voice rumbled out as he walked toward
the man. What could he want at this hour?

Sheriff Gentry's sharp eyes took in the cabin, the corral
and newly repaired fence and the frame of the big house
before meeting Jeff's gaze. "I just heard you're working for
Kennedy."

"That's right." Jeff kept his voice level, but the muscles
up his back tightened. What did the man want?

Gentry stroked his mustache. "You planning on making
that a permanent job?"

Wariness strummed Jeff's nerves. He narrowed his eyes at Gentry. "You didn't come out to pass the time with me, Sheriff."

"I've got a bad feeling about you." The sheriff spit out the words like he'd swallowed rotten swill.

Jeff heard a creak as the cabin door opened behind him. He stepped closer to Gentry, keeping his voice low. "Do you have a complaint?"

"Listen to this real good, Grant." Gentry stepped up to him, his dark eyes burning into Jeff's. "I don't want any trouble outta you. I'm gonna watch you like a fox in a henhouse."

"I'll consider that a warning." Awareness prickled Jeff's neck. Someone—Abby or one of the girls—was now standing in the doorway of the cabin.

Gentry nodded then turned on his heel. "That'd be mighty smart."

Jeff watched the man ride away, anger gnawing in his gut. Behind him, he could feel watchful eyes. He turned.

Abby stood in the doorway, her mouth pinched and tight. Her violet eyes locked on him, steady, condemning. Jeff swore under his breath and headed for the barn.

He heard her speak to the girls. He strode into the barn, her voice fading. In the corner of the gray's stall, Jeff reached for the can of nails he sought. The air suddenly hummed. He froze.

Abby was in the barn. He could feel her, and he could smell the faint powdery scent of her, something he was beginning to recognize.

He grabbed up the can, the nails rattling noisily as he turned for the door. He planned to walk out, just pass right by her, but as he neared she drew away from him.

Pricked by her action, he stopped. "You going to town?"

"Yes. Tom Ardington is bringing in Mr. Sweeney today."

Jeff wished he hadn't noticed the dark shadows of fatigue under her eyes or the tension in her face. Or remembered the silky feel of her neck under his tongue. Now he noticed a small circle of redness, like a rash, marring her neck. "Think you'll be able to figure out what was wrong with him?"

"I hope so." Her voice was quiet and cool, her eyes averted. The milk cows pushed their noses through the slats of their stall and followed Abby's movements. At the opposite wall, she took down the gray's harness. "You're working on the house?"

"Yeah." His chest tightened for a moment, his anger softening at the awkwardness of her words. He stared at the redness on her neck and wondered what had caused it. "I figured we could use the extra space."

"Yes." She slipped the bit into the gray's mouth, adjusting the harness over the horse's ears.

Jeff couldn't forget the feel of her against him last night, the desperate way she'd met his kisses. He ran a hand over his beard, corralling his thoughts. His hand stilled as he realized that he might have caused the redness on Abby's neck. When her gaze lingered on his beard then shot away, he knew he was right.

Last night she'd been willing, more than eager. Now she was cold and withdrawn, as distant from him as she'd been when he'd come to claim the girls. Though it was obvious she was ready to be rid of him, he pressed on. "I'm surprised Jilly didn't have the house finished before now."

Abby's head snapped toward him and she frowned. "She had no money after selling the cattle to pay off the land."

The words bothered him more than her sharp tone. "This land?"

"Of course." She hooked the horse to the buggy.

A feeling of suspicion flickered in him. "I thought Dave had taken care of all that."

"He died before he could." Abby paused in dropping the reins over the lip of the buggy and studied Jeff for a moment, anger and hesitation on her features.

Jeff thought back to Jilly's letters, letters of hope and fruitfulness, good crops and independence, with no mention of trouble. His suspicion grew. "If she sold the cattle to pay for the land, how did she make a living?"

Abby dropped the reins and faced him, annoyance mingling with her uncertainty. Her words were slow. "She took in sewing."

"That's all?"

"Yes."

Abby looked at him curiously, but Jeff barely noticed. Shock rippled through him at this unexpected information. Jilly had lied about how well things were going. Why?

He turned and stepped outside the barn, his hand slipping into his pants pocket to finger the locket. His gaze moved slowly over the barn door he had yet to fix, the new fence posts gleaming out of place against the old, the broken, abandoned corral, the unfinished house.

His sister had been in bad straits and hadn't told him. With a startling stab in his gut, Jeff suddenly knew why.

After what their father had done, Jilly would never have demanded that Jeff come to her. She wouldn't have wanted him to feel obligated to care for her. She alone had understood the freedom he'd needed when he left home, the freedom to make his own choices, his own mistakes. Oh, yes, he knew why she had done it, and the knowledge drilled into his heart.

The doc's voice came from behind him, whisper-soft with pain and regret. "You really didn't know. That's why you never came."

Abby thought he'd known about Jilly's difficulties and purposely stayed away.

Her opinion sliced at him. Jeff clutched the can of nails, closed the locket in his other fist and walked away, his heart aching with regret. For Jilly, for the girls, even for him and Abby.

He was reminded in that instant of the depth of his sister's love for him. Jilly hadn't demanded change of him, even at risk to herself.

With bitter certainty, he knew that a woman like Abigail Welch *would* demand change. His gun was in direct conflict with her beliefs. She was a woman who had sworn to cherish life, to save it at any cost.

He knew now why she wouldn't admit to the attraction between them. Despite the strength of their desire, Abby was fighting more than his job. She truly believed that he was selfish and uncaring, driven by violence and the power of a gun.

The thought cooled the heat that had lingered within him since last night, as effectively as a frigid bath.

He hadn't changed for Marcus Grant, nor had he done it for his fiancée, Caroline Street. Two people who had claimed to love him for what he was.

He sure as hell wasn't going to change for Dr. Abby Welch.

The kiss, comforting yet arousing, taunted her. It hinted at deeper passion, restrained desire. Even the next day, Abby's blood sizzled with the heat.

She smeared Mr. Sweeney's blood on a sterilized piece of glass and slid it under the microscope. She had walked the girls to school and now stood at her examining table in the center of the clinic. Twisting the knob to focus, she was unable to stop the comparison that her thoughts were as cloudy as the picture.

She couldn't stop thinking about Jefferson. Not the kisses they'd shared last night or the disturbing things she'd learned about him this morning.

He hadn't known Jilly was in trouble. He hadn't known or he would've come. Abby didn't question how she knew that, but she was certain.

But he was a hired gun. He was hired to operate without emotion, to perform cruel tasks. He was practically a legend in the state of Texas.

She'd overheard the sheriff's warning, confirming everything she'd thought about him before . . .

Before the kiss? Partly. But also before she'd seen him with Hannah and his tender treatment of Rachel. Jefferson Grant was two different people, parts of him exactly as she'd suspected and feared, other parts completely unexpected.

Which man was he? Coldhearted, ruthless gun or a hurting and regretful man wanting to keep his sister's family together?

She thought she'd known which kind of man he was. Until today.

She stared into the microscope without seeing, reliving the heat that coursed through her body at his touch. Her lips tingled at the memory; her neck burned where his beard had scraped her.

She had never felt such desire with a man, never felt like a woman capable of evoking the kind of response she had evoked from Jefferson. In fact, she usually felt immune to passion, as sterile as her instruments. While the experience thrilled her, she knew it could not be repeated.

His beliefs, his principles were practically nonexistent, whereas she had built her life on principles, namely to save lives. She couldn't fall in love with a man she didn't respect or believe in.

Fragments of his tenderness with Rachel surfaced in her mind, but were erased by memories of Sheriff Gentry's warning to Jefferson this morning. The spark she'd felt died inside her. She forced thoughts of him away, focusing on the sample under the microscope.

Her blood froze. She stared for a moment, not wanting to believe what she saw. Large rod-shaped bacteria. No, it couldn't be.

She blinked then looked again for long seconds. Her breath knotted in her chest. She spun and ran out the door.

A few minutes later, her father leaned over the microscope then looked up, his face drawn in solemn lines. His usually laughing eyes clouded with disquiet. "I think you're right, Abby."

"Anthrax?" she whispered, her stomach twisting. Just the single word could cause hysteria and chaos as well as ruin to the cattle industry of the Panhandle. She leaned down for another look, praying she was wrong, swallowing hard when she saw the same thing she had before.

She shook her head, confusion and panic billowing inside her. "Mr. Sweeney's lungs were blocked and there were lesions on them, but there were no external ulcerations."

"Every symptom doesn't always appear. You know that." Her father draped his arm around her shoulder and drew her close. "I think you should send a sample to Austin, to the university."

"Yes, I will. I've got to be sure." She paced in front of the table, wadding her apron into a ball. "Shouldn't I warn Mr. Kennedy? Recommend quarantine?"

"He won't like it." Distaste crossed Lionel's features. "I'll go with you if you want."

"No." Abby met her father's gaze, her stomach already knotting. "I'll do it."

Abby slanted a look at the hired gun riding beside her. Murdoch was the only name he'd given. He'd met her at the entrance to the immense ranch and ridden with her to the big house.

He had been polite, but firm. No one talked to Mr. Kennedy without Murdoch knowing about it. Abby was thankful Jefferson wasn't here. She didn't want him to be involved.

Murdoch had shown her nothing except courtesy, but Abby still repressed a shiver every time he looked her way. His thin dark hair was slicked back neatly under a spotless black felt hat, and his dark shirt and britches were clean and neatly mended. It was his eyes. They were dark and alert, but cold, remote. Void.

And they were perpetually slitted, whether from the sun or suspicion, she didn't know.

He waited for her to step down from the wagon then led her inside. The sprawling frame house was cool and spacious on the inside, with stone floors and adobe walls. Murdoch disappeared for a moment then reappeared before she had time to do more than notice a portrait of a stunning redhead over the fireplace.

Abby followed Murdoch into a large office outfitted with a heavy oak desk and rolling chair. Strat Kennedy sat in the chair behind the desk, fingers steepled under his chin. Impatience radiated from him.

Abby noted that Murdoch closed the door and stepped in behind her. She turned. "I really need to speak with Mr. Kennedy alone."

"He stays, miss." Kennedy leaned forward in the chair, the back of which rose above his head a good six inches. "What is it? Did you come about Sweeney?"

"Yes, I did." Her voice dropped and she moved closer to the desk, annoyed at his attitude. Murdoch stepped up beside her and she frowned over her shoulder. A grin twitched at one corner of his mouth. "You really might want to hear this in private."

"Murdoch stays."

Whiskey-colored eyes bored into hers, and Abby bit back a sigh. "Very well. I believe Mr. Sweeney died of anthrax."

"Anthrax!" Murdoch hissed beside her.

Strat Kennedy exploded out of his seat, sending the chair rolling across the floor into one of the glass-front bookshelves along the wall. Books and ledgers inside rattled with the impact.

"Are you out of your mind? If there was anthrax here, I'd know it. Hell, the whole county would. What are you trying to do?"

"I can't be sure until I get the sample back from Austin, but I've seen the signs."

Kennedy pointed at Abby, his arm shaking, his eyes widening until she thought his skin would split. "Get her out of here, Murdoch. Ger her out before I throw her out myself. Damn crazy woman!"

"Mr. Kennedy, please listen—"

"Maybe you should, Boss," Murdoch put in.

Kennedy's gaze swung to Murdoch, who didn't flinch at the razor-sharp glare.

Abby controlled her surprise at the support from the hired gun. She placed her palms flat on Kennedy's desk and leaned forward. "Where was Mr. Sweeney from? How long had he worked for you?"

"Not long. He came from New Mexico," Murdoch supplied.

"It's possible Mr. Sweeney brought it with him. Have any other men been sick?"

"Hell, no!" Kennedy glared at her, then at Murdoch. "Murdoch—"

"We need to work fast, Mr. Kennedy. I'll need blood samples from the cattle, and I'll also need to check the pastures." Abby stared thoughtfully over Kennedy's head, through the large windows behind the desk.

Kennedy's eyes slitted on her, and his face grew another shade of red. He came around the desk toward her. "There's no anthrax here."

"There's been no news of an epidemic anywhere," Abby said more to herself than to him. "Until I can get the results on the sample, quarantine would be the best thing."

The room stilled as though swept of life. Behind her, Murdoch puffed out a loud breath.

Mr. Kennedy's voice came low and stilted, throttled by rage. "You're wantin' me to close off my cattle?" His next words thundered in the room. "And cancel my trip to Dodge City? I've got a sale comin' up, lady. Just because you think I've got some disease you can't even prove? Sorry, Miss Welch, but your credit ain't too good with me right now. Sweeney did *die* under your care."

Fear burst inside her. If there was anthrax and he refused to cooperate— "You stand to lose everything if you don't take some precaution. If you would only quarantine and try to discover the source, you could save not only your herd, but perhaps some other men as well."

Kennedy's fist slammed the edge of the desk, scattering papers and jostling the oil lamp. "I said no! Now, get the hell out before I have Murdoch carry you out."

"Don't dismiss this." Abby's voice was sharper than she'd intended, but her blood was boiling. "This might only take a few days. Just tell me if Mr. Sweeney brought in any new cattle and where he worked. Who he was around."

"I've got to get to Dodge City. I can't miss this sale. What with them cowboys striking back in the spring, it put me far behind for the year. Maybe you don't understand how ranching works, Miss Welch, but on a ranch you sell cattle."

"You're a fool if you take any cattle or men out of here that haven't been checked. Anthrax is highly contagious, Mr. Kennedy. If not discovered, it can live for months. In grass, on animal hides."

"Live? Miss Welch, it ain't no critter. You make it sound like a wolf coming after my cattle."

"In a way, it is. At least that's Mr. Pasteur's theory about the disease, and I think he's right."

"You want me to cancel my trip on a theory? I don't even known any *Pasteurs*," Kennedy choked out. His eyes bulged, and Abby thought he might have quit breathing. "Murdoch, get her out of here."

Kennedy turned away and started around his desk.

Murdoch took her arm, pulling her toward the door.

She planted her heels on the floor, but she was no match for the gunman's strength. She slid across the polished stone floor. "You know what it would do to your ranch if I let it be known how Mr. Sweeney died? Everyone knew he worked for you."

If the news got out, the entire community might revolt. Abby had heard of people converging on ranches and burning them entirely to the ground, slaughtering cattle and anyone who got in the way.

Kennedy followed them to the door and studied her silently, anger boiling on his face, which grew redder and more mottled as though about to explode. "They'd think you're crazy, just like I do."

"We still have time if we act now. Just let me take some blood samples. Isolate your cattle into one pasture."

Kennedy exchanged a heavy look with Murdoch then slammed his office door.

Abby exhaled, muttering under her breath. They reached the door and Murdoch opened it, finally releasing her arm from his bruising grip.

"Good day, ma'am."

She looked up into his sun-beaten face and thought she saw a flicker of admiration. She would have preferred to have his help.

She would find another way. She wasn't giving up yet. Her mind spinning with possibilities, she climbed into the buggy and turned for town.

Martin Phipps stared in the mirror, his stomach no longer

revolting at the sight of his right eye. Or the place where his eye used to be, he corrected. He slanted the bandanna across the empty socket, pleased to note that the red streaks had finally disappeared. His head, however, still throbbed as though being jabbed from the inside.

Outside his hotel room, cowboys hollered and whooped at saloon girls. Guns fired and the street teemed with the bellows of passing cattle. Dust churned in a constant whirlwind outside the window, coating everything with a red film.

The barber in Tascosa was drunk more than he was sober, but he had managed to save Marty's life. He swore he'd never seen anything like it. Marty should've been dead before he reached Tascosa, but he had no intention of dying. Not until that bastard Grant had paid for killing Billy.

Marty had had plenty of time to think, holed up in this stinking, sweaty cow town, and he'd made plans for Jefferson Grant. He had no idea where Grant was, but he knew Grant was alive, knew it with every beat of hate in his body.

That hate had been his succor, his strength in the past days. It fed him, emboldened him and, Marty believed, healed him.

Now he would be able to find that bastard Jefferson Grant. And Marty knew exactly how.

SEVEN

Despite the hours that had passed since Jeff's revealing conversation with Abby in the barn, anger still simmered inside him. Who was she to judge him so harshly? It wasn't only his job and reputation. Part of her resentment toward him stemmed from the fact that she thought he had deserted Jilly.

His anger hadn't diminished and neither had his determination. Jeff flat refused to become involved with her, physically or otherwise, and that meant keeping his hands off. Because of the girls, he was tied to her, but he had no intention of any woman, any*one,* making demands on him again.

Water doused his face, and he sputtered, jerking his thoughts to the urchin in the tub. "Hey!" He reached out and splashed Hannah.

She giggled and twisted away, sloshing water over the edge of the oblong wooden bath. She asked in a singsong voice, "We'll be clean when Abby gets home?"

"Yep." Jeff swiped at a spot behind her ear, and she wrinkled up her nose at him.

Rachel made a soft sound, and Jeff saw a quick smile flash across her face. She stood next to the wall a few feet away, combing her damp hair.

Jeff grinned and flicked some more water at Hannah.

She squealed and ducked under the water.

He reached for her, soaking the shirtsleeves that were already rolled up to his elbows. He pulled her up, tickling her slippery ribs.

"Jeff-stop-it-stop-it," she panted, giggling. She thrashed around in the water, spraying the floor and drenching him. She reached for his beard and tweaked his whiskers.

He laughed. "Okay, I give. You're too much for me."

He palmed water from his face and shoved his now dripping hair away from his forehead. Hannah took the towel he offered and pressed it to her face. She lowered it and peered over the edge of the tub.

"Oh-oh, we made a mess."

Jeff glanced down, feeling the water soak through his denims and into the dirt floor where he knelt beside the tub. "Yep. We better get this cleaned up."

"Before Abby gets home," Hannah added. She climbed out of the tub and, with Rachel's help, wrapped the towel around her chubby body.

Rachel handed Jeff another towel, and he stood, rubbing it over his face and hair. Mud caked his britches to his knees.

The door creaked open and Abby stepped inside. The girls sidled next to Jeff and all of them froze guiltily. "Abby!"

"Hello, girls." Her smile was weary and forced, though her eyes lit up. She opened her arms and Hannah and Rachel rushed to her.

Jeff's gaze skipped over her, and he felt the familiar burn of desire she always induced. He reminded himself of his earlier vow.

Abby hugged each of the girls then kissed them on the head. "Time for bed already?"

"We've had a bath," Hannah announced, tucking the towel in more securely under her arm. "Jeff had one, too."

Without even a glance at Jeff, Abby walked over to the pantry, her smile vague. "How nice." She opened the door, stilled one of her prized teacups as it danced on the shelf, and pulled out a thick, heavy book from the bottom shelf.

Rachel reached around Abby's waist and hugged her again. "There's leftover ham and potatoes in the stove," she said softly. "Good night, Abby."

"Thanks. Good night, sweetheart." Abby hugged Rachel, kissed her again and flipped open the book. "I love you."

Hannah tugged on Abby's skirt until Abby looked down. A smile bloomed on her face, softening the tired features, warming her eyes. "Good night, Hannah. I love you, too."

"Love you, Abby. Don't let the bedbugs bite."

Abby smiled. "Certainly not."

Jeff plucked Hannah up and strode into the girls' bedroom. Rachel helped Hannah into her nightdress, and Jeff listened to the girls' prayers. Rachel finished quickly, but Hannah named everything in the room, on the farm and in town, including Reverend Carhart's new puppies.

Finally she was finished. He tucked the sheets around them, his heart clenching when Rachel turned away and faced the wall.

Hannah sat up and smacked a wet kiss on his cheek. It eased his bruised ego, and he kissed her on the forehead. "'Night, girls."

"Good night, Jeff," Hannah mumbled, already drowsy.

He doused the lamp and walked to the door.

"Good night." Rachel's voice echoed in the stillness, and a big grin spread across Jeff's face.

He walked out and closed the door. Abby sat at the table, a thick raggedy-bound book spread open in front of her. Just the sight of her heated Jeff's blood, not completely in anger. His smile faded. Recalling his intent to stay clear of her, he picked up the tub and dumped the water outside.

He stood at the door, debating whether to go to the barn or back to work on the house. He couldn't stay in here with Abby. Water from Hannah's bath slid down his chest, tickling him and soaking his shirt. He unbuttoned it and dragged it over his head.

"You gave the girls a bath?" Abby sounded mildly

surprised. She turned another page, leaning closer to the book.

Balling the shirt in his fist, Jeff used it to swipe at the wet hair lying against his neck and the rivulets of water running over his shoulder. "More like they gave me one."

She didn't respond. Jeff moved his shirt slowly down his neck and chest, studying her, imagining her hands on his body even though his mind urged him to stop.

Her head was bowed and the lamplight stroked her skin. The satiny skin of her neck and jaw glowed pearly in the light. Shadows outlined the thrust of her breasts and, beneath the table, the flare of her skirts.

Fire sparked within him, and Jeff rubbed harder at his wet hair, wishing he could erase this longing for her. "Did you find out anything about Sweeney today?"

"What?" She glanced up sharply, looking startled. Almost guilty. "No," she answered slowly. Too slowly. "Not yet."

Jeff ran the towel across his belly, suspicious of her guarded answer. "What's that you're studying? Some doctor book?"

She didn't answer, and he glanced up to find her looking at him. His throat closed up.

Her gaze was trained on his belly, and desire softened her face, clouded her eyes. Want slammed into Jeff's gut, probing, shredding his willpower.

Was she really looking at him? He moved the towel across his chest, shoulder to shoulder. Her gaze followed, intent, hot.

His breath locked in his chest, as much in astonishment as in arousal. Fire smoldered in his veins, and he couldn't resist playing, testing her, discovering how far he could lead her. He moved the towel to his navel and down, back and forth across his lower abdomen. Her gaze followed there as well, lingering on his body as though mesmerized.

Lust knifed through him, and he swelled painfully, rigidly against his denims. His belly burned. He clenched his fist tight on the towel.

Just then her gaze shot up and locked on him. He read desire there and confusion and . . . a plea? He gritted his teeth. Hadn't he sworn to leave her be? He was tied to her because of the girls. If she made demands on him, there was no easy escape. Certainly not one that would leave the girls unharmed.

Her purple gaze locked with his, and quicksilver fire flashed between them. What was she thinking? Desire thickened in the room, heavy with the perfume of want. Want. Need. Jeff could no longer distinguish the two.

Her breath tore out of her in tiny gasps, and he could feel it as if it were his own. He could see the white of her knuckles as she gripped the book just as he gripped the towel. That damned invisible force she exuded pulled at him. Desire hammered at him, pulsing away all reason, all his earlier anger. She rose slowly and stepped toward him.

His breath tightened in his chest, burned down lower. In that instant, he damned everything he'd sworn. He wanted to hold her, to touch her, taste her again.

She exhaled and halted a few feet away from him. A few easily breached feet. Her voice was low and rough. "I've got to go." She turned for the door, drawing the line between them again.

Startled, Jeff angled his body toward her, his voice harsh with need. "Go? Go where?"

She hesitated, her hand on the door. "I need to check on a patient."

She flung open the door and disappeared outside.

Jeff was on the porch before he realized he was going after her. He stopped, gripping the rough-hewn door frame. If he touched her now, he wouldn't stop. She was running away, and that was exactly what he wanted, right? Right.

Then why couldn't he douse the flames licking at his belly, arousing him to the point of pain?

With a muttered curse, he left a light burning on the table, took another lamp and went out back to work on the other house, hoping his damp clothes would cool his blood.

She wanted him, wanted to know every inch of bronze muscled flesh, wanted him to know every inch of her. Especially that. A shiver rippled through her.

Abby couldn't stop thinking about Jefferson even in the middle of Strat Kennedy's pasture, hiding in the moon-dappled darkness like a criminal. Covered from head to toe in a dark dress and gloves and surrounded by tall prairie grass, she could still feel Jeff's gaze on her as though it were his hands.

She couldn't banish the picture of him as he'd stood in front of her at the cabin. The sleek planes of his chest, washed in amber light and dampness, were burned into her memory. Her hands itched to touch that smooth, warm skin again and her nipples tightened at the thought.

What was wrong with her? How could just a look from him shatter her reason, make her long for his kiss, his touch? How could she want a man she didn't even respect?

That wasn't exactly true. She did respect his way with the girls, but not his way of life.

Confusion twisted through her, sharpening the desire she still felt.

Her legs ached, and she shifted as slowly as possible, careful not to disturb the shadows on the ground. She tried again to urge her mind to something other than Jeff, back to the reason she'd come.

Her palms sweated as much from the gloves as from nervousness. She would get the samples and escape. No one need ever know, unless there was proof of anthrax.

For at least an hour, Abby had crouched next to an old cottonwood, buried in prairie grass, waiting for the cowboy on watch to ride to another section of the pasture. At this rate, she'd be here all right. Rocking K cattle milled around, brown-gray in the moonlight, the patches of white on their faces and their long curved horns glinting ivory.

She had so wanted to tell Jeff, to ask for his help. He would've known how to avoid the man who was now circling around her like a hawk searching for a mouse.

But involving Jeff could compromise his job. He also might be forced to turn her over to Strat, which was not a chance she could take.

Abby uttered a silent prayer and waited. The scents of sweet grass and dirt and clean air tickled her nostrils. A lone cloud scudded across the translucent moon. The grass swayed around her in the soft night breeze and rasped against the cows' legs as they moved slowly from clump to clump. Their teeth ground the cud, over and over, a slurping, chomping sound that raked her nerves.

She replayed her meeting with Mr. Kennedy, saw again the horrible sight under his microscope that had caused her to come out tonight and try to get the samples.

Steal the samples, she corrected, for that's what she was doing. Again, she wished she had been able to tell Jefferson. To escape more thoughts of him, she thought of the girls and her collection of teacups and even tried to conjure up Neil, but Jeff returned over and over again.

His image hovered like a shadow, stalking her, tempting her.

The lanky man on horseback passed in front of her again, snagging her attention. She waited with locked breath as he finally disappeared over the ridge. Wasting no time, she clipped a clump of grass with the scissors she'd brought and stuffed both into a canvas bag. She removed the syringe from her pocket, checked over her shoulder to make sure she was still alone, and angled for the cattle only a few yards away.

She kept low to the ground, her silhouette melting into the shadows of the cattle. A large bull swung his head toward her, black, pebble-hard eyes staring at her. She stilled, her heart racing. He shook his head. Moonlight glinted off his lethal ivory horns. After a moment, the animal blew noisily and resumed eating.

Abby moved around a clump of sage and found a cow who looked soft-eyed and harmless. Swiftly, she jabbed the needle into the animal's rump and drew a blood sample. The cow kicked, bawling. Abby bit back a yelp of surprise, yanked out the needle and lunged behind the bush, jamming the syringe into her bag.

The cow hobbled off down the rise. Abby waited for a few more seconds, glancing around to make sure she was alone. She gave a sigh of relief and stood, turning for the next pasture.

"Evenin' there." The lanky man stared down at her from atop his stringy horse. "I guess you know you're trespassin'?"

Abby's breath jammed in her chest and her gaze darted behind him, gauging her chances for escape.

"Whatcha doin' with that bag? Gettin' yoreself a little beef?"

"No! No, I'm not." Abby licked her suddenly dry lips and attempted a smile. The man wore a gun as Jeff did, low on his hip, and his hand rested on his thigh, close to the weapon. She felt a niggle of recognition, but couldn't place him.

Pale light slanted across his face, slashing at a tomahawk nose and carved cheeks. He eased himself down stiffly from the horse.

Abby registered signs of arthritis even as her mind raced for a plan.

"I ain't never seen no woman rustler before. This is gonna make some story."

"I'm not a rustler. I'm a doctor," Abby stated, drawing herself up to her full height, wondering if she should try to reason her way out or lie. She couldn't let him turn her over to Mr. Kennedy.

"A woman doctor?" He peered hard at her, eyes glinting like silver in the moonlight. "Hey, you ain't that woman what killed Sweeney?"

"I did not kill him," she retorted hotly then swept around him as if to leave.

"Yore Grant's wife." The man's hand shot out and grabbed for her.

Abby jumped, careful to escape his reach. *Wife*. The word jarred her, but she nodded, taking another cautious step back. "Look, Mr.—"

"Tandy." He shifted, pulling his holster around to the front of his leg. His hand hovered above the gun.

"Mr. Tandy. You must work with my . . . husband." She wished she were adept at batting her eyelashes and wriggling her way coquettishly out of tight situations with men, but she never had been. "Surely you don't believe I was stealing anything?" *Nothing that will be missed anyway.*

"*What* were you doin'?" His stony gaze pricked her.

Abby, torn between her desire to explain and her need to keep silent until she had proof of anthrax, chose to lie. "I was out for a walk."

"With the cattle? Let me see that bag." He advanced on her, motioning with his fingers for her to turn it over. "C'mon, give it to me." He reached for her.

"No!" Panic flickered and she jerked away from him. She couldn't let him touch her. If there were anthrax here, it was all over her. "There's a . . . poisonous weed in here."

"A poisonous weed?" He scowled and glanced around at the waist-high grass. "For what?"

Inwardly she groaned, but she wouldn't back down now. She took another step back and hoped she could bluff her way through. "I was gathering it for medicine." Which was close to the truth.

"Medicine? No wonder Sweeney died," the older man muttered. Louder, he said, "See here, I'm gettin' tired of this. How's about I take you home and we'll let yore man handle you?"

Jeff was supposed to "handle" her? The idea set her blood sizzling, but she kept her tone even. She took another step back and narrowly missed a hole. "There's really no need. I told you the truth."

"Mr. Kennedy's gone over to Tascosa or I'd haul yore carcass up there." His steely eyes looked her up and down. He slid the pistol from the holster and waved the gun at her. "Let's go."

Abby swallowed and measured her chances for running, wondering if he would really use that *thing* on her. "There's no need for the gun," she gritted out.

He holstered the weapon and grabbed the saddle horn to mount. "You just mount up behind me and we'll see—hey!"

Abby took advantage of his slow movements and set off at a dead run. She leapt across a protruding tree root, wheeled around a scraggly bush and stumbled up the hill toward home. The grass whipped at her arms, tangled in her skirt, but she pushed on.

Drat, drat, drat. Abby grabbed up her skirts with one hand and clutched the canvas bag with the other. She half-skidded, half-ran down the other side of the steep hill. The bag bumped against her hip. Pebbles pricked through the worn soles of her shoes, but she didn't slow.

After all she'd done to keep Jeff out of this, that bowlegged raisin of a cowboy back there was not going to ruin her plan.

Jeff had it all planned out. The next time he saw Abby, he would just ignore her. He picked up the second pane of window glass and went across the porch of the new house.

A blur of movement drew his attention. He turned and heard the thundering hoofbeats at the same time. What the devil!

Abby raced down the rise toward the cabin, her features only partially visible in the dusky light. Directly behind, a horse appeared and shot down the small hill after her.

Fear sliced through Jeff. The glass slipped out of his suddenly sweaty hands and shattered on the newly finished porch. With a curse, he grabbed for his gun and sprinted for Abby, his boots crunching on the glass as he leapt over the steps.

She stumbled to a stop next to the corral. Her shoulders were heaving as she struggled to breathe.

Jeff jarred to a halt beside her. "Abby? Are you all right? What the—"

The rider thundered up behind him, pulling the horse to a skidding stop. Jeff spun, cocking his gun. "Back up, mister and give me some room or I'm going to nail you right between the— Tandy?"

Jeff's eyes widened in surprise. "What's going on here?" He looked from Abby to the old man.

"This here yore woman?" Tandy panted as he laced his wrists atop the saddle horn and leaned forward.

Abby stepped out from behind Jeff, holding her ribs and

gasping for air. She muttered something under her breath. Even in the darkness, Jeff could see the fire in her eyes.

She didn't appear to be hurt and his initial fear faded. Jeff grinned at Tandy's reference to "his" woman. "I guess she's mine. Why?"

"Caught her at the ranch." A stream of spit zinged between the old man's teeth. "I think she was tryin' to kill the cattle."

"Oh, for pity's sake, I was not." Abby rolled her eyes.

Jeff's gaze sliced to her. "You were at the Rocking K?"

She pressed her lips together and looked away.

Jeff's eyes blazed into her, studying her stubborn jaw. He turned to Tandy. "I think I can handle it from here. Thanks for bringing her home."

"I didn't know what to do with her. Mr. Kennedy's in Tascosa." He leaned toward Jeff and spoke in a near whisper. "She said she was gatherin' some kind of poisonous weed."

The old man thought Abby was crazy. Jeff bit back a smile. Knowing he'd get no answer, he refrained from asking her what she'd been doing at the ranch. "I appreciate you bringing her home."

"She shouldn't be out by herself at night. It's dangerous, ya know. I dang near shot her when I came upon her in the grass."

"She'll be more careful, won't you?" Jeff grated, reaching for Abby.

She sidestepped him and bit out, "Of course. Thank you, Mr. Tandy, for a lovely evening."

Jeff glanced at her then walked over to the old man's horse. "If you don't mind, let's just keep it between ourselves. No need to involve Strat."

"I don't mind, but you better watch out for her." Tandy scratched his head and stared at Abby. "You got yoreself a handful, Grant. Loo-ney." He wheeled his horse around and disappeared over the rise.

Jeff waited until he could no longer hear Tandy's horse then spun on his heel and advanced on Abby. "Poisonous weeds?"

"Now, Jeff." Abby circled around him, putting her back to the corral.

"What the hell were you doing over there? Did Tandy pull a gun on you?"

"Yes, but I'm fine. He thought I was a rustler, but I explained. Partly anyway." She backed up, holding her hand out in front of her to stay him. "Don't touch me, Jeff."

"I ought to turn you over my knee. Going over there was a damn fool thing, especially at night. You could've been killed."

"I didn't know you cared," she snapped, angling her chin at him.

"I was thinking of the girls," he bit out. He reached for her again and she slipped away. "Abby, what's going on? Why were you over there? Do you know what would've happened if he'd shot first then looked to see who you were?"

"Yes, I do know. I had to go." She stilled, gripping the rough wood of the corral fence. She watched him the way a deer watched a hunter, wary and trying to guess his next move.

He noticed then that she was wearing gloves. Apprehension skittered up his spine. He didn't want to get involved with this, and yet he knew he would. Hell, he already was! "You're not going to tell me why, are you?"

She winced at that, a bare movement he almost missed. She shook her head, confirming his guess.

"You're lucky you're not lying on the ground over there with a bullet through you."

"I know." She shuddered.

Jeff took another step toward her. "What *is* in that bag?"

"Grass." She met his gaze, searching his eyes, willing him to believe her.

Stunned, Jeff frowned. "Grass?"

"Please don't ask me any more." She squeezed her eyes shut, as though she wanted to tell him, but couldn't.

"Don't ask you? You come running in here with Tandy on your heels and you don't want me to know what's going on?"

"Jeff, please—"

"Fine," he bit out. *Back off now or you'll regret it.* "But in the future, why don't you show a little more concern for the girls? They've already lost one family. They don't need you up and dying on them, too."

He pivoted and strode for the house.

Abby's voice was low and thick with tears. "Thank you, Jeff."

"Yeah," he muttered.

Women! He wanted to dismiss her—he was walking away, wasn't he?—but he knew he was already involved.

What was she up to? And why wouldn't she tell him? He knew why. She didn't like or trust him. Like a lot of people he'd known over the years, he added. But for the first time since he'd left home, Jeff felt regret at the realization.

He reached the porch of the cabin and stopped, glancing over his shoulder at the barn. Abby disappeared around the corner. Jeff stood there, aching for the night to cool his blood.

He paused, telling himself to go inside, to mind his own business, to put Abby Welch out of his mind. An orange glow appeared behind the barn. A fireglow.

Jeff could no more walk away from her than he could call back the years he'd lost with Jilly. Lured by the flames, he walked to the back of the barn.

Abby stood in a small area that had been cleared of grass and leaves and bordered with rocks. A small pit, used for branding fires, had been dug in the earth that was now scorched hard from old fires and age. She was outlined by black night, bathed in amber light and shadow.

Her shoulders were bare, creamy ivory above the rough texture of a blanket. She was naked under there. Jeff's gut clenched.

Strands of her hair, loosened from her braid, streamed onto her cheek and the back of her neck. Something about her profile, chin lifted, lips pressed firmly together, pulled at him. What was it about this woman that drew him like a boy to mud?

A warning clanged in his head, but he ignored it. Stepping

up beside her, he silently watched the flames devour a pile of clothes.

"Jefferson?" Her voice wafted through the night, soft and plaintive, as confused as she felt. She clutched the blanket together over her breasts.

"Hmmm." Jeff's throat was dry and his insides burned, but he didn't betray it with his voice.

She watched the fire. He watched her.

Caressed by the pale orange light, her features were soft. Her strong jaw curved beguilingly into her neck. The shell of her ear peeked out from her hair. He wanted to press his lips to the curve where her shoulders and neck met. Magnolia white skin beckoned him. Even with the dirt and the earthy smells of manure floating from the barn, her powdery scent wrapped around him, scorching his insides, dimming the vow he'd made.

Her face was milk pale in the shadows, tinged with a flush of heat from the small fire. Worry and longing marked her features.

Before he could stop himself, he reached over and cupped her shoulder. He noted with great surprise that his hand was shaking. She didn't move away. Being this close to her kicked his gut like too-new tequila.

Abby shivered, longing for his touch, yet wishing he would go away. She hadn't wanted to compromise his job, didn't still. How long would it be before he figured out something terrible threatened?

Wrapping the scratchy blanket around her nakedness, she watched her clothes burn. Bitter smoke curled into the darkness. Despite the warmth of the night and the heat of the blanket, a chill skipped over her. Jeff was right. She could've been killed, but she felt more loss at the distance she'd imposed on them tonight, though she didn't understand why.

His voice was low and harsh. "You risked your life tonight, Doc. Tandy could've killed you."

"Yes."

His thumb moved in a tantalizing circle at the base of her neck, and she turned to face him, her eyes seeking his.

"I know," he said in a gravelly voice, "you won't tell me what's going on."

She continued to stare at him, willing him to leave and not ask any questions. A frown marred her brow and clouded her eyes.

Jeff's entire body hummed as though she'd stroked him. He read uncertainty and concern in her eyes, but also hunger.

An invisible current jumped between them. Jeff remembered how it was the other time he had taken her in his arms. She had burned him alive. "I know something's going on, Abby. And I know it's bad."

"I want you to leave it alone. Please."

"There aren't very many reasons people burn their clothes."

She looked away, licking her lips and staring at the fire.

He sighed. "You've found something. A disease or something?"

She shrugged, keeping her head averted. Still he saw a flicker of alarm.

He wondered if his imaginings were as bad as the real thing. "Tandy said he thought you were trying to kill the cattle. You were checking them, weren't you?"

She turned her head away, her breathing shallow now. If he guessed the truth, her face would give it away.

He knew he was right. Even in the amber light, he could see her skin go pale.

Anthrax? Could it be that or some other devastating disease? He didn't say the word, couldn't bring himself to compromise her. Even unspoken, the word seemed to taint the air.

Jeff was silent for a while then his head snapped toward her. "Did you get what you need?"

"Jeff, please."

"Tonight, at the ranch?"

She closed her eyes and hitched the blanket up higher, causing her breasts to swell.

He clenched his teeth against the urge to stroke the creamy flesh. He shook his head, not even telling himself to stay out of it. It was too late. "I can help. I can get what you need or talk to Kennedy."

"No!" Her eyes widened in disbelief and she choked out, "It might compromise you. Oh, no. I won't be accused of that."

"Is that why you didn't tell me? Because you didn't want to put me in an awkward position with Strat?" Jeff asked slowly, incredulous, taking a step toward her. A warmth spread in his chest, and he fought it.

She shifted, as though uncomfortable with his speculation. "It's not your problem. I can handle it."

"That's why, isn't it?"

She looked at his boots, his hands, the moon, everything but his face. She turned to leave.

He stepped in front of her, crowding her, blocking her in. "You thought it might risk my job?" he repeated, though he already knew the answer. He felt again that unfamiliar warmth and at the same time suffocated, as if water were closing over his head.

He told himself to step away. Away from her powdery scent wrapped in the musky smell of night, away from the temptation of her lips, of holding her to make sure she was all right.

But her gaze was trained on his mouth, locked there as though she couldn't tear it away. Yearning flickered across her face and his blood heated. The current of want sang between them. He shifted and dipped his head.

His breath touched hers, heat and mint and wonderfully caressing. Desire lanced him. His lips brushed the satin softness of hers. He was slipping into weakness, losing the edge of control. Instincts, from hard-learned lessons, awoke with startling sharpness within him.

He jerked back, feeling the same confusion he saw in her eyes. He was rigid from his neck to his knees. He throbbed with want for her, but he couldn't give in. She would demand too much. In that respect, she was no different than any other woman, was she?

She stared up at him, biting her lip. Pain flashed through her eyes then she straightened, masking the emotion.

Gathering the blanket tight around her, Abby stepped to the stall gate. "Thank you for your offer. There's no need for you to do it."

"It won't be long before others figure it out."

She stared at him, the battle waging clearly on her face. To tell him or not to tell him.

"At least if I'd been the one to find you tonight, I wouldn't have pulled a gun on you," he said dryly, hoping for a smile. Or an answer.

She shook her head and skirted him to walk back to the house.

Her name ached in his throat. He wanted to call her back, apologize, soothe her with his hands and lips. But he wouldn't.

She wouldn't trust him with the truth, and yet Jeff's guts gnarled with want.

It hammered at him, causing a fine sweat to break out on his brow. He wanted her, wanted to bury himself inside her and kiss her senseless, which he doubted anyone had ever done to the sensible Dr. Welch.

But he wouldn't give her that kind of power over him, and he instinctively knew it *would* give her power.

He walked, aching, back to the new house. On the porch, glass crunched beneath his boots, and it was then he realized that the pane glass had shattered. Just like his vow to remain uninvolved.

EIGHT

Abby didn't know how, but somehow she made it back inside the cabin. Her body throbbed with a dull pain, as though she had left part of herself with Jeff. She had certainly left her heart.

Only when she closed the bedroom door did she allow herself to breathe, great racking breaths from deep inside that clenched and tore at her muscles.

She wouldn't fall in love with him.

She couldn't love a man who hired out his gun.

It was desire and nothing more.

Abby told herself all of these things. She spent long hours into the night trying to make herself believe them. It was nearly dawn when she drifted into a fitful sleep, and she awoke almost immediately.

Jeff could be in danger! The thought rushed at her. Why hadn't she thought of it last night? She had been so concerned with first Tandy, then with keeping her suspicions from Jeff that it hadn't occurred to her that he and his horse had ridden all over the Rocking K. If anthrax were thriving on the ranch, Jeff and his horse could be infected.

She had to warn him, though she knew he might be as skeptical as Kennedy had been. On the other hand, he just might believe her. His astute guess had dismayed her last night, but it might be her salvation today.

Without even taking time to pull on her wrapper, Abby scrambled out of bed, rushed out of the bedroom and threw open the cabin door. Her gaze fixed on the new sun breaking over the rise. There was no sign of Jeff, and she knew without looking that his horse wouldn't be in the barn.

"Happy morning, Abby."

Hannah's sleepy voice caused Abby to turn. She tamped down her disappointment at finding Jeff gone. Hannah stood next to the table, rubbing her eyes and peering at Abby.

The smell of eggs and coffee wafted her. Rachel filled the coffeepot at the pump. "Jeff was gone when we got up. Are you ready to eat?"

"Yes, thank you. Happy morning, girls." Abby smiled as she leaned against the door. At least Jeff hadn't exposed the girls. Impatience brushed at her to find him, but she walked to the table and hugged both girls.

As soon as she took them to school, she had to find Jeff. She would warn him about the danger to himself and his mount, but she couldn't drag him into this mess with Kennedy. No matter how tempting his offer to help last night, she couldn't accept it.

He would never forgive her if she caused him to lose his job.

"How long will you be gone, Abigail?" Lionel Welch stood in the clinic, the shock at what Abby had just revealed finally leaving his face. "Don't you think I should go with you?"

"No, Papa." Abby held up a small, opaque vial of vaccine and studied the contents. She stuffed it into her bag along with a syringe she had sterilized with carbolic acid. "I'm not sure how long it will take me to find Jeff. I need you to stay here in case anyone comes by."

"But what about Kennedy?"

"I plan to talk to him again," she said firmly, snapping her bag shut and spinning for the door in a flurry of skirts. "This time, I won't take no for an answer. I've already sent the samples to Austin. Anthrax is too dangerous for his pride to get in the way."

"You be careful." Her father gripped her arm and turned her to face him. "That Tandy character could've blown you clear to kingdom come. You're lucky Jeff was there to help you."

"I know." Despite the fact that Abby hadn't wanted it, Jeff had helped her. She was determined to return the favor without involving him in her battle with Kennedy. She just prayed it wasn't too late. Why, oh why, hadn't she thought of the danger to him last night?

She kissed her father and hurried out the door. Once in the buggy, she gave the gray free rein and they raced off toward the Rocking K.

Doubts hammered at her, shushing through her mind with the rhythm of the buggy wheels.

Tell him. Don't tell him. Tell him. Don't tell him.

She was past the point of choice, though Abby didn't like the fact.

Dust billowed around her, filtering into her blue-and-white striped day dress. Winter wheat and prairie grass rippled in the wind like a velvet wave. Potent sunshine fingered its way through the open sides of the buggy, hot and clinging. Her hair hung in a heavy braid down the middle of her back, and a fine sweat pebbled her upper lip.

The closer she got to the Rocking K, the stronger she felt the urge to turn back. Her hands gripped the reins tighter, and almost imperceptibly the horse slowed.

Abby urged the gray on, feeling that she was talking to herself more than she was instructing the horse. Going to Jeff was the right thing. She just prayed her delay hadn't further endangered him or his gelding.

She dodged ruts in the road and careened over the hill leading away from the cabin. The buggy flew over packed dirt and grass, hopping a fallen log and jostling Abby to the corner.

Just as she topped the rise leading to the Rocking K, a horse and rider thundered straight at her. The gray snorted angrily, reared and jerked to the right, slamming Abby into one of the cap's supporting rods. They jarred to a stop.

Her ears ringing, Abby shook her head and regained her grip on the reins.

"Ho there, Dr. Grant! Ho!"

At the man's voice, she frowned. She peered around the cap of the buggy and saw Murdoch riding toward her. He halted beside her, his face flushed with heat and exertion. The black stallion he rode, a different horse from the one she'd seen before, rolled his eyes and pranced to the side. His ebony coat glistened in the sun. The stallion's black eyes surveyed Abby with wary suspicion, as though she were trespassing.

"Mr. Murdoch?" Abby took a firmer hand on the reins, quieting the gray. "You're in quite a hurry."

"I was comin' to see you. It's my horse, ma'am."

"Your horse?" Alarm skipped through her. "What is it?"

"He's dead. I went out this morning, gettin' ready to go town, and he was layin' in the stall. Just dead. Just layin' there dead."

Fear crawled in her throat.

Murdoch's slitted eyes twitched. Abby thought she saw pain flash through his eyes, then he pulled his black hat lower on his head. "Will you come?"

"Yes."

He wheeled the stallion, and Abby snapped the reins on the gray's rump, racing behind him.

Less than ten minutes later, she pulled on her gloves and stood over the dead horse. Murdoch waited outside the barn door as she'd asked.

She found the telltale signs within seconds. Ulcerating lesions ate away the skin under the horse's chin and down his muscular neck. "Is anyone else here sick? Any other animals?"

"No, ma'am. Not that I know of."

Abby carefully peeled off the gloves and walked outside, squinting against the sunlight. "I'm sorry, Mr. Murdoch. You'll need to burn the animal."

He considered her words silently, staring off over the

double corrals and across the vast expanse of prairie that stretched beyond. He shifted beside her. "I remember what you said to Mr. Kennedy the other day about . . . you know." Black eyes bored into hers. "Do you think that's what killed my horse?"

"I'm afraid so." Anger at her helplessness flared through her. She turned and stared at the big house. From this distance, she could see two men on the porch. She strode through the gate.

Murdoch caught up with her, matching her steps. "You goin' to talk to him again?"

"Yes." Abby set her jaw. This time, Strat Kennedy would not put her off. If she had to tell the whole of Donley County herself, she would force him to act responsibly. As they neared, she could distinguish Kennedy and Tom Ardington on the porch. "Do you think you could find Jefferson? I need to talk to him as well."

"He ain't here. He was supposed to go up to the north pasture today."

She halted, her heartbeat locking for an instant. "Is that where you've been riding?"

"No. I've been down in the south all week."

Jeff might still be safe, though she cautioned herself not to hope. She quickened her steps to the porch.

"Dammit, Strat. This is folly!" Ardington's voice rang out. As she approached, the lean cowboy moved in front of Kennedy, his hands fisted on his hips, legs straddled wide as though in anticipation of a fight. "I tell you that bull died, the one Sweeney brought in. And another one of the cows is acting poorly."

Abby stopped at the bottom of the steps, a heavy weight settling over her at the news.

Kennedy saw her and lunged to the edge of the porch. "What the hell do you want? Murdoch, get her out of here."

"Not today, Boss." The gunman halted beside her, a solid presence that wouldn't be moved.

Tom Ardington turned, surprise flickering in his eyes as he saw Abby. "Dr. Welch."

"Hello, Tom." She shifted her gaze to the ranch owner.

"I'm not wasting any time today, Mr. Kennedy. We can have this conversation in private or not, but we're having it."

"Don't think you're going to deal me more ultimatums, miss—"

"That's exactly what I'm going to do." Abby cut him off and walked up the steps to stand nose to nose with him. "Mr. Murdoch's horse died this morning. Now I hear that one of your bulls has, too."

"The bull Sweeney brought," Ardington put in.

"It's more than coincidence, don't you see?" Abby pleaded. "You've got to do something. You can't let this go on. I've seen Murdoch's horse and I know how it died."

"You weren't sure how Sweeney died, but you're sure of how a horse died?" Kennedy challenged, his face heating to florid red.

"Mr. Sweeney didn't have external lesions. The horse does. You've got to do something and now."

"Or you'll threaten to tell the whole county again, I suppose?" he jeered.

Abby shook her head, fighting the sadness and anger that tightened her chest. "I won't need to. They'll find out on their own, in the worst way possible."

"Yesterday you weren't sure of anything. Now you're tellin' me you know it's anthrax."

"I don't have positive proof, but the signs are there. You can't wait until I get results from Austin." She registered the sound of hoofbeats behind her, the flurry of dust from the corner of her eye, but all her attention focused on the man in front of her. "How many will you let the disease kill before you take action?"

"Get off my land!" Kennedy advanced on her, his thick hands curling into fists. His gaze flickered over her head and he stilled, relief evident in his face. "Grant, good. Get her out of here."

Abby spun. Jeff strode toward her, worry drawing creases around her eyes.

"Jeff, thank goodness. I was coming to find you and I saw Mr. Murdoch and—"

"Are the girls all right? I saw you ride in." His one stride covered two steps, and he gripped her shoulders. Crystal-blue eyes searched hers. His palms warmed her shoulders, offering strength and reassurance. She wondered why she'd wanted to see Kennedy alone.

"They're fine. I came about . . . you."

Jeff frowned and slid his hands down her arms. She shivered in response. "Me?"

"Grant, this woman's trespassin'." Kennedy thrust out his chest like a striking rooster and slitted his eyes. "You know what to do."

Tom Ardington spoke in a quiet voice. "You better listen to her, Strat, or all the animals will die."

"The animals?" Jeff turned to Abby, his gaze questioning. "What's going on?"

"My horse died this morning, Grant," Murdoch put in. "And Ardington here just told Mr. Kennedy that the bull Sweeney brought in, the one in the south pasture, was found dead this morning."

"You were right." Jeff's words were low, for her ears only. His face was bleak with comprehension.

"Maybe," she admitted, glad he was here, part of her wishing he hadn't been put in the middle. This was exactly what she had wanted to avoid. Still, he hadn't questioned her opinion and that boosted her confidence. "Mr. Kennedy, what are you going to do?"

Kennedy looked from Abby's worried features to Ardington's apprehensive face to Murdoch's stubborn stance. Defeat settled over Kennedy's expression. "All right. Tell me."

Relief skated through her. She turned to Ardington. "How many cattle are in the south pasture?"

"About twenty-five head right now."

"Where are the rest?"

Ardington stepped closer to the porch, a frown furrowing his brow. "The boys are bringing 'em down from the north. And across the creek."

"The bull is the only animal you've found dead?"

"So far."

"Dammit, Dr. Welch, if you're gonna do somethin', do

it!" Kennedy exploded, rocking back on his heels and throwing his arms in the air.

"Hold off, Strat," Jeff bit out. He turned to Abby. "We should keep the cattle separated."

"Yes." Her mind raced. "I need to look at that bull as well."

Murdoch and Ardington nodded.

Jeff eased closer, his heat wrapping around her, letting her know she wasn't alone.

She laid a hand on his arm. "Have you been in the south pasture today?"

"No. Not all week."

"Good."

"What about the cattle in the south pasture? Is there anything you can do for them?" Kennedy's voice was gruff, with a slight tinge of fear.

Abby tore her gaze from Jeff. "It will take a while. I'll have to order the vaccine from Leavenworth."

"What! I thought you could make your own medicine." He slammed an open palm against the sturdy column of the porch. "What kind of doctor doesn't know how to do that?"

"Watch it, Strat." Jeff stepped forward, his hand sliding toward his gun.

"It's all right, Jeff." Abby stepped up, her hip nudging his. She looked at Strat. "I can make some, but not enough for all twenty-five head. We'll vaccinate them first."

Murdoch spoke from behind Abby. "I can put that order through for you, Doc."

"Thank you." She gave him the name of St. John's Hospital in Leavenworth.

"Will this . . . vaccine cure them?" Kennedy rubbed his hands together as though assuaging a nervous itch.

"I'm not sure." She braced herself for Kennedy's reaction. "It's fairly new."

"You're not sure!" Kennedy's face turned purple with rage, and he stepped toward her. A thick vein popped out on his neck.

Jeff moved quick as lightning, shielding her body with his.

Abby put her hand on his arm, grateful for his strength, but hating to draw him in so deeply. "You should know, Mr. Kennedy, this vaccine could kill the cattle. It's a form of the virus."

"You mean you're givin' them anthrax!" His face paled. Only two bright slashes of color, high on his cheeks, remained on his face. "I don't believe this. You *are* crazy."

Jeff leveled a glare at him and urged Abby on. "What happens then?"

"The animal uses the germ cell to make its own protection. The animal may become ill, but could recover."

"You want to try that on twenty-five of my prize cattle which may or may not already have this disease?" Kennedy snorted, a harsh laugh between bitterness and disbelief. "What if you kill my cattle?"

"If you don't do something, Strat, they *will* die," Jeff pointed out tersely.

Kennedy paced, his boots echoing hollowly on the stone porch. His gaze settled on Abby, measured, then moved to Jeff. Murdoch and Ardington stepped closer to the porch, forming a tight knot of support.

Finally Kennedy huffed out a breath. "Go ahead then. Get it over with. My men will help you. How long will it take to know if it's going to work?"

"Mr. Kennedy, I don't have a supply large enough for all of them. I was able to make a vaccine from the culture I took from Mr. Sweeney, but it's only enough for one animal, maybe two. And even then . . ." Her voice trailed off.

"Even then what?" He demanded, his gaze narrowing on her again.

"Even then, I haven't seen it proven. I've only read about it."

"You mean this could all be for nothing?" he choked out.

"Possibly. Or it might be too late for the dosage to help them."

Astonishment and disbelief mingled on his features. "So I can let you try it out on them and probably kill 'em or I can take the chance that there's no anthrax here?"

"I'm fairly certain there is anthrax—"

"That's what you're telling me, isn't it?" Kennedy pushed. "If you're riskin' my cattle, lady, say so."

Jeff stepped between them, his broad shoulders blocking out her sight of Kennedy. He locked gazes with Abby. "You can try it on my horse."

Abby's breath caught in her chest.

Kennedy's head swiveled toward Jeff. "You're out of your cotton-pickin' mind, Grant."

Warmth spread through Abby like a shot of liquor, tilting her reason for an instant. Jeff trusted her, even when she wouldn't tell him everything. "Are you sure? Your horse may or may not be already infected. You, too."

Shock flickered in his eyes. He was silent for a long moment, his eyes fastened on hers. "What do we do?"

We. Abby's stomach fluttered. "I can watch you for signs of illness, but I can't watch all the animals."

"Can the vaccine work on animals if they already have it?"

"Yes, but—"

"Do it then. On my horse."

She looked into his eyes, and her skin heated as though he had taken her in his arms.

His gaze burned into hers, steady and believing. Then he turned, took the steps in a leap and grabbed up his reins, offering them to her. "Now, Doc."

Her throat burned. By helping her, Jeff was risking not only his job, but also the life of his horse.

"What do we do in the meantime?" Kennedy grumbled, coming down the steps toward her.

Abby smiled at Jeff, wishing she could kiss him full on the lips. His gaze dropped to her lips and he grinned. He knew what she was thinking. A blush burned her cheeks as she turned to Mr. Kennedy. "Quarantine the cattle as we discussed. Mr. Murdoch—"

"On my way, Doc." The gunman sprinted toward the second corral, where he'd left his horse.

Ardington strode off, calling over his shoulder, "I'll get the news to the boys. They should be getting close to the south pasture by now."

"I'll come with you," Jeff put in.

Kennedy snorted and stomped around Abby, jamming a wide-brimmed straw hat onto his red hair. "I'm comin', too."

As Strat Kennedy left, Abby stared solemnly at Jeff. Uncertainty warred with triumph. What if the vaccine didn't work? What if Jeff became ill? What if his horse died? What if the disease had spread to other parts of the ranch?

"Hey." Jeff covered the distance between them and touched her shoulder. "It's going to be fine."

She nodded, holding his gaze, taking the hope he offered. The doubts melted away. "I'll need to take your horse."

"Done. What else?"

"Pray." She met his gaze, wishing again for his arms to close around her, hold off the harsh realities of what they were facing. "Pray hard."

"You and prayer. Pretty lethal combination." Jeff smiled, then to Abby's complete surprise he leaned down and kissed her hard on the mouth. "Remind me not ever to go up against you."

Abby stared, a slow grin lifting the corners of her lips as he turned toward the barn. "Jeff?" she called softly.

He turned.

"Thank you."

His gaze stroked her face, touched on her lips then met her eyes. Warmth and desire lingered in the pure blue depths. Abby felt an answering tug low in her belly. Then he touched the brim of his hat and disappeared.

Uncertainty curled up her spine. Would he resent her for involving him? Despite her efforts, he was in as deep as she was. It hit her with the force of a stampede.

Abby's instructions were followed to the letter. Murdoch burned his horse and rode into town to send a wire to the hospital in Leavenworth. Kennedy held a meeting with the cowboys, ordering them to do as Abby requested. Jeff tied his gelding behind her buggy and rode off on another of Kennedy's horses.

Back at the cabin, she released the two milk cows and the

gray into the pasture beyond. She cleared old hay and straw from one of the stalls, led Jeff's chestnut gelding in, and locked the doors that led to the corral from the barn. Keeping other animals away was essential. The gelding's flanks quivered as she injected the vaccine, and Abby uttered a silent prayer.

She rode back to the Rocking K and examined the bull, wearing a bandanna over her nose and mouth. She was relieved to see that none of the carcass had been eaten away by animals, but lesions spotted the bull's matted hide. Just like Murdoch's horse.

The sun set, streaming red and gold over the flat land. Abby was surprised at how quickly the time had flown.

The next hours stretched like long, frayed ropes holding a condemned man who hoped for pardon. Each hour brought more pressure, building and boiling inside all of them, enough to test even the most gentle nature.

Day crawled into night; night eeked into day. Abby watched. And waited.

Despite Jeff's faith in her, she didn't want to give him false hope or let him down. Neither slept. They skirted around each other, afraid to ask the questions that wouldn't be answered until the horse took sick.

On the second night, Jeff ordered her to bed and swore he would wake her if anything happened to the gelding. She hadn't slept more than a few hours, and neither had he. She finally agreed, on the condition that he sleep when she woke.

She stripped off her clothes, donned her nightdress and tumbled into bed without even unpinning her hair. Visions of Jeff's warm blue eyes, Murdoch's stunned face, Kennedy's anger-mottled features swirled in her head before she finally dozed.

She woke with a jerk, and the fog of sleep slipped away.

She had heard nothing, yet she knew. Jeff was in the room.

She could feel him. His potent strength reached out to her,

enveloping her, stroking, making her yearn for the feel of his body, of his arms. Was it a dream?

She rolled over slowly and met his gaze. He stood by the bed, smelling like a fresh prairie breeze, a real flesh-and-blood man holding the lantern high. Soft gold light spilled across the bed, arcing him in shadow. His eyes glowed like blue flame in the half-lit room.

Abby propped herself up on her elbows, swallowing as her stomach quivered nervously.

She wanted him in this bed with her. The admission washed over her with the same caressing heat as his gaze. Her voice was husky with sleep and denied desire, seductive in a way she'd never heard. "Jeff?"

He moved closer, lowering the lamp so she could see his face more clearly. His features were drawn and haggard, his beard untrimmed from the last couple of days. Blue eyes, raw with hunger, speared her. His voice rasped out, uncertain and rough, "It's the gelding, Doc. He's collapsed."

The vaccine.

Without thinking, she held out her hand, and Jeff took it. Warmth flowed between them, and with it strength and hope. Still gripping his hand, Abby scooted out of bed and stood in front of him.

His chest brushed hers and her skin prickled. Her breasts grew heavy. Loose hair, streaming in disarray from her chignon, tickled her cheek and eyes. She pushed the strands from her face and looked up at him.

In his eyes lurked the same uncertainty she felt. She wanted to reassure him, show him that his faith in her hadn't been misplaced, but she could offer no guarantees. His features sharpened with yearning, and her heart thrummed in response.

She knew, in that moment, that her future was forever linked to his. A bubble of panic fluttered within her then disappeared.

He squeezed her hand and broke the invisible web around them. She forsook stockings, put on shoes and followed him out of the bedroom and through the front door. Once outside, he took her hand again and together they walked to the barn.

Indian summer night closed around them, a cool breeze swirling through the heat. Once in the barn, Jeff followed Abby to the stall. She took her gloves from the post at the gate and walked inside.

The huge gelding lay motionless on his side. Clods of dirt littered the area. Deep gouges runneled the earthen floor, indicating that he'd gone wild with fever. His sides heaved; muscles quivered beneath his sleek brown hide. Abby knelt, angling herself so that the light from the lantern Jeff held would fall on the horse.

"Be careful." Jeff's voice was hoarse with concern and uncertainty.

The gelding's eyes were closed. Abby checked them, noting the dilated pupils, wide and wild with fever. Sweat soaked the horse's dark brown coat, making it appear dull and matted in the lantern light. He tried to raise his head, and it fell back weakly, his jaw knocking her knee. Pity squeezed Abby's heart. *Fight, boy. Fight.*

She rose and walked back outside the stall to Jeff. She placed her gloves on the top post and turned. "All we can do is wait."

"What should I look for?" Jeff stared helplessly at the huge animal, now as weak as a newborn calf. Tension drew tight across Jeff's cheekbones. Abby noticed a fine sheen of sweat on his neck.

She touched his arm. "He'll probably convulse, like he would if he had a bad fever."

"Is there anything we can do?"

"Just try to keep him from hurting himself. He's so weak now, I don't think he'll be able to move."

Jeff turned toward her, worry clouding his eyes. "How long do you think it will be before we know?"

"It depends on him. He's strong. We might know by morning."

"You mean, he might die by morning." His voice was harsh, just like his features in the soft light and shadows.

"He might not," she reminded gently.

Jeff nodded and walked to the stall across from the gelding. He hung the lantern on the crossbeam overhead and slid to the floor. "I'll let you know."

Abby sank to the floor beside him. "I'm not going anywhere."

His gaze swerved to her and held. Disbelief, gratitude, relief all passed through his eyes. Under the tight scrutiny, her skin heated but she held his gaze.

Finally his voice came low and raw. "Thanks, Doc."

NINE

Jeff slitted open one eye and stared at the woman to his left. Her soft scent floated to him, and a whole new barrage of feelings assaulted him—frustration, arousal, tenderness. He hadn't thought he could get any more impressed with her after the way she had stood up to Kennedy, but he'd been wrong.

His admiration had grown in the past few hours. Hours in which Jeff had discovered he not only wanted her fiercely, but also liked her, playing havoc with his determination to keep a distance.

His determination seemed about as strong as gnawed rope these days. When Abby Welch Grant was around, reason collided with desire. Thus far, neither had won.

He appreciated her willingness to stay, to see the gelding through the night. Yet the state of her dress or lack thereof made his blood sizzle.

The lantern hanging overhead cast a crescent of amber light just beyond the length of his legs and deepened the shadows at his back, throwing into relief the woman beside him.

She was asleep, her head resting against the slats of the stall behind them. The tilt of her head exposed her throat and the elegant line of her neck. Slender, yet not frail.

Darkness and light played upon her skin, softening the stubborn jaw, sliding over the thrust of her breasts. Whether it was shadow or real flesh, he couldn't tell, but dark circles pushed against the thin material of her nightdress. Her breasts, free and rounded and full, rose and fell gently, and Jeff found each breath harder to pull.

Desire rushed in a white-hot flash to harden him. The burn in his belly and loins gripped him deeper, twisting his gut. He reached out and gently brushed a wayward strand of dark hair away from her mouth. She didn't stir, and Jeff felt an odd sensation clench tight in his chest. He looked away, replaying the argument he'd had with himself at least ten times.

He wanted her, but the consequences could prove to be too great. He had a family again, and he didn't want to risk it on a woman who couldn't accept him as he was.

The last few weeks he'd come to realize exactly what Jilly had left to him. First he'd stayed because of a pledge. Now he stayed because he loved the girls. Hannah because she'd been so open and loving with him and, strangely enough, Rachel because she hadn't. He understood her pain and was willing to give her time. He believed she would come around. He had to believe it.

"Is there any change?" Abby shifted beside him, her shoulder grazing his as she leaned forward to stare at the gelding in the stall across from them. "I didn't mean to fall asleep."

"He's thrashed around a bit, but for the most part he's just been laying there. Is that a good sign?"

"I'll check him." She rose, her nightdress riding up her leg to reveal a shapely calf and knee. Her gown clung to the firm curves of her rounded bottom before the material shook away with her steps.

Lust stabbed Jeff low in the belly, and he shifted, restlessness clawing through him.

Abby returned quickly and slid back down beside him. Her arm skimmed his. "His breathing seems more harsh, but I didn't see any lesions."

Jeff stared straight ahead, controlling his breathing and

moving his left arm away from hers. It was a damn shame he couldn't keep his mind on his horse instead of this woman. "Thanks, Doc. If you want to go in now, I don't mind."

"I'm not going." She wiggled beside him, her breast grazing his arm as she rearranged her nightdress, tugging it to her ankles. "I'm staying with you."

At her touch, fire brushed along his arm and skipped down his elbow. Jeff's throat dried up.

"Thank you for standing up to Kennedy." Her voice was soft, stroking his insides, tangling his reason. "I appreciate the faith you showed in me."

He angled one shoulder against the stall, trying to move away from her body, the shadow-feel of her breast against his arm, her thigh molded to his. "You're welcome."

"You took a risk."

"I thought you were right about the anthrax, Doc." The words were impatient, made sharp by her infernal moving around.

She nodded then drew her knees up, draping her wrists over them. "Could I ask you something?"

He nodded sharply, easing away another fraction. Her soft powder scent tortured him, mingled with a lighter, more womanly scent that hinted at rumpled sheets and warm skin. His body throbbed with a heavy cadence, starting in his chest and traveling in pounding waves to his toes. His reason wavered. He wanted her so badly his throat tightened and his belly clenched, but he fought the urge to reach for her.

"Why are you a hired gun?"

He froze, staring at the gold and washed silver of lantern light and moonlight mingling on the ground. Why did she want to know? Slowly he turned his head and met her gaze. "Why are you a doctor?"

"I've always wanted to be one," she answered simply. "My father used to take me with him to the hospital and to see patients. I never questioned it, although other people did." She grinned, giving her strong features an impishness he'd never seen before. "And I'm good at it."

"You make it sound like an easy choice. It can't have been, for a woman."

She looked down for an instant. Longing swept across her features, and her voice tightened with remembrance. "No, it wasn't. But I had my father's support. I think it made all the difference."

Father's support. The words cornered Jeff with regret and bitterness. He'd had his father's support only as long as his wishes had fallen in line with Marcus Grant's. "Your mother must have approved, too."

"Actually," Abby said on a sigh, "Mother only came around a few months before she passed on. She thought my father had corrupted me, taking me around with him. It was disgraceful to her. My sister, Amelia, is the only one who encouraged me. My brothers, Charles and Royce, thought it was great fun, but they didn't take me seriously. At first."

Jeff had only wanted to draw the subject away from himself, but he found he was truly interested. Plus it kept his gaze centered on her eyes, not her soft rose lips. "What changed their minds?"

She shrugged, staring into the dim light as though she saw something there besides dirt and bits of straw and hay. "How serious I was, I guess. Mother was the hardest to convince, but one day, after I'd assisted in my first surgery, she told me how proud she was. From then on, she was a staunch supporter."

"What are you doing out here? Why didn't you take over your father's practice in Philadelphia?"

She smiled though sadness touched her eyes. "Not everyone is as accepting as my family."

He could vouch for that. Thoughts of his own family scraped across memories and raw nerves. "I thought the East was supposed to be progressive," Jeff said lightly.

"Yes, well." She was silent for a moment then wrapped her arms around her knees. "A lot of people back there were just like Strat Kennedy. Even my fiancé."

"Your fiancé?" His head swerved toward her. "You were engaged!"

"There are things more farfetched," she retorted dryly.

Jeff shook his head, still surprised. "I didn't mean that. I just . . . didn't know."

"And couldn't imagine?" she chided softly, her gaze meeting his, demanding the truth.

"Oh, no. I think you're plenty of woman," he admitted in a rush, then wished he hadn't. But he enjoyed the look of pleasure that streaked through her eyes. He jammed a hand through his hair then locked eyes with her. "What happened?"

Her nostrils flared with a silent indrawn breath, and for a moment Jeff thought she wouldn't answer.

Her voice was light when she did, belying the pain he knew she must have felt. "Neil thought of me as a novelty, not a doctor."

"How do you mean?" Jeff rested one wrist over his drawn-up knee and shifted toward her.

Abby grimaced. "I met him in medical college. He was the first person to welcome me and was my champion for that first sixteen weeks. But once he learned I planned to practice medicine, just as he did, he couldn't accept it. He liked the idea of being with a woman who was different, one who had defied convention, but when it came to a wife defying convention—well, that was something he couldn't accept."

"And so you came out here?"

"Yes. I was running away at first. But I was running to something as well. Out here, I've been able to make it on my own, and I think I'm slowly finding a place." She smiled and plucked a piece of straw from the barn floor, worrying it between her fingers. "Now will you answer my question?"

He stared blankly at her, focused on the fact that she had faced prejudice just as he had. She had felt the pain of rejection just as he had.

"Why are you a hired gun?" she reminded him softly.

Jeff suddenly felt caged. Danger hummed at this unexpected connection with her. Though their lives were about things completely different, he'd discovered a link that he perversely felt compelled to break. "I like what I do." A smile touched his lips as he repeated her earlier words. "And I'm good at it."

She tilted her head and stared at him. "I think it's more than that."

Where was the distance she always imposed at mention of his gun? Where was that frigid look that seemed especially reserved for him at those times? Jeff found he wanted to tell her the truth, part of him hoping the fear and disgust would come back, part of him wishing it wouldn't.

Once she knew the truth, the wall between them would return. But he didn't want her thinking he was something he wasn't. Though his guts twisted, he knowingly made the decision to keep the wall between them. "I fell into it by accident, but once I'd done a couple of jobs, I found I liked it and I was fast with a gun. After my first job, offers started coming in and I took them."

"How did you get into it?"

Jeff's throat worked, and he fingered the locket through his vest pocket. He had told only Jilly that story. "There was a woman in Fort Smith. I was green and stupid. She and her partner weren't. They set me up one night during a card game. Stole my money and my one possession."

He could still remember the raw metal taste of fear in his mouth when he'd awakened, his head pounding from too much rye, and realized that the locket containing pictures of his mother and sister was gone. Fanny Sanford and her partner had taken his past, his identity. His one tie to home. Cold, slicing rage had sent him after the pair.

"I caught them in Oklahoma Territory and took them back to the law in Fort Smith. It turned out they had a string of aliases and robberies across the country. The marshal offered me a job, and I learned as much as I could from him. When a family passed through on their way to Texas a few months later, looking for a guard to ride with them, I took the job."

"And it grew from there?"

There was none of the condemnation he'd expected, just a curiosity and a wistful quality to her voice that tightened his chest. He looked at her, making his voice hard and unyielding. "It was a choice I made. I wasn't seeking revenge. I wasn't a victim who decided to strike out in bitterness. I wasn't forced at all."

Abby watched him carefully, her eyes wide with speculation. "I see."

He wondered if she really did. Memories of his fiancée ripped at him, reminding him that another woman had said she understood, had sworn to accept him and forsake all others for him. In the end, she hadn't. He knew just how to coax that cold look back into Abby's violet eyes. "I like how I live, Abby. I like my job. No one, *no one,* is going to take that away from me."

"Someone tried to, besides your father." It wasn't a question. He supposed it wasn't even a guess. Abby was much too perceptive.

His eyes narrowed. How could he make her see? He didn't want to tell her about Caroline, but maybe that was the only way. "I had a fiancée, too."

He glanced over to see if she was surprised, but her face revealed nothing.

"I didn't want to settle on her daddy's ranch and work for him the rest of my life. She couldn't understand that. We saw a lot of things differently. I always thought my woman would support me, go where I went, be my partner. She didn't want to leave. I didn't want to stay." There was no pain now, just a resentment that, strangely, had increased toward his father. "That's all."

"No one has the right to change who you are," Abby said quietly. Her words were heavy with meaning—she hadn't been accepted for who she was either—but there was something about the yearning under the words that made apprehension prickle his spine. He pressed his shoulders into the coarse wood behind him and glanced at her.

The look in her eyes was neither cold nor distant, but full of understanding and regret. Was it for herself? Or him? Could she really accept him, the way he was?

The possibility dangled before him, teasing and taunting him with hope. It soothed him like balm on a burn, but Jeff knew the hope could shatter, be crushed into nothingness by the weight of reality.

Suddenly the air was stifling, closing around him like a thick velvet net. He rose, his legs tingling with sudden feeling at the movement. "I'm going to get some air."

"I wouldn't have made you choose, Jeff." The whispered words appeared from nowhere yet Abby knew they were true. It was with an effort that she kept from calling him back.

As she watched him go, she realized how much they shared besides the girls. A chill skipped over her. Despite the heat of the late summer night, she wrapped her arms around her waist and huddled inside the thin material of her nightdress.

She knew what it was to be shunned and mocked because of her decision to become a doctor. As much as she hated his way of life, for her, for the girls, for what it meant to others, she had no right to ask him to change.

There was so much more to him than the fact that he hired out his gun for a living. Yet that was such an important part to Abby.

She understood more about him now than she'd ever anticipated, and the knowledge simply served to confuse her. Her feelings were a jumble of denial and understanding, regret and hope.

There was something different between them now, a deeper understanding that somehow sharpened the vulnerability she felt with him.

He was unapologetic about what he did for a living. Abby, much to her consternation, admired his attitude.

She knew he wanted her. Even with her limited experience, she could read the heat in his eyes, the yearning in his voice. She felt it. She wanted it, too.

And like him, she wouldn't compromise. The future stretched bleak and black before her.

The attraction between them had been forceful from the beginning, but she had dodged the admission until now.

She wanted a future with him, a real family. Even knowing what she did about him, she wanted that.

She was in danger of falling in love with Jefferson Grant.

No matter how much she liked him, she didn't see how she could live with herself if that happened.

The realization pricked at her through the long day, caused her to straddle the line between her conscience and her heart.

She understood the need to be loved and accepted by the people who claimed to care about you. That lack of acceptance had caused the rift with Jeff's father. Abby wished she could accept him, job and all, pretend the difference of life versus death didn't yawn between them, but she couldn't.

This new understanding between them was underlined by the awareness she'd felt since she'd first met him. In the barn, her nerves had sizzled, feeling every hungry gaze Jeff had branded on her. She ached with wanting him, fighting the need to merge her body with his even as the bond between their minds grew.

The kiss they had shared a few days ago remained in the forefront of her mind all day. She could remember the sense of rightness when he'd come into her bedroom this morning, the heaviness in her breasts. The taunting memory sliced through her resolve and scrambled her thoughts.

When she arrived home late that afternoon, she found the girls playing with a stick and ball out behind the cabin, close to the new house. After checking to see that they were all right, she hurried to the barn, hoping for a good sign about the gelding.

Jeff was already there. He stood at the horse's stall, arms draped over the rough-planed wood. He turned toward her, his weary features easing with a smile.

She hesitated in the doorway and soaked in the coolness of the barn as her eyes adjusted to the dusky light. Blue eyes glowed at her, warm with heat and pleasure.

Her stomach fluttered and she walked toward him. "Is there any change? Is he better?"

"Come see." Jeff turned back to the stall.

Abby reached his right side and gripped the splintery wood of the gate, pulling herself to a stop. Her breast brushed Jeff's arm and pleasure stabbed her. Beside her, he stiffened, his arm and shoulder and thigh as rigid as the bluff overlooking Carroll Creek. She inched carefully away, peering over the stall fence.

The gelding stood weakly in the corner, head drooping as though too heavy for his neck. His brown eyes were milky with sickness, but alert.

"Is he going to be all right?" Jeff asked eagerly, not looking away from the horse.

She swallowed, feeling the heat stir low in her belly, and walked around him to pluck her gloves from the gatepost. Slipping them on, she let herself in and crooned softly to the gelding. He manuevered his head toward her in a sluggish movement, but his eyes were bright.

"Hello, boy," she crooned. "How are you today?" She gently smoothed a hand down his muzzle. He shifted, one knee wobbling and causing him to stagger. Abby gripped his head and he stood quietly, a slight shiver rippling down his back. A quick exam revealed no sign of lesions and that the fever was gone. His eyes were dilated normally.

"Hey, boy."

The horse nickered at Jeff's familiar voice.

Abby patted the gelding on the neck and walked outside, peeling off the gloves. She stared at the horse, hoping the cattle would fare the same way. "I think it worked," she said slowly. "I think he's going to be okay."

Jeff reached for her, and before she realized it, he had plucked her up in his arms. He swung her in a circle. "Oooweee, Doc. You are something else! I thought he was a goner for sure, but you saved him."

Abby laughed, relief bubbling up inside her. Jeff's infectious joy spread. His heat branded her through her gray-and-white checked day dress. "This is wonderful! There's been limited success with the vaccine. I just can't believe we did it!" She wrapped her arms around Jeff's neck.

His own arms locked around her, melding her breasts to

the solid planes of his chest. He kissed her quick and hard on the lips, his beard scraping her skin. Though the touch was brief, heat shot through Abby and her gaze rose to his. His breath mingled with hers, his lips a fraction away. Awareness hummed between them.

She felt Jeff's shoulders go rigid, his back stiffen.

He set her on the ground and released her so quickly that she stumbled back.

A black emptiness swept through her, centered in her gut, and propelled her forward, with no thought for caution, straight into his arms.

"Abby, think—"

Her arms latched around his neck and his voice died. The rational part of her mind screamed at her to step back, to remember that he would never change and she had no right to ask him. But the need in her burned brighter, flamed into reason-burning fury.

The moist heat of his sweat tingled at her nipples. Liquid fire funneled through her. His breath, released from deep within his chest, brushed her cheeks.

Warmth rained over her, bathing her skin, making her want to feel the heated smoothness of his back, touch the chiseled contours of his chest. His mouth was close, a promise away. She knew he could fill her, feed her, make her more than she had ever been.

His hands curled into her waist, shooting streams of feeling down her sides and into her toes. His eyes burned into hers, wary, yearning, uncertain.

Abby lifted up on tiptoe, guided by a force she didn't understand but wouldn't question. Her lips brushed his, tentative at first then more firmly as memory of their other kisses flooded back. He crushed her to him, his hands gliding down the length of her spine and over the curve of her bottom.

Desire uncoiled in her belly. Heat flicked at her neck, her breasts, between her legs. She pressed herself closer to him and opened her mouth as his tongue delved deep inside. Need bucked through her, driving her.

In a haze of frenzied passion and movement, she felt

Jeff's hands at her bodice, loosening the buttons. Her fingers fumbled at his shirt. She wouldn't take her lips from his, wanting more of the fire and slick, sweet caress of his tongue. Her heart hammered against her ribs. She could feel its echo in Jeff's chest. His scent, musky and tantalizing, pulled at her, coaxing surrender.

Jeff pulled his lips from hers, slanted his head at another angle and muttered. "Lord, Doc!"

"I know." A dark sweetness rose within her. His hands were on her back, curving up her sides to cup her breasts. Heavy, calloused palms kneaded her. A bud of heat curled in her belly. His thumb scraped over her nipple, drawing it into a tight knot.

She ached for him, burned with a pent-up longing that erased all caution, all uncertainty. One touch and she shattered for him. She wanted to touch him, naked beneath her. She wanted his hands to roam over her, igniting this delicious wildness, stripping away her inhibitions.

"I want you, Doc," he growled, his voice coarse with passion.

"Me, too," she panted. "Yes, yes." She flattened herself against his powerful frame, meeting his tongue as it dipped inside her mouth once again.

She couldn't unfasten the buttons of his shirt and made a sound of protest deep in her throat. She wanted to feel him pour inside her like slow, thick molasses, his hands sluicing over her with heat and gentleness.

His fingers slipped the buttons from their loops, one, two, three. Cooler air brushed her skin, now fevered from his touch and the need for more. His arousal pressed into her abdomen, hard, throbbing for her.

Then he stopped. He pushed her away, gently yet firmly. She groaned in protest and leaned toward him, gripping his biceps. His hands clamped tighter on her shoulders, halting her. Slowly she opened her eyes and stared at the solid wall of chambray-covered chest in front of her. Only a hint of passion lingered in the clear blue eyes. His gaze was solemn, almost warning, and it was then she heard the girls.

"Hardy Musgrove slobbered all over my face one time

and Rachel punched him." Hannah was talking, though the words were fuzzy to Abby.

With shaking hands, she quickly redid the buttons on her bodice, using Jeff's body as a shield. Mortified that the girls had caught them, embarrassed at what had just happened, Abby shot a pleading look to Jeff.

He turned to the girls, still hiding her body with his. "You shouldn't let boys 'slobber' all over you, Hannah. If you ever have that trouble again, you come to me."

"'kay, Jeff." Hannah shuffled around between them and looked up at Abby. "Was Jeff slobberin' on you, Abby?"

"No, sweetheart." Abby's face flamed, and she was glad of the dim light of the barn. "No, he certainly wasn't."

Appalled at her behavior, Abby snuck a glance at Jeff and was relieved to see that he looked as stunned as she felt.

"It's okay if he was, 'cause ya'll're married." Having given her blessing, Hannah skipped to the stall.

Rachel followed, her gaze hopscotching from Abby to Jeff.

Abby smiled feebly, certain Rachel could deduce what had happened between her and Jeff. She was still swamped by the memory of Jeff's arms around her, his lips sealed to hers, the deliciously unbearable stroke of his tongue.

"Is the horse better?" Hannah climbed up to the second post and peered inside.

Abby moved to her side and curled an arm around the little girl's waist. "I think he's going to be just fine."

"That medicine worked?" Rachel asked, taking the place next to Hannah.

Jeff moved up behind Rachel, his hand resting on the top post of the stall.

His gaze met Abby's over the girls' heads and locked, searching. Abby tried to determine if Jeff regretted what had just happened. She had thrown herself at him, for goodness' sakes, but she could read nothing from his stone-polished eyes and tight features.

His gaze skittered over her, paused on her breasts then jerked away. A muscle jumped in his jaw and Abby felt his emotional withdrawal as certainly as she had his physical one only minutes before.

She wanted him and had very nearly given herself to him without regard for the strongest conviction of her life. She wished she could erase that kiss.

Misery settled over her. She wished she wanted to.

"Please, please," the woman cried in a thick German accent. She knelt in front of the torched barn, where her dead husband lay inside. Tears streaked her face, making runnels in the soot on her cheeks and nose. "Don't shoot the gun on us. My boy, he only ten. Please, I beg you."

Martin Phipps guided the stallion to stand in front of her, keeping the bandanna firmly over his nose and lower face. For a moment, he watched the spastic flicks of light in the barn, orange to yellow, a flash of blue. Then a surge of fire, an explosion of light, and the frame building caught in a sharp crackle. Smoke snaked from the building and tinged the air with bitterness. Anticipation kicked in his gut. "Give me some food."

The woman instructed the boy in some coarse language, and he disappeared into the tiny sod house, returning moments later with a half loaf of fresh bread and a grayish piece of mottled sausage. Marty grabbed the food and stuffed it into his bag.

The boy plastered himself to his mother's side, his eyes bugging with fright. Marty thought he might actually enjoy this if he wasn't so intent on Jefferson Grant.

He rested one elbow on the saddle horn and leaned down, leveling the pistol between the woman's eyebrows. Fear dilated her eyes. The boy locked his arms around her waist and whimpered.

Despite the dull throbbing behind his lost eye, Marty grinned and lowered the pistol. "You can thank me for sparing you. Your man's dead and that's enough."

The woman's eyes widened in shock, but she stood silently, her breath heaving out in harsh pants. The boy watched, his face gray and drawn. His eyes kept darting to the side, to the vast expanse of empty prairie where darkness settled over the land in slow-spreading waves of black to gray to silver and blue. Marty could read the boy's thoughts as though they were printed on his forehead.

He grinned, feeling a rush that his plan was coming together. The boy would head for the nearest law as soon as Marty left.

Smoke spiraled from the barn, bigger and bigger plumes, until it blanketed the air with an acrid-smelling fog. The fire grew, crackling and snapping, hissing as it hit greener wood.

"Warn your neighbors I'm comin', lady. Tell 'em to watch out for Jefferson Grant."

He wheeled the horse and spurred him over the rise. Cries of alarm and anger pierced the night behind him. He chuckled softly behind the bandanna. Marty had no idea where Grant was, but that didn't matter.

He was laying a plan, and in a few weeks, Grant would find *him*. Then Marty would finish what Grant had started.

TEN

Abby wanted him. She'd admitted it in the barn as her breath was mingling with his.

Desire pulsed through Jeff, stirring the feel of her, the imprint of her body against his. If the girls hadn't interrupted, he would've taken her there on the barn floor. Stupid in more ways than one, but true.

Jeff had made his decision. He had to stay away from her, but he couldn't stop thinking about her, feeling again those soft, warm lips sliding under his, her sweet tongue stroking the gentle abrasion of his. Lust bored a hole through his middle. Images of her, undressed and sheened with a fine mist of sweat, swarmed in his head.

He hadn't seen her since last night. He'd made himself scarce until after supper then had worked until nearly midnight on the new house. His self-control was in tatters, his resolve wobbling, but the house was coming along just fine, he thought ruefully.

He'd managed to keep a distance from her, wouldn't allow himself to be drawn in. All night and even this morning the possibilities of a real family had haunted him. Of all the women he'd known, he never would've guessed Abby Welch would be the one to accept him as he was.

He caught himself as he had several times through the

night. The danger of a trap loomed. He knew her stance on his job—she had never made it a secret. He also knew she wanted him. Right now, satisfying the desires of their bodies, relieving the frustration would be enough, but when it waned? Jeff knew her resentment would return. Her convictions were too strong.

Just as his were. So he'd vowed to keep as much distance between them as possible. When they finally did consummate this forceful, confusing passion between them—he had no doubt they would someday—he would call the terms.

Of course, Kennedy sending him into town this morning with a list of questions for Abby wasn't going to help, but Jeff would do it.

He rode into Clarendon from the west, crossing the salt fork of the Red River and steering his horse onto the well-used road that led from town to Tascosa. The sun glowed full force, drenching the brown-red streets and storefronts with vivid yellow light. Blinding rays bounced from the plate glass windows of the Rosenfield store. Sweat pebbled Jeff's neck.

He would simply leave the questions for her to answer and return later. His mind on Abby, it took Jeff a moment to register what he saw outside her office.

Voices droned like lazy bees, and a mass of people stood outside the clinic. The doors were crammed with them. Through the window he could see bodies, hats with feathers, bowlers and short-brimmed straw, hair slick with oil. He reined in his horse, borrowed from Kennedy, and slowly dismounted.

People crowded even out here and gave him barely a glance as he walked up to the edge of the mass. Scents of sweat, dirt and cologne edged in. Voices tangled in such a cacophony of sound that Jeff could not distinguish even one. People jostled and elbowed their way to the door. A stair creaked with the weight. The sudden shattering of glass quieted the crowd for a brief second and sent alarm knifing through Jeff.

He pushed and shoved his way through the crowd until he

stepped inside. The roar of voices intensified. At first he couldn't see Abby, but he could see his father. And Lionel Welch. Both were talking, red in the face with the frustration of not being heard. Harriet Beasley stood close to his father, gesturing wildly and jabbing a finger at a man in a white suit.

Jeff quickly scanned for the girls. He saw no sign of them and hoped they were already at school. So why wasn't Harriet?

He spotted Abby. Frustration and despair marked her features, and Jeff felt a tug of compassion as well as a bite of desire at the memory of the last time he'd seen her. She was talking, her strained features attesting to the fact that she was yelling. She kept shaking her head, either in denial or because she couldn't hear what was said. The noise swelled louder, rushing in on him like the grind and chug of a nearing locomotive.

Jeff's thoughts blanked for an instant, cut off by too much sound. Abby caught sight of him, and relief swept her features. He elbowed his way through more people, catching snippets of conversation.

". . . damn woman doctor . . ."

"Somethin' like that . . . killed everybody . . ."

". . . Kennedy . . . hang her . . ."

The conversation swirled around Jeff, and he realized that somehow these people had found out about the anthrax.

People crushed him from both sides. A hefty woman with a plumed hat stood in front of him, her feather jabbing at his face. He shoved it aside and tried to move her. She didn't budge.

He could recognize his father's voice now, though he couldn't understand the words. He could hear Harriet as well, yelling for peace and order.

Abby held up her hands in silent supplication and quit talking, staring into the crowd with frustration and apology clearly stamped on her face. Her eyes glittered with unshed tears.

Jeff was close, only a few rows of people away, when a

man in the front reached toward Abby. Thick hands grabbed at her shoulder, and Jeff reacted instinctively.

Whipping his gun from the holster, he fired two shots toward the ceiling in rapid succession.

Silence fell immediately, so quickly that the room still rang with the vestiges of noise.

The tight crowd slackened, and Jeff elbowed his way to Abby's side. "Get away from the doc. What's going on here?"

Abby looked stunned, but she locked onto his arm like a drowning woman. Her face was as colorless as fog, her eyes standing out in startling relief against the paleness of her skin. Alarm skittered through Jeff again, and a strange protectiveness he'd never felt for anyone until this woman.

Murmurs rippled through the crowd. Jeff caught enough to know they were about him.

The man who'd reached for Abby earlier pushed his way to the front of the crowd. Jeff turned toward him, letting his pistol do the warning for him.

The man stilled, but pointed a finger at Abby. "She knew about the anthrax at Strat's place and didn't tell us. She could've gotten us all killed."

"Yeah!" came a voice from behind the man. "Why didn't she tell us? What if our cattle's got it, too?"

"This is as good as murder!" a woman cried from near the window.

Jeff raised his gun in the air again, and this time just the sight was enough to quiet the crowd. How the hell had they all found out? "Why don't you let the doc explain?"

Abby's fingers pinched into Jeff's arm, but she lifted her chin and stepped up beside him. He slanted a glance at her, worried at her ashen features, the sheen of sweat on her face and the shudders he could feel tripping through her body.

Someone mumbled from the middle of the room, but almost everyone remained silent.

Abby's voice wobbled out then became stronger. "I'm sorry you all had to find out. It's true that Mr. Kennedy has anthrax at his place."

As one, the crowd drew its breath, a collective gasp. Air

dwindled in the room. Jeff noted that his father and Harriet Beasley pinned their startled gazes to Abby, as did everyone else. A quick glance at Lionel Welch showed the man's features drawn in compassion for his daughter.

Jeff angled his body so that his chest cushioned her right shoulder, a silent pledge of support.

Her voice strengthened. "The anthrax has been contained, and I'm waiting for vaccine from Leavenworth. I saw no need to alarm everyone."

"No need?" someone exploded from the back. "That stuff travels like a prairie fire."

"Yes," Abby admitted. "But I know where it came from, and the areas and animals affected are limited."

Jackson Swimmer pushed his way forward. "Did anthrax kill Sweeney?"

Abby's fingers tightened on Jeff's arm, but she nodded.

"Jum-pin' Je-hoshaphat!" the barber exclaimed.

Abby's breath shuddered out of her, but she faced the crowd, shoulders back, chin high. "I apologize if you think I endangered you, but truly the disease is contained."

"For now," someone interjected bitterly.

Abby turned toward the voice. "If any of you see signs of chills or fever in your animals, if they collapse, or you spot sores on them, come to me. And don't go near the Rocking K. I didn't want to alarm the whole town, especially if I wasn't sure."

"When were you sure? Has anybody else died? How about on the Rocking K?"

The questions pelted her like stones from a slingshot, and Abby answered them all. "I wasn't sure until an animal died on the Rocking K. So far, a bull and one horse are dead. No more men."

"What's this vaccine you're waitin' on?"

She explained the vaccine and its purpose.

"Whoever heard of a disease curin' a disease." The man in the front, who had reached for Abby, snapped.

"It worked on my horse," Jeff said quietly.

A rumble rolled through the crowd. Every gaze sliced to him.

Abby stared up at him, a sweet half smile hovering at her lips. Gratitude warmed her eyes.

"Your horse was sick and this medicine cured him?" Jackson Swimmer demanded.

Jeff glanced at Abby for agreement, and she nodded. "As you all know, I work for Strat," Jeff said in a dry voice, reminding them all of the day he'd gone into Rosenfield's store and been shunned. "I offered to let Abby test the vaccine on the gelding to prove to Strat that it would work. The horse was sick for a couple of days, and now he's fine."

"Why should we believe you?" Jackson Swimmer arched a woolly white eyebrow at Jeff.

He shrugged. "Don't. Just watch Strat's cattle. The vaccine should arrive soon. Judge for yourselves."

A plaintive voice rose from the back of the room. "So in the meantime, we just wait?"

"That's all we can do." Abby searched the faces in front of her. "If you would like, I can check your animals."

Sheriff Gentry shouldered his way through the crowd. "That's enough, folks. Dr. Welch has told you what she knows. If you have problems, come see her, one at a time. Let's go now."

Abby threw a grateful glance at the sheriff, and Jeff nodded sharply. He was more concerned with Abby. He could feel the tremors still shaking her body. Her face hadn't regained its color, and now her eyes darted around the room.

"The girls?" she whispered.

"They're here?" Jeff asked sharply, his gaze narrowing on the crowd.

Abby nodded, her eyes bright with alarm.

People funneled out the door, shuffling and moving as slowly as water after a freeze. The clinic was a shambles. A pane of glass from the door had shattered on the floor. Jeff's father and Harriet righted the overturned beds and examining table. Lionel Welch hurried to Abby and held her close against his chest. She hugged him, nodding in response to something he said.

Jeff searched the dissipating crowd, hoping the girls had escaped into the hallway and were waiting for Abby. As the crowd thinned, he spotted a small, dark head in the corner next to the front window.

Leaving Abby with her father, he strode over. Rachel had her back to him, and he touched her gently on the shoulder.

She turned, tears staining her cheeks. Her gray eyes shimmered with tears. "Un-Uncle Jeff?"

Blood oozed from a scratch on her right cheek, and a bruise was forming on her jaw. Fear dilated her eyes and anger exploded in his chest.

Jeff went down on one knee, his hand shaking. "Are you okay, Pumpkin?"

She nodded, catching her bottom lip with her teeth. It was then he noticed Hannah. She was huddled against the wall, and Jeff realized Rachel had shielded her little sister with her body. Hannah turned around, her eyes mirroring the same fear as Rachel's.

"Jeff, are we okay?" Her quivering voice tore at him, and he scooped her up against his chest.

Rachel eyed him warily then inched closer. With his other arm, he drew her in. Cradling them both against his heart, he could feel theirs beating a tiny tit-tat against his chest, smell the sweet scent of baby sweat, feel the dampness of their hair. Relief and anger swelled within him at once. "You're okay now. Everything's going to be fine."

"Girls?" Abby's voice quivered behind him, and Jeff turned, loosening his grip. They bounded to Abby, wrapping their arms around her waist and burying their faces in her skirts. She dropped to her knees, hugging them to her, her dark head bent close to theirs. She murmured soothing, gentle words to them, though Jeff couldn't tell what they were. A warmth shifted through him, piercing his chest and stinging his eyes.

After several long seconds, Abby released the girls and set them away from her. "Are you all right?" Her eyes darkened as her gaze fell on Rachel's face. "Oh, Rachel, what happened?"

"I'm okay, I think." Rachel attempted a brave smile. "Somebody bumped me into the wall."

Abby's eyes filled with tears as she gently turned Rachel's

face more fully into the light. Her strong jaw clenched, and Jeff felt the anger she tried to rein in.

Lionel, Marcus and Harriet all hurried over.

Lionel laid a hand on Abby's shoulder and bent down to the girls. "How're my little fillies?"

Hannah giggled, and Rachel managed a half-smile, wincing at the bruise on her face.

Marcus stepped up beside Lionel and reached over to squeeze the little girls' shoulders.

Harriet dabbed at her eyes then clasped her hands together. "You girls will have quite the story for school, won't you?"

Jeff watched silently, battling the anger that still rampaged through his body. He wanted to corral all the townspeople and lash out at them for hurting his girls. He knew it hadn't been deliberate, but that didn't dilute the anger.

Abby carefully examined Rachel and Hannah. Hannah, thanks to her sister, was unharmed. Rachel's scratch was minor, but Abby worried over the bruised jaw until her father told her she was hovering. Hannah, with the resilience of youth, began to retell the event. Rachel stayed glued to Abby's side, holding her hand.

As Jeff's blood began to cool, he noticed Abby. She stood quietly, staring at the girls with a mixture of relief and fear. Her face was pasty white, her eyes dark and battle-weary.

She hugged the girls once again and bent to right a chair that had been overturned. Her face was devoid of emotion now, her eyes the only living thing in her face.

"I think she's in shock." Marcus's voice rumbled in Jeff's ear. "Why don't you take her home? I'll watch out for the girls."

Jeff glanced at his father, surprised that he felt only a spurt of the old animosity. Harriet was listening as Rachel began to interrupt Hannah with her version of the story. Lionel stood close, one hand on Rachel's shoulder and one on Hannah's head.

Abby walked around the room, looking dazed and disoriented. With wooden movements, she picked up the microscope that had been shoved to the floor. Though the lens was tilted, she barely gave it a second look.

One of the doors of the glass-front cabinet had been broken. She walked through the glass, unaware of the grating slide of the broken pieces against the wooden floor, on her way to straighten her medical certificate on the wall.

Alarm skittered up Jeff's spine. His father was right. Abby was in shock. Sadness flitted through Marcus's eyes, and Jeff said in a gruff voice, "Thanks. I think I will take her home."

His father met Jeff's gaze. For a moment he looked as though he would say something else, and Jeff stiffened. In the end, Marcus only nodded and walked toward Harriet.

Jeff stared after him, admitting the longing he felt to make amends. Was it too late? They'd both been stubborn, too keen on not compromising.

Abby caught his attention again, and he hurried toward her, pushing aside other thoughts. She stared at him, eyes dusty purple with shock.

He took her hand, noting how clammy and cold it was in the heat of his. "Let's go home," he said gently.

"The medicine will be here soon." She stared at him gravely, as if she'd just answered a question.

He nodded, cupping her elbow and guiding her to the door.

"I left the carbolic solution in the bucket in the closet," she mumbled.

Concern pricked at Jeff.

"Abby, do we have to go to school today?" Hannah demanded.

Abby stared at her, a sweet smile breaking her wan features, but she said nothing.

Jeff exchanged a frown with Lionel and Marcus.

Harriet stepped in. "Today you can stay here and watch your Grandpa Lionel carve something special for you."

Jeff threw a grateful glance at his father and steered Abby out the door. She moved easily under his direction, stepping into the buggy and settling herself there. But she said not one word.

He tried to keep the panic at bay, but she hadn't spoken for several minutes. She seemed completely distanced, completely shut off.

"I'll drive, if you don't mind. I'd like to keep the buggy in one piece," he teased, trying to draw her out.

She turned her face to his, but looked through him, not at him. "Thank you."

She didn't rise to the bait. Jeff considered what was the best way to handle her. He wanted her to snap out of it, react with the anger he'd felt at seeing the girls hurt and afraid. But she rode silently, her vacant gaze focused straight ahead.

Her body was beside him, but there was no essence of the woman within. Alarm tugged at him. How could he reach her? Should he try?

Dimly, he realized he cared about her, really cared. Despite the distance he'd sworn to keep, this time he couldn't turn away.

Shock rippled through Abby, dulling her senses. Her father's voice was distant and distorted, as though echoing in a canyon. Marcus and Harriet's voices blended, becoming a rumble of sound punctuated by the sweet tenor of the girls.

Abby was vaguely aware of Jeff taking her arm and leading her to the buggy, lifting her up and taking the place beside her. Rachel's face, cut and bruised, kept flashing through Abby's mind, flickering like a flame that wouldn't catch. The fear in Rachel and Hannah's eyes haunted Abby.

She knew what had happened, and yet she felt as though she had walked in on a finished conversation, that her mind hadn't caught up with the ugly reality of the mob who had invaded her office and threatened her girls just like the vicious virus that had killed two animals and Mr. Sweeney.

The buggy rolled quickly over the road, through long stretches of prairie broken by a hill in the distance. Vaguely, she realized they were going to the cabin. On the wind, she caught a faint scent of man and sweat. In fragmented flashes, she was aware of the passing blur of green and brown grass and dirt, spots of yellow weeds and sunflowers, the annoying croak of a raven as it circled overhead as if to taunt her.

Your fault. It was your fault. The words stemmed from her mind, but they could've come from Jeff as well.

Muscles rigid, his jaw rock-hard, he sat beside her. The distance between them was as cold and tangible as a stone wall. Anger vibrated from him.

Abby squeezed her eyes shut, wishing she could reach out to Jeff, knowing that if she did she would unravel completely. She caught him looking at her once, but could form no words to respond to the frozen fire in his blue eyes.

A chill knotted low in her belly and spread. Despite the choking heat of the day, she shivered. Her hands were clammy, and she curled them into fists to warm them, her nails digging crescents into the soft flesh of her palms.

Guilt warred with denial. The girls had been frightened and Rachel injured. All because of her job.

The realization stunned her, and for a moment she stared blindly at Jeff. He stood at her side of the buggy, holding out a hand to help her down. She blinked, stunned to see the cabin already. "Why are we here?"

"I thought you should rest." His words were clipped. He reached out for her, impatience marking his features.

She wanted suddenly to cry out her frustrations, lay the blame on him, but the blame lay solidly on her. After all the time she'd worried about his job threatening the girls, it had been hers that had endangered them.

Because of her. Regret and fear stabbed deep within her breast, brought a sting to her eyes and throat. Jeff stared curiously at her then frowned, lifting her down.

His grip bit into her waist. The hard strength of his hands cleared some of the fog from her mind. Fury turned his eyes cold, dead. He blamed her, too. And he should. But she couldn't bear it if he lashed out at her now.

Her throat burning, she pulled away and walked into the cabin. The chill gouged deeper in her body, turned her knees to the consistency of a poultice.

"Abby?" Jeff followed, his voice taut and level.

She sailed into the bedroom, taking a deep breath to

steady her racing heartbeat. She was running. She knew she was, but she couldn't break down in front of him. If she did, the anger and regret building inside her would explode. How could she have let it happen? What could she have done differently?

Jeff stepped into the bedroom. She felt caged, stalked. His blue gaze captured her like a net. Abby wanted to shroud himself in denial, escape the guilt and shock that tore at her. "I'm sure you have work to do."

His jaw clenched and he gripped the doorknob. "Yes."

"Good." The word scraped her throat. She wanted him to hold her, to share the pain with her, but knew he wouldn't. Words bubbled up in her, excuses, apologies. Tears stung her eyes and she blinked them away.

Jeff's open palm slammed against the door. Abby jumped, her hand going to her throat and clutching at the buttons on her bodice. She took a wary step back.

"They could've been seriously injured." His voice was raw with pain.

His words lashed at her, laying open the wound of guilt. Words she'd tried to keep inside rushed out. "I had no idea people would react that way. I'm so sorry—"

"I've never been so scared in my life. When I saw Rachel's face . . ." His words trailed off, horror sour in the air.

Abby's control shattered. "I'm so sorry." She buried her face in her hands. "I never meant for this to happen. I should've prevented it," she said fiercely.

Jeff turned, blue eyes blazing into hers. "What do you mean? You had no—"

"It's my fault. I know it is. You know it, too." Her voice cracked. Her heart hammered her ribs, fast enough to cause an ache in her chest. "I don't blame you for being angry at me. I'm angry, too."

"I'm not angry at you." He frowned, taking a step toward her.

"I didn't know what to do. I made the wrong decision and the girls paid for it."

"Abby, I'm not angry at you. I don't blame you." He

cupped her elbows, dragging her to him. "It wasn't your fault."

His words finally penetrated, but didn't lessen her guilt and misery.

She stared at him, seeing for the first time the concern in his eyes, concern for her. Her words were a raspy whisper. "My own family was in danger. They could've been trampled or . . . worse." Impotent anger, the same she'd felt when Sweeney died, crashed through her. This time it was directed at herself.

Afraid to look at Jeff, to see the earlier ruthlessness directed at her, she tried to turn away from him. "Please go," she whispered.

She couldn't bear for him to look at her, could barely tolerate herself. He stepped back, his gaze still intent on her. The pressure in her chest eased at his distance.

But he didn't leave. He guided her to the bed and seated her.

"Jeff, please. I need to be alone."

He didn't speak. Instead he knelt and unlaced her shoes, gently pulling them off and placing them next to the bed. "Try to rest. I'll be outside if you need anything." He squeezed her foot in silent comfort.

Tears burned her throat. Pain stabbed her chest and she caught back a gasp. He rose and turned, his boots scraping the floor.

Guilt, denial, regret lashed at her. She forced her body to remain rigid, not go to him. Over and over again she replayed the surge of people into her office, the fear in Rachel's face.

Jeff reached the door. "It wasn't your fault."

She labored with the words, guilt sandwiched with shock. "They were hurt because of me."

"Abby, no." Jeff pivoted and reached the bed in one long stride, going down on one knee. Blue eyes burned into hers, zealous with conviction, trying to convince her.

The pressure in her chest squeezed harder. Tears clotted in her throat, and she forced herself to look at him, to face the blame she expected to find there. Blue eyes, indigo dark with anger and compassion for her, stared back.

"I'm angry, too, Abby, that those people would run roughshod over two little girls, but Rachel and Hannah are fine. They're just fine and you will be, too."

Anger came in a rush, making her raw and vulnerable. "I thought I was doing the right thing."

"What do you mean?" he exclaimed. "What else were you supposed to do?"

She surged off the bed, slamming a fist into her palm. "I didn't handle Kennedy right. I don't know what I would've done differently. My father would've known."

"Your father would've done the same thing." Jeff stood, facing her. "Hell, any doctor would've. If you had told those people without any proof, they would've lynched you."

"I should've trusted them with my suspicions. This is exactly what I wanted to avoid. By not telling everyone, I made it worse."

"You *did* the right thing, Abby."

"Then why were the girls hurt?" she cried, her voice choking.

Jeff gripped her shoulders. "This is not your fault."

She shook her head, wanting to believe him, but her conscience hammered at her.

"It *wasn't*, Abby. Look at me." He pulled her closer, shaking her slightly until she looked at him. "I, of all people, wouldn't lie to you."

"Wouldn't you? To protect the girls?"

"That's not what we're talking about," he said harshly.

Her thoughts and reason clouded. She pulled away from him and rubbed her forehead as though trying to solve a puzzle. "I always thought it would be you."

"What would?" Jeff tensed. She felt a coolness shift between them.

Abby continued, frustration burning through her. "If the girls were ever in danger, I always thought it would be because of *your* job."

"Thanks a lot," he said dryly.

Abby's head snapped up. He didn't even sound insulted. He sounded . . . like he understood.

That understanding nudged her toward the edge of panic. "I withheld information that could have saved lives."

"You were trying to be sure. There's nothing wrong in that."

"I hurt my family. It could've been worse."

"There are no guarantees with anything, Abby. Especially out here. You should know that by now."

Jeff gave no ground. Did he really not hold her responsible?

"My mother was right," she declared. "I should've learned things the way Amelia did, sewing and cooking and playing the piano, but I didn't."

"Well, maybe the cooking," Jeff conceded dryly.

Abby didn't acknowledge his attempt to lighten the situation. All this time, she'd held prejudice against his job. Now the girls had been threatened because of her job. It was more than Abby could take in. All her life she'd been so sure of what she wanted, so certain that she had done the right thing, even when people wouldn't accept her. But today had proved something different to her. "Neil was right. I never should've—"

"No!" Jeff thundered. He gripped her shoulders and hauled her close, arching her body against his until his belt buckle nudged her belly. Hot, moist breath brushed her cheeks. "Stop this. It wasn't your fault any more than it was mine. You can't take responsibility for those people in town. You're a damn good doctor. You did what any doctor would've done."

"Jeff—"

"You made a decision with everyone's best interests at heart. I won't stand here and listen to you degrade yourself this way. You're the smartest, most compassionate woman I know. This town would be a lot worse off if you weren't who you are." He stopped, his chest heaving, his eyes burning with fervor.

Abby stared, for the first time since the incident realizing that he really didn't blame her, that he was angry *for* the girls, *for* her.

Jeff returned her gaze, swallowing hard. A red flush crept up his neck and he shifted. Suddenly his hands dropped from her arms and he cleared his throat. "I guess that's all I had to say."

Warmth seeped into her body. "Did you mean it?"

"All of it," he answered without hesitation. His gaze held hers.

A smile broke on Abby's face, and Jeff answered with one of his own. For long seconds, she was lost in the slow honey-smoothness of it. Tingles raced down her legs.

She spoke first, slowly becoming enmeshed in the web of awareness weaving around her. Caution surfaced. "Thank you. I'm sorry I went on so. I'm just so shocked."

"Probably normal, Abby." His voice was rusty, tinged with kindness and now a hint of desire. "I feel badly about the girls, too."

"Of course you do. I didn't mean to imply—"

"It could easily have been because of me and my job. You shouldn't forget that. Neither one of us should." His words erected the barrier again.

Abby chafed at the imposed distance between them. Frustration clouded his eyes, and she wondered if Jeff felt the same. "I'm sorry I said that, about your job."

Her heart thumped slowly. The yearning returned, throbbing, beating in time to regret.

Jeff searched her eyes, his own unreadable. His jaw tightened and he turned away.

"Jeff?" Her voice was low, his name grating in the eerily still room.

He answered, rough and angry. "What?"

"Would you—" The words jammed in her throat. On the brink of shock, Abby realized how desperately she needed him. ". . . hold me?"

He froze, as though hobbled to the spot. Stunned that she had asked, Abby's heart sputtered to a stop. She couldn't turn away and couldn't survive if he did.

He braced one arm against the door frame and bowed his head. "Lord, I want to, Abby, but if I do, I'm not letting go."

He turned to stare at her, his gaze challenging and sharp with torture. "I'm not walking out of this room. I'm not sleeping on the floor tonight."

Relief and uncertainty warred then blossomed in a slow-warming wave through her chest. She stepped toward him and said softly, "Promise?"

ELEVEN

Jeff's heart slammed his ribs. Her soft voice burned through his restraint, and the feel of her hand on his arm weakened his knees. "Abby, you don't know what you're saying. You'll regret this in the daylight."

"It *is* daylight, Jefferson," she reminded him softly, the smile in her voice tugging at him. "I know what I'm doing. I know that I need you."

He spun, his gaze boring into hers, his breath folding in his chest. "We can never go back, Abby," he said harshly, hanging onto tenuous control. "Things between us—they haven't changed."

"They have," she insisted, drawing closer. Sunlight filtered around her and danced on her shoulders, sketching a pale glow on her hair.

"I'm not talking about this . . . thing between us," he gritted out, trying to draw the distinction in his own mind and explain it to her. "I'm talking about me. I'm not changing, Abby."

"I'm not asking you to." Her words battered at his carefully constructed wall. *Caroline.* His mind screamed at him, dredging up her name and all the hurt from the past, tainting the moment with bitterness. He stepped back, knees stiff, muscles drawn tight.

Abby eased closer, her breasts brushing his chest and clouding his thoughts. "You need me, too. Don't you?"

Jeff sucked in a deep breath, wanting to deny it, but the lie wouldn't even form. "Abby—"

She placed her fingers on his lips. Her hands were trembling, just like his. His throat went dry. Uncertainty wavered in her eyes, but there was also desire and the same piercing need he felt in his gut.

A need he could no longer ignore, a need he felt just as strongly as she did. He knew he should walk away or laugh at her and make *her* walk away, but he couldn't ignore the slow, shifting awareness that turned her eyes from violet to smoky amethyst. She dragged her fingers from his lips, leaving a burning imprint.

Willpower seeped out of him, one tearing inch at a time. He was caught in a trap he didn't want to escape. The brush of her hand, the slight drift of her scent mingling with his sliced at his resolve.

He clenched his hands, fighting the urge to close them around her waist and draw her near. She leaned up, brushing her petal-soft lips against his, and covered his next breath with hers.

Reason fled in the wake of desire and hunger. Even while his mind screamed *no,* Jeff's arms locked around her and he slanted his lips across hers, molding, tasting, teasing. Her hands moved over his neck, her nails scraping lightly. Slender fingers glided into his hair, stroked his scalp and drew him closer.

Her mouth opened, sealed to his in a fevered dance. His tongue delved inside and stroked the dark sweetness. The velvet of her tongue rasped along the slight roughness of his. Nerves shattered with a climbing fire.

Liquid ribbons of icy heat burned him from the inside out, gnawing a hole in his heart, destroying the barriers he'd built against her. He wanted to imprint his scent on her body and feel her legs wrapped around his hips, baring her most sensitive flesh to him.

Even through their clothes he could feel the wild rhythm of her heartbeat meeting his, her tight nipples beading

against his chest. A shudder racked him from his shoulders
to the base of his spine.

She gripped him tighter, her full breasts cushioning the
harder planes of his chest. Keeping his mouth a fraction
from hers, he raised his head, inhaling her light, powdery
scent. Her lips intoxicated like mulled wine, funneling heat
through his veins with a slow, ragged throb and making him
crave more. The taste of her destroyed his judgment and
drew him like a curious man to the edge of a cliff.

He shifted and felt his legs moving, taking them somehow to the bed. Gently he laid her down and followed,
stretching his length atop hers. A rainbow of colors washed
over him, warm pink, soothing yellow, fevered red. Abby
shifted beneath him and her hands curved over his face, as
though memorizing every detail. Her sweet breath mingled
with his, making his throat tighten.

She watched him. Wonder and solemn curiosity played
through her eyes. This was all new to her. With a jolt, Jeff
realized it was somehow new to him as well. He'd never
before felt protective of and yet hungry for a woman.

Intent on going at her pace, he rolled to his back and
pulled her on top of him, pressing her into the building
power of his arousal. She continued her exploration. Soft
fingers traced his eyebrows and eyes, tickled the bridge of
his nose and rested on his cheeks. All the while she kept her
lips pressed to his.

Fire washed through his body, pumping life, power,
sharpening the edge of desire. His hands itched to touch and
he bunched her skirt, gathering it up over her hips. The tapes
of her drawers gave easily, and he tugged the snowy
garments down her legs and shoved them to the floor.

She made a sound between a moan and a whimper and
snuggled closer on his chest, spreading her thighs fraction-
ally.

He growled and rolled her onto her back, coming over
her. The heat of her skin soaked through his shirt and
denims, steaming his chest, scalding his thighs. "Abby." His
voice was thick, distorted. "I want you."

"You have me," she answered dreamily against his mouth, pulling his head back down to hers.

He choked back his restlessness and tried to control the lust clawing through his belly. That unfamiliar protectiveness surged forward, reining him in.

She shifted beneath him, fitting her thighs trustingly to his, opening to him that most vulnerable and intimate part of herself. Surrender and uncertainty softened her eyes as she stared up at him. He was suddenly overcome with the desire to give to her, to make her know that he accepted her for everything she was.

Pricks of pleasure-pain nicked at him, and he struggled for reason through the haze of desire. Gently he undid the buttons of her bodice and below her waist, slipping the dress from her shoulders. He slid his hands to her back, his rough palms molding to the creamy softness of her skin.

"That feels good," she murmured in a throaty whisper. She smiled up at him, her eyes smoky purple with desire.

Need lanced him. Gently he framed her face with his hands, placing a soft kiss on her lips then her nose then her brow. He ran a calloused thumb across the crest of her cheek. "Tell me what you like, what you want."

She caught her breath, and Jeff saw the wonder and excitement in her eyes. He nibbled her lower lip, needing the succor. She responded in kind, hesitantly at first then with a bold nip. His body hummed.

This woman was his, and he wanted every muscle and fiber of her body to know his touch.

Her fingers tugged at his shirt, released the buttons and scraped the fabric away from him. Her hands played over him, igniting fire and branding him just as he wanted to do to her. "Is this all right?" Her eyes gleamed, teasing and seductive. "Can I touch you where I want?"

"Wherever you want," he choked. The heat whipped at him, driving relentlessly, binding their hearts, beckoning their bodies with invisible force. Jeff's hands shook as he raised them to the buttons on her camisole. Pale veil-thin material parted to reveal full breasts, lush and rose-tipped.

His breath jammed and he lowered his head, breathing in the musky scent of her body warmed by his.

He caught one nipple, already beaded, in his mouth, circling it with his tongue. She arched beneath him, her breath hissing out from between her teeth. "Oh . . . Jeff."

He slid his hands up to her scalp, cradling her head in his palms. He filled his mouth with her breast, guided by the ragged sighs she made, the rapid brush of her chest against his cheek as she panted.

Her hair, walnut-dark and sheened by sunlight, fanned out on the quilt, and strands of it coiled around his forearm. He felt weak and strong at the same time. She curled her hands into his hair. "Is it . . . supposed to feel . . . this good?"

He smiled against her breast, loving the husky change in her voice. Her thighs bracketed his. His arousal nudged the vee of her thighs, hot and moist and welcoming. He throbbed harder, heat spiraling in a tightening wave though his body.

He wanted her first time to be perfect so he tamped down the rage of desire. Trailing his lips over the swell of her breast, he laved and nipped at her collarbone, the sensitive skin behind her ear.

"Ummmm." The moan came from deep in her throat. She moved restlessly beneath him, her hands kneading his shoulders, begging for more.

He captured her lips with his in a slow, tantalizing seduction. Spreading his fingers in her hair, he cupped her scalp and tilted her head back. She arched against him, her throat bare to him, her tongue meeting each deep thrust of his. Her breath changed from slow and steady to a ragged sound of need.

She needed him, as desperately as he needed her. *Him,* not just any man. The realization pulled his breath tight across his chest.

In a rush of white heat and frustration, he shucked off his boots then reached for his belt buckle. His gun and holster hit the earth floor with a thud, a vibration he heard as much as felt. Her hands were at his waist, pulling at the buttons of his denims.

His muscles burned, straining with the effort to keep his weight from her until he could strip the camisole and stockings from her. Smooth skin, creamy ivory in sunlight, was revealed an inch at a time as he pushed the thin covering from her breasts and palmed practical cotton stockings from her firm slender thighs.

She lay naked beneath him. Her heart thumped visibly in her chest. His heartbeat, painfully erratic, mirrored hers. Wet and tight from his mouth, her nipples glistened. His throat tightened. With one finger, he stroked the taut bud of one breast.

She drew in her breath. "Can I . . . touch . . . you?"

He nodded. The torturous heat between his legs intensified, stripping the edge of his control. She wasn't ready yet. *He* wasn't ready. He wanted to touch every part of her first, wanted her to touch him.

She reached for him, bringing his head down to hers and meeting his lips with her own. Her hands, those competent doctor's hands, skimmed over the roped muscles of his back. They hesitated on the puckered flesh of his recent gunshot wound.

Jeff's breath jammed in his chest. The scar was a blatant reminder of their differences. Would she turn away, reject him when he was swollen to the point of pain?

To his surprise, her fingers gently traced the scar then continued down to his flanks. Her legs tightened around his and her feet skimmed his ankles. His hair-roughened belly, moist with sweat, met the satiny tautness of her.

Jeff's muscles clenched and he felt a spurt of heat give way, edging to the throbbing base of his arousal. Her nails scraped over his thighs, tickling the hair there, then slid around to the cleft of his hips.

He fought for time, to hold off the mind-slaking pressure that pulled at him. His mouth, greedy, demanding, closed on one nipple. Running his hands down her torso, he marveled at the water-smooth feel of her. He moved his lips from her breast and skimmed them over the sun-washed whiteness of her belly, the dark curls at the apex of her thighs. Gently he moved his hands up the inside of her thighs. She jerked and his muscles clenched.

His hand nestled in the curls between her legs, and he focused on Abby's eyes. "Okay?" His voice was gritty and hoarse with passion.

Her eyes darkened, purple like the last strip of sunset, then dilated as he slid his hand over her, cupping her. Surprise and pleasure flared in her eyes. She tilted, fitting herself more perfectly in his hand. "Oh—that is . . . wonderful."

His chest burned at the trust she gave him. Passion merged with control in her features.

He slipped a finger inside her. Sleek, wet, hot, she closed around him. Abby arched her back, drawing his finger deeper. She nipped at his shoulder, dipping her tongue into the hollow of his collarbone.

His breath crashed through his lungs. He felt her total surrender and knew he would surrender just as completely. She was his. He was hers without reservation. She possessed his heart, even his soul. More than he'd ever offered or given any other woman. Strangely he didn't feel trapped. Rather he felt wild, unfettered.

He captured her lips with his and tasted salt from his skin, the sweet powder of hers. Easing back, he watched the play of pleasure and passion caress her features.

Sunlight poured through the window, staining the room gold, illuminating Abby's skin to translucence. The light glistened in shades of lighter brown on her dark hair, a streak at her temple, over her forehead. Fine, nearly blond hairs traced her hairline. A deeper blue mixed with violet in her eyes. He could see faint dustings of gold on the tips of her thick, dark lashes.

Shards of fire sliced at him, urging him on. He caressed her, stroking her deep and full until she moaned and her eyes fluttered shut. Her hands closed on his biceps and she began to move against him, her body stretching down his.

Slow and deep, quick, shallow—she followed him. He watched the quick flutter of her pulse at the base of her throat, felt the subtle clench and relaxing of her stomach muscles against his, the fine mist of sweat that sheened her body and made it glimmer like a polished pearl in the full light of day.

Jeff gritted his teeth, knowing he couldn't wait much longer.

She reached for him. Her gaze mirrored his, dark with desire on the border of pleasure and hysteria, the near-panic, the desperation. He shifted above her, feeling her close tight around his fingers, plucking at his self-control.

She ran her hands over him, quick flutters that branded him in all the same places he'd touched her. She scraped her nails across his nipples then wiggled down to lave them with her tongue. Lightning lashed his body and he squeezed his eyes shut, struggling for a few more moments of sanity.

He wanted her to know his body as he knew hers. He'd never wanted that, not even with Caroline. He measured his breath, striving for control. Her fingers curled around his burning, pulsing length. He bucked, his back and arms taut with the effort not to surge into her.

Her startled gaze flew to his and she pulled her hand away. "I didn't . . . hurt you?"

He pressed her hand against him, roughly demanding the blissful fire of her touch. "No," he said harshly, striving for reason. He swelled in her hand, pounding with unmerciful sensation. She was hot and wet around his fingers. He ached to be inside her.

Slowly she stroked him, learning him with her hands. Her eyes fluttered shut as her fingers shaped him with angel-soft caresses. She circled him and slid her hand down, measuring his length. Then up again, driving all thoughts from his mind save her rhythm.

He clenched a fist in the quilt, gritting his teeth as she satisfied her curiosity and tortured him with pleasure.

When her fingers skimmed his length to touch the most sensitive part of him, his restraint snapped. He surged backward, rising on his knees and hauling her toward him. Hands splayed on the smooth damp skin of her back, he pulled her into him.

Her breasts drilled his chest. This time his kiss was

frantic. His tongue probed deep inside her mouth, miming the motion another part of his body ached to make. She met his kisses with fever of her own, arms locked around him, the hot, moist center of her pressed against his arousal. His blood centered there in a searing pulse.

She moved against him, shifting her thighs to brace her feet flat on the mattress. "Jeff . . . can't we . . . please?"

She was sleek, ready, burning against him. "Follow-me-Doc."

She nodded, moving with him as he turned to sit on the edge of the bed. He drew her onto his lap, straddling him. She pressed reckless kisses on his eyes and beard and cheek. On the edge of the mattress, Jeff planted his feet on the floor, trying to steady his world. He cradled her hips with his hands and guided her down.

Her gaze locked with his, eyes fired with hunger and trust. Her thighs stiffened.

"Don't . . . fight . . . me."

"Hurry Jeff." Her hands slid over his shoulders, hot skin to hot, and she kissed him, lingering.

His heat met hers. Desire and warmth swelled through him. Holding her steady, he pushed inside, surrounded by heat and dark velvet wetness. Tight and searing, she closed around him. He inched forward then withdrew, wanting her to be as ready as possible. Once he was sheathed inside her, his control would disappear.

She gasped, but her features changed in pleasure, not pain. She kept her gaze locked on his. He pushed again, panting with the effort to go slowly and not tear her apart. He tasted the first bit of heaven then withdrew, thigh muscles and arms quivering.

"Ohhhh." Her breath rushed out and she stilled, urging him on by stroking his face.

He probed again, deeper this time, fitting his body to hers like skin over muscle. She braced her hands on his shoulders and looked down to where their bodies joined, light and dark, smooth and coarse. Heat rushed through Jeff, leaving him dazed and grasping for control.

He moved again, inching deeper. Sleek wetness shielded

him. She gasped and her gaze snapped to his. This time when he ventured inside, she met him, pressing down and crying out as he pierced the tender barrier of her virginity.

His breath rasped out in a husky moan. His heart raced as though he'd just faced a faster gun than his. He watched her face crease, first in pain then in pleasure as he filled her. Blood crashed through him in a molten wave, pounding at the place where their bodies joined. He waited for a sign from her that she was all right.

She shifted, leaning full into his chest and meeting his gaze. Her eyes were glazed with passion and impatience. He gripped her hips. Hands slick with his sweat and hers, he began to move.

With subtle movements of his legs, he showed her how to follow him. Slow at first, with long steady strokes, stoking the fire, pulling in and out with mind-blanking slowness. Wet heat gloved him. She caught his rhythm and found his mouth with hers. Her tongue played against his, moving in time to his strokes. Then the rhythm changed and grew desperate and fast.

He hovered on the edge of control, holding her tight. She wrapped her arms around him. Her breasts rubbed against his chest, branding him with each stroke of her nipples. His pounding heartbeat echoed in his head and rippled down his body.

Plunge and retreat, plunge and retreat. Faster and faster they moved, skimming over light and reason, spinning in a world with no sound until she cried out his name and threw back her head.

He groaned her name, surrendering himself finally to a state that operated only by feel and touch and smell. A dull roaring crashed in his ears. Abby's head was tilted back, her eyes slitted shut, desire pulling her features taut. She looked so vulnerable, so fragile that it hurt his chest to look at her.

He moved, driven by his own body this time, gauging his movements by the subtle tension of hers, telling him when to slow, when to speed. She drew a rhythm from him, rocking at first then slow, steady strokes. In, out. In, out. His heart thudded in time with hers.

Her hands clasped his shoulders and slid over his back, gripping as he pumped faster. Heat whipped at him, building to razor-edged hunger, a craving that burst inside him and erased all thought. His body sought to meld with hers, to assuage the desperate need that slammed into him with each thrust of his body, each meeting arch of hers.

"Jeff!" Her voice was ragged. He felt her tighten. Tiny convulsions rippled through her innermost depths, pulsing around him.

He threw his head back and allowed his own release. Searing, burning, from his soul to hers. His mind blanked, perched between awareness and thought, able to register neither. Stars exploded behind his eyes. He held her close during the last violent throes, then he stilled.

For a long moment, there was only the sound of harsh breathing in the room, the tiptoe of sunlight across her breasts and belly, highlighting the coarseness of his work-roughened hands where they still fitted to her taut waist.

Sweat glistened on their bodies. His hands were dark against the magnolia whiteness of her skin. Her nipples were dusky, her skin flushed pink with passion and marked with scattered red scratches from his beard.

Abby opened her eyes and smiled. Desire coiled through him again, tightened in his belly. He wished he could do something about it, but he was weak with fatigue. He fell back on the bed, taking Abby with him.

They rolled to their sides facing each other, still joined. Sweat bonded their bodies. He gathered her close. Her nipples pressed against his chest and set off a deep-reaching warmth to his toes. Feeling spent, he managed to open one eye and look at her.

Her eyes glowed with tenderness and vestiges of desire. "I think I agree."

"With what?" With one finger, he moved a strand of hair from her mouth.

She snuggled against him, her hands stroking his back. "You're not sleeping on the floor anymore." She grinned. "To think I got you in this bed and I wasn't naked *or* begging."

He laughed, a full-throated sound that echoed in the room. Kissing her full on the lips, he rolled to his back and pulled her on top of him. They lay entwined, sandwiched together with afternoon sun splaying over them.

The sun's heat infused their bodies and they made love again, slowly, gently, exploring each other with fingers and lips.

Uncertainty nudged at Abby, but she refused to acknowledge it. Jeff's body was warm against hers, his hands stroking up and down her back with lazy strength. She had never felt so complete, so loved. Jeff had made clear to her that he admired her as a doctor *and* desired her as a woman.

Why, oh why, couldn't she do the same for him? The thought sliced into her happiness and she shoved it away.

She had made love knowing exactly where they stood. *Made love?* Yes, that's what they had done, though there had been no words of love spoken. The act itself had changed nothing between them, not their convictions, not the desire to be accepted flaws and all.

All too soon, reality would intrude.

Desperate to keep the world at bay, she wrapped her arms around his neck and pressed her lips to his. He pulled her closer and slid his tongue into her mouth. She sighed, reveling in the heat that stirred down low, the desire that shifted up her body.

She wasn't sorry. Never would she regret what had just happened with Jeff, Abby told herself fiercely.

Doubts nudged at her, trying to coax her mind back to the conflict between them, but she refused to think about it. Certainly not now, not after he'd just made her cry with his reverent possession of her body.

Red and gold light streamed through the window, the last rays of the sun merging in a crisscross pattern on the floor of the bedroom. Abby finished buttoning her bodice and glanced over her shoulder at Jeff. He stuffed his shirt into his denims, staring at her, hunger sparking his blue eyes to flame.

Liquid heat pooled low in her belly and Abby glanced away, feeling her cheeks flush.

She felt him move up behind her. He pulled her hair away from her neck and leaned down to plant a hot kiss at the slope where her shoulder curved into her neck. Heated honey moved through her legs, and she leaned against him for support. His hands moved around her waist and rested on her stomach.

Did he regret what had happened between them? Did he have doubts, too? She couldn't bring herself to ask. She had needed him on a basic level, a need that went beyond their differences.

She tilted her head, giving him easier access to her neck. Hot lips skimmed up to her ear, setting her nerves ablaze.

Their lazy play was shattered by a shout from outside, then the jingle of a harness. Abby jumped and Jeff stiffened.

He reached for the doorknob and she smoothed her hair back.

They stepped into the front room just as the cabin door was flung open.

"Abby! Uncle Jeff!" Hannah bolted into the room, rushing straight for them.

"Girls!" Abby caught the little girl up in a hug and squeezed tight. Rachel followed on her heels, grabbing Abby around the waist and holding on for life.

Abby passed Hannah to Jeff. The little girl locked her arms around his neck and hugged him hard.

"I missed you, tadpole. You okay?" Jeff asked, planting a kiss on the top of her head.

Abby knelt down and gathered Rachel in her arms. Guilt stabbed at her as she examined the little girl's bruised jaw and scratched cheek.

"I'm all right, Abby," Rachel hurried to assure her, as though she could read the blame in Abby's eyes. "Grandpa Lionel fixed me right up."

"Oh, honey, I'm so sorry that happened to you."

"Me, too, Rachel." Jeff stepped up behind Abby, his heat closing around her. "You sure you're okay?"

She nodded then shyly raised her eyes to his and smiled.

Lionel Welch followed the girls inside, walking to Abby. "Abigail?"

"I'm fine, Papa."

Harriet Beasley stepped into the doorway. Her gaze skipped over Abby then moved to Jeff. Surprise flared in her green eyes, and a tiny smile played at her mouth.

Abby was then aware of hair flowing loose around her shoulders, her wrinkled bodice and the fact that Jeff's shirt was tucked into the front of his waistband but not the back. Heat flushed her cheeks, and she hoped her father wouldn't notice.

A knock sounded at the open door, and Abby looked up to see Marcus Grant. "Mr. Grant, come in."

Tension erupted in the room like a sudden burst of cold air. Jeff shifted beside Abby, his jaw tight, features unyielding.

Marcus Grant stepped inside, and his gaze skated to his son. His voice was uncertain, yet tense. "I just wondered if everyone was okay."

He looked at Abby, but she felt he was talking to Jeff. She dared a glance at the man behind her. Those blue eyes, so hot a moment ago, were steel cold, almost gray with anger. She had wanted to avoid thoughts of his job as long as possible, but with his father here, the differences between Abby and Jeff returned. Her pleasure in the moments they'd shared dimmed.

When Jeff remained stoically silent, she smiled. "We're all fine. Thank you for asking."

"You had quite a shock, I think." Her father peered hard at her, searching her eyes, his expression clinical. "Did you rest?"

She tried not to look at Jeff as she answered. "Yes, Papa."

"Do you want me to give you something? I brought my bag."

"No, I'm fine."

"Need something to help you sleep?"

Behind her, Jeff coughed, and Abby bit at her bottom lip. "No, I don't think so."

Harriet's sharp gaze measured the situation. "We wanted

to check on you, and the girls were ready to come home. We'll be going now."

"Thank you." Abby smiled, trying to convey with her eyes that she appreciated Harriet taking Lionel and Marcus back to town.

Lionel, however, seemed oblivious to the tension between Marcus and Jeff and the obvious fact that he'd interrupted his daughter and her husband. He angled his way around Jeff and Hannah, heading for the stove. "Why don't you let me fix you some dinner? You probably haven't eaten all day."

"Lionel, I think we should go." Harriet moved gracefully around the table and slipped her arm through his. She led him back to the door. "It's been a long day, and the girls probably need to get to bed."

"You sure you're all right, honey?" Lionel hugged his daughter once again.

Abby could feel Jeff's eyes bore into her, and she tried to concentrate on her father's words. Instead she remembered the feel of Jeff's hands on her bare skin. "Yes, Papa. I'm fine."

"I thought you handled those people in town very well." He pinched her cheek, as he used to when she was little. "That's my girl."

"Thank you." Despite her best intentions, Abby sobered at the reminder of the incident in her clinic.

Harriet tugged Lionel to the door. Marcus followed more slowly, his stern expression trained on his son.

Rachel stood at Abby's side. Abby ran a hand over the little girl's dark hair, still feeling twinges of guilt despite Jeff's earlier words of reassurance and the boost of confidence from her father.

Her gaze roamed back to Jeff's, her husband now in every way. His eyes were hard, locked on his father's in a silent, private battle.

Marcus looked from Jeff to Abby, speculation darkening his gray eyes. He frowned. Walking outside, he caught Harriet's arm. "I think something's going on with those two."

"I certainly hope so," Harriet said spiritedly, taking Lionel's hand to step into the buggy.

Marcus stared up at her with a combination of shock and confusion. She flashed him an impatient look and motioned him up beside her. He climbed in, looking dazed, and Abby grinned.

Jeff moved behind her, close but not touching. Tension still hovered in the air, bringing back reminders that things really hadn't changed between them. Her throat burned. The smile faded.

Not yet, Jeff. Don't leave me yet. She wanted to plead, but kept her mouth shut and a smile on her face as her father drove away with Harriet and Marcus.

She turned to Jeff, hoping to see the heat back in his eyes, but he watched her solemnly. He seemed as distant and unfamiliar as the man she'd first met. Frustration and sadness surged through her. Did he still want her? Did he regret their lovemaking? She didn't know where to go from here or how to reach him.

Several hours later, she still wasn't sure. The girls had been fed and put to bed. Jeff had helped with all of it, including reading them a story and tucking them in for the night. Even Rachel seemed to want him near.

As Abby washed the skillet, Jeff closed the door to the girls' bedroom. She felt his gaze boring into her and willed herself to turn around, bracing herself for rejection or distance.

She couldn't discern the look in his eyes. Shadowed by the hazy circles of the lamplight, they were dark and unreadable. He walked to the door and opened it.

Panic shot through her. "Will you be back?"

His voice was gruff, though not unkind. "Yes."

He slipped out the door and Abby laid down the pan, starting after him. No, she told herself. Don't go.

Her heart ached to follow, to learn where they stood now, but she had some pride. She wiped her hands on the apron then untied it and placed it on a chair back.

Her body was tired and sore, a legacy of her time with Jeff. She decided she would go to bed and read until he returned. Perhaps he hadn't been as affected by their lovemaking as she had, but she'd thought . . .

He'd been so gentle, so patient. The heat in his eyes had mingled with tenderness and concern. Had she read that wrong? Her heart couldn't accept it. So where was he? Would he return at all tonight?

Questions buzzed round in her head, torturing her and making her want to put him out of her mind completely.

Blowing out the lamp, she watched the smoke twine in a silver curl into the darkness. She laid aside her dog-eared hand-me-down copy of the *British Medical Journal* and rolled over on her side. She forced herself to concentrate on the article by Joseph Lister she'd just read, entitled "On the Antiseptic System of Treatment in Surgery."

Then the door opened. She sat up and turned, her breath jammed in her throat. Jeff walked inside, his boots making soft dragging sounds on the dirt floor. She searched his eyes, needing a sign.

"I didn't know if you— what you were going to do," she finished quietly.

He walked toward, her, stripping off his shirt. Moonlight filtered into the room and skittered across the planes of his chest, the rounded muscles of his pectorals and biceps, shading the hair on his abdomen to even darker black. "Got room in there for me?"

He shucked off his boots and stopped, waiting for her answer. "I know we didn't talk about this, Abby. If you want me to leave, I will."

"No," she answered quickly then held up a corner of the sheet in silent invitation. "Where have you been? I thought you might have changed your mind. About this afternoon."

His belt buckle jingled as he unfastened it then slid his pants down his hips. Moonlight slanted over him, highlighting the upper portion of his powerful thick thighs, the dark dusting of hair, the masculine part of him that strained toward him. "I did *not* change my mind."

He slid one knee onto the bed, and Abby raised a hand to his face, caressing his bearded jaw. In the hazy light, his features were strong and almost threatening, but she could see the desire in his eyes, the gentleness. Her heart skittered wildly.

He eased down beside her, his hot hands curving at her waist and sliding up to cup her breast. Bending his head, he nuzzled her neck, whispering. "My beard is making marks on you."

"No—"

"Yes," he breathed against her cheek, cutting off her words. His hand touched the swell of her breast. "Here." Then her neck. "And here." His fingers glided lower, over her navel. "And here." Gentle lips followed his fingers, kissing each spot. The hair of his beard tickled.

She framed his face, rubbing her thumb over his lips, basking in the heat of his blue eyes. Her heart caught, and she realized she was in danger of falling in love with him.

Her conscience hurled images at her—memories of the shots he'd fired to break up the crowd in her office, the tension between him and his father, his face, drawn and tortured as he told her he wouldn't change. Not for her. Not for anyone.

Abby knew she couldn't escape her principles. She would have to choose, but she couldn't. Not yet. No one except Jeff had ever made her feel like a desirable woman.

She blanked her mind, giving herself up to the wicked heat of his mouth and hands.

TWELVE

He could walk away from her anytime he wanted. Lord knew he'd had enough practice walking away, first from his father, then from Caroline.

So why didn't you walk away last night?

Anger seethed inside Jeff. He was no stripling lad to be courted and teased to the point of pain, but it was as though he craved more than her body, as though he craved a part of her that somehow completed him.

Damnation! He wasn't falling in love with Abigail Welch Grant, just in lust. Abby was his wife in every way now. He could have her anytime he wanted. Anywhere.

But that visit from his father yesterday had set past demons loose. It was part of the reason he hadn't been able to stay away from Abby last night, when he should have. She soothed the ragged edges of his soul even while she aroused his body beyond reason. Because of that, Jeff had been deliberately distant to Abby this morning. A flicker of regret passed through him, but Jeff shoved it away.

He didn't regret the sex. Even now his body craved her with an intensity that gnarled his guts. Instead of feeling sated, he felt impatient, restless for more of her.

And once she decided she could not accept him on his terms?

He would be able to dismiss her just as he had Caroline and his father.

The vow clattered empty and dull through Jeff's mind, a repetition of times past. But this time wasn't like any other time.

He shrugged off his musings and swung the stallion east toward town to pick up the girls.

They were his concern right now, but soon he would have to deal with Abby. A chill of dread inched up his spine. Something—danger—threaded through the air, threatening like a lighted stick of dynamite he couldn't see. It would explode, but he wouldn't know when or where.

He might want Abby like a blind man craves light, but he wouldn't allow himself to be vulnerable to her. So far he was calling the shots.

There had been no talk of love between them. Jeff reluctantly admitted he could fall in love with her. Hell, he was already half in love with her, but he couldn't make a commitment to her. If he did, she would have to choose between him and her principles, and Jeff was not at all sure he would win.

Anger needled him. He liked the idea of them being a family, liked the idea of coming home to Abby and the girls every day, but could that ever really be?

He'd meant what he'd told Abby last night about not changing. And he didn't see how a woman like her could completely accept his way of life.

He reached the school yard, chuckling as a hefty boy of about eight ducked under his horse and sprinted past the blacksmith's stall for Carroll Creek. The last clang of the bell sawed in the air, and Jeff dismounted, dropping the reins and striding up the steps for the girls.

Abby had ridden over to Armstrong County today to check on a woman who was close to term in her pregnancy. Jeff had volunteered to pick up the girls.

Children, dwarf people ranging in height from Jeff's thigh to his shoulder, streamed out the door of the schoolhouse. Two boys, both redheaded and wiry, stopped to stare at him.

"It's him," one whispered in awe, brown eyes stretching wide.

The other one stopped, mouth agape. "The hired gun?"

"Yeah."

Jeff shot them an irritated look, and both boys scurried off. He made his way up the steps of the building that doubled as the church and schoolhouse.

Standing in the doorway, he removed his hat, then he stepped inside. He squinted against the hazy, dimmer light of the room and blinked to focus. Sunlight flowed through the windows, where the shades were drawn to half-mast.

Rachel stood at the chalkboard.

Hannah jumped up from a seat across the room and zigzagged her way through the chairs to him. "Hi, Jeff."

"Hey, tadpole."

She stopped in front of him and swiped at a chalk mark on her nose. "Mrs. Beasley's gettin' Rachel in trouble."

Jeff tugged at the little girl's braid then shifted his gaze to Rachel. She cast a pitiful glance his way then turned back to face the board, stretching on tiptoe to reach the top. Chalk scraped across the slate surface.

A partial sentence appeared, letters wavy and slanting up the board. "Young ladies do not—"

He stepped closer and frowned. "Rachel?"

"Jeff?" Harriet Beasley's voice came from behind him.

He turned, his fingers digging into the soft felt of his hat. "What's going on, Mrs. Beasley? Is there a problem with Rachel?"

Rachel cast a furtive glance over her shoulder and resumed her writing.

More of the sentence was revealed. "Young ladies do not punch young gentlemen in the—"

Harriet motioned outside. "May we talk?"

Alarm thumped in Jeff's chest. He forced himself to remain calm, assuring himself that Rachel appeared to be fine. Had she hit someone? Why?

After instructing Hannah to stay inside, he stepped onto the porch with Harriet and followed her down the few steps.

The schoolteacher tucked a newspaper under one arm and

clasped her hands, the picture of prim shock, but devilment danced in her green eyes.

His confusion grew. "What's this about, Harriet?"

"Rachel was in a fight today."

"A fight?" Jeff stared blankly at the teacher for a moment then whirled, ready to go back in.

Harriet stayed him with a hand on his arm. "She's fine. Unfortunately, Dewayne Musgrove isn't. I think she knocked out only one tooth—"

"Knocked out a *tooth*? Why?" he exploded. "Rachel has never done anything like this. At least I don't think she has. It doesn't seem like her at all."

"I agree." Harriet nodded, her eyes still glowing.

"Harriet?" Jeff asked in amazement. "You act like you're enjoying this."

"Well, it's not funny, I suppose. Except that Dewayne can be such a bully sometimes. Regardless, I am punishing her."

"I suppose I should, too," he said, knowing it would be the thing to do as a parent and squirming at the thought.

Harriet hesitated then held the newspaper out to him. "Perhaps you should look at this then hear Rachel's side of the story."

Jeff frowned, taking the copy of the *Clarendon News*. The motto underneath the name read: "Christianity, Education, Temperance, Civilization—Westward." An uneasy feeling jabbed Jeff as he scanned the page.

"What am I looking—"

He broke off as his gaze lit on the section of the paper devoted to the citizens of the town. Jeff had a paragraph all to himself, set off with white space under "Mr. Parks is home after a few days in Mobeetie." and "Mr. Osborne brought in another large antelope from his hunting expedition this past weekend."

Glaring at him, from the pages of the tiny town newspaper, was a full report of his "pulling a gun on the entire town during a meeting in the *Mrs.* Dr. Grant's clinic. Mr. Jefferson Grant, a renowned hired gun, not only shot a hole in the clinic's ceiling, but scared several of the ladies into a fainting spell."

He groaned and looked up at Harriet. "Rachel saw this?"

"Actually, Dewayne read it to the entire class at recess. From what I understand, when he wouldn't stop, Rachel stepped in."

Jeff shook his head, alarmed yet fighting the urge to grin. Rachel had defended him. He never would've believed it. One corner of his mouth tugged up. Harriet leveled him with a look and Jeff choked back a cough.

Still, he didn't think Rachel should have resorted to fighting, especially knocking out Dewayne's tooth. "I'll talk to her. It won't happen again."

"I hope not," Harriet said quietly, preceding Jeff up the steps. "Although I've never seen a better punch. Right on the money. It was quite amazing."

She entered the schoolhouse, and Jeff stared after her for a moment. A grin stretched across his features, but he sobered when he saw Rachel place the chalk back in the tray.

At least a dozen sentences slanted across the board. "Young ladies do not punch young gentlemen in the mouth."

Jeff wondered where young ladies did punch young gentlemen, but decided it would not be prudent to ask. Rachel walked toward him, her feet dragging. As she neared, fear flared in her eyes and she tucked her chin into her chest.

"Ready?" he asked gently, his heart tugging at the woeful expression on her face.

She nodded, drawing in her bottom lip with her teeth.

Hannah clutched two sets of books to her tiny chest and watched Rachel and Jeff with wide, curious eyes. "Is she going to get a spankeen?"

"It's *spanking,* silly," Rachel corrected then looked horrified. She fell silent again.

Jeff bit back a grin and tossed an apologetic look at Harriet. She smiled, her eyes glowing, then turned and began erasing the blackboard.

Once outside, he set Hannah in the front of the saddle and Rachel behind.

He had one foot in the stirrup when someone called his name.

Jeff lowered his foot to the ground and laid a hand on the horse's flank, watching as Sheriff Gentry strode toward him.

He nodded a stiff greeting, wondering if the lawman's business could have anything to do with the shots Jeff had fired in Abby's clinic yesterday. "Sheriff. What can I do for you?"

Gentry glanced at the girls then frowned. "Can I talk to you for a minute?"

Apprehension slithered up Jeff's spine. He told the girls to stay put then walked a few feet away with the sheriff, to stand under a wild apple tree. "What is it?"

"I gotta show you something." Sheriff Gentry pulled a handful of papers from the back pocket of his britches. He smoothed them out and thrust them at Jeff. "I've been getting these in on you."

Jeff took the papers, his gaze scanning them.

"This one says you were south of Palo Duro Canyon and murdered a man, torched his barn." Gentry jabbed at the papers in Jeff's hand. "Fifteen miles east of there, you killed two men and a bull on their way to Dodge City. Stole their horses and sold them south."

The accusations slammed into Jeff, left him dazed as he tried to make sense of what he saw. His name was branded big and bold on every sheet of paper. Two of the notices were posters with his picture and the offer of a reward. Jeff shook his head, flipping through the crumpled papers. "What the hell are you talking about? What is this?"

"I got eight reports here. All sightings of you within the last two weeks, and I know for a damn fact that you've been here in Clarendon the whole time. What's going on?"

"There's obviously been some mistake," Jeff said coldly. "You yourself said you know I was here." Suspicion charged through his mind and he froze. "Hell."

"You don't have a twin running around somewhere, do you?"

"Phipps." The word was broken and rusty. Fear knotted Jeff's gut. Sweat slicked his palms. *Abby. The girls.* He glanced back. The girls stared solemnly at him and he smiled uncertainly, trying to reassure them.

Gentry lowered his voice. "Who's Phipps? Would you tell me what's going on?"

With building fury, Jeff quickly explained his suspicion, telling Gentry about killing Billy Phipps and the run-in with Marty just before he'd arrived in Clarendon.

"He's trying awful bad to tell you something." Gentry took the sheaf of papers from Jeff and thumbed through them. "All the raids are within a fifty-mile radius of here. Think he's coming after you?"

"If he knew where I was, he'd be here." An unwilling admiration for the outlaw's cunning dawned on Jeff, and he said slowly, "He's trying to draw me out."

"He wants you to find him, all right."

"Or perhaps *he* wants to find *me*." Feelings of anger and frustration and fear for the girls shifted through him. That frigid gust of dread returned. He would have to deal with Abby sooner than he'd wanted.

Gentry stroked his mustache, confusion in his dark eyes. "He wants to find you? But how?"

Jeff checked the girls again then held out a hand to the sheriff. "Thanks for telling me."

Gentry shook Jeff's hand and frowned. "What are you going to do?"

"I'm not sure yet."

Gentry held Jeff's gaze, measuring. "If I can help, let me know."

Jeff stared for a moment then touched the brim of his hat in salute. "I appreciate that."

The girls seemed to understand that something had just happened. Rachel and Hannah were quiet as they rode past the sheriff and passed through town. Jeff could feel the burn of concealed gazes, heavy and accusing on them. Whispers, muffled voices followed them on the way out of town. Was everyone looking at him? Had they, too, heard the reports of his supposed crimes?

The news from Gentry rattled Jeff. It wasn't until they topped the rise to the cabin that he remembered Rachel's fight. He said over his shoulder, "Want to tell me what happened at school?"

Hannah twisted around to peer up at him. "Dewayne Musgrove was making fun of you and saying—"

"Hannah, I was asking Rachel," he admonished gently.

She clamped her lips together and sighed.

Rachel squirmed behind him. "It's like Hannah said."

Jeff wasn't quite sure how to respond. "Honey, I'm a big man. I don't need you to fight for me. You could've been hurt."

"Yessir," she said, her voice low and sad.

Jeff felt like a heel. "People can't hurt you by what they say, only by what they do."

"He said you were a hellion and would only . . . make things hard on us and Abby," Rachel cried out, as though she couldn't bear repeating it.

Hannah gasped and whipped around. "Rachel, you fibber! Dewayne said Jeff would get us killed."

Rachel's arms tightened around Jeff's middle, and his jaw tensed. He was used to hearing such things about himself, being followed by whispers and rumors, but the girls were innocent. They shouldn't have to pay for his life or the decisions he'd made.

He battered down his anger. "Honey, I appreciate why you did what you did, but I don't think fighting is the best way to handle things."

"What about you? You fight, don't you, Jeff?" Hannah asked matter-of-factly, her blue eyes innocent as they lifted to his.

Jeff stared down at her, wincing at her trademark directness. He shifted uncomfortably. "I fight if I need to, Hannah. And only when I need to. You can't just go around hitting everybody who makes you mad."

"Even Dewayne Musgrove?" Hannah wrinkled up her nose in distaste.

Jeff couldn't help a laugh. "Even Dewayne."

"I'm sorry, Uncle Jeff," Rachel said, "but it just wasn't right."

"Sometimes it takes more strength to turn away, Rach."

"I suppose so," she admitted quietly. Then hesitantly, "Are you going to tell Abby?"

"I think maybe you should tell her," he suggested.

Hannah leaned around him to look at Rachel, shaking her head vehemently. "Don't do it, Rachel."

Jeff squeezed Hannah around the middle, silencing her. "She's going to find out anyway, Rach. Wouldn't you rather it be from you?"

Rachel didn't respond. Jeff could almost hear her weighing the options.

"I'll be right beside you," he offered.

"Okay." She sounded dejected and laid her cheek against his back.

Love swelled to an ache in Jeff's heart. With a jolt, he realized that somehow, sometime, the two little girls had come to mean more than his life. They had been his first thought when he'd realized Phipps wanted him.

A cold chill of fear shuddered through him again.

He had violated the one unforgivable rule of his profession. He now had an Achilles' heel.

With the instinctive nose of a hound trained to scent fear and exploit that weakness, Phipps would realize what the girls and Abby meant to Jeff. And it wouldn't take him nearly as long as it had taken Jeff to figure it out.

With that brutal stab of reality, the warmth in Jeff's chest evaporated. The apprehension he'd been feeling exploded full force. He had to distance himself from Abby and the girls, for their protection and for his. Whether he walked away or they did, there was now no other choice.

And he had to start with Abby.

Abby's body throbbed, tormenting her with thoughts of Jeff's hands on her. Her mind prodded her to remember the oath she had taken to save lives, the oath that was in direct opposition to his profession.

She stood in the kitchen, putting away the last of the dinner dishes and listening as Rachel explained about a fight she'd had at school. Abby straddled the line between conscience and heart, wanting Jeff to be what he wasn't, almost wishing she were different, too.

Since she'd left for Armstrong County this morning, until she'd returned home late this afternoon, indecision had nagged her. At times it flared into a pain that shifted its way through her body, pulling her first one way then the other.

Just as strong and more potent were the memories of Jeff's body over hers, the wild desperation she had seen in his eyes as he made love to her.

How was she supposed to forget that? She couldn't. She also couldn't ask him to change.

But could she herself change? Relax the rigid principles she'd lived with for so long? The question had slipped in unexpectedly several times today.

It surfaced now as she watched Jeff with Rachel. He stood beside the little girl, his big hand curled protectively around her small one, offering unspoken support.

". . . but it was only one tooth," Rachel repeated, regarding Abby with a mixture of dread and hope.

Secretly Abby thought Dewayne Musgrove a bully, but Rachel couldn't be allowed to go unpunished. Abby's gaze lifted to Jeff's, and again she was struck by the remoteness of his blue eyes, the cold tension that stroked down her spine. Perhaps he was just worried about Rachel. His eyes hadn't changed since supper.

"Mrs. Beasley punished you at school, I take it?" Abby paced to the stove and back.

Rachel nodded, her Adam's apple jutting out as she swallowed hard. She edged closer to Jeff, and Abby wondered why he hadn't taken care of the matter. "Why in the world would you do something like that, Rachel?"

Hannah and Rachel spoke at the same time. "Dewayne was making fun of—"

"It wasn't unprovoked." Jeff cut them both off. "But I told Rachel hitting wasn't the best way to handle it."

Abby frowned at Jeff's sudden interruption, wondering what the fight had been about.

Rachel nodded vehemently. "I promised Uncle Jeff I wouldn't do it again."

"I didn't promise," Hannah said.

Jeff's lips twitched and he looked away.

"And I already wrote on the board twelve times," Rachel pointed out hopefully.

Abby studied her with what she hoped was a stern look. "I'm not sure what to do with you. What does your Uncle Jeff say?"

Rachel glanced up at him, searching for approval. "He told me to tell you. I . . . I suppose I should get a switch?"

Jeff stroked a knuckle across Rachel's cheek, and the little girl smiled up at him. Abby stared for a moment, a burn working through her heart. It seemed he had finally broken through Rachel's reserve.

Jeff's gaze locked with Abby's, and she searched for some sign of emotion, some signal that he was experiencing the same struggle about their relationship that she was. But when he looked at her, his eyes were as empty as a cold wind, his gaze dark and unreadable. Alarm flicked across her neck.

She sighed and tilted Rachel's chin up, staring somberly into her gray eyes. "No punishment this time, but if it happens again . . ."

"It won't," Rachel agreed eagerly, latching her arms around Abby's waist and hugging her. "I promise."

"I'll hold you to it," Abby said.

Rachel turned to Jeff, and he scooped her up in his arms, holding her close. As he looked at the little girl, his eyes warmed to sun-polished brilliance. The ache returned to Abby's chest.

Jeff returned her look over Rachel's head. His eyes were dark with secrets and pain. Did he want more, as she did, but was afraid their differences were too great?

Watching him with Rachel, Abby realized how much she, *they,* needed him in their lives. Could she live with Jeff just as he was, without condemnation, without resentment? Could she forget about his way of life and concentrate on what a wonderful father he was to the girls, what a difference he was making in her own life?

Abby wasn't sure, but she suddenly knew she couldn't live without him.

Jeff set Rachel gently on the floor, ruffled her hair and walked out. The chill in his eyes lingered in the room and pulled Abby to the door of the cabin.

As he stepped off the porch and walked around the corner, she stared at him. His white shirt molded to his brawny shoulders, outlining the power of his body and making him appear invincible, completely self-reliant.

The scent of rain teased the air. Yellow-green grass fluttered in the wind. The last blood-red rays of the sun fanned out over the prairie, lighting the dirt to bronze. Abby didn't know if she could completely accept him as he was, but she was willing to try. She yanked off the apron and followed Jeff to the new house.

Stopping at the bottom of the steps, she glanced around. New panes of glass shimmered in the sunset. The porch was fresh and slick with its coat of white paint. The front door swung open noiselessly at a touch of her fingers.

She spied a man's shirt draped over the handle of a wooden toolbox. At the staircase, Jeff stood with his broad bare back to her, sweat gleaming between his shoulder blades.

Abby's throat dried up. Fire flickered to life inside her belly as she watched him plane the banister rail. With slow, even strokes, his arm traveled down the wood, leveling, smoothing. Muscle and sinew flexed in his shoulders, corded in a lean line down his side to his taut waist.

Her gaze moved up the steel of his spine and over to the widening flare of his shoulder, the swell of muscle that flowed from his shoulder down his arm. Now that she was here, her resolve wavered. What if he didn't feel the same need she felt?

She conjured up again the hungry look in his eyes when he had come to her bed last night. That counted for something, didn't it?

"Jeff?" Her voice rang hollowly in the empty room, underlined by the sliding hiss of the plane as it moved down the banister. Wood strips curled and floated to the floor.

He stopped and turned, loneliness flashing through his eyes. "Oh, good. I need to talk to you." His voice was tired, guarded.

A sudden apprehension crawled up Abby's spine, but she offered a tentative smile. "I wanted to talk to you, too."

He stared at her for a moment, an unfathomable look in his eyes, then he turned away. Her smile faded. With another long stroke, he brought the plane down the banister again. "I spoke to Gentry today."

"About Rachel?" She stepped forward, frowning.

He shook his head, leaning down to eye the rail and gauge its levelness. "No. About me."

"Oh?" She kept her gaze pinned to his back. And waited. Seconds scraped by, coiling tension through her shoulders, drawing her nerves tight. "Well?"

Without turning, he spoke in a toneless voice. "Someone's looking for me."

"Looking for you? Why? For a job?" She hated saying the words so casually, as if his job were carpentry or moving cattle, but if she was going to accept him, she had to start now. "I suppose Sheriff Gentry told them where to find you."

"Not for a job, Abby." His voice lashed at her. He turned, spearing her with a rough gaze.

There was a weariness, almost a defeat, in the blue eyes that drilled into her. A chill started from deep inside her as realization bloomed. "Someone . . . someone . . ." The words came in a quick ragged gasp. ". . . who-wants-to-kill-you?"

"Yes."

She bit at her lip and tried to keep from moaning with horror, tried not to scream that this was what she had feared all along. "What are we going to do?"

"*We?*" He bit off the word, a flash of fury scuttling across his features.

"Yes, I can help."

"There won't be any 'we,' Abby. I can't have you and the girls in danger."

Fear throbbed with each beat of her heart, but she moved

toward him. "Jeff, I won't let you face this alone. We're a family now. At least I'd like us to be."

Yearning flared in his eyes then was gone. His voice cracked through the room with brutal force, striking at her uncertainty and opening a raw vulnerability inside her. "Don't you want to know why he's coming? I killed his brother, Abby. Shot him."

"Why?"

"*Why?*" Jeff repeated the word, the crease between his brow deepening as if he thought her crazy. "He was rustling cattle from my boss."

"Was he unarmed?"

"No."

"I don't believe you shot him in cold blood."

"Hell, Abby! Does it matter?" Jeff growled, frustration firing his eyes. "Martin Phipps is coming for revenge, not tea."

Her face heated with anger that he thought her so naive. "I understand that."

"Just because we made love doesn't mean anything else changed."

I did. It hurt that their joining hadn't been as powerful for him. "I know that," she said quietly, not ready to give up. "But I want to try. Don't you?"

Yearning flickered again in his eyes, then they went cold. His throat worked as he dropped the plane into the toolbox. "Do you think you can accept that a man is hunting me? That when he finds me he will kill me?"

She shook her head, her heart twisting in her chest. "Jeff, please—"

"That I will kill him first, given the opportunity?"

"Jeff!" Abby took a step back, frightened and alarmed at the ruthless stranger he was becoming.

Jeff advanced on her, his eyes sharp points of steel. "I want you to take the girls and move to town, to the clinic."

"No!"

His steps forced her to the wall. Abby placed one hand behind her, flattening her palm against the smooth wood surface for support.

He dipped his head, each word deliberate and cold. "Just because we made love, Abby, it doesn't mean you own me. Or that I owe you anything."

She tossed her head, her fear quickly being crushed by fury. "What about what happened between us last night?"

"That was—"

She saw the struggle in his eyes, hoped fervently he would admit that his feelings were as strong as hers.

"Not something I planned on," he finished mildly.

Abby's vision hazed. "Not something you planned on?"

She struggled to control her temper, not to launch herself at him and punch him just as Rachel had Dewayne Musgrove. "What does that mean? You'll share my bed, but nothing else?"

His gaze flickered from hers briefly, long enough for her to glimpse the pain and . . . fear? Something more was going on here.

She pushed against him, resisting the urge to slide her palms up his muscular chest and kiss him until they both forgot what was happening. "I tell you I'm willing to try, to accept you for what you are, and you're telling me no. Not only no, but that you hadn't *planned* on last night?" Her voice rose, and she clenched her fists at her sides.

Jeff stared back unflinching, his jaw tight.

"And since this is what *you* want, I'm just supposed to do it?"

"I wasn't expecting miracles," he muttered dryly, a flash of humor glinting in his eyes.

She ground her teeth. "I'm glad you can find something to be amused about. I happen to think we're becoming a family. I saw how you were with Rachel earlier. I know how you were with me last night." Despite her fury, her tone softened. "I think families stay together, no matter what."

"Abby, this is different." This time there was a hint of a plea in his voice.

His concern caused a shaft of fear to pass through her. Abby's eyes met his, as she tried to ignore the alarm she heard in his voice. "Because you want it to be different?"

"No. You can't stay with me because it's dangerous. Only

a fool would stay and you're no fool. At least I didn't think so."

"I trust you. I know you'll do everything you can to protect us."

He closed his eyes, torture ravaging his features. Gripping her shoulders, he hauled her to him. "Listen to me. If you stay, you are putting the girls in jeopardy."

She lifted her chin. "They were in jeopardy in my own clinic. Together we can—"

"I mean it. Phipps is coming after me, as sure as I'm standing here. And if you're here, he will go for the girls or you, anything to get to me. It's not a chance I will take."

"He would really hurt the girls?" she whispered. The room spun for a moment, and she clutched at the solid strength of Jeff's arms.

His voice was hard, driving. "I killed this man's brother. Revenge is part of my job like healing is part of yours. You would never forgive yourself if something happened to the girls. You sure as hell would never forgive me."

"Jeff, stop." Fear mounted, knotting in her belly. She didn't want to go, didn't want to leave him when she had finally convinced herself they could become a real family.

"Can you accept what I do?" He pushed her to the wall, thighs imprisoning hers, chest hard and unyielding against her softer one. His eyes seared into her.

Abby hesitated, knowing the question involved so much more than a yes or no answer. She raised her hands to his chest, wanting to implore him, needing to feel the gentleness she had felt last night.

Reluctance and warmth flickered in his eyes then were replaced by a cold void. "No, you can't."

"Jeff—"

"You took a vow, a solemn pledge, Abby, to save lives. It's in your hands to save the girls." His voice rose, marked by frustration and impatience.

Desperate and fighting panic, her voice rose, too. "And lose you?"

Pain darkened his crystal-blue eyes. His nostrils flared.

Tension drew tight around his mouth as the words rasped out. "You never had me."

Pain sheared through her and tears glazed her vision. Abby pressed her lips together, refusing to cry out. "You don't mean that"

"I'm telling you the way it has to be. For all our sakes, you should go." His voice was ragged, as ancient and raspy as hers.

For an instant, her fingers dug into Jeff's arms, then she released him. His arms fell back to his sides, and he stepped away.

"What will you do?" Her voice was faint, her throat clotted with pain. "If we go to town?"

"I'm not sure yet."

They both knew he would kill Phipps when the time came.

"And then?"

She wanted to know if they could try for a future, if Jeff was willing, but he didn't answer. The silence wound between them, tighter and tighter, like a noose closing around their necks. "Just go, Abby."

"Don't fight." Rachel's voice, high and shaky, sounded from the doorway.

Jeff and Abby moved apart.

"You told us not to fight." Hannah bounded past Rachel and came inside. The tie to her pinafore, streaked with dirt and grass stains, dragged on the ground.

Rachel followed Hannah, uncertainty clouding her eyes as she looked from Jeff to Abby.

Abby blinked back tears of fury and pasted on a bright smile. "We're not fighting exactly."

"How would you girls like to stay in town for a while with your Grandpa Lionel?" Jeff asked, keeping his eyes focused on Abby, deliberately using the girls against her.

Abby glared. He stared back, a muscle flexing in his jaw. Regret hollowed his eyes before his mask of indifference returned.

"Can we, Abby?" Hannah jumped up and down, clapping her hands.

Rachel's gray eyes were serious and knowing. She took Hannah's hand, quieting her and drawing her outside.

Hannah glanced back, frowning.

"Jeff, please," Abby choked out. She couldn't bear to leave him, yet she knew she couldn't stay. Not at such a great risk to the girls.

"If you stay and he finds me, he finds you. All of you could be hurt," he said bluntly, jamming a hand into his dark hair. His eyes were bleak, winter-hard. "Is that what you want?"

"You know it isn't." Sadness sheared through her. Her throat burned; her chest ached from lack of air.

Jeff cared for her, just as much as she cared for him. But he wouldn't allow her or the girls to be endangered. If he didn't put down his gun and change his way of life, nothing would ever be any different.

She dragged her gaze from his unforgiving one and walked out the door.

THIRTEEN

You never had me. Anger shifted through Abby, mixed with layers of doubt and hope and a deep stab of abandonment. Had he really meant that? She couldn't accept it.

"Why do we have to leave, Abby?" Hannah interrupted Abby's thoughts. In lieu of folding, the little girl wound her pink flowered nightdress around her arm and stuffed the tube of material into Abby's portmanteau.

Abby sighed, struggling to control her raging emotions. Drat the man! Drat his late-blooming protective attitude, his reason-shattering touch, his blasted job! "It's only for a while, honey. Uncle Jeff's expecting some trouble, and he doesn't want us to get hurt."

She wouldn't lie to the girls, though she didn't see how they could possibly understand the truth. And all its implications.

Rachel stacked her primer and slate board atop the bed and then sank down beside them. Her fingers drummed a hollow rhythm against the slate, and she lifted her gaze to Abby's.

The pain and confusion in Rachel's gray eyes tugged at Abby's heart, sharpened the ache that was growing deeper, an ache she felt not only for the girls, but for Jeff as well. She knew how hard it must be for him to separate himself from them, especially now when it seemed they were finally becoming a real family.

Frustration needled at her, and she turned away, unable to face the haunted look in Rachel's eyes. Silence choked the room, tight and thick with the threat of danger and loss and panic.

The man wouldn't let her stay, claimed not to want her. And a part of her, the long-doubting woman who'd never been considered attractive by rugged hard-core men like Jeff, believed him. But the other part, the part he had loved and changed, didn't.

There was nothing she could do. Abby couldn't argue with the need to protect the girls, and she couldn't leave them alone in town to deal with . . . whatever might happen to Jeff.

Fear tore at her, a cold chill of nausea that swept over her with mind-numbing ruthlessness. She'd skirted the issue of Jeff's danger for as long as she could. Her throat clenched convulsively. What would she do if something awful did happen to him?

She staunched the thought and jammed her stockings into her bag, then threw in her brush.

Rachel's voice trembled in the emptiness. "Is a bad man coming after Uncle Jeff?"

Abby's vision blurred, and she blinked away the burn of tears. She kept her voice calm, even while inwardly cursing Jeff. "He thinks so, honey. But he'll be all right. Your Uncle Jeff is pretty smart."

"And a fast draw," Hannah quipped.

"Hannah!" Abby whirled from stuffing a chemise into her bag. "Where did you hear that?"

"Hardy Musgrove and Ty Rosenfield were talking about him," the little girl explained, her attention on the carved toy Grandpa Lionel had given her. She marched the cow up her leg and back down again. "They said he was the fastest draw in Texas. And that's when Dewayne said it didn't count if you pulled a gun on a bunch of old ladies. And that's when Rachel hit—"

"I understand," Abby broke in, struggling to keep her

voice even. Horror streaked through her that the girls had heard such things about their uncle.

Even if it's all true? her conscience niggled.

Abby had agreed that the girls should stay in town with her father and Marcus Grant. The threat of danger made her blood run cold, and she knew Jeff was right to protect the girls any way possible. But *she* wanted to be with him.

It didn't matter what she wanted. Jeff had told her, in no uncertain terms, that he didn't want the same thing. She knew he cared for her, or he wouldn't be so adamant about her staying in town, too. What tore at her was the growing suspicion that once he had dealt with this Phipps character, Jeff was going to leave. Forever.

She wadded up her nightdress, stuffed it inside the bag then snapped it shut.

"Ready?" Jeff's voice, forced and tired, came low from the doorway.

Abby turned, willing herself not to look into his blue eyes, not to let him see the quiver of her chin. Swinging a look at the girls, she held out an arm and gathered them to her, guiding them out into the front room.

"Uncle Jeff, when we get back, will you take us fishing like you promised? I know I can catch that old ghost catfish." Hannah beamed up at him and slipped her hand into his.

Abby didn't miss the tightening of his jaw or the way he looked quickly away. "Sure enough, tadpole."

The air shriveled suddenly and panic burst inside her. Abby's heart chugged, laboring for each beat as though she couldn't gather any oxygen. She hurried out the door and threw her bag into the backseat of the buggy.

She turned just as Jeff scooped Hannah up in his arms and buried his face in her neck. "*Grrrrr,* that's a big bear hug and should last you until tomorrow."

The little girl drew back in his arms to look at him. "You'll come see us tomorrow?"

"Yep." He set her in the buggy and turned for Rachel.

Her face was impassive, yet the struggle and pain were clear in her eyes. She drew in her bottom lip with her teeth and threw herself at him, wrapping her arms around his waist. "Oh, Un-Uncle J-Jeff, do-we-have-to-go?"

"Shhh, Pumpkin. It's all right. It's only for a little while." He picked her up and nestled her close, his powerful arms cradling her narrow shoulders.

Tears burned Abby's eyes, and she felt her heart twist in her chest.

Jeff thumbed the tears from Rachel's cheeks. "You won't even have time to miss me. I'll be slaving like a dog and you'll be in town, getting toys and candy from your Grandpa Lionel, teasing boys and helping Abby with her patients."

She sniffled. "Will you really come see us?"

"Of course I will. Now you promise, no more punching boys."

She nodded, her face solemn with the oath.

Jeff smiled, but to Abby it seemed more a grimace of pain. He set Rachel in the buggy next to her sister then turned to Abby, his hands dropping awkwardly to his sides.

Words of longing and pleading rose to Abby's lips. The moment stretched between them, rife with pain and regret and the yearning that even now had her clenching her hands so as not to touch him. He watched her, pain driven from his eyes to be replaced with that damn remoteness.

"If you need anything—"

"We'll be fine," she choked out. Turning, she climbed into the buggy, moving woodenly, feeling only the piercing stab in her heart. Teetering on the edge of hysteria and fury, she quickly slapped the reins against the gray's rump, and the buggy tore off down the road.

Abby looked back, hoping he would stop them, knowing he wouldn't. She couldn't even see the startling blue of his eyes. Jeff was a blur of tears and dust.

He hated himself. Hated that he'd had to make them leave, but knew if he hadn't, and something happened to them, he would hate himself more. And Abby would despise him, something he could not live with.

Jeff stepped outside Sheriff Gentry's jail and stared across the street at Abby's clinic. He'd slept damn little last night and wondered if she'd fared any better. All night his body kept imagining the satiny soft press of her skin against his, the kneading drag of long fingers and nails across his back, her lips feathering kisses over his face.

Or he would jerk at the slightest sound, thinking he heard the girls' bed creak or the hollow thud of little footsteps across the dirt floor of the kitchen. Loneliness clawed at him, the way it had when he first left home and fought against returning to his father only by sheer stubbornness and hurt.

In the middle of the night, he'd gone back out with the lantern to work on the new house. The banister was completed. He could start on the stairs today after he was finished at the Rocking K.

After he told Abby about his plan with Gentry.

Gentry had said he could meet Jeff in half an hour back here at the jail to discuss their plan in detail. With a last glance back at the sheriff's door, Jeff tugged his hat brim lower and stepped into the street.

Gentry had turned out to be a surprise. Not only was the man clever, but now he was also an ally. This plan would allow Jeff the freedom to move around, to prepare for Phipps, and might also provide the element of surprise.

Phipps's arrival hovered over Jeff's head like a giant railroad hammer, driving the spike of apprehension a little deeper with each passing hour. It was the reason he'd had to get the girls away from the house. The reason he had to talk to Abby. And, as Jeff had realized last night, the reason he would have to leave the girls—and Abby—when the matter was settled.

All three of them had become too important to him. Abby in a way very different from the girls. And he realized now that the way he'd chosen to live would cling to him like a rotten scent for the rest of his life.

His was a life where the present made the future and the past would always ride his tail.

He wouldn't subject the girls or Abby to that. That realization had stormed him while talking to Abby in the new house, but he hadn't been able to bring himself to tell her.

Hell, he could hardly bring himself to think about it. Just the thought of never again rocking the girls to sleep or holding Abby torched his body with a searing pain.

He had time to see the girls before he met Gentry again. A few minutes later, Jeff strode out of Rosenfield's Mercantile, holding a bag of peppermint candy, one of lemon drops, and a bag with two hair ribbons.

The town bustled with noon-hour activity. The stage from Clarendon to Old Mobeetie and Fort Elliot waited at the stage stand. Wiry bronc mules, already harnessed to the stage, waited patiently as two people boarded the regulation coach and settled themselves in facing swaybacked seats.

Mrs. Carhart and Mrs. Garley swept around Jeff to walk into the store.

Mrs. Carhart smiled. "Good day, Mr. Grant. Shopping for the girls?"

"Yes'm." He bobbed his head and smiled at one of the few women who had welcomed him to town.

Mrs. Garley dipped her head and stared intently at the weathered plank porch, anywhere but at Jeff.

He bit back a smile. "Mrs. Garley."

"How do," she said stiffly, her freckles standing out in relief against her milky skin.

The women moved on into the store, and Jeff stepped off the planked porch front and edged around back, walking toward the school house. He waited at the back corner of Rosenfield's for the girls to be let out for lunch.

The bell clanged three times. Children scampered out of the building and down the steps like a litter of puppies, dodging here and there as though they couldn't decide where to go. Sound erupted, laughter and voices trickling with the sun through the leaves of the wild apple tree. Jeff saw Hannah and Rachel walk down the steps and take their lunch pails over to a group of girls under the tree.

Two boys standing nearby slanted glances at the girls then moved away. Jeff supposed this had to do with Rachel's fight with Dewayne Musgrove. He stifled a grin.

Hannah meticulously dusted off the ground and settled herself. Jeff grinned and strode over to the tree. "Well, look who I found here."

"Uncle Jeff," Hannah shrieked, springing up from her seat on the ground and launching herself at him.

He caught her under the arms and hoisted her up.

Rachel carefully set her pail down and ran to him as well. "Uncle Jeff, can we come home now?" Her arms locked around his waist and he felt his heart swell. How could he bear to leave them? How could he not leave? Staying would only put them under the threat of constant danger.

He kept his voice light as he slid Hannah to the ground. "Not yet, Pumpkin. Look, I brought you something." He held out the bags of candy first, peppermint for Rachel, lemon drops for Hannah.

Each girl peered into her sack and beamed up at him. Warmth shifted through him at the pure pleasure that streaked across their faces.

"Candy?" Rachel asked. "In the middle of the day?"

"Don't tell Abby," they all chorused in unison then laughed.

Hannah popped a lemon drop into her mouth and spoke around the candy. "Thank you, Uncle Jeff."

"Yes, thank you." Rachel rolled the top of her brown paper bag down neatly to save the treat for later.

Jeff knelt on one knee and peered into the other bag, frowning. "Now, let's see, who should get the blue ribbon?"

"Ribbons, too?" Rachel's eyes grew wide. She leaned toward him trying to catch a glimpse inside the bag.

Hannah bounced up and down, her candy sack bobbing and crackling against her dress. "Me. Me. Give me the blue one. I have blue eyes like yours."

Jeff laughed and pulled out the blue ribbon. Hannah clutched it in her hand, beaming. He handed the yellow one to Rachel.

She stared at it for a long moment, her small fingers stroking the fabric.

An ache pierced his chest. Jeff shifted, reaching out to

finger the sleek satin. "I wasn't sure you'd like it. If you want another color—"

"No!" Her small fingers clutched the ribbon tightly. She leaned over and kissed him on the cheek. "It's perfect. Thank you."

Hannah put the ribbon in her pinafore pocket. "Did you come to check on Abby? I heard her crying— Ouch!" Hannah whirled on Rachel, who had jerked her braid.

Unease prickled Jeff's neck. Abby crying? He'd only seen her do that one time. He smiled at Hannah and poked her playfully in the stomach. "I'll check on her, how's that? Now, you girls better eat your lunch before it's time to go back in."

"'kay." Hannah smacked a sticky kiss on his cheek and walked back over to her seat under the apple tree.

Rachel smiled shyly, pleasure turning her eyes clear gray. "Thanks for the candy and the ribbon."

"You're welcome. I'll see you soon."

He straightened, watching as Rachel joined Hannah and the other girls. A tightness cinched his chest and throat. Already he missed them and he hadn't even left yet. He cut off the thought, not wanting to dwell on what would happen once he finished with Phipps. Intending to head for the clinic, he turned toward Rosenfield's store and pulled up short.

Abby stood in the alley between the bleached walls of the mercantile and the blacksmith's barn, staring at him with hungry, haunted eyes.

Desire and regret drilled into Jeff, twining like dusk and darkness until he couldn't distinguish one from the other. She drew herself up as he neared, eyes bitter with pain, and made to walk around him.

"Abby, wait."

She froze, features tight, her brow knotting into a frown. Jeff's heart kicked against his ribs, and he realized that she was looking at something over his shoulder.

He glanced around, alarm thumping at the base of his skull. What he saw made him pivot.

The girls who before had sat with Rachel and Hannah had

moved several feet away and turned their backs to the sisters. Another group of children huddled at a distance, glancing stealthily at the girls and whispering.

Hannah looked up at Rachel, confusion marking her features. Pain flared in Rachel's eyes and her chin quivered. She pasted on a smile and grabbed Hannah's hand.

Fury bubbled up inside Jeff as he scanned the small clusters of children. All sat apart from his girls, with either their backs turned or their faces looking away. What was going on? Why were those kids treating Hannah and Rachel this way?

A primal instinct to protect what was his slashed through him. He turned, intending to head straight for the girls.

"You'll only make it worse." Abby's voice was hoarse and gritty behind him.

Jeff hesitated, knowing she was right yet itching to get to Hannah and Rachel. Two boys stood whispering behind the girls. When they saw Jeff looking at them, they bolted for the schoolhouse.

Jeff's gaze followed them and met Harriet's. She stood on the steps, the sadness in her eyes clearly revealing that she had seen what he had. Regardless of Abby's warning, he started back toward the girls, long, angry strides propelling him across the hard ground.

He didn't wait for Abby to follow, but heard the swish of her skirts behind him, the purposeful tap of her shoes on the packed earth.

Harriet rang the bell signaling the end of lunch. Jeff and Abby drew to a halt at the bottom of the stairs. The children filed past, edging to the opposite side of the steps as they went inside. Rachel and Hannah gave him and Abby brilliant smiles—too brilliant—as they passed. Jeff touched their heads, rage burning through his chest.

He followed them up the steps, staring after them as they walked to the front of the classroom and each took a seat. Abby moved up beside him, her arm brushing his.

Even at the brief touch, lightning flared through him. He moved slightly away, noting that Abby had drawn up like a startled sand spider. He spoke to Harriet, "It's because of me, isn't it?"

"It could be because of Rachel's fight with Dewayne," she said gently, looking from him to Abby.

"Which was because of me, too," he reminded bitterly. Muscles clenched in his jaw, stringing tight down his neck and shoulders.

"Children can be so cruel." Abby's voice shook with hurt.

Jeff clenched his jaw, staunching the urge to slam his fist into the sturdy wooden doors of the schoolhouse.

Harriet touched his arm, took Abby's, and guided them down the steps. "I'd like to hit something, too. It hurts."

Jeff arched his neck and stared the glaring sun full in the face. "I guess it wouldn't be the thing to do since I told them not to hit people."

"Example is a powerful teacher," she agreed. But he saw the anxiety in her green eyes, as if she were afraid he might charge into the classroom like a water-starved bull and destroy everything in his path.

The edge of his fury dulled, and he said ruefully, "Kids change you, don't they?"

"Yes, they do. That's just what your fath—" She broke off, her cheeks pink. "I'm glad you stopped by."

Jeff nodded, studying her. A sudden realization stung him, making him feel foolish and a little dense. The words jumped between them. "You love him, don't you?"

Abby's eyes swerved to him then settled on Harriet.

The schoolteacher met Jeff's gaze, her eyes still soft, her cheeks rouge pink. "Yes, I do."

"I'll be." Jeff rubbed his beard, trying to shrug into the idea of his father with another woman, the idea of another woman wanting his father.

Harriet smiled, her eyes a gentle spring green, and walked back into the classroom.

Abby turned to him, concern clouding her purple eyes. "What are we going to do?"

"About the girls?" He searched her expression for the condemnation he expected, but found only pain that mirrored his own. He looked down to her lips, soft and full.

She realized where he was looking, and impatience flickered across her features. She turned away from him. He caught her arm.

She stopped and stared down at the ground, her body held stiffly away from him. He felt a faint quiver run through her.

The incident with the girls had strangled the hope of any ease between them, and Jeff knew he must still tell Abby about his plan with Gentry. Panic tickled his throat, like he'd just fired off his last shot in the face of a charging platoon. "I'm not sure if there's anything we can do for the girls, except be there. I need to talk to you. About Phipps."

The tension that had fringed their words since Abby had shown up exploded full force at mention of the outlaw's name.

She jerked her arm away, tilting her chin at him. "Have you killed him already? Are you ready to tell the girls to come back to the house so you can send them away again?"

Shame and guilt bit into Jeff. He lashed back, his voice harsh. "I haven't killed anybody today, *yet.*"

"I'm sorry." She buried her face in her hands then looked at him, shoving a few wayward tendrils of hair away from her cheeks. "I'm sorry. It just bothers me."

"What those kids did to the girls?"

"That. Leaving the cabin. All of it." She shook her head, frustration stamped on her features. "I'm sorry I snapped at you. What did you want to say?"

Jeff braced himself, uncertain of her, annoyed at this reluctance he felt in telling her. "Gentry and I have come up with a plan."

After he explained it to her, she stared at him with incredulous eyes. He detected a hint of disappointment, but couldn't be sure if it was for him or her.

She wrapped her arms tight around her waist, closing herself off from him. "Sheriff Gentry's going to send out a notice that he's captured you and that you're awaiting trial here?"

"Yes."

"And then?"

"I think Phipps is trying to draw me out. I would bet this will get him to come here, try to make a play for me."

"But you won't be in jail, so you'll be ready for him? What if he doesn't come?" Panic scored her voice and she turned away, her shoulders tight. "What if he *does* come and finds out you're not in jail?"

Jeff wanted to touch her, to hold her and tell her everything would be all right. But he didn't really know that, did he? And he didn't think she would respond favorably to his touch right now. "I'll be ready for him, Abby. If he learns I'm not in jail, he won't know where I am. *Whatever* he finds out, he won't know about you or the girls."

She looked at him, face ashen, eyes glowing purple fire. "And if he never comes, Jeff? Have you thought about that?"

He frowned, stepping toward her. "What do you mean?"

She glared at him. "Will you always have to worry about him? Or someone like him?"

"Yes, dammit." Her words were no different from ones he'd said to himself, yet they plowed up a latent rage inside him. Jeff had the same feeling he did when his father looked at him with condemning eyes, but there was only anger in Abby's. "That's the sacrifice I've made for my job. I'm always looking over my shoulder, and I can't be doing it for anybody except me."

She flinched, a tiny movement that she checked almost as soon as it happened. Pain flashed through her eyes then was masked by dullness.

He wanted to call back the words, but he didn't. They were the truth, the reason he couldn't live with Abby, why she would eventually resent not only his job, but him.

"Thank you for telling me," she said quietly, stepping around him. "Good luck with your plan. You needn't worry about the girls. If anything else happens, I'll let you know."

"Don't come out to the cabin, Abby." The words split the air between them, cold and bitter. He didn't want her there, not only because he didn't want Phipps to get to her, but also because she distracted him with thoughts of pleasure and guilt all at once. "Not until the thing with Phipps is settled."

"Very well." She stared straight through him, a deep emptiness in her eyes. After a long pause, she walked away.

"I mean it, Abby. Stay clear." Jeff's voice cracked through the air.

She didn't turn, but he saw her spine stiffen and her shoulders jut back in silent hurt.

He clenched his teeth against an apology.

If Phipps discovered Jeff's relationship with Abby and the girls, Jeff would not be able to live with himself. Abby had looked at him with anger and pain and condemnation, but not hate. If anything happened to the girls because of him, that would change.

No matter how tempted he was, he couldn't get close to her or them. He couldn't risk the consequences. Jeff strode up the alley and turned for the jail, cursing himself the whole way.

Fury blinded her. Abby made her way across the street and back to the clinic strictly by instinct. The loud roaring in her ears only increased as she neared the office, marched up the stairs and rocked to a stop inside as though yanked like a puppet in a funnel cloud.

Half of her wanted to strangle Jeff and blame him for what had just happened to the girls.

But the other half of her remembered the naked pain on his face, as though he were the one being shunned. Conflicting images skittered through her mind, rolling, flipping, turning black to white, good to bad, raking her insides with frustration and indecision.

The girls had been shunned because of Jeff's job and reputation. Even he knew it and admitted it. Abby never, *never* wanted that to happen to Rachel and Hannah again.

And she knew Jeff didn't either. She couldn't erase the image of his eyes bleak with pain, his face ravaged with shock and rage. He had hurt as much as they had, maybe more because he hadn't been able to do anything about it.

She didn't want to understand, didn't want to excuse him.

A red haze clouded her vision. She closed her eyes and tried to control her breathing. Her heart thundered against her ribs. Sweat prickled her nape and between her breasts, and her skin felt cooked from the inside out.

With slow, methodical movements, seeking control, she replaced the microscope in the glass-front cabinet. She blanked her mind, trying to forget the wrenching agony on the girls' faces, her own horror at the cruelty of children, the denial and hurt in Jeff's eyes.

She carefully replaced two glass slides in a partitioned wooden box and set them next to the microscope. Her hands shook. Instead of lessening, the rage built in intensity, shooting through her like the sting of a needle, the first prick steepling into searing heat.

Her hand closed over the brass tongue depressor, holding one edge of the L-shaped instrument. Her knuckles paled and her bones stretched the skin as she clutched the instrument, embedding a sharp corner into her palm.

Flickering like remnants of a bad dream were the girls' horrified faces, Rachel's brave smile, the other children's taunting whispers growing louder and louder.

"No!" In a sudden burst of frustration and helplessness, she whirled and launched the tongue depressor toward the door.

"Whoa!" In the doorway, Marcus Grant ducked.

The instrument somersaulted over his head and clattered onto the porch.

He straightened, glanced at the porch then back at Abby, his gray brows arching high.

"Oh, I'm so sorry, Marcus." She hurried toward him, wiping her sweaty palms down the front of her faded blue cotton dress. Her face heated, this time from embarrassment. She bent and retrieved the instrument. "Are you all right? I'm so sorry."

"I'm fine. Are you?"

Abby jammed the tongue depressor into her pocket, suddenly wary at the deep concern in his voice. Had he heard about the incident at school? As angry as she was at

Jeff, she knew he already blamed himself. She couldn't bear for his father to blame him also. "I'm fine. May I help you?"

"I'm looking for Jeff."

She walked back to the examining table, reluctant to look at Jeff's father, afraid to give anything away. "He said something about going over to the jail."

"The jail?"

"To speak with Sheriff Gentry." She knew Marcus wanted more, but she couldn't bring herself to tell him.

"Oh."

Disappointment weighed his voice. What did he want with Jeff? She busied herself making up a carbolic acid solution to sterilize the tongue depressor and other instruments.

"Abby, I—" Marcus shifted from one foot to the other, as though the spacious room suddenly crowded his wide shoulders.

Abby lifted her gaze to his. She had never seen him uncertain or hesitant. She knew with sudden dread that his mood had to do with Jeff.

"I just saw Harriet. She told me what happened."

His words rang like the slam of a judge's gavel. Startled, her breath locked in her chest. "She did?" Her voice was a hoarse croak. Abby cleared her throat, tamping down her plea to Marcus not to confront Jeff, not to lay any more blame at his feet.

She didn't want to understand Jeff's pain. She wanted to blame him, but she knew the struggle he had experienced to not pull Hannah and Rachel away from those children. *It wasn't Jeff's fault.* She wanted to defend Jeff to his father, but still smarting with anger and hurt, Abby kept her lips sealed tight on the words.

"I need to speak with him." Marcus sighed and sought her gaze with his kind gray one. "It's probably not a good idea, is it?"

"Probably not." She frowned, feeling a combination of frustration and helplessness and a surge of hope.

"Doc! Doc!" Hayward Suddity from the stage stand barreled onto the porch and skidded to a stop in the doorway behind Marcus. "The-stage-is-here," he panted. "Pa wanted me to tell you that your boxes are on it!"

"Boxes? The medicine?" Abby's heart jumped.

The boy nodded. "Yes, ma'am. From Leavenworth. Ain't that right?"

"Yes. Yes, it is." Abby set aside the enamel-painted metal bowl full of Lister's carbolic acid and water, wiped her hands on her skirt and started for the door.

Marcus Grant followed her outside. When Abby reached the porch, he stepped onto the street.

He tipped his hat to her. "I hope you're all right, Abby. Tell the girls I'll see them tonight for supper." He shifted and asked hesitantly, "If I'm still accepted at the table?"

"Of course you are."

"Until this evening, then." He wheeled and strode purposefully next door. Toward the jail.

Abby's gaze followed him before she walked in the opposite direction, to the stage stand. As usual, with anything concerning Jefferson Grant, her mind and heart warred.

She wanted to go after Marcus, defend Jeff to him, and yet didn't she blame him for the same things?

George Suddity, sturdy with bulk despite the loss of one arm, hauled up one of the wooden crates and pried off the top. Veins bulged on a forearm made granite-hard from compensating for the loss of his other arm. "This here's what you been waitin' on?"

"Yes, I think so." She dragged her gaze from Marcus Grant's back and stared down inside the neatly packaged carton.

Carefully Abby lifted out a clear, heavy bottle of vaccine— hopefully the cure for a deadly disease, and peace of mind for a community. She stared, overcome with a sudden image of herself years ago, as a woman who clawed and struggled to become a doctor. Uneasiness about herself and her relationship with Jeff draped over her.

She had taken an oath to heal people, to try and save lives, make them better. Jeff's chosen profession was to make things more convenient for people, regardless of what was involved, even the taking of life. They were too different, as she'd known all along.

"Doc!" George's voice blasted through her thoughts. "I said, it won't be much longer, will it?" He turned to drag another box from the top of the stage.

"Oh, no, it shouldn't be." She smiled an apology. "I'll get started today." Her excitement over the arrival of the vaccine was overrun by her earlier encounter with Jeff.

Since they'd made love, she'd let the heat of his touch, the wicked honey of his tongue seduce her into thinking they had a future.

He was a sweet poison in her blood, lulling her senses, dimming her reason until she had convinced herself they had a future.

Jeff had made it clear that they had no future, and Abby knew she had to forget him.

Because Jefferson Grant was either going to die or leave. How many lifetimes would it take to rid her blood of this craving for him? Worse yet, how was she going to explain it to the girls?

She'd been drawn into the marriage because of a pledge to her dear friend. But now her heart was at risk and, just as important, so were the girls' hearts. It would kill them if Jeff left. Abby could try to forget him, but what about the girls?

It wasn't fair to expect them to do the same. Anger flared again within her, only to be snuffed out by sadness. And an overwhelming sense of loneliness.

FOURTEEN

Abby's words spun through Jeff's head. *I'm willing to try. We're becoming a family. Families stay together.*

It was so damn tempting. Jeff wanted the same things she did, felt the same way she did. Maybe he *could* protect them.

His gut tightened in denial, but the possibility loomed. He'd finally found someone who wanted to accept him for exactly who he was, and he couldn't have her or their family. He couldn't subject them to the risks.

The realization brought a wry twist to his lips.

He was tired of denial, tired of being lonely, tired of fighting every battle on his own. As soon as he and Gentry finished at the jail, Jeff was going to see Abby again. He couldn't let her come back to the cabin, not until he was finished with Phipps, but he had to see her.

He strode down the street and back to the jail, glancing at the clinic as he passed. The door was open and Jeff saw his father talking to Abby. He hesitated, curious as to why Marcus was in the clinic, hungry for a glimpse of Abby.

Gentry's voice shattered his musings. "Hey, Grant, come on in." The sheriff stood on the porch of the jailhouse, motioning Jeff over.

He followed the sheriff inside and closed the door.

The deputy sheriff, W. H. Oliver—"Bally" to those who

knew him—stared blankly at Sheriff Gentry. "You're sayin' that you're arrestin' Mr. Grant, but you're not really?"

"Yes," Gentry affirmed patiently then turned to Jeff. "I'll have to go to Mobeetie to send the wires. They've got the only telegraph office in the Panhandle."

"All right." Jeff nodded, fighting impatience to get back to Abby.

"This here Mr. Grant?" Bally's wide handlebar mustache drooped to his chin. His brown gaze slid in confusion from Sheriff Gentry to Jeff.

"Yes. The whole town doesn't need to know what's going on, but you do."

Bally nodded, a dazed look still on his face.

Gentry turned toward Jeff, leaning his hip against the counter. "You know, it occurred to me that we could have other interested parties besides Phipps."

"Bounty hunters." Jeff glanced out the window, watching for his father to leave the clinic, hoping Abby would come out on the porch.

"And Rangers."

"You think we'll get that much interest?" He shifted to look at Gentry. Jeff should've thought of that himself, but he'd been too preoccupied with thoughts of Abby.

"There were quite a few posters on you, several more since I showed you those. And Walter Durbin, who used to drive the stage from here to Old Mobeetie and Fort Elliot, is a Ranger now. He's always interested in any goings-on up this way."

"Damn." Jeff pulled his attention to the sheriff, though not quite able to dismiss Abby completely. He wanted to see her, convince her that everything would be all right between them. His chest swelled in anticipation, but caution bloomed as well.

"I don't really think we'll have problems, but I happened to consider that. If any lawmen show up, we'll just explain the situation to them. Shouldn't have any trouble once they realize what's really going on."

"That'd be fine." Jeff's neck tightened. He was taking a gamble hoping for Phipps to come to him. He didn't need a bunch of lawmen converging on him like a swarm of locusts on a field.

"I'll get going then." From a peg on the wall, Sheriff Gentry lifted his hat and settled it on his head. "Bally, I should be back in a few hours."

"All right, Al. I'll keep an eye on things."

Jeff stepped outside with Sheriff Gentry, who unlooped his horse's reins from the hitching post. "I appreciate this, Gentry."

"This could be a hell of a plan to pull off." Gentry swung into the saddle, excitement lighting his eyes. "I hope it works."

"So do I. And soon." Jeff stared over the horizon, wondering where Phipps was and what he was doing. Was he close? Was he right this minute committing another robbery or murder in Jeff's name? "Without any lawmen joining in."

Gentry touched the brim of his hat in salute and headed north around Miss Van Horn's Ready-to-Wear. Past her store, he urged the roan to a gallop. Jeff watched rider and mount disappear in a blur of dust and sunshine on the road to Mobeetie.

Impatience scraped at him and he turned, intending to head for Abby's clinic. He stopped short at the sight of his father.

"Jeff." Marcus stood a few feet away, shoulders braced, eyes guarded. "Is there some kind of trouble?"

Jeff's stomach muscles bunched as though he'd been hit. His hands clenched into fists. "Don't you mean, Am I at the jail of my own free will?"

"No, that's not what I meant." Marcus shifted from one foot to the other, the worry in his eyes turning them the color of wet river stone. "I heard about what happened with the girls. In town."

"Did Abby tell you about that?" Suspicion sharpened his tone. Though he couldn't imagine Abby blurting out the incident, he also didn't want her telling his father about something that Jeff considered his own fault.

Marcus leveled a gaze on him. "No. Harriet told me."

Jeff's gaze locked with his father's. Suspicion drummed at him and he narrowed his eyes. "And?"

His father's voice came soft and rusty. "I'm sorry."

Sorry? The word slammed into Jeff. He tried not to show the surprise he felt. Silence, corroded from years of unresolved anger, ticked in the air between the two. Each clop of a horses' hooves, the far-off low of a cow, the gentle blow of the wind through the grass fed the silence, spawning tension, anger, a futile frustration.

Jeff's eyes scanned the street as he searched for something to say, trying to understand the anger that mushroomed inside him. What did his father want?

Marcus Grant turned away.

"Why did you come?"

"For that." His father halted and spoke over his shoulder.

Something perverse pricked Jeff, old anger with a new twist that gouged his conscience. "No, you didn't. You came to tell me it's my fault."

Marcus turned slowly, his gray eyes seeming suddenly ancient, wasted with pain. "I said what I came to say."

Jeff's eyes narrowed in suspicion. "Those kids were taunting Hannah and Rachel because of me, because of what happened in Abby's clinic."

"Does that have anything to do with why you were in the sheriff's office?"

Jeff's jaw tightened and he looked away. He knew he had to tell his father, though it was more out of duty than courtesy.

"Sorry," his father said, turning away again.

"There's an outlaw coming for me." Jeff bit out the words, low and hard, waiting for the condemnation. "He's been making his way around Texas, doing murder and robbery, introducing himself as *me*."

"A Jesse James trademark?"

"Yes."

Murcas turned, facing Jeff with concern etched on his features. He hesitated then asked, "What are you going to do?"

Jeff was surprised by the question. He'd been expecting his father to tell *him* what to do or to blame Jeff for Phipps's actions. "Gentry and I came up with the idea of arresting me in order to pull Phipps in."

"If he's arresting you, then what are you doing out here?"

Bleak humor glinted in his father's iron-hard eyes. "And where was he riding off to when I walked up?"

"He's sending out wires to that effect, but—"

"It's a trap." His father's eyes warmed with the realization, and a smile crept over his face. "Pretty clever."

"If it works." Jeff's words came slowly. He shook his head, his skin itching as if he were about to be jumped from behind. Where was the merciless judgment he usually saw in his father's eyes? Why wasn't Marcus berating him? Pointing out that if Jeff hadn't started out on this path, such measures wouldn't be necessary?

He waited for the harsh words, for the judgment and anger. Instead his father said, "Is there anything I can do to help?"

Suspicion and uncertainty collided in Jeff. His restraint snapped. "What the hell is this? Where's the old speech about how selfish I am and how my irresponsibility is going to get people killed? Those girls are your grandchildren. Don't tell me you don't blame me."

"I've learned some things in the years you've been gone, son." Marcus took a step toward him, his eyes dark with apology.

"What does that mean? You think my job's okay now? That's a damn lie! If you thought that, why did you force me to marry Abby?"

"I didn't say I approved," his father shot back, his voice razor-edged. "And I see now I shouldn't have forced you and Abby into that marriage. It's just—I thought . . . maybe it would keep you here."

"I told you I wasn't going anywhere," Jeff gritted through clenched teeth, trying to keep his voice down. "But you didn't believe me."

"The marriage hasn't turned out to be so bad, which you would admit if you weren't so angry."

"Oh, you think not? Not even now that it's put Abby and the girls in danger?" Jeff's guts gnarled. Regret and pain and guilt prodded him to say the words his father wouldn't, words Jeff knew to be true. He also knew he wouldn't be able to go back to Abby, that he wouldn't be able to stay as he'd allowed himself to hope. "I figure you came here to tell me to stay away from them. Well, you don't have to. I do have some sense of integrity, even though it may not be the same as yours."

"I didn't come to say that. I came because—"

"If it weren't for my job, they'd be safe, right?"

"Jefferson, stop it." Though it was surprisingly gentle, his father's voice lashed at him.

"You've been wanting to say it since you got here," Jeff pushed, swamped with feelings of frustration and inadequacy. His conscience pounded him with guilt. "Go ahead"

"Sometimes, no matter what we do, we can't keep our children completely safe."

Where was that hellfire tongue, the self-righteous indignation, the blame? Lord knew, Jeff blamed himself for what had happened to the girls. There was no reason why his father shouldn't blame him, too.

Hope, disbelief, remnants of anger swirled through Jeff. He stared at the man in front of him, wanting to believe that his father was *not* judging him. The little voice inside his head grew louder, and Jeff flinched at his own words. "The girls wouldn't be in danger now if it weren't for me. You know it. I know it."

"Technically speaking." His father's deep voice rolled out, smooth and strong like new sunshine on a spring day, almost soothing. "People are ultimately responsible for their own actions."

"Just what I said." Jeff frowned, feeling trapped in unfamiliar territory.

His father continued. "Take those children in town, for instance. They're the ones who turned their backs on the girls, who shunned and hurt them."

"It was because of something I am," Jeff reminded his father mutinously, uncertainty attacking him again.

Marcus conceded with a nod. "It could be argued."

"Would you argue it the other way?" Jeff barked, his chest suddenly feeling too small, the air around him tight and scarce.

His father's eyes gentled on his face, a look that Jeff achingly remembered from his boyhood. "I would."

With that, Marcus Grant turned and walked back to the clinic, leaving Jeff to stare.

Feeling winded, he stood on the porch of the jailhouse for long seconds. What had just happened here? Had his father made an attempt to forgive the past, to accept Jeff the way he was? The way Abby told him she was willing to try? Was it actually possible that he could have a family once again?

The possibility teased him, beckoning him with the image of a soft pair of lips and amethyst eyes.

He blanked out the picture. Jeff couldn't have it, any of it.

The only way to save Abby and the girls was to leave, after he'd dealt with Phipps.

If Phipps found out about Jeff's newfound family, he would destroy Abby and the girls.

The guilt would destroy Jeff.

Distance was what he needed from Abby. One look into those violet eyes would crumble his defenses. He turned away from the clinic and vaulted into the saddle, riding out of town without looking back.

Abby could fight another woman. She could fight prejudice. But she couldn't fight him.

Jeff was leaving.

He had never said he was, never hinted that he would, and yet she knew.

He wasn't leaving because he couldn't accept her. He was leaving because of his own job. It was ironic that he was leaving *her* for that reason and not the other way around.

She had wanted to stay with him, believing that was her place, and he had pushed her away. With every breath she took, the knowledge gouged deeper. She would survive, though the loneliness in her would never be filled.

But Abby couldn't imagine what it would do to the girls to lose him. Hannah and Rachel had become very close to him. Abby was slightly more worried about how Rachel would deal with his absence. It had taken her so long to warm up to him. It would wound her sorely when he left.

For the girls' sakes, Abby wanted to confront him, but caution held her back. In all fairness, she realized that no one knew when this Phipps character would show up. Jeff's plan was sound and made sense. And Abby didn't like it one bit.

She didn't like being away from him, didn't like missing him, and abhorred the way her body would soften and heat at just the thought of him.

So she determined to forget Jefferson Grant and spent the next two days doing exactly that. The arrival of the medicine proved to be a godsend in more way than one.

Armed with syringes, gloves, Lister's carbolic acid and the three crates of vaccine, Abby left the clinic and drove out to the Rocking K.

After a short conference with Strat Kennedy and Mr. Murdoch, Abby followed them to the bunkhouse, where she gave a demonstration of what she would do. The cowboys would be responsible for rounding up the cattle, putting them through the chute where she would inject them, then taking them to another part of the pasture.

Tandy, the old man who'd chased her from Kennedy's the night she had taken the samples, handed her a bottle of vaccine. "Here you go, Doc. Hope it works."

"Me, too, Tandy."

There was plenty of occupy her mind, and it should have been focused fully on the cattle. But as her hands moved over the tough, hair-slicked hide of the animals, images of Jeff invaded her mind.

Of him lying weak and powerless on her examining table as she stitched him up. Of him holding her in comfort the night Sweeney died. The haunted, tortured look on his face when he said good-bye to the girls.

Automatically her hands moved, filling the syringe with vaccine, jabbing the needle into a hip. The cow shifted and stomped. Abby pulled her foot out of the way just in time.

"Yah!" Tandy slapped the animal on the rump, and he lumbered through the chute gate to the other side.

Around the barn, a cow bawled. The sawing refrain was taken up by dozens of others as they crowded into the area, awaiting their turn in the chute. Abby tried to drown out thoughts of Jeff with the lowing sound of the cattle, the occasional sharp sting of a twitching tail against her cheek.

Pictures of the harder man shifted through her memory.
Jeff holding the gun on her that night in the kitchen; his
words to her in the barn about how he would never give up
his job for anyone or anything.

The images played through her mind, jumbling her
senses. She focused on each head of livestock that clam-
bered through the chute, trying to sort her tangled thoughts,
trying to banish memories of Jefferson Grant.

"You're mighty quick with that needle, Doc." Admiration
sounded grudgingly in the old man's words.

Abby flashed him a surprised smile. "Practice, Tandy."
She reached down for another bottle of vaccine and handed
the empty one to him.

The air around her suddenly changed, became raw with
an electric stillness just as it did in the seconds before a
twister hit the ground.

She knew Jeff was behind her.

Her heart thumped wildly against her ribs, stealing her
breath and shredding her resolve. She could feel his gaze on
her, compelling, demanding. Seeming to move at his command, not hers, she turned.

Atop his horse, he towered over her. His gray hat was
pulled low over his face. His long shadow, broad and hard,
stretched over the ground and merged with hers. His hair
and beard were streaked with sand and dirt. Blue eyes
blazed at her, heating her skin, stroking her nerves as he
dragged his gaze over every inch of her.

Her breath folded in her chest. An ache grew and spread
in heating waves through her body, tightening her nipples,
swelling her breasts. She lifted her chin and stared back at
him, refusing to turn away.

But each place his gaze touched went cold then hot. A
moist fire grew between her legs. As though he had touched
her, chills slid under her skin.

She pressed her lips together and tried to erase the teasing
sensation of his lips on hers, his breath misting her skin.
Even though he still sat his horse, the distance between them
shrank.

At first she could read nothing in the piercing blue depths of his eyes. Then she saw them change, glow with heat. For her.

He was reminding her of the night they had shared. As if she could ever forget. Abby felt her own gaze change from defiant to soft and hated herself for it. A muscle flexed in his jaw. He wheeled the horse, and thundered off into the distance.

She would never get over Jefferson Grant.

The admission left her with a sudden stab of loneliness. Why had he come? If he wanted her to leave him be, then why didn't he do the same?

Questions hammered at her and dredged up anger. She dodged them all, concentrating on the cattle, working steadily until dark.

She fell into bed exhausted, having no thoughts of him, but haunted by a pair of clear blue eyes.

The next morning, she was at the chute before the sun. It was dusk before Abby dropped the syringe into a crate and peeled off her gloves. The last of the cattle had been vaccinated. Now, just as she had with Jeff's horse, she would have to wait.

Abby had already decided to stay at the Rocking K. If an animal went down in the next few days, she wanted to be nearby. Time was of the essence. Just because Jeff's gelding had responded didn't mean the cattle would.

She massaged the ache in her lower back, letting her eyes scan the horizon. Jeff hadn't returned to the barn. She hadn't heard or seen him since yesterday.

She should be glad, shouldn't she? He'd told her why he wanted her to leave. He had put her safety and that of the girls ahead of his own desires. It was a noble thing to do.

And Abby hated it.

How could something so right hurt so desperately?

Marty watched the old man for an hour before he made a move.

His horse had gone lame, and he'd headed over to Fort Elliot to "borrow" a fresh one. Then he'd stumbled across this rangy white-haired man alone by a camp fire.

A platinum moon hung low and heavy in the clear black

sky. Stars glittered like diamond dust. The night was still,
fringes of smoke curling into the air from the old man's
camp fire. The scent of roasting meat filtered through the
air. Marty's mouth watered.

From his point behind a gnarled cottonwood tree, he
could see a bay stallion tethered to a line. No sense in
wasting this opportunity.

Marty adjusted the patch over his right eye then pulled his
gun. Pain, almost constant since his run-in with Grant,
throbbed behind his eyes. Slipping in two bullets to fill up
his six-chamber, he sauntered out from behind the tree.
"Don't let me disturb your supper. Just need to borrow some
of that chow and your horse."

The old man moved in a blur, surprising Marty with his
speed. An old Colt was leveled at him, glinting a wicked
silver in the pale light.

Marty raised his aim to the knot of wrinkles between the
man's eyes. "Don't be stupid. I ain't aiming for no trouble,
just some food and the use of your horse."

"Well, I'm using that horse. And I don't cotton to
strangers walkin' into my camp with a loaded pistol on me."

Marty edged closer, his thumb stroking the hammer of his
gun. "I'll just relieve you of this." Lashing out with one leg,
he kicked at the old man's wrist and dislodged the Colt.

The man squeezed the trigger. The gun fired as it toppled
from his hand. He scrambled for it, but Marty slammed his
boot on the man's bony wrist and stuck the barrel of his
pistol in the man's ear. "Don't move."

The old man's hand clenched on the ground, then he stilled.

"That's better," Marty said in a low voice. "I didn't want
to have to shoot you just yet."

"You're pretty cocky for a two-bit horse thief," the old
man observed calmly.

Marty leaned in close, angry that the man seemed so at
ease. The old coot wasn't even sweating. "I ain't no horse
thief. Bet you've even heard of me. The name's Grant.
Jefferson Grant."

"Grant?" The old man's head snapped back. In the hazy
shadows, Marty could see comprehension in the dark eyes.

He grinned, shifting his weight. "I see you recognize my name."

"I guess so!" the man expelled with a huff. "I was coming after you."

"Coming after me?" Marty shifted so his boot heel ground the man's wrist into the hard earth. So his plan had been working. "What're you? A bounty hunter? You must've seen some posters on me."

"How'd you get out of jail? You kill that sheriff in Clarendon?"

"I'm asking the questions—" Marty blinked. Grant was in jail? In Clarendon? A grin spread over his face. "Naw, I didn't kill the sheriff, but I can see I'm going to have to kill you."

"That must've been the shortest jail stay in history. I only heard about your capture a couple of days ago myself."

"Is that right?" Marty bit back a laugh. So Grant *was* in jail. It had to be due to Marty's shrewd plan. And this old man was even on his way to take a piece out of Grant's hide.

Too late, he saw the old man's fingers inching toward the gun. The Colt whipped through the air with lightning speed. Marty cocked his pistol, lunged and rolled. The guns fired at the same time.

A bullet whistled past Marty's head and buried itself with a *splat* in the tree beyond, spraying a flurry of bark. Gun smoke twined with fire smoke, bitter silver in the moonlight. Marty heard a grunt of pain and turned toward the old man. He lay motionless, a dark stain soaking the ground beneath him.

Marty pushed himself to his feet and stepped over to the old man. With one foot he rolled the body over. The man's eyes were closed, his face creased in pain. Blood stained the front of his white shirt an inky black.

"Hmmmph." Marty jammed his pistol into the holster and turned to the fire, taking the rabbit from the spit. He wrapped it in his bandanna and headed for the horse.

With one hand, he threw on the striped blanket and the saddle. Crooning softly to the horse, he mounted and nudged the bay out of the trees. He tore off a bit of meat and smiled, heading south for Clarendon.

FIFTEEN

He'd had to see her one last time, and now Jeff couldn't get Abby out of his mind.

Not knowing when Phipps would show, Jeff had to be careful, but he'd gone to the chute where she was vaccinating the cattle. Just looking at her released memories he'd kept caged. The satin ripple of her hair against his chest, her light, fresh scent, the burning touch of her eager hands on his skin, the intoxicating sweetness of her lips. And another more surprising memory: the complete freedom he'd felt when they made love, a sense of belonging.

And she remembered, too. The smoke of passion in her eyes ripped his insides. Even now steel-sharp talons of need hooked into him.

He was ready to be finished with Phipps. And he wanted to be prepared for anything when the outlaw showed up. To that end, he'd been working every spare moment on the house.

Inside and out was finished. There was one more special thing he planned to do for the girls, something to remind them of him.

The conversation with his father had only fanned the flames of frustration within him. Marcus hadn't condemned Jeff for what had happened to the girls or what he planned to do about Phipps. The acceptance from his father, so long in coming, tightened the longing in Jeff's chest.

He wanted to stay with Abby and the girls. Finally he allowed a dangerous thought to surface. *What if he laid down his gun? For good?*

The question had torn at him since the incident in town with the girls. Where before he'd been so certain of leaving, now he was doubtful. But experience and common sense overrode the doubt, made him crush the thought.

Even if he gave up his gun, changed his way of life, there was no guarantee that men would stop coming after him. Despite his feelings for Abby and the girls, because of them really, leaving was his only option.

Four days passed before Tandy, Murdoch and Ardington came to her. She was in the barn unhitching her buggy after checking the cattle in the south pasture, the ones affected first.

She turned, and the three men stood in the doorway, their faces drawn with dark seriousness.

Tandy walked inside the barn and stopped beside her.

Ardington's voice rumbled out, deep with uncertainty. "They're down, Doc. At least a dozen head collapsed a few minutes ago."

Tandy took the harness from her and she walked toward the door. "The rest of the men are with them?"

"Yes, ma'am." Murdoch stepped aside to let her pass between him and Ardington. Harness jingled in the barn as Tandy finished with the buggy and rushed to join them.

"What do we do now, Doc?" The old man fell into step beside them.

"Have you told Mr. Kennedy?"

Ardington nodded. "He's on his way to the pasture."

Abby let out a deep sigh. "Now we wait."

Night bled into day; day ground into night. Abby lost track of how long they waited for the vaccine to take effect.

Her eyes were gritty from lack of sleep. Sweat and dirt itched in her pores. The cattle came to know her touch and voice as well as they knew those of the men who worked them on a consistent basis.

Days passed. Four cattle died. Then seven more. Kennedy spent more and more time in the pasture, hovering at Abby's elbow, his face growing blacker and blacker with rage.

"I thought you said this would work. It worked on Grant's gelding."

Kennedy found her at dusk, kneeling in front of a dead yearling. Abby pushed herself up from the ground, her muscles protesting with fatigue and sweat and discouragement. "Mr. Kennedy, I told you we weren't sure. Some of these animals were either very susceptible to the disease or it hit them sooner than the others."

"I might as well shoot them all myself. I can't believe I let you come in here and kill my cattle."

Abby held on to her temper with an effort. She was tired and dirty and just as frustrated as he was. "I can't believe not one of them has responded. Jeff's horse—"

"Doc! Doc, come quick!" Murdoch raced to the top of the hill, waving his arms. He turned and disappeared back the way he'd come.

Abby's gaze sliced to Kennedy, who narrowed his eyes. "If another of those cattle is dead—"

She picked up her skirts and ran, her fatigue-weak legs pumping over the ground. Dry grass, brittle from summer heat, jabbed through her skirts and crackled under her feet. Skidding down the hill, she spotted Murdoch and Tandy gathered round a tree. And a cow. The cow was standing!

Energy pumped through her, and Abby raced toward the men and slid to a stop. "Is she—"

The cow stood, albeit on wobbly legs. She looked at Abby with dark, docile eyes, lucid eyes. Abby knelt in front of her and checked for lesions. There were none. The cows eyes were clear of fever. Abby listened with her stethoscope. No wheezing, no signs of labored breath. The cow turned her head impatiently and pulled up a clump of grass. Chomping noisily, she moved to the next clump and plucked up another.

Abby closed her eyes and sat down hard on the ground. "Oh, thank you. Thank you."

"Is she all right, Doc?" Kennedy boomed behind her. "Tell us what's going on."

"I think she's going to be fine." Abby pushed herself up, her movements slowed by exhaustion, but the thrill of triumph hummed through her veins. "She'll be weak for a couple of days, but—"

"Doc, over here!" Ardington galloped over a rise and pulled his horse to a stop in front of her. His gaze went to the cow meandering slowly around. "Is she up, too? I think we've got another one."

"Hot damn!" Kennedy exclaimed then shot a quick look at Abby. "Begging your pardon, Doc."

Abby started toward Ardington.

"One up!" Another cry came from the cowboys behind her.

Kennedy turned in a half circle then threw his hat in the air. "Ya-hoo!"

Abby stared, relief and victory thudding with each heartbeat as several cattle struggled to their feet. A loud cheer sounded. She turned with surprise to see the rise lined with men.

"Whoo-eee!" Kennedy yelled, jamming his hat back on his head. He rushed over to Abby, his whiskey-colored eyes glowing like fine brandy. "I'm, uh, real sorry about what I said over there."

"It's all right, Mr. Kennedy. I was just as frustrated as you were." Abby's gaze scanned the rise for Jeff, but there was no sign of him. Since she'd seen him last week, he'd made himself scarce. She'd learned from Murdoch that Jeff had switched shifts with the other hired gun and now worked nights.

She doused thoughts of Jeff and turned back to look at the cattle. Relief and excitement trickled through her. They were going to be all right. The vaccine had worked! Oh, if she could only share it with someone, with Jeff.

She spent the rest of the afternoon checking the cattle. More and more of them recovered, standing on weak legs and greedily gulping down water the cowboys brought to them. Several yet lay as still as death, their ribs rattling with each breath. In response to Kennedy's questions, Abby told him they would just have to wait and see. Every animal might not make it.

Just before nightfall, when the wind had shifted to a gentle, cool breeze and the moon was a transparent disc on the horizon, Kennedy came to her.

"Dr. Welch, I can't thank you enough." He extended his hand, his eyes warm and truly welcoming for the first time.

Abby shook his hand, relief finally edging out her apprehension that the cattle wouldn't survive. It looked as if the majority would. "Thank you for letting me try the vaccine. It took a lot of faith."

"I was backed into a corner and you know it, but thanks for being gracious." He hesitated, as if not quite certain how to continue. "I want to give you something."

"You paid for the vaccine. That should cover it."

"No. I want to pay you, but I also want you to have Caesar."

"The bull?" she squeaked, eyes wide. "But he's one of your prize studs."

"I know. I want you to know how grateful I am."

"I do know. It's not necessary to give me your bull. Perhaps you could just spread the word about the vaccine."

"Nope." He set his jaw. "I want you to have the bull." His eyes glinted with humor. "Maybe you'll let me use him sometime."

"Anytime you want," Abby said with a smile. What she was going to do with a bull she didn't know. But the gesture was incredibly generous.

"Good, that's settled. I'll have your husband bring him over tomorrow."

Her husband. The words slammed into her. She'd managed to keep thoughts of Jeff at bay for the last few hours. Kennedy's words brought all the hurt, the uncertainty, the want crashing back.

He didn't seem to notice that she answered only in monosyllables or that she took her leave quickly. He helped her into the buggy and pumped her arm in an exuberant handshake one last time.

Abby refused to let thoughts of Jeff dim her euphoria. The cattle, most of them, were going to be fine. Perhaps now new methods could be employed to deal with anthrax. Perhaps this would see an end to the slaughter and burning of animals and farmland.

Rolling along in the buggy, bathed by moonlight and a cool breeze, Abby reveled in the knowledge that her plan had worked. She knew part of the credit went to Jeff, and at that moment even the thought of him didn't spoil her excitement. Caught up in the heady warmth of victory, she suddenly realized that the buggy had stopped. She was at the top of the rise leading to the cabin.

Her heartbeat sputtered then resumed. The cabin sat dark, draped in pensive shadows. From the new house, light spilled out of the windows. Jeff was there, working.

She couldn't see him or a silhouette, but she could hear the occasional ring of a hammer shift across the prairie, echoing in the lonely night. She could go in, tell him the news and leave. He would be glad. Maybe he would ask her to stay.

Stop it.

She knew she shouldn't go in, if for no other reason than that Phipps could be watching even now. But the knowledge that Jeff was inside pulled at her, coaxing her with the memory of his smile, the soft abrasion of his beard on her skin, his lips on hers.

Caution won out. She cracked the reins on the gray's rump and sent the buggy hurtling past the house. Her excitement dimmed as she drove on, she'd wanted to tell Jeff of her success with the vaccine. But her father would be thrilled and understand exactly what it meant to modern medicine.

The gray flew toward town, and Abby reined to a halt in front of the clinic. Lamplight warmed the windows. Rushing up the steps, she threw open the door, refusing to let thoughts of Jeff further ruin her excitement. Expecting to see her father, she skidded to a stop in the doorway.

Harriet and Marcus jumped apart, a guilty flush staining their cheeks.

Abby stood in shocked silence for a moment, her gaze locked on them. She realized she was staring and jerked her eyes away. "Have . . . you seen my father?"

"He's down at Rosenfield's with the girls." Marcus picked up his hat from the floor and jammed it on his head. A red flush darkened his neck. Harriet stared at him with a mixture of exasperation and affection on her face.

Feeling awkward, Abby backed up a step. "I'll go find him."

"I'll go." Marcus said something in a low voice to Harriet then quickly walked out the door.

Abby turned, watching him rush down the street.

Harriet walked up beside her, frustration deepening the laugh crinkles around her green eyes.

"I interrupted something, didn't I?" Abby asked. "I'm so sorry. I didn't know."

"That man!" Harriet burst out then laughed weakly. "It's not your fault."

Abby grinned. "Harriet, are you and Marcus—"

"We would be if he didn't waste so much time being a gentleman."

Abby's eyes widened. "Harriet! Harriet, where are you going?" She followed her friend onto the porch of the clinic.

Harriet marched into the street and turned. "I'm too old for these courting games. I'm going after him and I'm going to tell him how I feel. Too much time has been wasted for me and him."

"Good for you." Abby smiled, a little shocked but more pleased at the notion of Harriet going after the man she wanted. "Let me know how it goes."

"If you see him with a black eye, you'll know," Harriet retorted as she started toward Rosenfield's.

Abby laughed and walked back inside the clinic. It was empty and quiet. Disappointment surged within her. Her father wasn't here, and in the surprise of finding Harriet and Marcus, she hadn't told them either about Kennedy's cattle.

She walked to the examining table and fingered the

smooth wood. Harriet's words hammered at her. *I'm going to tell him how I feel. Too much time has been wasted.*

Abby wanted to be with Jeff, didn't she? A burst of cleansing anger shot through her. Drat this Martin Phipps person and drat Jeff's job!

She spun, eyeing the door. Could she do it?

With a hard swallow, she strode outside, softly closed the door to the clinic and climbed inside the buggy.

Abby didn't allow a single thought to cross her mind and distract her from her purpose. She suspected that Jeff would leave when he was done with Phipps. She was going to try and stop him. At the very least, she was going to tell him how she felt.

But when she set the brake on the buggy and climbed down in front of the new house, she faltered. Soft yellow light splayed onto the porch. The night sang around her, ripe with the sounds of crickets and animals scurrying through the tall grass, but there was no hammer clang.

A shadow passed in front of the window. Her heart clenched. Before she could talk herself out of it, she stepped up to the door and pushed it open.

A lantern rested on the banister, sending warm light over the front room. She walked inside, scanning the room with growing apprehension. The wooden floors and walls had been sanded and shone smooth as a pebble in the flickering light. There were no curtains, but the windowsills and floors had been swept clean of sawdust. The banister and stairs were spotless and shiny with a new-wood sheen. An oblong box filled with tools sat next to the wall. The house was finished.

Abby heard a tapping from the room to her right and walked over.

Two beds, one on each side of the room, identified the girls' bedroom. Kneeling, Jeff faced the headboard of the bed next to the front window. Soft worn chambray stretched and bunched over his wide shoulders as he worked at something there. As Abby walked inside, her shoes scraped the floor and he glanced over his shoulder.

His eyes blazed at the sight of her, the hunger quickly masked. He lowered his arms and turned, eyes guarded. "Abby. What are you doing here? Is everything all right?"

"The girls are fine," she hastened to assure him. Her stomach jumped in a nervous knot, and she inched into the room. Just the sight of him fed the flames smoldering inside her. She felt her knees go soft. "I wanted to tell you . . . about the cattle."

The cattle? She inwardly groaned. But faced with his unrelenting stare and harsh features, she couldn't blurt out the real reason she'd come. And she did want to tell him about the vaccine.

"You shouldn't be here. Especially now, when the word's gone out about me." He eased off the bed, leashed power evident from the cord-tight lines of his neck down to his stiffly braced thighs.

"I know all that," she said impatiently. "I just wanted you to know about the cattle."

"Kennedy's cattle? The vaccine?"

"It worked, Jeff!" She moved into the room, clasping her hands in front of her so she wouldn't grab him as she wanted to. "Most of them responded to the vaccine today."

"I knew it would work." His voice softened with a smile, and for a moment they stared at each other. Then his eyes changed, wary, concerned, reminding her of Phipps. The silence strained and turned ragged, flicking at her nerves.

She spoke to cover the nervousness, to stall the time when she would have to go, to prevent him from asking her to leave. "Even Kennedy was surprised. He's going to give me Caesar, although I told him I had no use for a bull."

"Abby—"

"You *made* these beds, didn't you?" She walked closer and stroked the smooth wood footboard. A simple design scrolled around the edges of the sturdy elm piece. Both beds were identical, and Abby's gaze skimmed over the criss-cross of ropes that would hold the mattresses. "They're beautiful."

"You think the girls will like them?" He glanced uncertainly over his shoulder at the furniture.

"They'll *love* them."

Her gaze lit on the headboard. In each piece he'd carved one of the girls' names. Tears stung her eyes, as much for the gesture as for its underlying meaning. The work was simple, yet she knew how the girls would treasure it. "Oh, Jeff."

He shrugged, as though uncomfortable. "This way they won't fight over who gets which bed."

Despite his light tone, Abby knew what this gift meant. She looked up at him, her hands curling tightly over the footboard. "You're leaving, aren't you? After you've dealt with Phipps?"

He stared at her for a minute then turned away. "I never said that, did I?"

Abby gritted her teeth, fighting for strength. "Just tell me."

She kept her eyes focused on his back, the rigid whipcord strength of his neck. Seconds ticked by, scraping her nerves, feeding her fears. "Jeff?"

"I have to."

"No, you don't. When I told you I was willing to make this marriage work, I meant it."

He turned, dropped the hammer and chisel to the floor and swooped on her. Gripping her shoulders in a bruising hold, he held her away from him. "I can't put you and the girls in danger. I won't."

"You don't have to leave. Have you forgotten they were in danger because of my job?"

"What are you saying?"

"You never know what could happen. They could get bitten by a snake or fall into a well or—"

"I know what *wouldn't* happen if I was gone. This isn't something you and the girls should have to worry about. I would never forgive myself if something happened to them. Hell, you would never forgive me and you know it."

"Won't you even try?" She tried to keep the tears from her voice. Already they blurred her vision.

His voice was choked, raw with pain. "I can't, Abby. The risk is too great."

"Not even after Phipps is gone?"

"*If* Phipps is the one who leaves. That's what I'm trying to tell you. I could be the one who ends up dead."

She flinched when he said the words and hated herself for it, wanting to prove to him that she could stomach it, could stomach anything if he would only stay.

He shook his head. "See? You can't even stand for me to talk about it. Go, Abby. Go back to town."

She stared at him, aching from the torture in his eyes, the loneliness that scored his voice, feeling the same things herself. Could she walk out and never see those blue eyes burn for her? Never feel his touch on her skin again? Never laugh with him or see him with the girls?

Too much time has been wasted. Harriet's words circled round in her head. Abby turned for the door and closed it.

"What the hell!"

"Mr. Kennedy said something today that got me thinking."

"Abby, stop this." Jeff's voice lashed the room.

She turned to face him, fighting back the edge of panic. He couldn't leave her. Crystal-bright moonlight splashed through the window, circling them in paleness and shadows. His features were carved.

"He called you my husband."

Jeff frowned, confusion flaring in his eyes. "Well, I am, aren't I?"

"But I've never really thought of you that way." She walked toward him, pleading with her eyes for him to understand. "I've thought of you as a partner, yes. As a . . . lover, but not a husband. A wife's place is with her husband."

"Not in this case."

"In every case."

"Abby, it's dangerous for you to be here."

As if she needed to be reminded. She wished he would yell or try to force her to leave, but his voice was gentle, breaking her heart with the truth.

Her throat was tight and as dry as sand. "Were you going to tell the girls good-bye?"

"Of course I was!" he exploded, jamming a hand into his hair. He searched the room as though looking for escape.

Abby's voice was a hoarse whisper. "And me? Were you going to tell me?"

His gaze rose to hers, dark with longing and pain. Her eyes burned at the gentleness there. "I don't know *what* to say to you."

"You could say you'll stay."

His eyes closed, his face ravaged with misery. A low groan came from him. "Abby."

"Will you make love with me?"

His eyes flew open. The disbelief on his face was so comical she would've laughed any other time.

"If you're going to send me away, then at least give me that."

He backed against the wall, staring as if she'd lost her mind. "I can't believe you're saying this."

"Are you telling me you don't want to?" Her voice was soft, the words sticking in her throat. She had no experience at this, was appalled at her boldness, but she wasn't walking out that door without this one night to remember. "You're giving the girls a special gift. Can't you give me one, too?"

"We're hardly talking about carving wood, Abby."

She'd never seen such a look of sheer terror on a man's face, had never thought she would see it on Jefferson Grant's. A tiny smile played at her lips. Even as uncertain as she was, Harriet's words pushed her on. "Will you at least kiss me good-bye?"

He swallowed, uncertainty clouding his eyes.

"Then I'll leave." *Maybe.* She stepped toward him, stopping a hand's width from his chest. His heat webbed around her, throbbed low in her belly, tingled in her nipples. Uncertainty lodged in a wet, cold lump in her chest, but she stared up at him, reading the desire and confusion and frustration there. "It's not so much to ask, is it?"

Keeping his hands at his sides, he lowered his head and brushed her lips with his. Abby stood motionless, wanting to curl her arms around his neck and force him to kiss her until her knees gave out. She waited. His lips feathered over hers once, twice, then he groaned.

His arms went around her, and his tongue nudged her lips apart to plunge inside. Abby's heart swelled in her chest. She raised up on tiptoe and fitted her length to his. She clung to his shoulders, coveting the feel of his strength beneath her hands, the warmth from his body as it eddied against hers. Flames licked up her legs and centered in her core.

He ravaged her mouth, his tongue searching out sensitive hollows and stroking sinuously along the sleek darkness of her mouth.

Clinging to him like a second skin, Abby gave her heart willingly. Without reservation. She wanted him to know. He cupped her nape and tilted her head to give him freer access. The kiss told her what he wouldn't: he wanted her.

His chest heaved against hers. Her breath came in ragged gasps. He raised his head, his eyes smoky with desire. Need knifed through her.

"Thank you," she whispered.

He stood staring, his breath rasping out. The iron-hard planes of his chest stroked her breasts with each labored breath. His gaze tracked over her, rough and raw with hunger, but he didn't move to pull her closer.

She could see the desire fire his eyes, making them glow like heated gems. Apprehension stroked her insides and jammed her breath in her throat.

On a gamble, Abby pulled away from him and walked to the door. *Please don't let me leave, Jeff.* "Good-bye."

Her hand had closed on the doorknob when palms slammed the wood on either side of her. His chest covered her back; his arousal nudged her bottom. Abby closed her eyes in thanks and waited.

His voice trickled in a ragged whisper over her shoulder. "You sure know how to make a man lonesome."

Her heart tripped up its beat. She waited, her chest aching, wondering if he would indeed force her to walk out. *Tell me to stay. Ask me. Order me.*

Her breath jammed in her chest, straining against her breastbone. *Please, please don't let me leave, Jeff.*

How long they stood that way, Abby didn't know. Moonlight flitted in patterns around her feet, touched the hem of her skirt, slanted across the backs of Jeff's hands.

His chest pumped in rapid breaths against her back, and his arousal burned through her skirts. The scent of dust and man and sweat sharpened her senses. Need stabbed through her.

Her own breaths were short, harsh, as she struggled for control. His beard was coarse against her cheek, his breath hot on her neck. Still she waited, afraid to move and risk breaking the current between them.

One of his hands dropped from the door. Alarm raced up Abby's spine. It hadn't worked. He wasn't going to—

His hands closed over her breast and stopped the thought. Her breath seeped out of her, and tears stung her eyes.

His hand kneaded gently, pressing against her fullness and stroking her nipple with his thumb. He plastered his body to hers, chest to shoulder, his hard arousal fitting against her soft bottom, his knee to the back of her thigh.

He dragged his other hand down her throat, a blatantly possessive touch that branded her.

She stood unmoving in his embrace, locked in a trap of desire and heated touches, abandoning herself to the need that flooded her.

"Is this what you want, Abby?" His hand moved to the other breast, plucking her nipple tight even through the material of her dress. "Is this what you came for?"

"Yes, oh yes." She knew she sounded wanton and she didn't care. He was here. He was touching her. There had been no words of love spoken, but he couldn't deny this thing between them. She knew he loved her. If only she could get him to admit it, perhaps she could convince him to stay.

His nimble fingers worked the buttons free on her bodice and parted the material. Warm air stroked her, then moist heat from his mouth as he pressed his lips to the hollow in her collarbone.

She tilted her head back, pressing harder into his arousal, reaching around to grip his hip and hold on for dear life. Need washed through her, changed to a rocking crash that built and tore at her reserve, her control.

He turned her to face him, bringing her flush against him. His strength surrounded her. Hard thighs to her softer ones. Rigid chest to her tingling breasts. His eyes were hot and dark with the same need she felt. "I can't let you go," he said hoarsely, his gaze devouring her features. "I'm not that strong."

"Good," she said fervently, staring into his eyes. "I want to be with you."

"No matter what?"

"No matter what," she repeated firmly, refusing to allow thoughts of Phipps or anyone else to invade her time with Jeff. This night was just for them, one special untarnished night when they would love each other because of what they were, not in spite of it.

He crushed his lips to hers and she met him, her lips opening, molding to his. She sought the fire he stirred, the release he promised, release from this horrible uncertainty, the aching fear that he would leave.

The heat inched to the surface of her skin, itching, prodding her to fumble with the buttons on his shirt. Once they were released, she slipped her hands inside and touched the warm muscled expanse of chest. His shirt fell to the floor unheeded.

Her hands skimmed over him, learning the steel-hugged velvet of his muscles, the thundering beat of his heart against her palm. He peeled the dress from her shoulders, pushed it in a heap to the floor, then swept her against him.

Her hands glided up his arms, savoring the power there, the gentleness in his hands as he slipped the buttons free on her camisole. She tore off the garment, craving the feel of his brawny chest against hers, of sleek muscles beneath her hands, his fullness inside her.

His mouth left hers to press hot kisses on her neck, the

slope of her breasts, then take one turgid, throbbing peak into his mouth. She moaned and threw back her head, arching toward him in a plea for more.

Even before their joining, she felt fulfilled, complete. Invisible wires bound her to him, stroking her insides with pleasure, tightening with every touch of his lips on her breasts, the gentle skim of his hands down her belly. He loosened her drawers, and she was keenly aware of the seductive scratch of cotton as they slid down her hips. She reached for his belt buckle and jerked it loose, pulled at the buttons on his denims.

She struggled to push the heavy material down his legs, to bare his body to hers so she could feel every inch of him on her. Coarse hair on his thighs tickled her the smooth skin on hers. His hard and muscle-carved belly teased her soft one. Desire clawed through her, making her desperate for his touch, his kiss.

She wanted to feel his lips on hers, his hands stroking down her body. She lifted her head for his kiss and curled her hands into his hair.

He gently laid her on her back and covered her body with his. Slivers of sawdust and sand rubbed at her bare skin, but Abby focused all her attention, her world, on the man above her.

She gave Jeff her heart unconditionally. She could live without him, but didn't want to. She could accept him for everything he was and had been, as long as he didn't leave her.

His arousal probed between her thighs and she shifted, opening for him. Her fingers skipped over his back, kneading the thick muscles, loving the flex of supple steel. Strong arms cradled her, the calluses on his hands stroking a tender abrasion on her skin.

"Jeff, I need you." She cupped his face in her palms. "Please say you won't leave. Please tell me you won't."

"Abby," he groaned. "How can you even talk right now? Just love me. Let me love you."

"Yes, I want that, but—"

His lips cut off her words, and she gave herself up to the

fire reaching in long, burning tendrils through her body, curling around her heart. His touch burned away all thought, all reason. There was only him, moving above her, touching her with exquisite tenderness.

Moist heat coiled between her legs, burning for him. He slid inside and stared down at her. "Are you okay?" His voice was harsh with passion.

Abby nodded, flattening her palms on his back and dragging them up his shoulders, soaking in the feel of him, the sweat-musky smell of him. He slid in fully and she sighed, tightening her thighs around him.

His mouth covered hers, a gentle kiss, giving and taking at the same time. Nearly withdrawing, he moved his body in a long, torturingly delicious stroke. She gasped. Her muscles clenched around him. The knot in her belly tightened. He thrust inside her then began to move in a slow, steady rhythm. His gaze stayed locked on her face. He held her cradled against him, loving her body with his, worshipping her with his eyes.

Love ached in her breast. Her every breath and thought was tied to this man. She reached up and touched his face, her eyes fluttering shut in pleasure. She tightened her legs around him, and the rhythm changed to something fast, desperate, frantic. They moved together, chased by a whirlwind of fire, striving to become immersed in its heat.

He climaxed, groaning her name. He threw back his head and muscles corded on his neck. Then the coil of heat inside her split, unraveled through her body in hard-hitting waves, battering her insides. She held onto Jeff, aware of the sounds coming from the back of her throat.

The waves ebbed into a steady glow of heat. Jeff relaxed against her, his weight bearing her into the floor. Tiny grains of sand and wood itched her skin, but she welcomed the feel. Her nerves hummed with energy. She wrapped her arms and legs tighter around him and kissed his eyes, his nose, then his lips. "I love you."

"I love you, too."

"I knew it." She smiled and he smiled back, but she didn't

miss the shadows that came into his eyes or the worry that etched his words.

Her heart clenched tight, wanting to savor the memory of what had just happened, realizing it might never happen again.

He rolled to his side, taking her with him. For long moments, she nestled next to him, her cheek pressed to his sweat-dampened chest. His heart beat in a reassuring rhythm against her head. Moonlight tiptoed through the window in washed shades of gold and silver. Outside, a hawk called, and Abby lifted her gaze to Jeff's.

His eyes were closed, and there was such agony on his face that her heart caught. "Jeff?" She raised a hand to his cheek.

He took hold of it and pressed a kiss into her palm. "Abby, this doesn't change anything."

"You said that last time, too," she said with a gentle smile. "I didn't believe it then either."

"I mean it." He stared down into her eyes, willing her to look at him, to hear him. "I won't have you and the girls put in danger. We've been through this. If anything, tonight just makes me more determined to protect you."

"Why can't you understand that we want to be with you? Why won't you trust me enough to let us choose?"

He rolled away from her and rose, a towering golden shadow in the silver light. He jerked on his pants and buttoned them. "It has nothing to do with trust."

"It has everything to do with it." Suddenly aware of her nakedness, Abby leapt to her feet. She grabbed up her dress and pressed it to her body like a shield. "Do you think I'll go running off at the first sign of trouble? Or that I won't be able to accept you when I see you pull a gun? Maybe those things were true once, Jeff, but they're not anymore." Her voice cracked. "I'm willing to try. I'm willing to put aside things I thought I never would. Why won't you?"

"Because I know what men like Phipps are capable of. He's not the only one. Others might come. I won't have you and the girls exposed to that. I won't be responsible for what might happen."

"If you won't stay for me, at least consider the girls."

"I *am* considering the girls." His voice shook with frustration. "Abby, why do you have to make it so difficult?"

She took a deep breath, tempering her anger and her tears of frustration. "Didn't tonight mean anything to you?"

He grabbed her and hauled her to him, his words fiercely tender. "It meant everything to me. You are one hell of a woman, Abigail Grant, but you can't be *my* woman." He held her, pressing her face to his shoulder, resting his head atop hers. "It's not that I don't want you, Abby. But I can't risk losing you just because I'm too selfish to put precaution over emotion."

She looked up at him, memorizing the look of possession and torture in his blue eyes. "How can I convince you?"

"It's best this way, Abby. I know."

"It's not best for anybody," she declared hotly, pushing away from him. She jerked on her dress and gathered up her underthings and shoes. "I do think you're right about Phipps. For the girls' sake, I'll keep them away from here. But I won't give up on you. I want more of what we just shared, and I think you do, too."

He gave her a crooked smile, teeth flashing in the darkness, his chest damp and gleaming. "I hope I'm strong enough to resist that."

"I hope you're not." With that, she turned and left.

She waited until she was well over the rise before she stopped the buggy. Loneliness and frustration swamped her. She had so hoped Jeff would waver in his determination. It seemed she had only strengthened his decision to keep a distance from them all.

Until he had dealt with Phipps, Abby knew he wouldn't relent. Would he then?

SIXTEEN

Empty. The damn cell was empty.

Moonlight trickled inside it, slid into dark corners and confirmed what Marty resisted believing.

From his vantage point outside the barred window, he could see a lumpy mattress made of ticking on an old wooden Army cot. Nothing else. No new dents in the mattress to show that anyone had slept there. No empty plate or tin cup or even rats chasing crumbs on the floor to show that anyone had eaten there. No sign of Jefferson Grant anywhere.

The hair on the back of his neck prickled. The muscle in his injured eye twitched. He lifted his head into the cool night air, nostrils flaring as he remembered the oily stench of chains, the sweat-musty odor of a used cell. Alarm skittered up his spine, quickly followed by a chill of relief.

He'd nearly walked into a trap.

Anger flared in him. He'd been so close, although he shouldn't have expected it would be as easy as walking up and actually finding Grant. Was Clarendon's sheriff perhaps holding Grant somewhere else, for maximum security, or was he holding Grant at all?

From a solid oak door, portholed with a square window,

251

he could see the soft glimmer of light. A deep rumble of voices sounded through the door.

That telltale prickle itched the hairs on his neck again, and he slid into silver-blue shadow, making his way back to the horse he'd stolen from the old man.

Options circled in his mind. Perhaps Grant had already been picked up, even hanged. Frustration burned at that thought, and Marty pushed it away. He hadn't come all this way to find Grant already dead.

Feeling his way along the back wall of the sheriff's office, he inched toward the horse. Grant had to be here. Somebody had to know something about him.

The dapple gray stomped restlessly, moonlight gleaming on its shiny coat. Marty ran a hand down the sleek neck and quieted the animal. Sharp pain knifed through his temple, and he closed his eyes for a second.

His good eye still played doubles on him at times, and he found himself staring at four black-tipped ears and a fractured vision of the horse's jaw. Dizziness whipped through him, and he reached out a hand for the saddle horn to steady himself.

His fingers closed over the leather-covered pommel, and something jabbed his wrist. Steady once again, he eased closer for a better look. Something protruded from the seams at the front of the saddle. Thinking it was a piece of leather, Marty tugged at it.

A round disc slid out from between the seams, and he held it up to the light to better see it. At first he thought his good eye had failed him, too. He shifted the piece in his hand, studying the silver metal circle etched with a design and bearing the inscription "Texas Ranger." A badge. A Texas Ranger badge.

The old man he'd met on the trail had been a Ranger.

A low chuckle escaped Marty, and he folded his fist over the badge. Suddenly he knew how to find out about Grant.

He slid the badge into the pocket of his denims, raked his curly hair into a semblance of order and replaced his hat. Leading the gray, he walked around to the front of the sheriff's office and looped the reins around the hitching post.

He strode inside, closing the door softly behind him. "Good evening, gentlemen."

A whip-thin man, about six feet tall and wearing a neat mustache, rose from his place behind the desk. A shorter, thick-chested man with a long, woolly mustache jerked his booted feet from the desk and shot out of his chair, stroking the mustache nervously.

"Something we can do for you?" the thin man asked.

"I'm looking for the sheriff," Marty said politely, thumbing his hat back on his head. Both men stared at his eye patch, and he struggled to keep from touching it.

The neatly trimmed one nodded. "That'd be me. Sheriff Al Gentry. This is my deputy, Bally Oliver. And you are?"

"Abner Long." Marty fished in his denims for the badge. He flashed it and jammed it back in his pocket as though he wasn't concerned whether they saw it or not. "You got a prisoner by the name of Grant?"

"You a Ranger?" Oliver asked, broad gnarled hands on his hips, fingers drumming nervously against his holster belt.

Marty grinned, though his nerves stretched taut. Where the hell was Grant? His gaze swept the small office, noting posters on the wall behind the desk, an inkstand and quill layered with dust and a cedar cabinet housing that looked like a Sharpe rifle. "Yessir, nigh on ten years now."

Gentry stepped up, his eyes narrowing on the eye patch. "Did you come for Grant?"

"I surely did." Marty managed to keep the glee out of his voice, barely.

Gentry glanced at the deputy, who then scooted around and went out the front door. "There's something I need to tell you about that."

Well, hell. When Marty stepped outside a few minutes later, his hand gripped his gun until his knuckles ached. Thanks to the badge, he had learned that Grant lived around here. And was still alive. Waiting on him, no doubt.

Well, I'm onto you, Grant, you old bastard.

Anticipation inched up his spine, tickled his gut like lust. He would get Grant. In only a matter of time.

He couldn't be seen, not after he'd told the sheriff he'd be traveling on tomorrow morning. He'd find a place to hide and he'd see Jefferson Grant.

Marty wasn't leaving until he'd made Grant pay for killing Billy, for taking the only family Marty had left.

Indecision sawed at Jeff, dredged up old anger and wariness and a yearning for forgiveness he'd thought buried long ago.

Between his conversation with Abby and his last meeting with his father, Jeff could barely tolerate his own thoughts. He'd been right about his father wanting to make amends. Now it was Jeff's turn to reciprocate. Or not.

For two days, he seesawed back and forth. But the longing in his gut to call a truce tore at him. The knowledge that he was really leaving after he finished with Phipps finally dictated his decision. So, with apprehension and dread tingling up his spine, he rode into town to see his father. He purposedly went early, hoping to avoid running into Abby and the girls.

He couldn't see inside the clinic as he rode past, but he knew Abby was there. Every muscle tightened, every fiber in his body strained toward her, but he wouldn't allow himself to stop. Just the sight of those violet eyes shining at him weakened his resolve as effectively as the anthrax had weakened the cattle. He couldn't allow himself to waver from his purpose. So he rode past, keeping his eyes straight ahead, and ignoring the burning in his chest.

In front of his father's office, stationed in a small corner of the courthouse next to Rosenfield's store, Jeff tied his horse and took a deep breath. Old anger pulled at him, welled up. He didn't owe his father anything. He wouldn't apologize or stand for any censure this time. He would simply acknowledge his father's effort. Still he hesitated outside the door as though he were again a boy and his father waited for him with a strap.

Shoving aside the unreasonable apprehension, he strode

into the cool, dim interior of the courthouse and walked the
short hall to Marcus Grant's office. A scent of cigar smoke
lingered in the office, and sunlight streamed through a
four-paned window behind the mahogany desk.

His father sat in a leather and brass-tacked chair with
rollers, in front of an oak-and-glass bookcase. Marcus
Grant's brow was furrowed in concentration as he flipped
the pages of a heavy law book bound in burgundy. Spectacles, perched at the end of his nose, gave him a suddenly
haggard appearance. Or perhaps it was the sun on his hair
picking out the lines of gray that hadn't been there fifteen
years before.

Jeff suddenly felt tired and lonely and uncertain. He
rapped lightly on the door before he changed his mind. His
father swiveled around and peered over his spectacles.

"Jeff?" His eyes warmed briefly as he stood, then concern
tightened his features. "Something wrong?"

"No, nothing like that." Jeff walked inside, keeping his
back to the wall, not comfortable with leaving himself open
and vulnerable in the middle of the room. He thought about
making small talk, thought about asking if his father had
seen Abby and the girls, but in the end he said, "I've been
thinking about what you said the other day."

"And?" His father stood motionless, still holding the
large volume. Tension ticked in the room, a heavy, stagnant
pressure that shrank the air between them. Waiting swelled,
raw with hope and promise, wariness.

"I . . . appreciate what you said." Jeff's voice sounded
gravelly, coarse with age. "I wanted you to know that."

His father's face softened in a way Jeff hadn't seen since
he'd left home. "I meant it, you know?"

"I know. That's why I'm here."

"You're leaving, aren't you?" Marcus's voice was soft
with resignation and hurt.

Jeff swallowed, attempting a laugh. "You and Abby can
read me pretty well."

"Don't go."

The simple words stabbed Jeff's heart. If only his father
had made that request fifteen years ago. He squelched the

thought. That was in the past, time to forget and move on. "I have to. You know why."

"I think Abby would work with you. She loves you."

Jeff massaged the back of his neck, feeling uncomfortable with the conversation yet wanting to talk at the same time. "I can't do that to them. Always looking over my shoulder, making them live with the uncertainty." His voice fell to a hoarse croak. "Never knowing if they'll be all right, if it would be my fault."

"I think you should consider staying. Have you?"

Misery gnawed Jeff's gut. "Not much. Don't try to talk me into it. That's—that's not why I'm here."

His father raised silver brows, silently waiting. He placed the law book on the desk behind him and folded the spectacles to lay them on top.

Jeff took a deep breath, pushed by the fact that he was leaving, that he might never see his father again. When he left, he didn't want it to be the way it had been last time. "I want you to know I'm sorry for the way things happened. Can you forgive me? Or can we at least start over?"

His father's eyes glinted suspiciously bright. A heavy weight pushed against Jeff's chest, yet he stood there, his palms slick with sweat, heart thundering.

Marcus cleared his throat and a flush darkened his face. "I should be asking your forgiveness. I realized a long time ago what I'd done to you, done to myself and even your sister, by saying what I did that night. Now I'm not so sure you did the wrong thing."

"But—"

His father took a step toward him then stopped, folding his arms at his chest then unfolding them. He flashed a tight smile. "It wasn't that I resented you finding your own way, though I know it came across like that."

"You did want me to be a lawyer pretty desperately," Jeff reminded him gruffly, stung with memories of Justin and his law career.

"It wasn't that so much as I felt alone. You wanted to leave right after Justin and your mother— Well, I felt I was losing everything and didn't know how to hold on. And then, instead of coming to you, as I knew I should, I let stubbornness and pride get in the way. The years passed. It became easier to hold onto the anger, the hurt, than to come to you."

Jeff stared at his father, tightness cinching his chest. He understood exactly what his father was saying, because he'd felt the same way himself. For those very same reasons, he hadn't written or come home.

"So, I'm the one asking for forgiveness. Can you?"

His father's silver eyes, dark with regret and apology, burned into Jeff's.

"I think we're both due . . . Dad," Jeff managed to say around a lump of emotion in his throat. Slowly he held out his hand.

Relief and love warmed his father's eyes, and Marcus gripped Jeff's hand tight. A new bond of love, born of forgiveness, surged between them. Then Marcus pulled Jeff into a tight embrace. For a long moment, they stood, letting the anger of the years slip away, hesitant on new ground, uncertain about continuing.

They pulled away from each other, and Jeff looked down. It hurt his chest to see his father this happy, to know they'd made peace but that he would have to leave anyway.

"On the basis of our new beginning, can I try to talk you out of leaving?"

"No." Jeff answered abruptly. He was close to forfeiting the game anyway. Just the thought of never again seeing Abby's violet eyes light for him, or feeling her soft skin brand his, left Jeff shaken and lost. If his father tried to persuade him to stay, Marcus just might succeed. And Abby and the girls would be the ones to pay. "You know this is the right thing."

His father was silent, though there was denial in his eyes. Then he said hesitantly, "I think you'll make the right choice."

Jeff's doubts mushroomed and he turned away. "I'm glad we did this. I'll see you again."

"Maybe tomorrow night, for dinner?" His father followed him to the door.

Jeff turned, wary of a setup with Abby or the girls. "Just us?"

He saw the struggle in his father's eyes, then Marcus agreed reluctantly. "Just us."

They shook hands again and Jeff walked out the door.

Mired in thought and wishing he could stay, Jeff mounted and rode down the street. Trying to dodge thoughts of his father and their newfound peace, and the memory of the hurt in Abby's eyes last night when she'd left, he didn't hear the sheriff until the man grabbed his reins.

"Hey, Grant. Need to talk to you for a minute."

His attention honed in on Al Gentry with predatorlike swiftness. "News?"

"Not of Phipps, but I wanted to tell you that a Ranger showed up last night looking for you."

"Just like you said." Jeff relaxed, his eyes scanning the street, searching in spite of himself for Abby.

Gentry moved around in front of him. "I told him what was going on. Name was Long. Once he heard the story, he went on his way this morning."

Jeff pulled back to look at the sheriff. "Thanks, Gentry. I appreciate it."

"No problem. I just wish Phipps would hurry up. I'd hate to be explaining this to very many Rangers."

"Yeah."

Gentry turned to leave. "I'll let you know if anything happens."

"Appreciate it. Maybe you could keep an eye on Abby and the gir—"

"Uncle Jeff! Uncle Jeff!" Hannah's voice obliterated the rest of his sentence.

Jeff glanced up to see her and Rachel running toward him. Damn, where was Abby? How could she let the girls loose like this? She knew about Phipps. He climbed down from the horse, intent on sending them back to the clinic.

His heart tilted at the excitement in their voices, and when Hannah barreled into him, wrapping her arms around his legs, his resolve disappeared.

"I missed you. Did you miss me?" she demanded, lifting

her arms in silent command to be held. Rachel skidded to a stop behind her, her face flushed and eyes smiling.

He grinned and scooped them both up. "Who are you young ladies? Are you lost?"

"No, silly." Hannah giggled. "You know us. We're yours."

His heart caught at that. He hugged them tight then caught sight of Abby. He froze, his heart slowing to a painful thud. She walked toward them, slow and deliberate, moving as though she were picking her way through glass. Caution screamed through him, but relief and desire and love snuffed it out.

She looked so damn beautiful. Morning sun gilded her dark hair. Her eyes were wary, but glowed like polished amethyst. The sleeves of her white blouse were rolled past her elbows, emphasizing her delicate wrists and slender hands. In a painful stab of memory, Jeff again felt her hands on his body.

"Girls, come on. Uncle Jeff has to go somewhere."

Pain and bitterness tightened her voice. In her eyes, dull with loss and hurt, were remnants of what they'd shared last night.

His heart clenched, and pain funneled through his body. *If I could do it differently, Abby, I would.*

Her gaze slid away from his, and she stopped, close enough to touch if he dared. But he didn't.

Hannah and Rachel glanced from Abby to Jeff and back again. Abby's eyes rose to his. He wanted her to understand this was the only thing he could do, but in her expression, he saw that she didn't understand. There was only hurt and regret and anger.

"Come on, girls." She forced a smile and held out her arms for Hannah.

Emptiness swamped Jeff as Abby took the younger girl. He set Rachel on the ground beside him.

"Love you, Uncle Jeff." Hannah leaned forward in Abby's arms, her lips puckered.

"I love you too, tadpole." He leaned down and kissed her on the cheek, his jaw tightening at her baby-soft scent.

Rachel's hand slipped inside his. "Will you come see us tomorrow? Maybe for supper?"

He didn't miss the flattening of Abby's lips or the chill that swept through her eyes. She tilted her chin at him, challenging him to deny a seven year old.

"I can't, Rach. I'm having dinner with your Grandpa Marcus. Man talk, you know?"

He kept his voice light, his gaze fixed on Abby's. Surprise and questions flared in her eyes, but she hugged Hannah closer and motioned to Rachel.

"Bye, Uncle Jeff," Hannah sang, looping her arms around Abby's neck and dropping her chin to Abby's shoulder. She wriggled her fingers at him.

He lifted his hand, stormed by loss and loneliness and a painful urge to follow them, to ask them to come back to the cabin. Before he could stop himself, he reached out and squeezed Abby's elbow. Tears welled in her eyes, and she pulled away as though he'd burned her.

Rachel hugged him around the waist then skipped off behind Abby and Hannah. Jeff's eyes caressed Abby's trim back, willing her to look at him just once. She didn't.

From the dugout along the south end of Carroll Creek, Marty could see everything in town. And he couldn't believe what he saw.

An hour earlier, Grant had come into town. Minutes ago, he had started toward the creek when he was waylaid by two little girls and a lady.

From here, Marty could tell only that the children were girls, the woman pretty. But he could see the affection the little girls had for Grant and the tension that simmered between the two adults.

Marty knew then the surest way to torture Jefferson Grant. She had just walked into the doctor's clinic.

Fear and anger jabbed at her. By the time Abby had walked the girls to school and returned to the clinic, she still hadn't stopped shaking.

Why wouldn't he relent? How could he walk away from them?

When Hannah and Rachel had greeted him in the street, she'd seen a look of determination seal his features, but he'd faltered. His face had softened with love and pain, a fierce longing. Then that savage protectiveness had flared in his eyes and she'd known he would still leave, as he'd said he would.

Frustration clawed through her. She had greedily devoured the sight of him, not knowing if it would be her last. She wanted to beg him to stay, but had bitten off the words. He had to stay on his own, because he wanted her and a family with the girls. Not out of his sense of duty or out of guilt.

She walked inside the clinic, her movements forced and sluggish. She took the enamel-coated metal bowl from the examining table, filled it with carbolic acid and carried it to the bench under the window. Though it was time for the weekly scrubbing down of the entire clinic, Abby admitted she was doing it more to keep her mind off Jeff.

Her control wavered. She wanted to go after him, scream at him not to leave, but she feared that would drive him farther away. Sweat dampened her palms, and the bowl slipped onto the bench. Acid solution sloshed onto the wood and dripped over on the floor. She stared for a moment, her thoughts detached, unfinished, as though she were fatigued rather than angry. On unsteady legs, she moved to get a bucket of water to mix with the acid.

A shadow sliced through the bright morning light, and she turned. A short, wiry man leaned against the door frame, a black patch covering his right eye. Dirty blond hair curled to his shoulders. His good eye was dark brown and as devoid of warmth as a nail. Sudden caution inched down Abby's spine. "Yes?"

"Need-help," he rasped in a gruff voice.

Abby hurried to the door. "Here, come inside. Let me help you."

She gripped his elbow and he hesitated. Thinking to

reassure him, she smiled. "I'm a doctor, truly. What's the trouble?"

"Won't be any if you do what you're told." The man straightened abruptly, his left eye boring into her.

"What do you—?"

He whipped out a pistol, silencing her as effectively as if he'd clapped a hand over her mouth. Panic fluttered as she stared at the shiny barrel pointed straight at her. Abby swallowed and took a step backward.

With one foot, the man closed the door behind him. It swung silently shut on oiled hinges. Only the click echoed in the eerie stillness of the room. Abby searched desperately for the sound of footsteps outside, the sound of a voice, but could hear only her heart rushing in her ears.

"Wh-what do you want?"

With the gun, he motioned her back another step, glancing over his shoulder out the large plate window. "I want Jefferson Grant."

Abby drew in her breath, her heart kicking her ribs in a painful surge. "You're . . . Phipps."

"Ah, I see you've heard of me." Again with the pistol, he directed her against the examining table. "Where is he?"

Abby gripped the smooth wood of the table behind her. "I-I don't know."

Phipps edged closer to her, a feral smile curling his lip. "What're you to Grant? Not his sister, I'd wager."

How had he known about her at all? Abby licked her lips, stalling for time, wanting to deny her relationship with Jeff in order to protect him, but Phipps somehow already knew there was a connection between them.

His hard gaze darkened with malice and slid away from her, skimming over the room. "You the mother of those girls I saw with him?"

Abby's heart flipped. How did he know about the girls? "No."

"Don't matter. He'll come for you."

"H-he . . . won't." Fear tightened her throat and caused her to stumble over the words. "He knows me, but I'm only the town doctor."

He spat out a harsh sound and leaned into her face. "I ain't blind, lady. I know somethin's between you two. Those girls, if nothing else." He thrust the barrel into her stomach, and Abby wobbled from a surge of nausea. "Get over to the window."

Fear mixed with anger within her, and she looked at him. "What are you going to do?"

"Do what I say." He prodded her ribs for emphasis.

Knees shaking, her chest aching as though she'd had the wind knocked out of her, Abby moved slowly toward the window. Cold sweat slicked her palms, the back of her neck, slid between her breasts. Her eyes traced the street. She was relieved yet disappointed to find it empty.

He raised his right arm and she drew back, fearing he would strike her. Instead he jabbed his elbow through the window. The sound of breaking glass screeched through the room, and Abby stared, her heart beating a rapid staccato. He pushed away several remaining slivers embedded in the frame and drilled the gun barrel between her tenth and eleventh ribs. "Look pretty now."

Fear sliced a cold wake through her, and Abby felt the strength ebb out of her arms and legs. She braced her knees against the bench under the window for support and opened her mouth to scream for help.

He nudged the gun barrel harder into her ribs. "Won't help you any." He then turned and leaned out the window himself. "Sheriff!"

Abby's eyes widened in shock. What was he doing?

"Sheriff!"

She fought the urge to wrap her arms around herself, afraid he might fire at the slightest movement from her. She barely moved her head, her gaze slanting left and right, looking for someone, anyone.

"Sheriff!" The voice was louder this time, bordered with anger.

From the corner of her eye, Abby saw George Suddity and his son peer out of the stage stand then slowly walk out to stare. Other figures, blurry and indefinable, moved across the street. Abby didn't dare look at anyone.

Next door, the sheriff stepped onto the porch of the jailhouse. "What's all the racket?"

"Sheriff, you see what I got here?" By the sheer pressure of the weapon in her ribs, Phipps guided Abby around so that she faced the sheriff.

Sheriff Gentry's eyes stretched wide. "I'll be damned," he breathed. Anger slashed his features and he stepped off the porch. "You! What do you want?"

Phipps looped an arm around Abby's neck. "Not another step."

Her knees wobbled, and only the threat of the gun going off kept her upright.

Sheriff Gentry spread his hands in supplication. "All right, all right. Tell me what you want."

"Get Jeff Grant here within the hour."

"I'll send my deputy." Gentry turned to Bally Oliver, who stood slack-jawed beside him. He murmured something low and terse then ordered, "Go, Bally. Hurry."

The deputy nodded, jerked at the reins on the hitching post and scrambled up on his horse, kicking the animal into motion before he'd even gained his seat.

Gentry's attention snapped back to Phipps. "Let her go. Grant will come. I give you my word."

Phipps laughed, a short, cold sound that pierced Abby's small self-control. "I got all the insurance I need right here."

He tugged Abby backward toward the examining table and out of sight of the window.

"Wait!" Gentry called.

Phipps didn't answer. He removed his arm from around her neck, but kept the gun glued to her ribs. "Shouldn't be long now. Hot damn, would you look at all them people? They out there for you or for Grant?"

Abby glanced outside, appalled to see the street crowded with people. Mr. Suddity, rifle in hand, and his son now stood in the street in front of the clinic. Reverend Carhart and Morris Rosenfield stood next to them, concern and anger festering on their faces. The sun glinted off the barrel of a shotgun held at Rosenfield's side.

She could see Marcus and her father, but no sign of the

children or Harriet. She prayed all this would be over before the children heard of it.

Phipps moved closer to her, edging in front of her to peer at the crowd. "Where's those girls?" he muttered.

Panic exploded through her and she turned, an abrupt move that earned her a sharp jab in the ribs. "Please," she cried, ignoring the pressure of the weapon. "Don't kill him. He's the only family those girls have left. You can't kill him. Please."

"I don't aim to kill him," Phipps said slowly, swiveling his head around to stare at her. His one good eye glowed with malicious glee.

Abby's throat closed up. Danger prickled along her spine. "You don't?"

"Nope." A smile stretched across his features, and he actually seemed to relax. "I'm gonna kill you."

SEVENTEEN

I don't know what to do, Jilly. What's the right thing for the girls? For Abby?

Jeff stood on the porch of the finished house, aching as he studied the spanking fresh paint, the solid door in front of him. He wanted to live here with Abby and knew he never would. Ever since the visit with his father, Jeff had turned over doubts and guilt and anger in his mind. Leaving was the right thing, wasn't it? They wouldn't be safe if he stayed.

So why had his father urged him to stay, even knowing the risk? *Because even now he thinks he can change you.*

No. Because he thinks you'll change on your own.

The idea floated to the surface, and this time Jeff didn't push it away. It had come to him after he'd seen the girls shunned in town, but he had been so sure leaving was the answer. Could he change? Did he want to?

"Grant! Grant, come quick!"

An urgent voice sliced through Jeff's thoughts. He turned to see Bally Oliver careening over the rise toward him.

Alarm crawled through him. He vaulted the porch steps and ran toward the deputy. "What is it?"

"It's Phipps!" Bally jerked the bay to a stop, panting, his

voice high and nervous. "He's got Dr. Welch. I mean Dr. Grant. Your wife. He's got your wife."

Jeff's blood stopped cold in his veins. Icy fear jolted down his spine. "Is she all right?"

"She was when I left. He said he'd give you an hour." Bally held his heaving sides, which pooched out like overfilled bags. His face gleamed with sweat and his hat sat askew on his head.

Jeff was already sprinting for the corral, where he'd left his horse tied. He yanked the reins free and leapt into the saddle in one fluid motion. The chestnut gelding raced past Oliver, who wheeled and set his horse at a dead run to catch Jeff.

Bally's voice rose above the thundering hooves. "Phipps was the Ranger we talked to last night."

Jeff's gaze sliced to the deputy. "Damn!"

He jabbed a heel into his horse's flanks, laying low over the saddle as he urged the gelding to run faster. Wind whipped at Jeff's hat, stirring the panic that already sawed at the edges of his control.

He forced himself to concentrate on the ride, skirting a fallen log, a hole burrowed by a mole, the small leap over the creek as they rode into town.

Abby, Abby, Abby. Her name pounded through his head, in time to the thundering rhythm of the hooves and the broken rhythm of his heart. How long had Phipps been here? Long enough to learn that Jeff wasn't in jail, obviously. Jeff bit back a howl of frustration. If Phipps harmed her . . .

Hell, it didn't matter if he harmed her or not. Jeff was going to kill him as soon as he got the outlaw in his sights.

Don't come, Jeff. Don't come.

The words thundered in time to the ragged beat of her heart. Glass lay shattered across the floor, jagged shards reflecting the sun like miniature rainbows. Abby's gaze scanned the room, searching for a weapon, something to distract Phipps, anything to protect herself.

"Phipps, let her go." Jeff's voice, savage with fury, sounded almost unrecognizable.

He'd come. Twin forces of fear and relief tore through Abby's breast. She didn't want to be the cause of his death, nor did she want the girls to witness what Phipps had threatened.

Phipps laughed, a low chuckle that vibrated in her ears. "That's not how it works, is it, Doc?" To Jeff, he yelled, "Grant, move to the window. So you can see."

Abby swallowed, bracing herself for Phipps's next move, her gaze darting over the examining table, she glass-front cabinet, the bench, searching for something, anything—

Her gaze moved back to the bench in front of the window, littered with broken glass. Light shot through the pieces and created a pattern of muted colors on the wall and floor. The shattered glass didn't hold her attention; the enamel bowl full of Lister's carbolic acid did.

Phipps nudged her with the gun. She obeyed automatically, her gaze centered on the bowl now.

From the corner of her eye, she saw a movement and looked up. Jeff stood in the street, in front of the window. Guilt and anger marked his features. Under his beard she could see the flex of muscle, the cold, hard stare that promised retribution. She shivered, despite knowing Jeff was here to help *her*.

"Quit hiding behind the woman, Phipps," Jeff snarled. "Let her go."

"Abby! Abby!"

Rachel and Hannah cried out in unison, their voices high with fear and uncertainty. Abby winced and looked toward the crowd, only to find her movement halted by a squeezing grip to her arm. She searched the crowd, and her heart pounded with fear and apprehension. *No!*

She saw Hannah and Rachel first, with all the other schoolchildren gathered around. Her father held Hannah and Marcus held Rachel, preventing the girls from running toward Jeff.

Even from the window of the clinic, Abby could see the tears streaking Hannah's face. The little girl reached out toward Abby and Jeff, her features crumbling pitifully. Abby's heart clenched. Rachel locked her arms tight around Marcus's neck and buried her face against his shoulder.

Rage and frustration churned inside Abby, but she tamped it down, knowing she might have only one chance for escape.

Jeff's voice lashed the air. "The woman's innocent. I'm the one you want."

Abby could hear the desperate anger in Jeff's voice and hoped the outlaw couldn't."

Phipps halted at the window, Abby's knees pushing into the bench. "Here's how it's gonna be, Grant. I'm going to kill her. Just the way you killed Billy."

"Phipps, you yellow coward! This is between you and me!"

"No!" Phipps yelled, his fingers biting into Abby's upper arm, the gun drilling a hole in her side. Her breath came in tight, painful gasps and her head spun, but she kept her eyes glued to Jeff. Just the sight of him pumped caution into her. "She dies. I'm gonna take her from you the way you took my brother from me. You can suffer for the rest of your life knowing it was your fault."

No, Abby screamed silently. *Don't believe him, Jeff.* Jeff carried enough guilt already; Abby didn't want him blaming himself for whatever happened today.

"Phipps, you idiot. If you shoot her, at least five guns will level you where you stand." Jeff's voice was coldly matter-of-fact as he indicated the sheriff, the deputy, George Suddity and Morris Rosenfield. Only Jeff's eyes revealed the smoldering rage inside him.

Phipps hesitated then spat, "Even if that happens, I'll have killed the doc here and you'll have lost the same thing I did."

A stilted silence webbed the crowd outside the clinic. People exchanged glances, weighing stares.

Suddenly Jeff bellowed like a wounded coyote and charged the door. Gentry and Oliver managed each to grab a shoulder and hold on to him.

Phipps cocked the gun. Abby's mouth dried up as if she'd swallowed sand. *No! No! No!*

Jeff twisted and writhed as though chased by a branding iron. "Phipps, let her go, dammit!"

Abby felt the slight relaxation in Phipps's body as he inched forward to laugh at Jeff. She sprang, breaking free of his bruising grip, snatching up the bowl of acid solution and slinging it straight into Phipps's face.

The outlaw howled and grabbed his face with one hand, swinging the pistol toward her. She ducked, flew under his arm and wrenched open the clinic door. A gunshot cracked the air behind her, and the bullet whistled past her head, burying itself in the door frame, inches from her face.

She dove, her breath whooshing out of her body as she hit the unforgiving wood of the planked porch. A ripple of gunfire exploded over her head, three shots, four.

Sharp cries pierced the echoing sound of gunfire.

"He's hit!"

"Got Phipps!"

In a fuzzy blur, she saw Jeff fall as she scrambled to her knees and slid off the edge to huddle against the side of the clinic, out of sight.

Her breathing rattled in her chest, and her heartbeat roared in her ears. It was a few seconds before she realized those were the only sounds she heard.

Blessed silence shrouded the air. Taking a deep breath, Abby risked a peek around the corner.

Gentry and Oliver holstered their guns, their features stunned as they rushed inside. She scanned the faces in the crowd—her father, Marcus, Harriet, Reverend Carhart—and found the same dazed relief she felt.

She struggled to her feet on wobbly legs, looking for Jeff. "Uncle Jeff! Uncle Jeff!"

Hannah's broken cries jerked Abby's attention to the street. The little girl tore out of Lionel Welch's arms and raced toward her uncle. He was lying facedown in the street.

Abby's heart stopped. "Jeff?" She took a step forward, fear slashing through her. She wasn't seeing this, she told herself. She wasn't. "Jefferson?"

Rachel wriggled down from Marcus's arms and rushed to Jeff. She threw herself on him, sobbing. "Uncle Jeff, please."

Marcus followed, his face as pale as chalk. He stopped behind Rachel and stroked her head, looking as if he were garnering support from her.

Hannah knelt beside Rachel and leaned down to Jeff's ear, patting his shoulder. "Uncle Jeff, it's me. Tadpole. Wake up, silly. Wake up."

Abby moved, panic shooting through her body. *Jeff, no!* She darted around the porch toward him and fell to her knees.

Rachel choked back a sob. "Abby, do something. Is he going to—" *Die?* The word hung unspoken between them.

Abby leaned over, pressing two fingers to the carotid artery in his neck. A faint pulse flirted against her fingertips. Blood trickled down his temple and into one dark eyebrow. Was he only grazed?

"Uncle Jeff, wake up," Hannah crooned in his ear.

Abby was aware of tears burning her face, blurring her vision. She knew she should get him up, take him in the clinic and attend him. But she could only sit on her knees, her heart breaking, fear binding her hands like leather straps. Feeling as though her hand were floating out in front of her, she stroked Jeff's hair. "Jeff, can you hear me? Jeff?"

Gentry and Oliver came out of the clinic, carrying Phipps's body. They walked behind Abby and over to the jailhouse.

Her father laid a hand on her shoulder. "Abby, let me look at him."

"Oh, Papa," Abby cried, gripping his hand with her free one. "Do something. Please."

At Abby's knee, Jeff's hand clutched the folds of her skirt.

"Jefferson?" she said on a breath of hope.

He raised his head, dirt plastering one side of his face, his eyes groggy with pain. "Abby?"

"Uncle Jeff!" Rachel breathed beside him, reaching out to touch his shoulder.

Hannah beamed at Abby. "I told you he'd wake up."

He levered himself up and balanced one hand on the ground, blinking a few times as if he couldn't focus. Abby leaned toward him, fingers closing over his hard biceps to steady him. He smelled of sweat and dirt, a welcome reminder that he was alive.

Hannah stood and dusted off her hands, shaking a finger at him. "You scared us out of our wits, Uncle Jeff."

A smile tilted one corner of his mouth, and his gaze rose to Abby's. He shook his head, as if he couldn't quite orient himself. Then relief, pleasure, longing softened his eyes, and they burned into hers.

Before she knew what he was about, he reached out and snagged her bodice, drawing her toward him.

"Jeff—"

His lips covered hers, barely touching at first, as though to reassure himself she was there. Then they moved, hungry and relentless, plundering, demanding a response. She gave it freely, cupping his face in her palms, tasting the salt of her tears in the heat of their kiss.

"I think he's going to be fine," came Marcus Grant's dry voice.

Abby heard nothing else. Her world tilted, and she gripped Jeff's hard, dusty shoulder for stability. She couldn't let him go, not ever. He released her, staring into her eyes, the gentle flame in his gaze stirring a like one inside her.

"I'm so glad you're all right," she whispered, stroking his face.

Jeff smiled, reaching up to take her hand and twine his fingers with hers. He glanced at the girls and winked.

Hannah squirmed between Abby and Jeff, scrambling onto his lap. "Can we come back to the house now?"

Abby smiled into Jeff's eyes. "Yes, can we?"

His smile faded. Guilt and bitterness hardened his features. Abby felt him withdraw as surely as the sun on a rainy day. She saw pain flicker in his eyes and she knew what was coming. *No, Jeff, don't do this. It wasn't your fault.*

But it was too late. He struggled to his feet, aided by

Abby and her father, though he protested he was all right. Lionel ordered him inside the clinic, and Jeff followed, after thanking everyone for their help.

Lionel hitched one arm around Jeff's waist and helped him to the steps of the porch. Jeff stumbled and Marcus appeared beside him, offering his arm. Jeff hesitated, then took it.

Abby followed, noticing the difference in the relationship between the two men, hoping there would be a difference for her and Jeff, too. Her mind scrambled to think of ways to convince him to stay.

Shudders bucked through his body, great wracking things that pricked his skin and set his teeth to chattering. The same frigid revulsion that had attacked him every time he'd had to kill a man.

This time, Abby had nearly been killed.

Next time, she could be. Or the girls.

Guilt chewed at him, erasing any thought except the curses he leveled at himself, the ever-tightening knot in his belly that threatened to make him vomit.

His father sat outside the curtained cubicle, as he had since Abby had cleaned and bandaged the scrape on Jeff's head. Sheriff Gentry and Bally Oliver stepped inside and assured him that Phipps had been taken care of. Reverend and Mrs. Carhart expressed concern and wished him a speedy recovery. Mrs. Garley, in that nervous chicken-peck way she had, expressed her sympathy and brought him a jar of pear preserves. Even Morris Rosenfield welcomed him to town.

The whole time he could hear the soft, rhythmic fall of Abby's footsteps as she paced on the other side of the curtain.

He kept seeing the fear that dilated her violet eyes, turning them nearly black. The tortured cries of the girls echoed in his head. His own helplessness haunted him. He'd never felt so uncertain or utterly incompetent as when he'd seen Phipps's gun caressing Abby's ear.

Jeff attempted a smile and shook Rosenfield's hand before the man left. Then he closed his eyes, trying to banish the images of Abby with Phipps and cease the tremors still rocking his body.

Whether it was ten days from now or ten years, he couldn't put them through that terror again. Hell, *he* couldn't go through it again. His heart had stopped at least three times. He'd frozen up like a greenhorn. If it hadn't been for Abby's quick thinking, she could even now have been the one lying in this bed.

It was in Jeff's power to do something about that, and he would.

"Stop it."

Abby's voice lanced his breath. She stood at the end of the bed, her face gray with worry, her eyes burning with concern. Their gazes met, hers desperate and hungry, his bleak with the knowledge of what he had to do.

"I know what you're doing, Jeff. Stop blaming yourself."

"And who should I blame?" His voice was bitter and edged with fury. He squeezed his eyes shut, unable to look at her. She was innocent, had given her trust and her heart to him, and he'd nearly gotten her killed. It could just as easily have been the girls as well.

"Jeff, I'm fine. The girls are fine." She sat down on the edge of the cot, her heat slowly trickling over him, her light, powdery scent teasing his nostrils.

"This time." He clenched his jaw. "You surely don't kid yourself that it might never happen again?"

"It might not," came her soft reply.

He opened his eyes and jerked his gaze to her. He shook his head. "Don't fool yourself, Abby. It's not worth it."

"I happen to think *we* are worth it."

He turned his head away, unable to face the vestiges of fear in her eyes, the fierce determination.

She captured his hand and laced her slender fingers through his dirty, coarse ones. "I don't blame you for what happened. I don't want you to blame yourself either."

"How can you not blame me? He had a damn gun to your head, Doc."

"I was there, remember?" she said with a feeble attempt at humor. "Please, Jeff. I know you're going to use this as an excuse to leave."

"It's not an excuse." The words ached in his throat.

"Yes, it is," she cried. "I want you to stay with me. The girls want you. We're willing to do whatever it takes."

"Abby, stop it!" He pulled away from her and pushed up on his elbows. Sharp pain jabbed through his temple then subsided. "I will not risk you again. I . . . can't. I almost died out there watching you."

She smiled tenderly and touched his face. "And I'm sure I'll feel the same if I ever see you in that position, but—"

"No buts. Go. Go on and leave me alone."

"I won't." She took his hand again, clutching as though she could bind them together and leaning down to peer into his face. "You listen to me, Jefferson Grant. I love you. So do the girls. They don't blame you any more than I do. We realize things won't always be easy—"

"Easy?" he snorted. "Abby, we're talking about life and death here."

"You can't anticipate what might happen." She continued as if she hadn't heard him. "You said that yourself. Or I did. Anyway, anything could happen to any of us." She stared into his face, as though she could will him to believe it. And he wanted to.

Unable to look away, he stared, feeling her passion, her determination. His body thrummed with her nearness. Looking up into her soft violet eyes, he realized what he had gained.

He'd found a woman who vowed to accept him as he was. With the girls, they were a real family now, or at least on their way. Because of that, he wanted to protect them. The selfish desire to stay battled with the knowledge that he should leave.

"Trust me. Trust yourself." Her gaze held his, hers bright with unshed tears. "Give us a chance."

He wanted to, so desperately he could feel it burning his breastbone, knotting in his gut. The want strained at the boundaries of what he knew was right. And the right thing would be to leave, not see them again. But Abby's words confused him, infused him with the hope that it could work with them. But he knew differently.

"Phipps never would've known about you and the girls if I hadn't been here."

"And we wouldn't have ever known you either," she said softly, stroking his cheek.

He grabbed her hand, eyes stinging. "Abby, he saw me with you."

"Why is it your fault? He could've seen me when I came to the house last night."

"Abby—"

"Or even when we saw you in town this morning. Do you blame the girls for coming over to talk to you?"

"No, of course not." Jeff shook his head, confused. "That's absurd."

"Of course it is. The fact is, he found you. And us. It might happen again. It might not."

"And you can live with that?" he bit out dubiously, his breath catching in wait for her reply.

She let out a deep sigh. "I wouldn't like it, but I would rather risk that than you leaving."

He stared at her, fighting the urge to pull her on top of him, bury his face in her neck and pretend none of this had happened. But he was lying on this cot, with a bullet graze on his temple to prove that it had happened. "You don't mean that."

"Yes, I do. I love you, Jeff." She leaned down until her breath mingled with his, her soft skin almost caressing his cheek. His hand clenched in the linens on the bed so as not to grab her. "You love me. Please say you'll stay."

Then she kissed him, a gentle touch, of her soft lips against his, that twisted his heart. "Stay here with us and make a family."

Jeff had been gone for three days. When Abby had returned to check on him, the cot was empty. As empty and hollow with loneliness as her heart. Only the indentation in the pillow and the dark woodsy scent of him lingered.

She knew he wasn't gone forever, not yet, because he hadn't said good-bye to the girls. What was he doing? Would he trust her, believe that she loved him enough to accept anything if only he would stay?

She had bared her heart to him and didn't know what else to do to convince him.

At sunset on the third day, Abby rolled her instruments into a sterile white cloth and placed them in the glass-front cabinet. Jeff would return to say good-bye, wouldn't he? Doubts wormed in and she bowed her head, staring at the worn toe of her shoe peeking out from her dress. How could she convince him? Just the threat of him leaving frightened her as much as a repeat of the incident with Phipps would.

Uncertainty tore at her, burning her throat when she thought about him and the bleakness in his eyes when she'd last seen him. *Oh, Jeff, if I can do it, why can't you?*

"I'm looking for Dr. A. Welch."

The familiar voice froze Abby, floated over her and rooted her feet to the floor. A heavy weight slammed into her chest. A booted footstep landed on the floor, sending a tiny vibration under her shoes.

"Jefferson?" Her voice was whisper-bare, and she turned, afraid she had heard his voice because she wanted it so desperately.

He stood in the door, sun slanting behind him and blocking out the features she'd come to love so well. In his hand was a bouquet of wildflowers. She was aware of yellow, red, and blue blooms before she noticed the girls beside him. They stood quietly, excitement dancing in their eyes. She could read nothing in Jeff's eyes.

Abby's heart lurched. Was that a good sign or bad? Had he come to say good-bye or hello? She moved closer on weightless legs, desperate to touch him, to know he was really here. Her hand touched his chest, eyes closing in relief as she felt the solid power, the heat soaking through his shirt.

Joy exploded in her breast then was wiped out by uncertainty. She blinked, staring up at him. "Your beard?"

"I shaved it." He ran a dark hand over the newly shorn jaw. "I'm—"

"You have a scar on your lip, just like Hannah!" Abby exclaimed, raising her fingers to touch it. His lips burned her skin, and she drew away, trying to coordinate the familiar blue eyes and voice with the stranger's face looking back at her.

He still looked ruthless, but his features were leanly planed, his cheekbones weathered with creases, the skin there a lighter shade than that of the rest of his face.

He grinned and her stomach kicked. She recognized that, but it only served to whet her uncertainty. "W-What are you doing?"

He took a step toward her, his neck reddening. Earnest blue eyes met hers. "I'm a new man, Abby."

"He's gonna—"

Hannah stopped as Rachel elbowed her.

Hope flared, but Abby restrained herself. "A new man?"

"I want to stay. I'm going to change and I've already got a job. Dad wants me to build a house for him and Harriet."

"He's going to teach Grandpa Lionel how to *really* carve," Rachel put in, her hopeful gaze glued to Abby.

"Oh, Jeff!" Abby barreled into him, throwing her arms around his neck. "Really? You're staying?"

"Yes. I told Kennedy—"

She cut off his words with a quick kiss then pressed kisses over his face. "Told Kennedy what?"

"That'd I'd—" Kiss. "Have to—" A longer kiss on the corner of his mouth. His arms went around her as his body hardened against hers. "Quit."

He swooped down and captured her lips with his, twining his tongue around hers and tilting back her head to gain further access in her mouth.

Abby surrendered herself totally. The gentleness of his kiss bespoke of his surrender, too. To a new life, a new family, their love. She could feel the desire thrumming in his heart against her breasts, in the arousal straining against her belly, but his passion was restrained for now as he whispered her name.

She framed his face with her hands. "Don't change for me. I don't need that."

"It's not only for you. It's for me, too. When I came here, all I had in the world I was wearing or riding. You gave me something I thought I'd lost years ago. Now I have a place to belong, someone to belong to."

"Two someones," Hannah chimed.

Rachel added quietly, "Three someones."

"Three someones." Jeff smiled and tightened his arms around Abby. "I thought about what you said and I want to trust you. I can't promise others won't come—"

"I can't promise it will be easy."

"I'll try to keep my gun away from the girls, maybe only for hunting and so it won't remind you."

"I can live with reminders, Jeff. I just can't live without you."

His gaze gentled on her face. The flowers fell to the floor. Hard, hot hands rubbed up and down her back, drawing her into him, letting her feel the thud of his heart next to hers. "I love you, Abby."

"I love you, too."

"You're not gonna kiss again, are you?" Hannah grimaced and eased up beside them.

Jeff grinned and lowered his head to Abby's, slanting his mouth across hers. She gave herself up to the kiss, secure in the knowledge that whatever happened he would stay. They would be a family.

"Oh-my-gosh! Rachel, look! They're—"

Hannah's words were abruptly cut off. Abby pulled away from the heat of Jeff's kiss and peered over his shoulder. Jeff's gaze followed hers.

Rachel stared up at them, eyes wide with angelic innocence, her hand clapped over Hannah's mouth. Hannah squirmed against the restraint and Abby laughed.

A low chuckle rumbled from Jeff's chest and he hugged her to him.

Hannah squeezed between them and beamed up at Abby.

"Uncle Jeff says we're gonna be a real family now. Does that mean we're all gonna live together forever and ever?"

Rachel pressed against Jeff's other side, her gray eyes searching Abby's face.

Abby raised her gaze to Jeff's. His was hot with desire and love and gentle triumph. "Yes, forever and ever."

Author's Note

Clarendon, Texas, or Saints' Roost as it was dubbed by cowboys, is one of three original colonies of the Panhandle. Several of the characters in this story actually were settlers there.

For story purposes, my heroine was the first doctor in the Panhandle. In fact, Dr. Jerome J. Stocking was the first physician in the area, but didn't arrive until 1885. Today, the spot of the original settlement is a lake. In 1887, the townsite moved in cooperation with the railroad and in 1890, it moved again to its present day location.

The two remaining original Panhandle settlements, Tascosa and Mobeetie, vanished. Old Mobeetie was literally blown away by a "big cyclone" in 1898, and in 1915, Tascosa became a ghost town. Clarendon, with all the characteristic grit and stamina of Texans, is the sole survivor.